,000 miles - 8 months

ONE WATCH
AT A TIME

ONE WATCH AT A TIME

AROUND THE WORLD WITH **DRUM** ON THE WHITBREAD RACE

SKIP NOVAK

W. W. NORTON & COMPANY
New York   London

ACKNOWLEDGEMENTS
Ron Holland Yacht Design for supplying the drawings of *Drum*
Ted Lonsdale and Brian Etheridge for reading the proofs
Photographers Kos, Rick Tomlinson and Chris Barker
for making their material available
Julian Fuller for his log book
Drum's crew for their log books

Illustrated by De Etheridge

ISBN 0-393-02498-9

W.W. Norton & Company, Inc.,
500 Fifth Avenue, New York, NY 10110
W.W. Norton & Company, Ltd.,
37 Great Russell Street, London WC1B 3NU

Printed in Great Britain

1 2 3 4 5 6 7 8 9 0

Contents

Introduction

It all began with an air of romanticism one winter's day in a pub on the Isle of Wight in 1976. I was an American abroad, 26 years old and had just finished a ski season in Austria which left me financially destitute. With no plans nor prospects I fetched up on the South Coast of England, the most likely place to find some casual work.

Sailing, yacht racing and delivering big sailboats were my meal tickets for adventure and travel. And Cowes, Isle of Wight, the historical center of yachting in the 'Old World,' was at the time a clearing house for transients like myself.

"Go have a chat to that Australian down at the end of the bar," someone suggested. "He's doing the Whitbread Round-the-World Race on a 65-footer called *King's Legend* down in the marina." I had certainly heard about this race. In 1973/4 a fleet of 16 boats had set out from Portsmouth, England to race each other around the world. Organized by the Royal Naval Sailing Association and sponsored by Whitbread Breweries the yachts, ranging in size from 40 to 75 feet, had sailed 27,000 miles during seven months and had made scheduled stops in Cape Town, Sydney and Rio. Two boats failed to make it all the way, and three crewmen were swept overboard in the wastes of the Southern Ocean and lost at sea. In spite of the tragedy, the organizers were planning another Round-the-World Race due to start that coming summer and the event was recognized as one of the last great sailing adventures.

The conversation with the Aussie was brusque and to the point. I had to talk to the owner of the boat who was coming down that weekend from his home in Suffolk. We had a few beers on it. A week later I landed the navigator's berth on the British cutter and little did I know it then, this was the start of an eight year involvement during the next three Whitbread Races that were subsequently scheduled every four years.

For the general public, racing sailboats easily lends itself to the popular conception of an activity drifting somewhere between sport and a casual pastime for the well-to-do. Indeed, for many the word 'yacht' alone immediately conjures up images of wealth, leisure and people who by their very appearance seem to say, "I've made it."

But 'yacht racing,' if not 'yachting' alone, can take on a variety of forms and the terms have long since become nebulous. The portly, yacht owner/skipper balancing the tiller in one hand and a gin and tonic in the other has, in his casual approach to the sport, laid the groundwork for more serious endeavour by the purists. He has, in effect, provided the vehicle by which the competitive experts reared in the racing dinghy and Olympic class boats have become 'yachtsmen' of exceptionally high caliber.

This marriage of big money and talent is best exemplified by the penultimate event in a yachting career which is participating in the America's Cup. The extremes in dedication of the crews and the financial expense of winning this regatta have long since transcended the simple pleasures of being on the water under sail and it has become what one observer cynically describes as "An egotistical management exercise between the syndicates which by chance happens to have sailing as a focal point."

There can be no doubt that involvement in some form of yachting is a 'social elevator' and the route from impressing friends and associates at the club level through to the lofty heights of the America's Cup syndicates is clearly defined. No less so is the same exercise for the sailor as he graduates in stages from the racing dinghy to the helm of a 12 meter. Alan Bond, syndicate head for the victorious Australian challenge of 1983, and an active yachtsman, has, in the course of four consecutive campaigns to win the 'Cup' from the Americans, become not only a household word in Australia, but a celebrity in the circles he will travel in internationally for the near future. Dennis Conner, two times skipper of the American defenders, is the best in his business. He has admitted he has never cruised nor sailed purely for pleasure.

But yacht racing has decidedly another side. The 'ocean race,' unlike the short course races in the America's Cup, is a long distance event sailed between two ports of call and by the nature of the exercise is little understood and an under publicized phenomenon. You could certainly make a case for the lack of publicity due to the nature of the game itself, where instead of the courtroom and in the press conference, it's between the starting and finishing guns where the drama is played out on an ocean race. Out of sight of land and most likely out of sight of even the other competitors, the people involved are out there, in large part, for 'the sailing.'

Brought up spending our free time as a family on Chicago's lakefront I can remember being around boats all my life. While barely a teenager I left behind an interest in competitive dinghy sailing and gravitated toward the longer offshore races on Lake Michigan on board the larger cruiser/racer sailboats. Not yet able to pull my own weight I was off on the weekend forays to the resort towns to the north that dotted the Michigan and Wisconsin shoreline. I enjoyed what was there considered to be extended periods offshore and the chance to see new places. For a boy who spent his formative years at school locked in the gridwork of the western suburbs of Chicago, this was a natural escape and a chance to travel. It was the combination that lead me to a nomadic life at sea that has lasted for the better part of fifteen years.

It didn't take me long to find the ocean, and before I was twenty I had become a regular in a small group of colorful sailors that made their precarious living by maintaining and pushing racing sailboats in and around American coastal waters. Living out of a seabag and literally able to make a decision and 'move out' within hours I could be off on a boat delivery to the Caribbean, on to race in Long Island Sound, or up to some boatyard in the Great Lakes for repair work; if it was to a new destination or with a different boat, fine, and the longer the haul, the better.

As thousands of sea miles clocked up I came to know and enjoy days on the open ocean especially well. Whether it was a full-blown storm or the boredom of a dead calm the passage would always be a gratifying experience with the prospect of another new port to explore. These pleasures had always been enjoyed by the serious world cruising sailor as a matter of course, but I was no cruiser. There was too much to accomplish in the racing world first.

The first Whitbread, almost a race–cum–rally went by all but unnoticed in America. When I first heard about it I was fascinated. It didn't take me long to realize Europe was the place to be.

We mounted a serious campaign for the race in 1977/78 in a mixed fleet of racers and cruisers and finished a credible 2nd place on *King's Legend*. Beaten by the organizational skills of a Dutchman, the owner of *Flyer* had, by high finance and meticulous planning, raised the ante of the contest to a level that would practically exclude lower budgeted cruising boats for the next time around.

The Whitbread Race began to gain credibility, but the costs were escalating beyond the means of the self-proclaimed amateurs of sailing: Enter "sponsorship", at the time almost a dirty word to the Corinthian set. With budgets topping $2 million dollars for the 1981/2 campaign, sponsors became a necessity for the race's survival.

For that contest I signed on board the first American entry called *Alaska Eagle*. The California-based project was a 'hemisphere' away in the ideas and management skills necessary to run a Whitbread campaign. Fraught with internal politics, the wrong crew and a slow boat, we got what we deserved finishing a disappointing 9th place out of 27 starters.

Having blown the last attempt I was now firmly hooked on doing this race again, but vowed I wouldn't attempt it without three requisites; a maximum size boat, plenty of financial backing and enough time to plan, build and campaign the boat before the Whitbread started. While several of the previous skippers already had projects underway and were building new boats, I desperately looked for a sponsor in America. Fund-raising in Manhattan can be a demoralizing experience and like so many amateur actors who come to Hollywood for the first time looking for work, I went away completely disillusioned. By September of 1984, with the start only one year away, I had given up all hope.

But then, at the 11th hour, a rock music star named Simon Le Bon from the British group Duran Duran had announced he intended to enter a boat in the forthcoming race. I applied for the skipper's job without a moment's hesitation. (Far stranger things have happened in the sport.) In spite of being American on a British boat, I got the job. Soon after we bought the 78-foot hull of a Maxi boat originally conceived for the race, and began to finish the construction in earnest. That was in January, 1985. Le Bon had the money, we now had the Maxi boat, but we were far short of time for the 'ideal' schedule I had dreamed about years before. The start was only nine months away. The pressure of time would have dire consequences.

This was the beginning of the *Drum* project – the fitting out and preparing of a yacht called *Drum*, owned by Simon Le Bon. *Drum* was built to what the pessimists described as an 'impossible schedule', capsized in the Fastnet Race when her keel had 'fallen off,' and was miraculously salvaged and refitted for the start in 5 weeks. Things got worse before they got better, and in Cape Town we labored over another refit and with doubts that we would 'ever make it.' But 'make it' we did, and with style.

This is not so much the story of *Drum* as it is about the people who built her, the people who believed in her and the crew who sailed her. And it's not the story of a major victory. We didn't win the race; we didn't even win a leg. But there were countless, other victories; like making it to the next stage when all seemed hopeless, so many times along the way. And with every setback, we seemed to grow stronger, intent on finishing something we had started and that would take over a year. A year together fighting battles with equipment, against the sea, with each other and within ourselves.

That's what the Whitbread Race is all about; sticking it out in bad times as well as in the good; and taking it one leg, one day, and then one watch at a time.

WELCOME ABOARD!

1 · They Said Something Like This Might Happen

Interviewer: *You said in Portsmouth you were certain of* Drum's *integrity.*
Interviewee: *I did.*
Interviewer: *You obviously were mistaken.*
Interviewee: *I was.*

Roger is standing in the main hatch waist deep in water. He looks at me like it is all my fault. The water laps up over the gunwhale and begins swirling in and around the deck coamings. She's going down alright and there's not a damn thing we can do. A voice calls out, muffled and distant, "Time to go on watch, you've got 20 minutes."

I wrestle with the sleeping bag, drenched in sweat. With the pipe cot hard up against the deckhead I am totally disorientated port from starboard and bow from stern and then I finally realize where I am and that we are still plugging along. It was the first bad dream I'd had since the capsize. I let the bunk tackle out just the few inches I need to slip out and on to the pile of sails in the alleyway. Collapsing at the chart table I slowly put on my gear, while Roger briefs me on the situation. I'm still half asleep and can remember nothing of what he says. Mug of coffee in hand, I make an entry in my personal log:

October 27th   position 27° 30′ South 01° 00′ East
0200
It's a rugged night with the unpleasant prospect of a dead beat into the wind all the way to the finish in Cape Town. Even more so because the boat is really starting to take a hammering in these building seas. I know I'm feeling the strain. Frankly, I'm a nervous wreck. I'm sure all 17 of us on board are asking ourselves the same question: "If the last 1,000 miles turns into an endurance test, can 'Drum' survive it?"

It was like a chamber of horrors down below; the bearings supporting the rudder shaft were suspect and crackled away, getting dramatically worse as the seas increased. Overhead, the traveller track that supports the load of the mainsail was visibly pumping the deck beam and surrounding deck and making its own particular alarming brand of noise. You lie in your pipe cot and try to sleep, but your ears are alert to the slightest variation in the background clutter of familiar pings and groans of the sheets, wires and blocks coming under load. But it's when the helmsman misses a wave and all 78 feet of *Drum* launches herself into the air at 9½ knots and then lands in the trough with a belly flop and an indescribable splitting noise, that you think your little self-contained world is flying to pieces. It's supposedly impossible to keep your eyes open while sneezing and I find it hard to do the same during these unplanned maneuvers.

The night before in the early hours we had our first major gear failure of Leg One; the genoa tack fitting, a hefty piece of 16mm stainless steel round bar, sheared off at the deck with a loud bang. 'Filthy' Phil' spent most of the morning in an immersion suit, jury-rigging a wire strop passed down through the holes. Working right up at the bow, he would frequently disappear from view as the seas combed the foredeck. When the wash had cleared he was often found at the full length of his life harness tether grappling back to finish a job well done. I thought at the time, if that's all that goes wrong I'll be happy.

Several of us were showing the wear and tear. Owner Mike Berrow had been complaining of pains in the gut so Dr Roger Nilsson shot him full of tetracycline and told him to hope for the best. We were still a long way from helicopter range if it was appendicitis. My hernia condition was definitely not improving heaving the sails around. As skipper I chose to stand a watch, and not being able to do my share of the work wasn't improving my disposition. After a few tacks that evening we headed back south on port.

1510 Log Entry
Broke a big 20mm rope genoa sheet this afternoon on the No. 3 jib. One of the guys had just clipped in a second, back-up sheet to the clew when the primary one parted – a few seconds later and the clew ring might have taken his head off.

Back on starboard tack heading east was the closer course to the finish by 15 to 20 degrees, but the pounding was dramatically worse as we hit the seas head on. Although the motion and the noise are always worse down below, up on deck it was bad enough. It was the mast we were all worried about. The lee shrouds were going incredibly slack when she hit a wave and the whole rig then gyrated like a piece of spaghetti.

I thought about *Equity and Law*, one of the smaller boats in the fleet. One of the best prepared boats in the race, she had suffered a failure in one little stainless steel fitting which rendered her mast useless and forced her crew to retire from the Leg and with it went all hopes of an overall victory. Three years of planning and work gone by the board.

October 28th   position: 28° 30′ South 05° 10′ East
1420 Log Entry:
Broke the port genoa halyard at 0400 this morning. "Down on the deck she came." Up went the No. 4 – plenty of sail. The boys are now hanking on the forestaysail anticipating the worst, always the prudent approach. With only one suspect genoa halyard in operation we have to change it to a new spare on the next sailchange; it's too risky sending someone aloft to run down a new starboard one.

Neil astutely observed, "Well, we've broken all three corners now, no problem with these Kevlar sails, only what they're attached to."

Two and half days to the coast. Two and half days to the critical tack south in the likely event that we won't make Cape Town on starboard. I'd like to say two and half days to sheltered waters, but if it's blowing south-southeast it will be hard into the wind all the way. Cape Town is reporting 60 knots in gusts out of the southeast.

Steering was getting to be downright dangerous. The helmsman would have to peel off course 20 to 30 degrees down the backsides of what seemed to be 'square shaped' waves, then struggle to lock the wheel so it didn't break his wrists when it spun back. Sometimes he had to let go and just hang on to avoid being launched out of the cockpit.

The crew sat perched about casually on the weather rail – not a lot to do with the small, No. 4 jib and a triple reefed main. Most of their thoughts were on the next off-watch coming up, where, if they could sleep, the time would pass painlessly.

Peter Kuttel, South African skipper of *Portatan* and one of our main competitors, was certainly right when he predicted a beat all the way, almost one week before. High pressure was still persisting southwest of the Cape near Tristan da Cunha. Our own Phil Wade, another local to these waters, had said those conditions never lasted more than a day or two. That day was the fifth.

Lion New Zealand and *Enterprise New Zealand* were 67 and 50 miles behind respectively, having taken a bad tack north of east after giving up the southerly option and have consolidated. The others were much the same as we, all 'starboard tackers' for the coast. *Portatan* was the only Maxi completely out of touch tactically at 132 miles ahead on our bow. *UBS Switzerland* and *Cote d'Or* to the north were looking good and would pass clear ahead of us in a tacking situation.

The tactics will now be obvious – breakdowns, however minor, will become the significant factor in determining the results.

We saw our first albatross yesterday at 28 Degrees South. Today, more of them herald our arrival in southern waters. What fortune will they bring? On deck the wind whistles at 35 knots, southern ocean style, and a cold draft finds its way down below through a partly cracked portlight, its glass already dripping with condensation. And down below, well, it's a fucking mess!

I wasn't due to come on watch until 1300 the next day on the 29th, but I was almost instinctively aroused by the crackling of the Single Side Band radio just aft of my bunk. Roger was tuning in to the 1100 GMT intership radio sched with the fleet. This was how we got the news every day, twice a day, and you could almost feel the tension in the radio waves. Pinned to the overhead in the upper starboard bunk it was obvious to me that conditions hadn't changed since I came below four hours before, as we took another slam that shook the boat in the now familiar way.

"*Cote d'Or* is running off with a delaminated bow section," was the first reply that came over. I had to admit to a fleeting sense of joy at their misfortune, as if to say, "Well, there's one down." The next bit of news was that *NZI* had broken their main halyard and was unable to reeve a new one. They were already losing ground fast. "Two in the bag!" We were now looking at a solid third place into Cape Town.

Our elation was tempered by guilt and a sense of camaraderie with fellow seamen, and our half smiles soon faded as we flew off another wave at speed and began to worry about our own state of affairs.

While cooking breakfast the bullish Englishman Richard Freeman had stuck his head out of the hatch to tell Rick, "Hey. It sounds like someone is frying eggs up in the forepeak." It was as if God Almighty had caught us red handed in our delight in the misfortune of others and retribution was exacted almost immediately. As I crawled out of my bunk, Rick Tomlinson, one of the boatbuilders hailing from the Isle of Man, in his usual inaudible tone of voice informed me that, "We've got a problem up faarward . . ."

Still groggy from a deep sleep I followed him along the length of the boat, heeled over at 25 degrees and bucking like a bronco. The sails were piled high on the starboard side to balance the trim and it was a crawl space past rows of bunk modules, two men in each who were still fast asleep. Amidships and to leeward Richard, ankle deep in what looked like raw sewerage, was busy pumping out his galley bilge area. Opposite to weather was the head compartment and with the danger of urinating overboard in the rough weather this little cubicle of horrors now smelled of its intended purpose. The forepeak forward was a dark cavern of pipes, frames and sail bins and by the time we reached the mast I heard the noise. It sounded like someone ripping velcroe tape apart.

In the dim light from an overhead fixture and aided by flashlights Rick didn't need to point out the problem. Four of the hull panels, about 15 square foot sections defined by transverse frames and fore and aft longitudinal stringers on the port side at waterline level, were simply panting like slack bass drums everytime we hit a wave. The hull construction was a 'state of the art' layup of inner and outer skins of Kevlar cloth that sandwiched 30mm of Nomex Honeycomb core material, which is similar in appearance to corrugated cardboard impregnated with epoxy resin. The pounding sea conditions had obviously delaminated the skins and the core material in between was being crushed.

I immediately called for first mate Phil Wade and the watch on deck to drop the No. 4 Jib and 15 minutes later the mainsail had to come down as well. The forward way had to be taken right off to relieve some of the deflection. It was serious – we were right out of the race, in danger of foundering if the hull breached, still 300 miles offshore.

The word quickly got out and our crew gathered around Rick and I to watch the hull panels breathe in and out as *Drum* wallowed in the sea. You couldn't help but think, "What if the hull opens up, this thing will sink!" But your reason tells you no, wait a minute; this is Kevlar, you know, the stuff they make bullet proof vests out of. And then you speculate, "But the builder must have made a bad job out of it; a bad lamination, not enough resin, the wrong material?" And as if to almost ignore it, you convince yourself with absolutely no foundation, that "It will be alright." Most of the crew were speechless for some minutes, each harboring their own theories.

"I'll tell ya something right now, if that panel continues to flex like

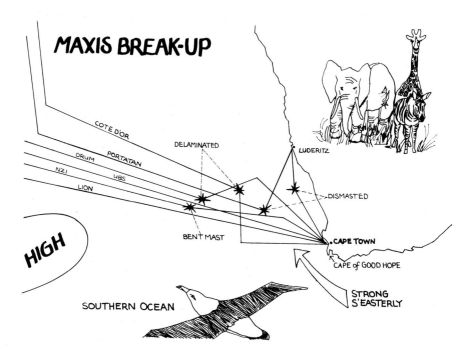

that, those Kevlar fibers will fatigue, just like a piece of steel wire and break", said Chris Barker. "The resin will shake right out of the cloth and that'll be it!" A New Zealand boat builder, Chris was outspoken and sure in his reasoning. Out of all of us he had the most experience working with the material.

Chris and Rick, in almost a panic, began to shore up the panels by laying in a soft bedding of sailbags, spinnaker material and cushions followed by floorboards braced to the deckhead by the jockey poles, pipe cot tubing and even the ensign staff, a piece of equipment that someone pointed out was being put to its first practical use.

I couldn't imagine how this makeshift 'sponge' as it were, would stop a flood under pressure, but it certainly served as a psychological barrier for the time being and was a positive move. While the crew in turns came below to inspect the damage I put on our wetsuit and was lowered over the side to check the outside skin at the waterline. Only paint and filler cracks were visible and I was convinced we were in no immediate danger.

By the time I dried off and changed into warm gear the controversy was raging. Chris advocated that we stop completely, sure in his knowledge that no matter how little the Kevlar flexes it will eventually fracture with time. Like a magician pulling a rabbit out of his sleeve, he produced a piece of resinated Kevlar fiber (one would think in preparation for just such an occasion) and began bending it back and forth for the quiet crowd of spectators. Sure enough, the spell of hope I had intended to offer was already broken as his sample snapped smartly in two, thereby proving his point.

I quickly realized that if we were to make it to the finish (or even to shore) under our own steam I had to quickly stem the rising tide of pessimism and gain some supporters. I found it hard to believe the hull would just open up without further warning. We hoisted the staysail and crept along at 4 to 6 knots and it was obvious that at that speed the 'oil canning' was no worse than when lying dead in the water. We limped in the direction of the coast making well north of east. The Namibian fishing port of Luderitz was set as our destination, some 400 miles distant in the general direction we could maintain. So far so good.

Back at the chart table, Roger and I, who shared the navigational duties, looked at the options. On one hand, if we were confident in the boat not coming apart we should be on the other tack heading south as that one was closer to the finish. That option would keep us well offshore, however, and would not be a popular move. *Cote d'Or* was standing south, but we could never be sure of the extent of her damage. We tried the port tack testing the theory that it would lift the port bow section out of the water and relieve the slamming. Result; no appreciable difference. That attempt certainly raised the eyebrows of

Chris' camp and when I asked the advice of Phil Wade and Magnus Olsson, the other watch leader, and no doubt the most experienced on board, their response was non-commital. Phil was somewhat ambivilant and Magnus looked worried and could only muster an honest "I just don't know," and he didn't seem too sure about even that.

It was obvious to me that if the boat was repairable in the time we had in Cape Town before Leg Two, this crew would have to stick together. It was no good forcing any situation on them that wasn't in the majority and right now, that was to go back onto starboard tack and limp towards shore. Roger contacted the weather bureau in Pretoria who predicted a possibility of a light westerly wind on the coast within 48 hours which again strengthened this decision.

To keep the speed down it was only possible to fly a small staysail up forward. We tried the storm trysail on the mast which is only a handkerchief of a sail, but the speed would rocket to over 8 knots. The attendant pounding would then predictably trip the catch and like a 'Jack in the Box' Chris' head would pop out of the main hatch and wail to the watch on deck, "You've got to slow down!"

An ocean racer is required to carry comprehensive safety equipment including commercial standard liferafts to carry the crew in total. We had two ten-man rafts for our 17 crew, but one had been rendered useless two weeks ago when the gas cylinder that inflates it had leaked and blew open the liferaft locker lid. We had to bleed off the bottle and deflate the raft in order to stow it, and although it could be inflated with the hand pump, it would be useless in a panic. No one on board had to be reminded of this situation and Chris argued that in light of this we should think about calling out a rescue, or at least arrange to have a deepsea fishing boat come out to us to stand by.

Englishman Neil Cheston captured the ambiance on board that day in his journal:

Needless to say the prophets of doom are having a field day and Chris heads up the 'instant sinking school of thought.' One or two of the Swedes have gone a bit pale. Phil Wade is pretty unfazed, and I certainly value his opinion more highly than most. I learned in the Fastnet capsize which of the crew has the strongest survival instinct and I'm staying close to them.

We are all apprehensive – no question about that, but we are also very much aware of the need to be cool in the face of what appears to be a dangerous situation.

It's a tricky one for Skip, since he's the only one that everyone is watching closely, and any anxiety on his part is transmuted into doom and fear among the sea lawyers. Chris had made it clear that if we put into Luderitz for repair, he for one is getting off. This would mean that we would be disqualified from the leg, so we can't really let him.

As far as I was concerned, calling out a rescue was an extreme measure, under the circumstances. I still intended to finish this leg under sail and with no outside help, as I believe when you're on the open ocean you have a commitment to 'carry on' and only call out an already much abused rescue service when it is, in fact, the 'last resort.' In terms of lives at risk I would suppose this argument could have been construed as selfish, egotistical and smacking of misadventure, but luckily no one challenged the decision.

Back in the wetsuit, the crew lowered me over the side once again before nightfall to check the outer skin. I was happy to report no change and this news gave us confidence for at least the immediate future.

We changed the watch system to three hours on, six hours off as there was little to do. By 0700 the wind had freshened slightly and we had to change the staysail for the No. 6 Storm Jib, *Drum's* smallest sail, in order to maintain the required 4 to 6 knots. Since noon yesterday we had logged only 75 miles, roughly in the direction of Luderitz. But this haven of safety was still over 300 miles away.

By mid morning Dr. Roger Nilsson took charge of the forepeak with two able assistants and began to reshore the damaged panels properly with solid packers of floorboards, braced by wedges and tubing. No sooner had he started I could hear, from as far aft as the chart table, a tremendous argument raging up forward. Hans Bauer, one of the two sailmakers, Magnus and Roger were discoursing in their native Swedish and given the language as it is I found it hard to gage the mood as they spluttered away at each other, but it was obvious they were not discussing whether Borg could win another Wimbledon.

Apparently Hans had freaked out when he saw Roger removing the old shores and begged him to put them back lest the sea rush in and swallow them as they stood there. Eventually pacified, Hans, sometimes easily given to emotion, retired aft in a pitiful silence while the work continued.

An orthopaedic surgeon in his native Sweden, the Doctor was certainly adept in this major splinting job, training, he assured me, not from orthopaedics but from a stint in the Swedish Navy. Rick was the 'gopher' and as Roger sawed and banged away up forward, he would be searching out and measuring up pieces of the interior to provide him with the raw materials. Most of the floorboards were used and a lot of the overhead battening was cut into wedges. It was a fine repair and an improvement to the extent that most of the panting had stopped completely.

Just when things were settling down a bit, another 'black cloud' appeared, this time rising from the bilges. Most of us were suspicious of the hull-to-keel joint as there had been what the designers and builders described as an 'acceptable amount of movement' at the mast step, an area of enormous compression loading from the rigging tension. While underway at speed an obvious movement was there, but not dramatic. Now, with the way off, and the stabilizing effect of pressure removed the movement had dramatically increased as we wallowed in the seas.

With the forward panels temporarily forgotten, all attention was now riveted to the central bilges upon which stood the generator and battery boxes. These were plywood constructions, bolted and fiberglassed onto the transverse and fore and aft frames and visually hid the tops of the keel bolts underneath. We man-hauled the bags of sails out of the way that literally bury these compartments and with a clear view, the interior fittings seemed to come alive. Floorboards would lift and separate from their beds and the plywood boxes shifted and breathed in rhythm to the roll of the boat. We could only assume that the keel, an 8-foot fin weighing 14 tons, was acting like a huge pendulum and flexing the whole bottom sub-structure. A ¼-inch movement above the pivot point in the boat would indicate a 'flagging' distance approaching a foot at the bottom of the keel. It was alarming, to say the least.

Speculation was rife on how much damage had been done. It was not unreasonable to assume that the bottom skins of Kevlar and carbon fiber, although a solid laminate over 40mm thick in that area, just might be coming adrift like note paper. It was certain that whatever the problem was it had dramatically deteriorated lately, hence the slackness in the lee side shrouds; the mast compression was literally deflecting the bottom of the hull and trying to rip the keel off.

Drum's keel was an emotional issue for all of us and if we hadn't capsized only two months ago we might have looked at the present situation a little more stoically; perhaps I should say naively. Instead, the safety gear and the liferafts were made ready and talk, once again, turned towards rescue. For ten of us, it was hard to forget the drama when *Drum's* keel had fallen off in the Fastnet Race and she went upside down in a matter of 20 seconds. The others needed no convincing that if the same happened again, we were in big trouble.

You force yourself to look at it logically: 14 keel bolts hold that thing on. The part that failed last time is now overbuilt and 'bomb proof'. It's hard to imagine the bottom of the boat just 'dropping out', and as yet there's no water coming in. I offer my opinion, but I'm only the skipper, not a boatbuilder, not an engineer and I could hardly take offence that my words weren't accepted as gospel by a few. "Who was I kidding?" I thought to myself. "Given our history it's hard to look at anything logically anymore."

While I prepared to suit up and go over the side to dive on the keel, the midday radio sched brought more bad news. *Portatan*, when only

220 miles from the finish and having a sure victory in sight, was dismasted this morning and was proceeding under a jury rig, north, also towards Luderitz. There, they planned to erect a makeshift mast with local help already being organized in Cape Town and make another bid for the finish. With only a spinnaker pole set as a spar they couldn't make any headway to the south so this was their solution. We expected to see them in Luderitz.

It's a tricky job getting underneath a rolling boat in a big sea, but I managed to spend a few vital seconds inspecting the union of keel and hull and more importantly, the hull surface adjacent to the keel. I was happy to report that I could see no outward signs of deformation nor anything unusual in the joint.

Again the panic had blown over as quickly as it came, but now there was another controversy brewing. The boat, as a structure, was now suspect, and in view of the problem in the bilges it would be a tall order to repair it during the four weeks in Cape Town before the start of Leg Two. Many of the crew agreed it was best to reserve judgement until we hauled the boat out and surveyed the damage. Others, like Roger, looked at the problem and understandably decided that the logistics were impossible and lobbied for abandonment of the race. Roger was making his point with such fervor that he made hope of continuing seem foolhardy.

He wrote in his log that day:

I called all the relatives of our Swedish crew today to inform them what's happening before the media gets to them. Once again I called the hospital in Stockholm, like after the capsize, and once again I asked the head doctor about the chance of slipping back into my old job. As far as I was concerned, we were out of it.

I am amazed to hear Skip talking about the repair coming up; with an incredible will power, he has been on the radio all day furiously organizing things on shore for what will be a major rebuild. I still feel very doubtful that we will be able to restart.

Michael Berrow, one of the three owners of *Drum*, was with us on Leg One and I felt sorry for him then. It was difficult looking him in the eye and assuring him it would be alright. I wouldn't have blamed the owners in the least if they had dropped out of yachting altogether then and there. He had talked to his brother and partner Paul in London on the radio and explained the difficulties. Their credibility was at stake, not to mention the capital expense of yet another major repair. Mike and I sat back aft wedged into the sails expounding on any and all scenarios that came to mind. We agreed it was to everyone's benefit if we could continue. Beyond the personal sense of failure that we would feel if we had to drop out there was the matter of money.

In New Zealand, if we could get there, a high fee for a TV commercial waited for us. We needed the money for the rest of the race.

If the repairs were impossible in the time that would be available, the alternatives certainly were unattractive. We could repair the boat and then take it to the Caribbean or the Indian Ocean for the commercial, but it wouldn't be the same as being in the race. Mike knows the boat is not worth much if she does the race or not, but the simple fact is that so many other projects revolve around *Drum* that it was a nightmare to contemplate a write-off. In the off chance that the hull was a total loss we even considered selling the mast and rigging to *Portatan* and salvaging the electronics and other pieces of equipment for Paul's future cruising boat!

Like a rising tide that hides the remains of a shipwreck, each new idea or solution would temporarily lift our spirits. But as sure as the ebb tide rushes out to expose battered ribs and spars, the reality of our situation would sink in a little deeper and we'd sit there depressed, lost in thought.

With plenty of soul searching to do I wrote in my log that evening of the 30th of October:

No doubt serious thinking is going on in everyone's mind of what to do now, especially if she is a write-off for the race. I'm sure we've all worked out our personal contingency plans. For me, the worst case is to pack up in Cape Town and head back to the Hamble with De; I could think of worse. In the best case, to be retained by the Berrows and Simon to sort this boat out, and stick with it for at least a year in order to get myself back on a firm financial footing.

I can't imagine where I would start anew . . . Go and do another two-bit boat delivery? Work for some obnoxious wealthy boat-owner (these guys not included) as his 'captain?' I feel once again as I did after the capsize; melancholy and disheartened knowing that this chance-of-a-lifetime project (at least in the world of sailing) has been blown. Nowhere could I have gained as much credibility for the future as through this coming year. Now I feel as if I'm already fading into obscure mediocrity with the added weight of disaster hanging around my neck.

On the morning of the 31st the weather finally broke in our favor. The seas had eased considerably and the wind had swung into the south. By noon we were able to hoist the Storm Trysail and the No. 5 Jib and make good headway. The talk naturally veered in favor of scrapping the Luderitz plan and making directly for Cape Town 450 miles away. Sunny skies replaced the dismal blanket of cloud and, with the prospect now of reaching our destination, the crew's spirits soared. Our offical project photographer Rick Tomlinson wrote that day in a diary he was keeping for his parents:

Today we have been back to normal and I have taken my lifejacket off – much to the relief of the rest of the crew. Though I wasn't frightened by all of this, I took as many precautions as possible, i.e. lifejacket, harness, warm clothes, passport in plastic bag with 10 exposed films, waterproof camera with new batteries and five new films. Self preservation!

If the weather held in our favor there was actually a possibility of scoring a third place finish; *Cote d'Or* was well south and her position unreliable; *NZI* reported more mast damage with her topmast bent 30 degrees to the vertical and also limping in while *Portatan* had arrived in Luderitz at 1200 local time and was erecting what was described as a 'sewer pipe' for her jury rigged mast. Only *UBS* and *Lion* had come through the blow unscathed with only sail damage. Already reports were filtering through that skipper Peter Blake on *Lion*, not yet finished, was expounding to the press over the radio an "I told them so" story about *Lion's* solid construction and how he predicted that this would happen with the 'experimental' designs. I remember thinking sarcastically aloud, what they say for almost anything in New Zealand, "Gid on ya Peter!"

We had a long conversation with the then jovial Padda Kuttel, skipper of *Portatan*, earlier that morning when they were approaching Luderitz 8 miles off. A native to South Africa and the owner of one of their largest fishing fleets based in Cape Town, Kuttel knew Luderitz well as he had used this desolate, frontier community, once a diamond mining boom town, as a fishing port. He warned us about the aggressive barmaid in the only hotel in town. He explained that they reckoned one of their diagonal shrouds had broken when they had fallen off a wave yesterday morning. They had to cut the whole rig loose, as a mast tethered to the boat by its rigging could punch a hole in the hull. Yes, they planned to do the second leg was their response to the obvious question. By the race rules any yacht is allowed to enter port and take on any assistance without penalty and at this stage *Portatan* was still very much in the game.

All that afternoon our generator ran continuously to power up our single-side-band radio as Mike, Roger and I were on to Cape Town and England laying the ground work for the repair. We talked to the Race Chairman, Rear Admiral Charles Williams; our boat secretary Jackie in Cape Town and John Irving in the UK who was *Drum's* project manager during the construction; we contracted labor and requisitioned likely materials.

Butch Dalrymple-Smith would be arriving from Ireland representing designer Ron Holland who drew the lines of *Drum* and Adrian Thompson, designer of the structure and laminate as well as Rob Lipsett, the builder, were already on their way from England.

In the simplistic view you could say the builder was at fault and the crew, still in the heat of the moment made idle threats of things they would do when they saw Adrian and Rob. As far as we were concerned they had cost us the race. Mike Berrow wasted no words about how he felt. That afternoon, while on the wheel and feeling spirited he promised us he would remain in Cape Town in spite of pressing business back home, to "sort Lipsett out," and referring to one of Rob's earlier professions before becoming an entrepreneurial custom boat builder, Mike ended his dissertation describing him as "That fucking used car salesman."

I felt sorry for Lipsett as he would become the obvious scapegoat. I had gotten along well with him during the construction, and he did good work. As an insider I knew the responsibilities in *Drum's* failure would be difficult to pin down given the nature of the marine industry and especially the way in which the boat was originally conceived.

With every mile made good in the right direction more of the old *Drum* humour seemed to be returning. Roger, almost eccentric at the age of 37, appeared on deck in full foul weather gear for it seemed like the first time this leg. The navigator's job requires a lot of time below at the chart table and this privilege is always a sore point for the other crew who have to stay on deck, especially if it's wet and cold. They lost no time in berating him about the fact that his gear looked as though it had just come out of the plastic bag. "Strange," they said, "after 7,000 miles at sea." Possibly not seeing the humour he quickly disappeared back down his hatch like a performer realizing he was in the wrong costume in a second rate vaudeville act, the audience in fits of laughter.

By noon the next day we had full sail and were reaching in a light southwesterly to Cape Town. With those conditions it would have been only 36 hours to the finish. The radio sched that day was interesting: *Lion* and a deflated Peter Blake were just outside St. Helena Bay, still about 100 miles from the finish and in light airs; *UBS* would finish and win by a landslide, then only 8 miles offshore; *NZI* reported being close to *Lion*, but skipper Digby Taylor said it was a 'shaky', deadreckoned position; and *Cote d'Or* was 210 miles due west of Cape Town going at a reasonable speed. *Portatan* reported to be 50 miles behind us, having left Luderitz at 2100 the night before after a quick refit. They expected us to be pulling into Luderitz that morning and they were surprised at our 1100 position; they met the news with a dead silence. I'm sure they had hoped to beat at least us.

I had felt that only a head sea would give us more trouble, but I was wrong. The wind eased steadily during the next 24 hours and by the early hours of November 3rd we were still 140 miles out. *Lion* had finished at 0700 the previous morning, *Cote d'Or* at 1100 and *NZI* was due in soon. The only one in worse shape was *Portatan*, again dismasted. We could see her running lights and had them on radar only 3 miles away. They reported that their jury-rigged sewer pipe for a mast had come down when one of the shackles holding a shroud had broken. They were now under power and looking for fuel from any fishing boat they could find, having officially dropped out of the Leg. There was no humour in their radio voice. I decided I didn't want to be there when someone in a bar made a smart remark to these guys.

As the hours slipped away with the competition far ahead while we tacked into a light headwind, making little progress along the rhumb line, some old animosities resurfaced: "These guys get angry with me every time they ask me how far to the finish and I tell them," Roger said. "How can there still be 150 miles to go when you told us four hours ago there were 140?" they would say. These exchanges would usually start out with light humour, be misconstrued and wind up in lost tempers. We all needed to get in.

My log entry of 0100 on the 3rd:

Thirty-five tea bags left, coffee ran out yesterday and just about zero going in the snacks department. Richard the cook had one last chocolate cake up his sleeve tonight; now only 2 days of basic menu left.

My mind drifts to the arrival in Cape Town.

Our new problems will be easy fodder for the press. "You told us the boat's integrity was beyond question," – "How can you justify taking this boat down into the Southern Ocean with 17 crew without a proper sea trial?" I had better start thinking of some answers to some obvious forthcoming questions. I'm sure some people will try to discredit Drum and it will be difficult fending off the attacks. It all seems so crazy, now that we're sailing along again at 8 knots in a new southwesterly under clear skies and the crew sitting peacefully on deck. They too must be thinking of the hard times to come.

At 2130 on the night of November 3rd the twilight had come on fast. Below Richard had just cooked his last 'normal meal,' promising freeze dried 'brown rice risotto' for breakfast, as well as for lunch and dinner if we didn't get in the next day.

We spotted the light on Cape Columbine 25 miles away which put us about 70 miles from the finish. After stopping and starting all day enshrouded in sea smoke we were now reaching with the full size spinnaker heading for a towering cumulus cloud with an anvil top which had to be rising over Table Mountain. It was still brightly illuminated by the rays of the sun that had already set over the western horizon.

2 · Holding It All Together

Listen mate, if I were you I'd get off this boat while the gettin's good!
Lion New Zealand crew member

It was a cold, damp morning for that time of year as *Drum* shot out of an inshore squall and hauled up into Table Bay. The familiar landmarks of Table Mountain in the background and Signal Hill which from a distance are the unmistakable 'Lion's Head' and the 'Lion's Rump' of Cape Town were hidden under a layer of threatening stratus cloud.

At 0604 local time, in the first light of dawn, we crossed the finish line off Mouille Point and even the cannon the Race Committee fires for every yacht on arrival seemed muffled and subdued. There were none of the usual spectator boats coming out to escort us in, no photographs taken, and not much celebration on board except for the usual courtesies. It was as if the problem with the keel was a cargo of illicit goods in the bilges as we surreptitiously slipped through the seawalls under auxillary power and made for the reception jetty.

The few familiar faces were encouraging none-the-less. My girlfriend De was there as was fellow Chicagoan Bill Biewenea's Alice. Paul von Zalinsky, senior *Lion New Zealand* crewmember and two-times race veteran was the only one from the fleet present and considering the time of day this was much appreciated. Brian 'Mugsy' Hancock and his girlfriend Erin had just arrived from the States. A South African by birth, 'Mugsy' was scheduled to join us for Legs Two and Three. And another old friend was there at this miserable hour hefting over the lifelines a case of cold beer. I had met Richard 'Thirsty' Bertie a dozen years before while he was working on boats in America. Returning a few years later to his native Cape Town to pursue business and start a family he had been waiting on the dock on

opposite Shortly after the start of the Whitbread Race. Minutes later we would pass *UBS* off Cowes and lead the fleet through the Solent and out into the English Channel (*Photo by KOS*)

overleaf An inspiring sunrise the day we rounded Cape Horn (*Photo by Skip Novak*)

all three of my previous arrivals from England, no matter what the time or weather, bringing one of the two things a sailor has had none of during the long passage.

Race Chairman Rear Admiral Charles Williams was first on board to present me with the traditional bottle of warm, cheap champagne. The practice of the skipper spraying the joyous crowd is so well established that the good Admiral has a 'special' blue blazer for celebrations like this, which might occur two or three times a day.

I had a hard time managing the ceremonious duty with elan, but the drill was completed, more for the Admiral's benefit and the few press hounds who were now gathering, hoping for us to make some devastating announcement. As we milled about the deck I could see that both our crew and friends were asking themselves various versions of "Well, what happens now?"

As the reporters made a beeline to the forepeak to inspect our damage, the Admiral, a veteran of World War II, pulled me off to one side and from his lofty height of 6' 4", looked down on me, and with the gravity of one inquiring about the casualty report after the 'D' Day Landing, asked if I thought it was very serious. "It could be very bad for us," I answered. "It's not only the boat; the crew has lost all confidence in it. I will have a handful holding this thing together even if the yacht is repairable in time."

I could see what was going through his mind. As Race Chairman he was in a difficult position; *Drum* and *Côte d'Or* with serious hull damage, *Portatan* dismasted, and *NZI* with a massive rig failure, and this only after the first leg. He had to oversee repairs that could pass official scrutiny and be acceptable to the committee, and he had to shore up the reputation of the Race as a viable exercise. Although all the competitors sign waivers and releases against the race organization, if a boat went down out there and lives were lost the publicity would be as devastating for the Whitbread Race as a 'waiver' is useless in a public liability claim.

Cleared into the country without ceremony, we made our way to the Royal Cape Yacht Club, our host for the stay in Cape Town. There we had an English-style breakfast of eggs, bacon, sausages, tomatoes and mushrooms; washed down by real coffee and pints of lager. Jacky Dodd-Noble, our shoreside secretary, had briefed me on our transport and hotel arrangements. A portable office with telephone and telex had been set up on the dock. Our 20-foot seafreight container with all of our spare parts and tools had been custom cleared in advance by Jacky and our 'shore clothes' had already been taken to the hotel by the girls.

---

opposite In the Falmouth Dockyards, she was righted in seconds, as quickly as she had capsized only four days before (*Photos by Rick Tomlinson and Chris Barker*)

After making some on-the-spot inquiries about 'instant' help from some familiar faces, I announced to the crew that we would meet back on board at 1400 to strip the boat of its 22 sails, miles of running rigging and all personal gear and then pull out the mast. This is not usual practice after just having sailed 7,000 miles, and I'm sure there was some grumbling on the way to the hotel in the suburb of Sea Point down the coast. But without fail, they all turned up on time, knowing that every day in the four-week layover would be critical.

The fact that I had been there three times proved to be a great bonus. Between myself, Phil Wade, who attended the merchant marine academy in his native South Africa, and 'Mugsy,' who had raced in Cape Town before setting sail permanently from its shores in 1978, we had built up a solid network of contacts in the marine and heavy industries. We made no bones about the fact that for us to make the restart all the 'stops' would have to be pulled. With help from local transport and the Hood sail loft we managed to have everything offloaded and our mast craned out by early evening.

As is the sailor's privilege, most of the crew went on a rampage that night, over-eating and over-drinking, to the extent that a lot of them spent most of their next day off in bed with hangovers and stomach problems. Feeling shattered from the outset, De and I instead retired to our room to relax in comfort and have a nice bottle of South African wine in private. I had a full day of organizing the survey, the haulout and dealing with the press and the Committee so I had to keep my head reasonably straight. As the wine soaked in I began for the first time to contemplate our situation in an organized manner.

We had finished 5th out of the 7 Maxi boats in the total fleet of 15 that had started from England. The problem of course was not so much the placings, but the time that had elapsed from the finish of leaders until our arrival. It was cumulative time differences for the entire race which mattered most. *Lion*, our sister design, was just less than 48 hours ahead of us and *UBS Switzerland*, a wopping 63.

However, the major question before us was whether or not to continue at all, to take the risk when the odds seemed stacked against us. We had wanted a Maxi, and now in the limelight and in trouble, we certainly had one. For a race as costly as the Whitbread for both the organization and the entrants, sponsorship has become a financial necessity. Publicity, in its most grotesque form, thrives on disaster and it's a well-known joke in professional yacht racing that if you don't win outright, it's much better for your sponsor if you have what's known as a 'horror show,' rather than an honorable second.

On the morning of November 5th, I gave a brief press conference on *Drum's* behalf which was good fodder for the news. The rumour was circulating that we would have to drop out of the race altogether. Even Peter Blake, skipper of the *Lion*, was quoted as saying to the

New Zealand press that if he was in our shoes he wouldn't continue, which I felt was a bit unkind of him. I could only assure them that we would do our best to repair the damage in time and make the restart. The irony was that at that time few people knew about the problems with the keel.

That same morning I was summoned to the telephone to give a short interview that was aired live to the BBC 'Breakfast Time' show in England. It is a sad fact that all the news media dwells on the negative, but the British press seems to pursue it with special relish. As I answered the interviewer's gloomy questions, I imagined a bell tolling somewhere in the studio, further enhancing the British public's depression on another rainy, fall day. As I was trying to end what seemed like 'our last rites on a more positive note,' the interviewer cut me off in mid-sentence, his audience sated.

To cheer up, I only had to remind myself that by nature the Whitbread with all of its complications and the long, drawn out time frame, is almost an exercise in setting yourself up for failure. For all of Peter Blake's boasting he is one that knows this only too well. One of the few who have competed in all four events he had experienced hull damage while crewing on *Burton Cutter* in 1973 and had to miss Legs Two and Three, rejoining the Race in Rio. In 1977, as watch captain on the Maxi *Heaths Condor*, he watched the rig come down on Leg One, and in 1982 the same happened on his own *Ceramco New Zealand*, arguably robbing him of the overall victory. Capitalizing on disaster experience and a good sailor and organizer to boot, this time his *Lion* campaign was in his own words, "bomb proof."

While his *Lion* bobbed peacefully away at the warps, looking as if it could depart tomorrow, I spent the first few days in Cape Town laying the groundwork for massive repairs. The first task was to organize the haul-out. Yacht club members had offered their services to act as liaison officers, and one Dolf Tigler-Wybrandi, the sales chief at De Jong's Engineering, was appointed my man. De Jong's is one of Cape Town's largest ship repair services and Dolf's job was to drum up business from the heavy shipping traffic coming in and out of the Cape. With dry dock facilities able to cater to some of the world's largest merchant vessels, shipping companies would often opt for a repair or refit in Cape Town because it was close to a common trade route, had a reputation for good heavy industries, and South Africa, being what it is, plenty of cheap labor. "You must come with me naa!" said the man with a moderate Dutch accent, "We've got a helluva lot of people to see before you can aul dat boot aat."

The Cape Town docks area is entirely customs controlled. High barbed wire fences keep undesirables out and duty-free goods in, and every car has to pass through a customs inspection gate. It is common for the guard to order you to open the boot of your car, more often than not looking to confiscate banned, pornographic literature for his own enjoyment rather than searching for other illicit goods.

Four years ago I made the naive mistake of not only smuggling out a stack of Playboys and Penthouses for the South African friends I was staying with, but also several politically oriented paperbacks I had bought at an anti-apartheid center in London. "They probably would have just taken the porno, mon, but if they caught yooo with dat sheet, they'd just have locked yooo away," my shocked host had warned me when we got to his place. "They don't fuck around in Sout Afreeka!"

The South African Railways, a government institution, controls the entire port and trains are the chief transportation facility in, out, and around the dockyard. Only two years ago old steam locomotives had puffed their way around the docks between massive piles of coal, hauling the fuel and other cargo and serving as transport to the thousands of black workers that labor in and around the area. The steam engines have all gone now and with them the coal dust and soot everyone had always complained about. With them also went the only element of color in what is now just a drab, dockland area. They will be missed.

Our first stop of the uphill battle against the bureaucratic system was at Harbor Board. Here we applied for the permit to lift out a 'small boat'. There is no facility for yachts of our size in the area and we would have to be hauled by the 50-ton crane in the Sturrock Dry Dock at the north end of the port. The Port Captain, who has the first and last word for everything that moves in the compound, gladly gave us the go ahead. We could collect the necessary forms from one of his assistants. After overcoming the natural resistance by an Afrikaaner to anyone who addresses him in English, the assistant issued us the appropriate document.

Next stop was to the dockyard to see a Mr. Fenwick, the dock-master. A man far easier to talk to, in either language, he knew what we wanted and set the date to haul as that coming Saturday, the 9th of November. He pointed out the enormous derrick that would do the job. "But you now have to go see the Stevedores," he said as he slipped us another piece of paper. "Captain Clark will sort you out with lifting gear and labor, but mind, they don't like to work after hours and on weekends."

Back in the car, again to the other side of the port where Capt. Clark, an ex-merchant seaman and a man of the world, took the details down, confirmed the time and gave us more forms to fill in, in triplicate. The Stevedores run this port almost 'by hand.' I remember in 1977 when we hauled out *Kings Legend* on a large synchro-lift, rather than move the boat around the yard by winch power on the skids, the white 'Baases' would organize maybe a hundred blacks to push it around, boat, cradle and all. They would then stand around in groups, blending in quite successfully with the coal piles, soot and machinery, waiting for another task. One can protest against such antiquated labor practices, but it was obvious that one power winch could put one hundred men out of work. However, times hadn't changed much. The 'gangs' were still used and today, in what is considered an unfashionable opinion, I couldn't help but think that employers, who could easily have afforded the machine, were being benevolent.

Mr. Fenwick was glad to see us back in his office. "Now you have to pay," said he. I pulled out my wallet thinking we had arrived, but it was not to be. Instead, he sent us off to the customs building, a veritable labrynth of 'red tape,' where after several hours waiting they took our money and issued us with the all-important receipt. We were told that a bottle of whiskey for the crane driver would make the exercise complete come Saturday morning. After a stressful day of talking and cajolling we made our way to the nearest watering hole to have a beer on our success.

The Royal Cape Yacht Club is one of the friendliest I have known, and I've known many. Unfortunately, the club's grounds are fenced off – a compound within the compound of the port, fronting not on a beautiful, picturesque shoreline, but on a dirty commercial harbor. Like so many 'colonial' clubs around the conquered world, the Royal Cape is very much a social oasis in the troubled desert of South Africa. The club members are for the most part English South Africans or very liberal Dutch and the talk around the bar is seldom political. It is a place to go to forget the problems just outside the perimeter fence.

By the time we arrived most of the crews had gathered to swap stories, and the place was buzzing. In the far corner of the open air bar with Mike Berrow sat Adrian Thompson and Rob Lipsett, just having arrived from the UK. They had been on board and didn't look too happy. As designer of the structural layout and the builder respectively, they had their necks on the chopping block and they knew it. They didn't offer any excuses then, only Rob admitting to me in his Midland's accent, "I guess she's just not strung enooof."

Adrian Thompson, a lanky 6′ 5″ is an innovative boat builder and designer from Devon who is arguably the leading authority on composite constructions in the UK. Self educated, he has experimented in hybrid fibers and epoxy resins seeking what every designer strives for, a structure that is both ultra light and ultra strong. With curly black hair, an engaging smile and a disshevelled appearance he can rightly be described as what they call a 'boffin' in England; one with his head up in the clouds dreaming up impossible solutions to problems not yet envisaged.

Rob Lipsett, by contrast, is short, a bit stodgy, and brusquely to the point about everything. An apprenticed boatbuilder with entre-preneurial tastes in many areas, he is a go-getter and expediter of the first order. He is well known in the marine industry as a man willing to take on (and some say subject his workforce to) impossible schedules for building high-tech race boats. "Just get it doon!" was Rob's answer to every problem that cropped up, and, in a country suffering from the union work ethic, without his drive we never would have made the start.

Adrian Thompson and Rob Lipsett were what one of our crew members described as "The Laurel and Hardy Act of Ocean Racing", but they were the experts that had come down to put things right. They had already specified the repair for the bow sections and we had engaged a Cape Town boatbuilder to sort that out, it being a very straightforward case of replacing the Nomex core with balsa, relami-nating the skins and then adding two extra longitudinal stiffeners. Although they had a general idea of the problem in the keel, we all had to wait until *Drum* was hauled and the guts of the boat taken out.

Admiral Williams appointed Eric Bongers to monitor the repairs. Any solution would have to be acceptable to him if *Drum* were to be allowed to continue the race. Bongers had built *Portatan* and was the local authority on hull integrity. When he inspected *Drum's* radical construction he immediately proclaimed that the solution was to build a complete metal ring frame inside the hull and deck head to tie in all the loaded components. Although a conventional boat building system, this proposal was now out of the question. It was clear he would need gentle politicking for a plan that could be carried out in the time remaining to us. His problem was to help us without being in the position of approving a marginal solution.

The main point of controversy was that Adrian's structural concept was totally unprecedented in a boat of this size. The skin of the hull was a conventional combination of Kevlar undirectional fibers in both outer and inner skins sandwiching a Nomex honeycombed core in the topsides and a solid laminate of Kevlar and carbon below the water-line. The problem lay in the structural frames and longitudinals directly under the mast and over the keel.

'Conventional' is a word almost out of context in a custom-built yacht, but it had been 'accepted practice' to support and distribute the stresses of this highly loaded area through a metal 'H-Frame' bonded by fiberglass into the hull itself. This was normally an aluminium welded construction that formed a large 'ring frame' transversely inside the hull from the mast/deck union, out to the chainplates at the rail and then down to the butt of the mast. In conjunction with this 'ring,' a fore and aft metal frame bore the weight of the keel, which was bolted up through it, thereby insuring a rigid connection between itself and the hull.

Drum was conceived and built using virtually no metal parts but relied on her stiffness in this area on massive laminated carbon fiber ring frames. The main advantage to this system was to build an homogenous 'plastic' structure (as there had been problems in attaching metal bits to plastic hulls) and save weight, which in our case amounted to approximately 3,000 pounds. Theoretically it should have been as strong as the metal, and it probably was, but ironically the problem that would be revealed was exactly the one Adrian had tried to avoid – the metal to plastic interphase.

It was clear that we would need some configuration of a metal substructure, but not to the extent that Bongers wanted. I put heavy pressure on a local aluminium boatbuilder called Cenmarine to do the metal work for us. Only a few days before they had agreed to build a new keel for *Cote d'Or* and they panicked a bit when I explained the problem. The same company had helped us repair a few cracked frames on *Alaska Eagle* four year ago, and whether it was the talk of the 'good old days' or my persistance in ignoring their polite refusals they eventually gave in. The only man we were now waiting for was Butch Dalrymple-Smith from the design office of Ron Holland.

Ron Holland had conceived and designed the lines or shape of *Drum* and the structure was left to Adrian, but in the real world *Drum* was identified and known as a 'Ron Holland Maxi' and if the keel failure had not already done enough damage to Ron's credibility, the failure of the boat to continue the Whitbread Race, for whatever reason, would be even worse. So the final construction decisions were left to Butch's discretion. An Englishman who has been Ron's partner for over 10 years, Butch had done the first Whitbread on board the winning Mexican yacht *Sayula* and is still considered somewhat of a folk hero in these circles. One could select "thinking" as Butch's main hobby. With a charming sense of humour he takes great pleasure in devising solutions to difficult problems. Although not a trained engineer, he had accumulated a wealth of practical knowledge of yacht constructions as a yachtsman and designer. He also was a master at transmitting to others his confidence that all would be well. He had to summon all these powers to satisfy the likes of Rob, Adrian, Bongers and most important of all, our crew.

Crewman Neil Cheston recorded the mood in his diary of what Butch was up against:

The lads on the other boats seem to think we are going to chuck it all in and go home, which is a bit galling. Mind you, they could be right. Chris was right, the keel was in trouble, and according to the local shipwright could have easily come off again. It's all very well to take advice from the so-called experts, but from what knowledge are they speaking? So far they have been disastrously wrong, and so far as I'm concerned they can keep their advice. I'm going to take some convincing. Magnus seems to be unsure about carrying on, and so far he's been one of the few people around here to talk any sense.

Satisfied that the situation was well in hand, Mike Berrow treated the crew to dinner the night before he left for England. Feeling optimistic he talked about returning for Leg Two, even though he wasn't scheduled to go. He had realized that it would not look good if one of the three owners were not on board for this difficult next stage. Like-wise the situation was the same with Ron Holland's brother, Phil, who was scheduled for Leg Two. Phil, another one of the capsize veterans, had made it quite clear to me on the phone that he was not confident of coming down and was waiting to see "What Butch thinks." I had also found out later that there had been an almost macabre conversation between Ron and Paul Berrow at the time, to the effect that, "If my brother Michael is going on the second leg, you better make damn sure that Phil is there as well!"

Englishman Patrick Banfield, who had joined us only two days before the start of Leg One, was proving invaluable leading the team of Rick, Micky Olsson (another of our five Swedes) and Bill down below. A yacht designer by trade, he was certainly adept in demolition. They had already taken out the generator, the battery box and the water tanks in the center bilges by the time *Drum* was lifted out by her chain plates. The giant red hull of *Cote d'Or* was already 'on the hard' and the rumours were that Tabarly was opting for a new keel as they not only had some leaks around the hull (due to a severe grounding that summer in Britain) but the weight distribution and shape of the keel were making the boat dangerously 'bow down' in trim.

Gangs of stevedores heaved on long warps from the bow and stern as *Drum* swung dangerously in the fresh breeze dangling high over-head out of water and surreal as in a Dali painting. Still on the deck, Patrick, aka "death wish", looked uncharacteristically nervous 70 feet off the ground with the chainplates making funny noises. "Look," said the unshakable Bill Biewenga, "If it's going to go, it's going to go; not a damn thing to worry about." After much shouting and swearing, the hull was eventually cradled safely in two fiber slings strung between a steel girdered structure. Rather than have a fixed cradle this way we could raise and lower the hull in the likely event the keel would have to be dropped off.

J. J. Provoyouer, a local boat builder, was put in charge of the bow repair while Adrian and Rob spun off the keel bolt nuts and prised out the aluminium backing plates. After the whole area was shot blasted clean of paint and grease, one of our problems (cause and/or result) became clear. One of the main carbon fiber ring frames had cracked clean through on its vertical web, thus eliminating stiffness directly over the keel. Other, smaller cracks were discovered in the corners of the bays and went right through the flanges that were bonded to the hull. The keel bolt holes in the aluminium backing plates that filled the bays were elongated and cracked radially outward. It all indicated movement that was force enough to load parts of the carbon beams beyond their yield point and cause them to fracture.

After a day's work of stripping the inside of the hull right and poking around, our worst fears were over. There was no evidence of delamination in the hull adjacent to the keel and what we could see was certainly repairable.

Adrian and Rob thought it best to overlay the entire area with 12mm of fiberglass to create a new base. This would extend from beyond the keel forward, aft to its trailing edge and athwartships to the bunk fronts; in total about 150 square feet excluding the vertical faces of the beams and longitudinals. They reckoned it would take at least five days of continuous work.

Butch was due to arrive on Wednesday, the 13th of November and in the meantime the work would proceed despite much haggling between Bongers, Cenmarine et al. about the proposed metal work. The final solution was to be ready by Thursday and presented to the crew as a working plan.

After a week in port the fleet had dispersed itself around the docks for major overhaul and normal refitting. The place looked like a marine version of the pits in Formula One auto races. Boats, masts, and equipment were scattered around in pieces. *NZI* was still in the water, her old mast, broken in two sections, being stripped of fittings in anticipation of the new sections being flown in from New Zealand. *Portatan* was hauled out at Kuttel's fish factory at the south end of the harbor. Her keel had to come off to fill some old holes that were leaking and they also had to strengthen a few of the frames up forward and back aft near the steering post. Only *Lion* and *UBS* seemed to have little to do. Blake's crew were already proudly stowing the food on board for Leg Two and preparing to go on holiday. Most of the smaller boats had arrived with little damage.

Even with a month in port and disregarding our major difficulties, the crew had long worklists for normal servicing and jobs that had been left undone before the start of Leg One. Each man had a specific expertise and within days of arriving I had issued the master worklist from their suggestions with additions from the group as a whole. Although exhaustive, tedious and in areas unclear to an outsider it is worth listing here to demonstrate not only the workload we had to face, but also the complexity of a modern racing yacht.

Mast and Rigging   Magnus and Neil
inspection and lubricating of all fittings
redesign and fabricate new headboard cars

replace V1 shroud toggle, order new one from Navtec, USA
fabricate new fitting for inner forestay
install 'chicken stay' fittings for gooseneck
measure all turnbuckles and mark them
rig and check extra runners
reroute genoa halyards and run 'mouses' for both halyards as spares
improve shockcord system on diagonal shrouds
put in more prebend
install headstay pin one hole further down
modify genoa halyard chafe guards
plan routing of external spinnaker halyards
check sweep back of spreaders
improve exits for spinnaker halyards at mast head
change the 'U' bolts for spinnaker halyards
have spare clevis pins made for all standing rigging
install swivelling blocks for pole lifts
X-Ray any weldments on mast or fittings where necessary
install light shining up at halyards
order spare headstay to be sent to New Zealand
replace any sections of chafed Gemini foil
beef up forward inboard spreader ends if needed
reinforce forward end of boom
replace steel nuts on Baby Stay locking device with stainless
install steps on mast for reefing

Running Rigging   Filthy and Neil
check all rigging, make up new where needed
end for end all Kevlar and Gleistine sheets
make 8mm wire boom preventers
lanolin all wire
make new donuts for rope afterguys to fit the new pole ends
leather runner toggles and blocks with foam pads underneath
paint Nico Tool box, service tools
check steering cables
check bunk wires
change flattener and outhaul wires
rig spinnaker pole trip system
overhaul all Sparcraft shackles
make gooseneck 'chicken' stays
make sure vang strap goes on board
rig new spinnaker poles
rig boom with: tail bags, eyes and tackle for preventers, hooks for
   blooper sheets with protective flaps
modify custom pole ends
put handles on boom sheet jammers

order any running rigging for New Zealand
replace and make spare donuts for boom blooper leads
any mods to Mk 20 reefing system?
fit safety line on jockey pole
make sure pole guys are on board
splice Kevlar light sheets into drifter

Deck Dept and Hydraulics   Janne and Bill
overhaul all winches and deck gear
check and adjust headfoil
have new tack bail made
seal innerforestay and babystay
fix forehatch
replace two bent stanchions
tighten up lifelines, deck jackstays and genoa nets
install padeyes on rail for # 2 leads
change angle of padeyes forward for gooseneck stays
install jammers for down fuckers, etc.
leather or cover stanchion tops, etc.
modify runner tail keepers and sheet tail keepers
file or grind Nautor tracks
tighten up and check all tracks and deck fittings
grind machine screws on rail tracks
make up new double blank stops
locktight all grinder handles
glue in rubber track stop ends
make new system for standing up mainsheet blocks
install grabrail on mid foredeck
install new ball bearings for Barbarossa blocks
install shock cord for wind handle pockets
resecure winch handle pockets with stainless steel plates
rig stowage for new spinnaker poles with custom ends
lock babystay from swivelling
make plugs for breakwater
align and remark hydraulic valves
check hydraulic system
install safety bars across small hatches
install steeper footwedges amidships

Mechanical/Plumbing   Micky
service main engine, genny, watermaker
fit electric bilge pump with wandering lead
fit longer hoses for pumps forward
fix gas solenoid
overhaul water pressure pumps

clean seacocks and strainers
fix shower hose
check batteries
new system for taking out fuel
gymbal high pressure pump for water maker
refit broken heater ducts, lag all ducts
run in heater
fix genny stop solenoid
rethink bilge pump system, see Phil Wade
fix oil leak in water maker
overhaul head
fix lead in gas locker, solve problem of sea water coming in

Electrical   Phil Wade
fix luff light
fix switch for Branstedt
fix switch for head fan
rig hanging anodes
install light for hydraulic panel
fit inverter to make sewing machine run off batteries
check out battery charger

Safety Gear   Phil Wade
have liferafts serviced and repacked
install new catches for Dan-Buoy lids
assemble all safety gear for next inspection
install bracket for forward fire extinguisher
fit MOB strobe light amidships

Navigation and Medical   Roger
arrange roll for computer paper
change Sat Nav and test new one
repair Sonic Speed
fit new barometer
fit southern hemisphere compasses and swing
change #1 MFD
replace top Branstedt and fix reostat
check switch for mast head units
test telex and weather fax facility on Sharp 5000
clean up and oil sextant
check all charts and nav books for Leg Two
cut down on number of books by photocopying info
have appropriate sight reduction tables on board for high lat
check function of Decca
replace used medicines for Leg Two

correct rotating speed of barograph
calibrate wind instruments and both logs
install small alarm clock at chart table
install nonskid on ladder aft
install pencil and cup holder at radio station

Sails Hans and Mugsy
check all sails for damage and repair
install new luff tapes on #2 and M1
sew on all temporary patches
change checkline on Kevlar main
reinforce head and clews on 2.2 oz Xargo spinnaker
same on Xargo storm spinnaker
take delivery of three new spinnakers, check and mark
improve shape of top of Kevlar main
same on middle section of M1
reglue loose sticky back on diesel #3 and 4
install new water reef on M1 further forward
make canvas cover for forepeak
make bags and shelves for better personal stowage
service and check sewing machine
make spinnaker socks work better
check all turtles and bags
make canvas pouches for sail bins
check we have hanks on board
reinforce head and clew on 2.2 oz blooper
reinforce tops of all genoa luff tapes with Kevlar
devise better system to secure sewing machine
check and reinforce # 2 jib top for heavy running
discuss with crew sail selection for Leg Two

Galley and Provisioning Richard
note crew's suggestions for Leg Two
reprovision accordingly after checking with Skip
install light over sink
install fans
install course treadmaster in galley sole
raise fiddles in work areas
hinge bin top
move fire blanket to deckhead
install paper towel rack
move cutlery stowage
install extra fiddle on outboard side of oven
remove excess hose at hot water outlet
seal vent under cooker

round off galley locker fiddles
service cooking burners
redesign top of sewing machine top
design and have made articulating worktop

Interior and Stowage PJW/Rick/Patrick/Roger/Micky
fix all known deck leaks
install new drain plugs in forward bulkhead
make plywood safety top for quadrant
install bunk curtains
lower aft bottom bunks
fix padeyes for securing sails and equipment below
fit padeyes for lashing emergency tiller arms
repair and repaint floorboards
install hooks for harnesses
install individual mug rack
install overhead, rope grabrails amidships and forward
install foot wedges in sole forward of mast
buy or make up sleeping bag sheets
sort out stowage for oilskins
install door for drying locker
make sure drill press, bench vise and jigsaw are on board
install better mirrors in head
install net stowage forward for paper goods
devise vegetable bin stowage aft

Boatbuilding/Composite Work/Rating Rick and Patrick
check deck and hull throughout for other signs of strain
drop rudder, check bearings and blade, drill test hole for water
   intrusion
pull out and service both steering boxes
make new rudder flaps
change keel and shaft anodes
repair any graphics
touch up paint work on deck and hull
repair and improve liferaft locker lid
drill prop for wooden dowelling
check keel for water intrusion with test hole
research and subcontract construction of bow foils
rerate the boat

On Monday morning I had my hernia operation and the joke
around town was that not only was *Drum* falling to pieces, but the
skipper had 'delaminated' as well. Luckily, the no-nonsense doctor
said as long as I could stand the pain I could do what I please.

I checked out early the next morning and went straight to the boat. There, crew boss Phil Wade was in charge of lifting the hull off her keel. Without the help of any cranes, he rigged two chain blocks to the slings and with a lot of elbow grease took up enough tension so that the weight of the keel parted the joint between it and the hull. A native of Durban, Phil was used to dealing with the local labor practices. I noticed that a new crewmember was up on the deck polishing the metal work. "I hired 'Speedy' for ten Rand per day (about $3.50 at the time) to keep the boat clean," said Phil as he hauled on the chain hoist. "He's happy as a pig in shit to be here and he'll do anything we want him to." (I am not ashamed to say we were the only boat in the fleet to have used local black labor.)

To help myself get around, De had bought me a carved wooden walking stick in a curio shop and with it I tried to gesture commands to the crew while perched on a bit of concrete some yards away. I could hardly raise my voice for the pain in my groin and finally, like the troops of a shell-shocked colonel suffering from dementia, the 'foot soldiers' courteously took no notice, and I was finally ushered off the front line back to my quarters. By the next morning they had successfully dropped the keel and the boat floated buoyantly in her slings, free from her infamous burden once more.

The weather had broken clear and sunny a few days before we hauled *Drum*, and the panoramic view of Table Mountain against a cobalt blue sky was like an old friend. Although the winter and spring weather in the Cape can be stormy and gray, the strong southeasterly wind known here as the 'Cape Doctor' announces its arrival with the famous 'table cloth' that rolls up and over the backside of Table Mountain and spills over into the city side like a frothy vanilla milk shake. This is a sure sign of a clearing southeasterly and the arrival of a good blow.

Cape Town is naturally bounded on three sides by Table Mountain and the sea. Only to the north does it sprawl into vast industrial areas and the infamous shanty towns. Leading south from the city is the coast road to Port Llandudno and into Hout Bay, a spectacular coast drive with the Southern Ocean fetch breaking hard against rocky promontories on one side and on the other the mountain range called the Twelve Apostles, butting up close by the roadside. Rising to over 2,500 feet, these sandstone cliffs and peaks of orange, red and yellow lend a warm contrast of the late afternoon sun to the cold, blue sea below. It is one of the most beautiful drives I have ever seen, especially for one so close to a major city so easily enjoyed.

Geographically dynamic, South Africa labors under immense social and political problems that often cloud the country's natural beauty. *Drum* too is physically striking, and *Drum* too suffered from social problems within. Though the work was going reasonably well it was a juggling act monitoring the crew's attitudes which wavered from bright enthusiasm to utter gloom. Of course, it was difficult getting an honest opinion out of them because they found it difficult to admit to their skipper that they had doubts about the project. The situation was not helped by the fact that I was not always as communicative as I should have been with some of the crew.

One day Roger asked me to come to his room for a private chat. "Some of the crew have asked me to talk to you," he said, "Although I had not noticed these incidents during the leg, they were upset with some of your reactions when you came on deck and were not pleased with things. I know you and I have not gotten along as well as we did on *Alaska Eagle*, but then again, I think that's more a case of our tactical decision-making methods."

"I realize," I said to Roger, "That my behaviour has been different this time. I made a decision early on to distance myself from the crew. I think they believe I should be more personal, 'one of the guys,' but with a project this big, even though I'm coming from the same background as they are, I just have to stand aloof from them. I have to call it when things are not going the way I feel they should. As far as I'm concerned that is the skipper's necessary prerogative."

"Well," Roger said, "you should take it a bit easier on them. You know, they highly respect you, but it has reached the point at which they are afraid to come and talk to you."

Mugsy, an old friend who I had sailed over 50,000 miles with, was straightforward and confident. The crew talked freely among themselves, and he would let me know who was OK and who looked shaky. "I can't understand what's wrong with these guys. Hans is just moping around, just about useless in the sail loft. I came in there yesterday and he was asleep on a sailbag and admitted he just didn't feel good about the whole thing. Janne and Micky seem alright and so do Patrick and Filthy. But even Magnus is confused and Roger is advocating a copout on the project if he doesn't get some answers soon. Skip, all I can say for sure is that you can depend on me."

Sometimes it was easy to lose sight of the fact that it was easier for me to be confident than it was for them. I was in charge and telling everyone what to do next. Mugsy had not been on the capsize nor on the first leg. It was a simple case of tolerance as a function of the time put in. Some of the guys who had been on *Drum* since the beginning were coming to the end of their emotional tether.

Roger, despite the best intentions, became almost a preacher of doom. Like everyone, he was going through a personal crisis of decision, thinking aloud about his doubts and fears. He was under intense pressure from his mother, among others, to call it a day. "But Roger, if the keel fell off, what about the rest of the boat?" this 75-year-old woman living in the middle of Sweden had asked him before the start. He obviously had not given her the right answer.

Butch had arrived as planned and by Thursday, he and I conducted a meeting with the crew. I laid down the general plan and Butch went through the repair specifics. We all agreed that the boat must pass a sea trial offshore and our schedule had us going in the water one week prior to the start.

There had even been talk of getting some kind of written guarantee from the designer that this boat was now sea worthy, but of course this was impossible and quite worthless in practice, certainly in the middle of the ocean. No one offered a guarantee with financial ramifications. The best we could expect was an endorsement from Bongers good enough to satisfy the Race Committee.

I stressed the fact that everyone had to make up his own mind whether or not to continue. I pointed out that I had not tried to lobby for their support; they were all, in the end, responsible for their own lives. Although I was willing to take the responsibility of leading them out there, if the solution to *Drum's* repair was wrong there would be more at stake than just a few reputations. One thing I didn't want is for any sheep to come back and haunt the shepherd if things did go badly offshore. I told them that I would have to have everyone's decision by the coming weekend. Only one man in the group stared into the carpet with a furrowed brow.

Neil later wrote of his feelings after the meeting:

The general feeling among the boys seems to be one of relief that we can carry on, mixed with the trepidation that has become a natural part of sailing on Drum. The worst part of all this is pressure from friends to quit. Having decided to carry on I find I now have to justify my decision to anxious relatives, and can't think of convincing enough reasons.

Skip has succeeded in herding all of the doubters to the fold, although I think he considers us a bunch of frightened children rather than intelligent people faced with a difficult decision. It's easy to stand aside and heckle, but I'm glad I'm not in his shoes right now.

Butch stayed for four days while the steel was being fabricated and then had to return to Ireland confident that everything would be on schedule. Phil Wade was off to Durban to see family, and I became fit enough to work full days. Roger, Filthy, Mugsy and Bill took a four-day holiday to the game park Mugsy's brother manages in Bhoputhtswana, and although I encouraged everyone to take some days away, Neil, Magnus, Pat, Rick, Janne and Micky stayed on the job being content with occasional visits to the local fleshpots and night life of the Cape.

Equity and Law arrived on the 14th after her ordeal repairing her damaged spar in Monrovia. For all purposes out of the overall results, much the same as *Portatan*, her crew looked dejected and forlorn with over three-quarters of the Race yet to go. On a lighter note the smallest boat in the fleet, *Sas Baia Viking*, the 52-foot Danish entry, a home-built, steel boat and admittedly racing/cruising around the world, finished with no problems on the 18th, and the fleet was all accounted for.

There to meet them on the dock was the good Admiral, smelly blue blazer, champagne in hand. As is customary, he kissed any girls on board, and there were two beautiful Scandinavian blonds. However, he kissed a third, a long-haired blond who turned out to be named Klaus, which created an uproar and a fair bit of embarrassment!

That same night a 60-knot Cape Doctor blew through and created havoc at the docks. A few of the boats strained their warps and hit the concrete wall while our mast, an aluminium tube stripped of its rigging and spreaders and propped up on oil drums blew smartly over onto the ground, luckily without damage. Janne arrived just in time to catch *L'esprit d'Equip's* mast from blowing into the water. Our rudder, resting on some wooden horses for inspection, flew off and split its trailing edge. Although only minor damage was done, it was not a good omen.

By the 21st my hernia condition was dramatically better and De and I were able to take a long walk down Nordhoek Strand, a beautiful 3-mile, crescent-shaped beach south of Hout Bay. It was almost deserted. Only a few horses and their anonymous riders cantered up and down through the surf that gently rolled in from the Atlantic on this windless evening. It was a beautiful drive back up the coast road in the twilight and after a light meal in the village of Camps Bay, we made for our hotel feeling content that everything was going to work out fine, but Adrian, Rob and Rick were waiting for us, also having just arrived, and Rob came right to the point. "The keel can's fooocked, mate."

That morning I had asked Rick to scrape off the old joint compound on top of the aluminium spacer and prepare the surface for the keel to go back on that weekend. It was a gross oversight by everyone that this was not done before because when he cleaned the surface the four forward bolt holes all had hairline cracks radiating out from the centers and the top plate of the aluminium spacer, the part that had failed in the capsize incident, was visibly deflected with cracks in the bolt galleries. Rob and Adrian were adamant that we would have to have a new spacer made, this time out of steel, and they could see no way that trying to repair it was a viable solution.

I asked Rick not to tell anyone until I saw it and De and I made our way down to the docks by midnight with a flashlight. It was bad alright, but as far as I was concerned it had to be repaired as we were now out of time to build a new one, the start only two weeks away. I called up Fred Farmer from Cenmarine and asked him to be down at 0700 the next day to have a look. He was so used to being asked the impossible from all of us that he readily agreed to be there.

Fred, an engineer from the Tyneside, was used to ship repair and declared this little task a straightforward one, and he would get his man Dave, the Scotsman, on it right away. He reckoned that in two to three days he could sister another 20mm plate on the top and weld up all the cracks. But again, the repair was not the worry.

As the crew filtered in that morning the word 'keel' spread quickly, and as fast as they had bailed out of *Drum* when she had turned over that day in August, they came to the drydock to inspect this new-found damage. From the looks on their faces I knew we were in trouble.

Magnus, usually exuding sunshine, became a grey day, and Neil, who had come over from working on the mast, looked at it and was almost in tears. It was indeed fortunate that Roger was still away. I called another crew meeting for 1730 that evening. Meanwhile, I got right on the phone to Ron Holland's office and when I explained the problem there was a long sigh and silence on the line. Ron said he would contact the Wolfson Research Unit at the University of Southampton so they could, by telex, reiterate the study they had made last summer that the keel spacer's design was sound and also to specify the method and weld schedule for Cenmarine's repair. I had to have this information with me at the crew meeting that afternoon as I knew it would be very difficult talking this one through.

Down at the boat Adrian began bandying about the theory that the keel as specified by Ron was at fault and not his structure in the boat. His reasoning not being accepted, we had a minor row on the hard that morning. We finally agreed that it wasn't going to do any good to lay the blame and confuse the crew still further. As our telex machine smoked away all day with information, questions and reassurances flying back and forth from Europe to the Cape, the press caught wind of another meal on *Drum* and descended on us like a pack of jackals. And the implications were even more serious; *Lion's* keel spacer was actually a structure inferior to ours in a few details and Big Roy Mason, *Lion's* engineer, who came to inspect the cracks declared in an uneasy baritone, "Fuckin' hell," and walked away to go and tell Blake.

It was clear the project was about to fold there and then. "Was this boat really jinxed?" I asked myself. For the first time I had my doubts if we could hold it together, as the crew began to arrive at my apartment late that afternoon for the explanation. I thought back to the beginning of the *Drum* project, almost a year before, and although I had known that what we were attempting was a risky proposition, I had never thought it might end like this.

3 · Rock Around the World

"I know it's a lot of money – but it just took someone to say, Hey, we've got to do it!"

Simon Le Bon, January 1985

What was to become the *Drum* Project began in a very casual way, as do most yachting campaigns. People get together and 'talk boats.' Maybe a once-in-a-lifetime 'dream' is the motive for someone with enough money and who has gotten to the stage in his business life that the 'one year off' can wait no longer. The catalyst is often provided by the guys like myself who tell the sea stories and with a complete air of confidence say, "Yeah! Let's do it!"

I had been to many meetings with potential financial backers for sailing projects, some pretty bizarre, like setting up sailing schools for the Iranian Navy or a three-day airplane chase around middle Europe trying to pin an Austrian industrialist down about a Maxi Racer contract. Such pursuits have brought me some interesting projects over the years, although a vast majority turn out to be pipe dreams.

For a variety of reasons the *Alaska Eagle* Whitbread campaign was not a satisfying experience. In fact, a few crew members on that boat advised me to stick to single-handed sailing. However, I was determined to do the next Whitbread, this time as skipper in complete control of the crew and the running of the boat. The *King's Legend* tour had been my 'great adventure,' and the *Alaska Eagle* effort was supposed to be based on things learned from it. Instead, it turned out to be an abysmal failure. Sharing the management of the campaign with an incompatible project manager, I was at least partly to blame, if not for the boat's performance, then certainly for the animosity between two factions in the crew. I realize that I am not an easy person to live with at the best of times, but when I feel people are wasting my time, I have no qualms about making life miserable for them.

In 1979, not long after my first Whitbread Race on *King's Legend*, I had organized the crew, the fitting out, and the campaign of the Swan 65 *Independent Endeavour*. We entered and won the Parmelia Race in a 15-boat fleet. It was sailed from Plymouth, England, to Perth, Western Australia, with a two-week layover in Cape Town, it was a 'one off' race to commemorate the founding of the Swan River Colony in Perth by English settlers who had arrived there in the ship, *Parmelia.*

Not only did we win the race, but more importantly for me, our 11-man crew had finished the four-month project the best of friends. To this day we share fond memories of the experience which had convinced me that my management skills were sufficient for the successful management of a Whitbread campaign.

Soon after the *Alaska Eagle* debacle, with a clean slate and plenty of time in hand, a journalist friend and I set up a small fund-raising company to look for big money in America for the next Whitbread. Running low-budget mail shots to over 80 high profile American firms, we foolishly tried to raise interest in a race that neither starts, stops nor finishes in the United States. The few inquiries that went beyond the initial stages were usually by some executive who kept a boat on Long Island Sound and was interested in the project as a conversation piece over lunch. It became obvious that no one was going to risk the needed $2 million on a sailboat race that the American public had scarcely heard of. As time slipped away, so did the balance in my bank account. After too many unsuccessful forays into Manhattan we gave up hope.

By late fall of 1983, the nail seemed to be in the coffin. The serious entries, and there were several, already had their boats under construction with planned launchings during the fall and winter of next year allowing them a healthy 8 to 12 months of sea trial before the start in September, 1985. It was time for me to stop dreaming and look for a job.

There's only one place to find boatwork in England in the middle of winter. Anybody with anything to do with yachting in Europe is in London during the 10 days of the London Boat Show, possibly the most comprehensive boating trade fair in the world. The Earls Court Exhibition Center is the venue, but the center of insider activity is always the Guinness Drinking Stand. There, frustrated yacht brokers and marine salesmen go to relieve themselves of the general public. A veritable listening post for what's happening both there and abroad, it is also a moderately quiet meeting place in the general chaos of boats and equipment of all shapes, sizes and descriptions.

Although the mid-day drinking there starts out in a civilized manner, by late in the afternoon it is fast and furious, the floor wet and sticky from the spillage and air thick with cigarette smoke. By evening, brokers and salesmen take on an almost twisted appearance after their 5th pint of stout, obviously with a gutfull of talking to the mildly interested mass public all day, knowing full well that most of whom had not the slightest interest in buying whatever it is they were trying to sell.

My own base of operations was at the Nautor stand where Messrs. Irving and Liley, the UK agents, were displaying a Swan 46. Nautor of Finland lay claim to being at the outer limits of the production boat market with their fleet of solid fiberglass hulls ranging from 37 to 76 feet. Built by Finnish craftsmen, classified to Lloyds 100 A1 register and carrying a price tag that reinforces the old aphorism, "If you have to ask the price, you have no business owning one," the 'Swan' phenomenon began almost 20 years ago. Almost from their inception they had cornered the market for expensive cruising sailboats, possibly because they were true quality and, compared to many others, they looked and sailed like sailboats.

Much of the early success of Nautor was an advertising campaign based on their Swan 65 *Sayula* which had won that first Round-the-World Race in 1973. The campaign implied, truthfully, that "Safe to race around the world means safe for you and your family." It is a legend that is as true today as it was then.

John Irving pulled me to one side and said, "Can you fly to Paris tomorrow night? I've got a customer who wants to do the Whitbread on a Swan 651 and I need someone who can give him the 'Whitbread spiel'."

My association with Nautor had begun almost eight years before when I had berthed on *King's Legend* that winter's day in Cowes. We came in a creditable 2nd that year in the Whitbread and two years later was when we won the Parmelia Race on another Swan 65. I had worked on their behalf and for several of their clients as a consultant and had delivered their yachts worldwide, clocking well over 60,000 miles on Swan 65's alone. When Whitbread and Swans were mentioned in the same breath it was not surprising I was considered a Swan/Whitbread 'guru.'

"Sure," I said to John Irving. I had no real desire to race around the world in another Swan, but I smelled a good consultancy job. Besides, a meal in Paris is always a great idea. The brief was that the rockstar Simon Le Bon and his two managers, Mike and Paul Berrow, wanted to enter the race as a three man partnership for an exercise in adventure.

"Ever hear of Duran Duran?" asked Irving. I had to confess I had not. Since John was ten years my senior, I was a bit surprised that he had, until he reminded me of his teenage daughter. I thought to myself, "A rock music star on a racing yacht?" Then I thought about the Iranian Navy and that crazy Austrian and it didn't seem so hard to believe.

The next night we were on a plane to Paris, our destination the Hotel Rafael, a baroque structure in the middle of the capital that could have passed itself off as an art museum. John was dressed in his usual yacht broker's uniform of impeccable blue blazer, blue tie with little obscure symbols on it and gray slacks. While 'Irv' chain-smoked Marlboros furiously, I straightened my tie and checked that there were no labels still hanging from the sports jacket I had just bought. I was taking no chances; this could be a million dollar deal for Nautor.

Paul Berrow phoned to say he would be down in a minute. Three quarters of an hour later an unshaven, lanky Englishman appeared in a baggy multicolored sweater with holes in it. He ushered us upstairs where his brother Michael, shorter and of similar appearance, and Paul's beautiful girlfriend, Miranda, were waiting. I felt like a complete idiot in my jacket, but Irving, a hardened sales veteran who had cut his teeth on the insurance business as a broker for Lloyds of London, rambled on in his usual relaxed fashion.

Simon Le Bon wasn't at this meeting, but the brothers explained their desire to do the Whitbread and why. In their mid-thirties they had amassed a considerable fortune managing Duran Duran, as the group rose from obscurity to world fame. Simon and the brothers, now close friends, all had some sailing experience and they reckoned in two years the timing would be right to take 'that year off' and do something completely different. Although the brothers had cruised transatlantic, neither they nor Simon had ocean racing experience.

John Irving tried his best to stick to his Nautor sales pitch. Plans of the Swan were laid out, building schedules discussed and the point quite rightly brought home that the Swan would be a good investment after the Race, reconverted to a cruising boat.

What the brothers were really interested in was the race itself. "What's it really like out there?" they would ask in a variety of forms. I explained the conditions under which 16 to 18 men would live for approximately 35 days at sea. I ended on a positive note, dwelling on the people side of things and how important it is that they all are compatible. After a long evening of coffee and cognac back in the hotel, 'Irv' and I both felt we had done our job. Promising each other we would all be in touch, we returned to London the following morning.

During the next 12 months I heard very little from the Berrows. I spent a typical year freelancing my services in a variety of projects. The yacht charter business is not my forte, but I happily filled in as a charter skipper for two months in the Caribbean on a Swan 651, compliments of John Irving again. That spring I converted the 61-foot racing sloop *War Baby* for an extended, four-month cruise to Scotland, Northern Norway and Spitsbergen in which I took part. Two weeks after I returned to England, Nautor signed me up to spend the fall in Finland commissioning the Swan 651 *Fazer Finland* and training her crew in big boat sailing. *Fazer* was a firm entry for the Whitbread.

Joined by my old shipmate, Brian 'Mugsy' Hancock, our job was to get the boat and crew started at the beginning stages of their campaign. Initially I had spent a week at Nautor in mid-September going through the equipment lists and specifying the modifications needed to transform *Fazer* from a cruising to a racing mode. Being 'up' at Nautor, is an apt description, as this prestigious yacht constructer's factory is located at 63 degrees North, 10 miles inland from the Gulf of Bothnia and surrounded by the boreal forest of Northern Finland. By September, winter is already in the air and the fall deliveries of their yachts must be on their way out before the beginning of November before the sea ice closes in.

After a two-week commissioning period and sea trials, Mugsy, the owner/skipper Micky Berner, myself and the 15 crew set out from the Nautor home town of Pietarsaari in an ice-cold northerly of late October with snow flurries. We were bound directly for Helsinki where we would spend 10 days in a publicity campaign and promotion.

The purpose of the visit to Helsinki was promotion and further fund raising. It was a good example of how sponsorship in yachting works. Fazer, a 19th-century family firm producing confectionery and bakery goods was the main sponsor. Hence the name *Fazer Finland.* Although Micky Berner had bought the boat outright from Nautor, Fazer had provided the bulk of the capital.

Minor sponsors who contributed to the campaign had the right, strictly written and enforced by the race rules, to have the names of their companies on the side of the boat in four-inch letters, just below the sheer line. They could also have a spinnaker and a sail cover carrying their company logos. 'Colt' is a brand name of the Rettig Group, which deals in tobacco, brewing, metals and shipping, among other businesses. Union Bank of Finland is Finland's oldest commercial bank and the country's leading export bank. 'Sampo' is a group of insurance companies in Finland with international holdings abroad. Thousands of miles away from the oceans of the world, these companies from tiny Finland all chose to put money into what would become a national focal point in the months ahead.

In simple terms the sponsor buys advertising space on boats he hopes will make news. But the sponsorship game is much more complex. Equally important to these high profile companies is the corporate entertainment aspect. While in Helsinki on view for the public at large, the yacht served as a venue for breakfast meetings, luncheon parties (one day Marcus the cook had to prepare for the Finnish prime minister), and evening cocktail parties for business clients and executive groups. Not only would Fazer and her other sponsors show their company flags during the race, but this social aspect would continue in all of the ports and after the race back in Finland.

Mugsy and I agreed to help sail the boat to southern Spain and then compete in an ocean race from there to Santo Domingo in the Dominican Republic. This one was commemorative of Columbus' discovery of America and would trace his route via the Gulf of Cadiz, the Canary Islands (where he is rumoured to have visited a mistress), then transatlantic to the Island of San Salvador and on down the length of the Bahamas and through the Mona Passage.

After this race, in which we were the first to finish, we had logged over 10,000 miles with the *Fazer* crew. Along the way we taught them to splice wire to wire, how to mend sails at sea (Mugsy's speciality), break down and repair winches and hydraulics, and most important of all to handle the sails efficiently and safely in all conditions. For a group of young people who in their own circles were the elite of Finnish sailing, they did not always take kindly to the regimentation required to race a big boat and what I am sure they thought was my ruthless approach to yacht racing. It would be almost a year later when they were in a solid third place on handicap half-way around the world (far ahead of *Drum*), that they admitted to us that without our help in the beginning it would have turned out quite differently. This was a gratifying tribute to our methods.

Only a day before we left Spain in the wake of Columbus, I received an urgent message from John Irving. Simon and the Berrows had resurfaced and were now desperate to enter a boat in the Whitbread. I was in a dilemma, now committed to this race that would put me out of touch for a month while the seeds of one of the biggest projects in yachting were about to be sown in Britain.

John was also in a difficult position. The three-man syndicate was now considering a Maxi boat rather than the Swan, having realized that their public image needed a boat that would be out in front in high profile. When this news broke in the marine industry, they were immediately descended upon by yacht brokers from three continents. Maxi boats are few and far between and despite the adage that 'everything is for sale,' even fewer were readily available.

While at sea I was in constant radio communications with John Irving and the Berrows. The drift seemed to be logically going in favor of a Maxi hull and deck lying uncompleted in a shed in Plymouth. It was the Ron Holland-designed *Colt Cars* and had been designed specifically for the Whitbread. Construction had begun two years before, but eight months ago the project had been halted when the sponsor backed out. The rumour was that it could be had for a good price, along with a spare mast and 30 bags of sails bought from the Spanish Maxi *Xargo*, and an engine and other equipment from Mitsubishi. Not only was boat selection an unsettled question, but also my position. I knew only too well that others in Britain would be vying for the skipper's job and with me temporarily offshore and out of the way, the groundwork I had laid a year ago was shaky.

Ironically, and unknown to me, the day we started from Spain on December 4th, the *Standard* in London carried an article entitled: CHAY IN LINE FOR POP STAR'S YACHT. "Three of the world's top sailors are shortlisted for the job of skipper on pop star Simon Le Bon's boat in the next year's Whitbread Round-the-World Yacht Race . . . Names on this list so far are headed: Chay Blyth, Jeff Houlgrave, and the veteran American, Skip Novak . . . Jeff Houlgrave, the man who attempted to save Dame Naomi James's husband Rob from drowning nearly two years ago, has been closely linked to the Colt Cars Project. He would be a natural choice if Le Bon decided to buy the boat – presently bearing a £275,000 tag for just the hull and mast. But Chay Blyth – who has renounced his vow never to round Cape Horn again after being shipwrecked there last month – is strongly in the running. Skip Novak is a professional racing skipper whose main disqualification in this instance is the fact that he is American. There is nothing to stop Le Bon from putting him on his boat, but it would severely detract from the idea of a powerful British challenger, in a race which has become dominated by entries from overseas."

The day we landed in Santa Domingo I made for the airport, a little poorer after Micky Berner, who seemed quite relieved there would not be another Swan 651 in the Race, assessed my overseas telephone bill against my wages. With an interim stop in the States, I landed at Heathrow on the eve of another London Boat Show.

It was one of Britain's coldest Januarys on record. Four inches of snow had brought London to a temporary standstill. Outside of Earls Court I ran into Harold Cudmore who was raising money to skipper the British 12-meter for the next America's Cup campaign in 1987. Harold is an Irishman with a British passport and one of the foremost match racing helmsmen in the world. However, charm and Irish ability to tell a good story, were more useful to him at the Boat Show than his racing ability. He and British yachtsman and syndicate manager Graham Walker had to coax more than £5 million out of the business community in order to mount a credible campaign. It was not surprising that he was exhausted by endless rounds of talks, refusals, and further appeals.

We wished each other luck as I pushed my way into the teeming mass of humanity of the Boat Show. The familiar back room at the Nautor stand was smoke filled and steamy. The negotiations had already begun to buy the *Colt* hull, and John Irving was laboring under pressure, having decided to remain with the Le Bon project as business manager. If he had realized the committment this would entail further down the road, he might have had second thoughts. On the other hand, it is standard procedure in the yachting industry, especially in brokerage at this level, that a good, but aberrant customer should be nurtured along in hopes of his returning to the Swan fold eventually.

The first chapter of the Colt Cars story had ended in tragedy. British yachtsman Rob James had commissioned the design from Ron Holland back in early 1983. One of the most respected long-distance sailors in the country, Rob had competed in the Whitbread in 1973 as crew on *Second Life*. In 1977 he skippered the then already ageing *Great Britain II* with a controversial crew of inexperienced paying guests.

In 1978 his young wife, New Zealand-born Naomi, sailed alone around the world and establishing a new record. The pair were Britain's new sailing success story. They settled in southern Ireland soon after and began to plan future sailing projects while writing books about their past exploits. With due respect to the many "professional" yachtsmen of Britain, the James's were the first to approach the sport so seriously and with such acumen, that not only did they do an outstanding job of satisfying their sponsors, but also successfully publicized themselves in a graceful and highly successful manner.

For tax reasons, Ireland, particularly the south coast where the weather is mild, has become a haven for artists and authors. There, Rob, Naomi and Ron Holland, their well-known neighbor in the village of Currabinny, joined together on a new project. The rural atmosphere and the increasingly cosmopolitan aspect of the community almost lends itself to what an Irishman would describe as "fostering grand ideas."

Having missed the Whitbread in 1982, Rob commissioned Ron to design a 60-foot trimaran for transatlantic single- and short-handed racing. Rob had secured a full sponsorship program from the Colt Cars Company in the UK, a subsidiary of the Japanese giant Mitsubishi. The flamboyant Michael Orr was at the helm of the Colt company and pushing its resources to what appeared to be acceptable limits. The trimaran began with success, winning the Round Britain Race, a two-handed event in which Naomi was Rob's crew. While the trimaran was still racing a full schedule, Michael Orr gave the thumbs up sign to a Ron Holland 78-footer for the next Whitbread Round-the-World Race coming up in 1985. For Rob it was all too good to be true.

But Rob never saw the start of the construction. He was drowned while on a delivery from Cowes to Plymouth when he fell through the trimaran's safety net between the sponson and the main hull while taking down the mainsail. Mate Jeff Houlgrave was the only experienced man on board and with the mainsail down and having no engine it was difficult to maneuver the unwieldy multihull back to Rob in the predawn darkness. Jeff had gone over the side with a line around himself and at one point had a hold of Rob, who was then losing consciousness, but with the sea running and the boat under its own way he lost his grip. Rob's body was picked up later that morning, having been washed inshore. Despite the tragedy Michael Orr and Colt stood by the committment to the Maxi, and the project began as planned in March, 1983, with Jeff Houlgrave the designated skipper/ project manager.

One-off boat construction, especially in plastics, is usually accomplished by a do-it-yourself approach. Very little tooling is needed as in metal construction and to cut costs it is quite typical to find a shed (or build one) and set up your own management company.

From the beginning, the Colt construction was confused at the design stage. Although Ron Holland had drawn the lines or 'shape' of the boat and specified the sail areas, the structural analysis and design as well as any further involvement was taken out of his control. The primary reason was that Mitsubishi Maritime set up by Michael Orr, had wanted to depart from what they considered was Ron's overly conservative approach to construction. They felt that they had to have an edge somewhere to beat the competition. Rob Lipsett, who had been involved in the construction of the Colt trimaran, was hired as building supervisor and with him came Adrian Thompson, the foremost local expert on composite materials.

For their unprecedented structural plan, they commissioned a local engineering consultancy firm that specialized in composite plastics to undertake an extensive computerized stress analysis. Using a data base from Scicion Int., a British Petroleum subsidiary that catered to industry and finance, this scheme cost the project £40,000. Supplying the research center with basic, known data of the loads on a Maxi, they produced a computer model of hull loadings that translated into reams upon reams of computer print-outs. These, when interpreted, laid the foundation for the types of materials and their alignment in the structure and hull. In short they supplied all the information Adrian needed to design the structural components and the laminates.

During the winter of 1983/84 the project was in full swing as were the rumours of Michael Orr's unlimited spending. By April the hull shell was complete as well as the deck, built in separate moldings. One day of that same month the work force was told not to come in. Michael Orr had been eased out of Colt for corporate reasons, so the story goes, and with that Mitsubishi shut down its division of Mitsubishi Maritime in Plymouth; no more funds were available.

Not long after the shed door was closed, Adrian landed a contract to build a radical 60-foot trimaran and Rob established himself in Cowes with his newly formed Vision Yachts Company, and began building a string of smaller craft for the Admiral's Cup and level racing. A disappointed Jeff Houlgrave tried desperately to find another financial backer in Britain, but he had no luck.

It's not clear where the Le Bon/Berrows trio first heard about the *Colt* hull, but I surmise it must have been at the Swan World Cup in Sardinia that September. All three were invited down by John Irving to crew on a Swan 651 called *Yellowdrama*. The Swan World Cup, one of yachting's most prestigious social occasions, consists of a week of inshore racing based out of Porto Cervo. You can hardly see this little community from a few miles offshore, so well did the architects adhere to the concept of a typical Sardinian village that should blend in with the natural surroundings of scrub and granite outcroppings. Of things Sardinian, it stops there. The brainchild of the Aga Khan, sportsman, investor, and the spiritual leader of Shi'a Moslems, the resort is elite, extremely expensive and totally artificial. Boasting several hotels, restaurants, discotheques and an elaborate marina with a boatyard and an extravaganza of a yacht club, Porto Cervo makes St. Tropez and Ibiza look like cheap, bourgeois tourist traps.

Since the resort was established only 15 years ago, the Aga Khan, a yachtsman enjoying the luxuries of his many high speed motor craft, has been host to a yearly schedule of international yachting events including the Sardinia Cup, the Mediterranean Maxi Series, world dinghy championships and even a Twelve Meter World Championship. But it is the Swan World Cup that is the most successful of them all.

What is essentially one of the most clever marketing campaigns in yachting, Nautor has built up an aura of what they describe as 'The Supreme Sailing Experience.' Swan owners are adroitly recognized as a breed apart; yachtsmen, discerning consumers and very often repeat customers. The Swan Cup provides nothing more than a stylish venue where this set can get together, race their boats in a relaxed atmosphere and hob nob with the likes of European royalty while coming to the conclusion their 51-footer needs to be upgraded to a 65, "Like so and so's over there." "Thank you very much," says the friendly agent as he rubs his hands together.

I can imagine John Irving's reaction when he heard that the Berrows and Simon had found out that there was a Maxi hull, designed and built specifically for the Whitbread, lying in waiting in Plymouth. It must have been clear that Simon's already high profile would be enhanced if they entered a big boat with chances of being first to finish. All eyes would be on Simon, and it would be difficult for the general public to understand the concept of handicaps and the International Offshore Rules that determines them.

There was another circumstance that led toward a maxi-yacht for the Berrows and Simon. Great Britain still did not have a credible entry in the Race. A journalist called Bob Salmon had entered the ageing *Great Britain II* once more, but his campaign was clearly understood to be low budget with 'charter guests' as crew. Miranda del

Morgan was rumored to be heading an all-female effort, but its chances did not look promising either. With only a year to the start, and with first-class big-boat entries from New Zealand, Switzerland, Holland, France, Finland and South Africa already on the water or about to be launched, the outlook for this seafaring nation hosting the biggest ocean race in the world was embarrassing.

Thus, when it was rumored that Le Bon was considering doing the Race, Whitbread's public relations company immediately began to lobby for his participation with the British-built Colt Cars Maxi. They didn't have to be too clever to realize that if Le Bon was in, publicity for Whitbreads and the Race would be automatic.

During the week at the Boat Show, Irving and I had made a budget based on the purchase of the Colt hull right through to the end of the campaign. Figures rounded out at roughly 1.7 million pounds and although Le Bon and the Berrows had made sizable fortunes during the five years they had been with Duran Duran, they had no intention of paying for all of it themselves. Hugh Marriott, Public Relations director for Whitbreads, explained to them why they would not have to foot the entire bill. Charity concerts were proposed, donations in kind were promised and on this rhetoric and on what appeared to be a few well-timed leaks to the press, they were swept past the point of no return. The fact of the matter was that although sponsorship was there, it was far too late to expect any single company to come up with really big numbers. This we all found out much later, having turned down a fair number of lesser offers. And so Britain had its big entry in the Round-the-World Race.

While the financial wrangling continued, feasibility studies had shown that it was possible to finish the boat in time, and that it would speed up construction to bring in the same people who had begun the job. It was in Ron Holland's best interest to promise all support from the design and consultancy side. He had only one Maxi in the Race, *Lion*, while his arch rival Bruce Farr, another Kiwi, had three. Adrian still had the structural design of the ring frames and longitudinals to complete and although pressed by two other projects underway he agreed to give us priority attention. It was the same with Rob Lipsett. Currently building three Admiral's Cup boats for the summer, all on tight schedules, he agreed to hire more labor and rent another shed for what was then code-named the Argo Project.

Meanwhile, independent of our negotiations, the Colt hull was already on the move. It turned out that another syndicate was very close to purchasing the package and Mitsubishi had made arrangements to have the boat transported by truck down to Moody's Marina on the Hamble River. There it was to be launched and towed west through the Solent to Lymington where the Berthon Boat Company would broker it and then hopefully land the contract to finish it.

Luckily for us, the Berthon Boat Company is inaccessible for an overloaded truck making its way over the winding English country lanes. On January the 10th, the naked, white hull arrived at Moody's, was unloaded from the truck and put on hold while Irving dealt with Berthon's.

By this time the word had leaked out that a rockstar had entered the Whitbread Round-the-World Race. Rumours of Duran Duran concerts in every port and wild speculation about how Simon Le Bon would fare as a yachtsman were popular topics. A growing pessimism, fostered by a few individuals who were not involved but would have liked to have been, took root. They claimed that it was impossible to finish the boat in time for a needed sea trial. It is very 'British' to play down someone else's success, so I declared in my best Mid-Western accent, "Hey man, in America every thing is possible, we'll just have to work longer hours!"

To avoid having to explain what was still unofficial, I gave the Guinness Stand a wide berth on my way to Nautor HQ. I took a circuitous route through the motorboat aisles, outboards and engines, avoiding the areas where the sailmakers, hardware manufacturers, and yachting magazines were located, because I knew they would either give me the third degree to which I could only answer 'no comment,' or try to sell me something on spec!

On January 11th at the Boat Show, with all of the principals in attendance, we set a schedule that would see the boat launched in the middle of June. The plan was to tow the boat from Moody's to Rob's Vision Yachts in Cowes to finish the structure and then six weeks later tow it back to Moody's which had been awarded the contract of fitting her out with deck gear, interior, and machinery.

Although it was top secret that Simon was due to arrive at the Boat Show to meet everyone for the first time, the groupies, who seem to know what is going to happen before it is planned, had already gathered outside the velvet rope divider that separates the casual public from potential Swan customers who enter by advance appointment.

The door opened with a clank of chains and spurs, and Simon, clad from head to foot in black leather, his bleached blond plume of hair standing on end, came in and introduced himself. "Those boots may be a little hard on the fiberglass," some wise guy said under his breath, but big money ultimately commands respect, and he awaited his lordship's next move like the rest of us.

Although I didn't admit it to any one at the time, I had a great dread of becoming involved in what some visualized to be a circus project; rockstar buffoons sailing around the world strumming guitars in the southern ocean with the crew no more than props in some madcap publicity stunt. Although I can't recall what was said, I was pleasantly relieved that he was straightforward and easy to talk to. So far so good.

The project seemed to be set contingent on the negotiations with Mitsubishi, which were strung out and frustrating. On assurances that we could finish the boat in time and on Whitbread's promise that the sponsorship would be forthcoming, the Berrows and Simon took the "leap of faith." Realizing from this day forth, their reputations would be on the line, Paul Berrow made his feelings quite clear to me. "There is one thing that cannot happen," he said as he pointed his cigar at me like a gun, "We cannot come sixth out of six Maxis." I assured him we would not.

By January 20th the contract had been signed and the boat was ours. The Boat Show was over, and although we had not made the hoped-for announcement, the story hit the press on the 22nd that the boat was on the move to Cowes. In the same article the yachting journalist Tony Fairchild made it plain that this British project was being undermined by an American.

He wrote in the *Telegraph* that day, "Simon Le Bon, the lead singer with the pop group Duran Duran, is understood to be buying the boat – only legal niceties prevent full revelation of the facts, it seems – and with American "Skip" Novak to be in command. With respect to Novak, an experienced Round-the-World skipper, it will seem a pity if "British Pop" is not under the command of a Briton. The myth, being given wide credence, that there are no Britons capable of undertaking such a task as skipper is nonsense. There are a dozen who come to mind at once."

That bit of controversy went completely unnoticed and my place as skipper was officially confirmed. The boat was British, that was the main thing, and besides, after ten years abroad, I had lost most of my Mid-Western accent and was verbally unobtrusive.

John Irving and I left London and returned to the South Coast. While Simon and Mike and Paul Berrow would no doubt be thumbing through sailing manuals and sea adventure stories, I bought the latest Duran Duran albums and made a point to watch 'Top of the Pops' every Thursday night on the BBC. We all had a lot to learn.

---

opposite Navigator Roger brings the log and the positions of the other boats on deck in good weather in hope of explaining the tactical situation to the crew, during some pleasant sailing on Leg One (*Photo by Skip Novak*)

overleaf No one expected to be deeply reefed on Leg Two; once again, we lash up the foot of the mainsail, somewhere south of Kerguelen Island (*Photo by Skip Novak*)

4 · A Worldly Occupation

The Businessman: *Surely you can't go sailing your whole life.*
The Sailor: *I haven't really thought about it.*
The Businessman: *What's going to happen when you're too old?*
The Sailor: *I'll probably go into business.*

Competitive sailing is probably as old as sailing itself. Modern Yacht racing probably derived from competition between 19th-century sailing ship captains who raced not only by being first in with a cargo but also for their reputations among other captains. They formed an informal men's club which was the basis for what has gone on in yachting ever since.

In Clipper Ship days, the European trade was in silks, tea and spices. In America, the contest was to fight Cape Horn and make the California gold fields with general cargo. Until World War II, the Grain Race from South Australia had the last of the Windjammers making their long hauls back to Europe with wheat.

In 1852 no fewer that 15 Clipper Ships had set out during one month from New York and Boston bound for what the unfortunate crews popularized as 'Cape Stiff'. The *Wild Pigeon*, the *John Gilpin* and the *Flying Fish*, all crack Clippers of the day, made history that year when they sailed out in front of the others and in sight of each other on and off for a passage that lasted over three months. 93 days out the *John Gilpin* slid under the Golden Gate Bridge only a day ahead of the *Flying Fish* although the *Flying Fish's* time out of port was a day and a half less. Though the record still stood at 89 days 4 hours set by the *Flying Cloud* the year before, the glory of the moment went to the captain of the *Flying Fish* for having set the year's best elapsed time.

In 1866, English captains and shipowners had organized a similar contest of even grander proportions, with attendant wagers, rewards, and publicity. To be first in with China tea was the object of the exercise and a 10 shilling per ton premium was promised the winner.

---

opposite King Neptune meets us at the Equator as expected; our crew who had not crossed the 'line' before found the ritual less pleasant than those of us who had (*Photo by Skip Novak*)

Sixteen Clippers had rallied in Foochow that spring to load the first of the spring tea harvest from China. After a confused few days getting out of the river, five leaders took to the fore, but 21 days later by the Sunda Straits which separates Sumatra from Java and is the gateway to the Indian Ocean, all but two had dropped well astern. What followed during the next 78 days was a match race between the *Taeping* and the *Ariel*, all the way to the docks in London. The accounts of the 15,000 mile voyage leave no doubt about the speed and determination with which they changed sails and shifted ballast from tack to tack. It was a contest that rivalled, and surpassed, in terms of pure, hard work, any ocean race held since.

Racing as a 'gentlemanly' sport, also made its appearance at about the same time. In 1851 the English lost a silver mug to the Americans in a race around the Isle of Wight. The trophy became known as the America's Cup. It was, and remained until recently, the holy grail of Corinthian yachting. The Corinthians, by their own definition, saw themselves as amateurs, and this was correctly construed as a class distinction dividing them from professional sailors (in those days fishermen and merchant seamen). This was not surprising because, then as now, they needed boat loads of money to pay for their sailing.

Fifteen years later, three American schooners raced from New York to Cowes. At stake were gentlemanly wagers by the three owners, all captains of industry. In those days it was protocol to leave the sailing of a race to professional captains and sailors, and in this case it was even more understandably so because the three vessels left Sandy Hook in early December! J. Gordon Bennett Jr.'s *Henrietta* won that contest taking just less than 14 days to cross on the heels of some typically savage winter gales. Years later this impromptu event would be considered to have been the first offshore ocean yacht race.

Racing for shipowner's profits and captain's bonuses died with the last of the Windjammers in the 1930's. However, the celebrated J-Class yachts were jockeying around the America's Cup course for nothing more than the same silver trophy. When the J-boats had succumbed to World War II professional sailors went with them, leaving the Corinthians happy to race on by themselves.

After World War II, particularly in America, money was abundant, and where the old, established yacht clubs failed to liberalize their membership qualifications to include other than blue-blooded, white Anglo-Saxon Protestants, enthusiasts just got together and formed their own clubs. It was boom-time for a great leisure industry.

While sailing developed at every level from dinghy fleets to the new America's Cup 12-meter yachts, other yachtsmen were looking off-shore as a way of combining their desire for racing with a love of cruising to far away places. No less wealthy and determined than their sea-going predecessors, these captains of industry took the sport beyond that of a weekend pastime. They created a yearly circuit of regattas and passage-making races in almost every corner of the globe. The craft ranged in size from about 35 to 75 feet, were well equipped and crewed, and could cross any ocean in any weather with confidence.

Some of the races were annual or semi-annual events. Others were one-off affairs in conjunction with an organized cruise after the finish. The names were the stuff of a dockboy's dreams: The Bermuda Race, Transatlantic to Copenhagen, Sydney-to-Hobart, Cape Town to Rio, The Fastnet Race, Transpacific to Hawaii, Buenos Aires to Rio, Miami to Montego Bay, Hong Kong to Manila, Transatlantic to Cork. Crewed by a combination of transient hands and friends of the owner, a Transatlantic Race may have taken 16 to 18 days, the Sydney-to-Hobart, Bermuda Race and Fastnet only 3 or 4. At the end of the hard slog there were days of relentless celebration, a refit, and then, for the transients at least, off on a delivery to the next venue, which could be half way around the world.

In 1971, at the age of eighteen, I took a long Easter holiday from my university in the American Midwest and sailed my first ocean race from Miami to Montego Bay, Jamaica. The 40-footer took five days to log the 800 miles which skirted the edge of the Bahama Banks and then direct through the Windward Passage between Cuba and Haiti. For one who had only travelled locally, this first passage to a foreign land was a fantasy come alive. Warm seas, tropical islands with magical names, and dolphins riding the bow wave were certainly a change from the western suburbs of Chicago.

I went back to the cornfields of Illinois, full of stories and impressed with the lifestyle of the regulars on board those boats. As a result I put in less time on schooling and more on sailing. I spent the entire winter quarter racing in the Southern Ocean Racing Conference in Florida and Bahamian waters. In January I joined the professional boat hands preparing for the six-race series that is known the world over by yachtsmen as the SORC.

My job was on a 40-footer from Chicago and I was pleased to find many familiar faces on the other boats. Most of these 'professional' boat hands who maintained and delivered the bigger boats between races were foreigners at that time. Australians and New Zealanders were in the majority, with Englishmen, South Africans, and a few Americans rounding out this colorful mix of marine talent. They all had nicknames, 'The Fat Rabbit', 'The Abbo', 'Bruce The Goose', 'Chas from Tas', 'Sticky', 'The Flying Nun', 'Jocko' and 'Tom the Pom' were a few examples. They happily referred to themselves collectively as 'boatniggers'. Bruce Kendall, aka 'Bruce the Goose' was a classic, having skippered a succession of *Kialoas* for Jim Kilroy for over ten years, and is now a successful businessman in his own right. "He had three attributes necessary at the time," an observer once said. "He spoke with a foreign accent, played the guitar, and knew how to fix a Diesel engine."

The subject of a feature article in the Summer 1981 issue of *Nautical Quarterly*, Mike Levitt described 'boatniggers' in this way: "You know them by their righteous, self-satisfied smiles, facial messages that say 'I've got it made'. They have tans so indelible and deep their brains must be slow-cooked medium-rare. Their sundry UK accents can charm a publican out of a pint or a 'racer chaser' out of her knickers . . . Their lives seem an endless summer; their 'work' is what others consider play". For this American, a product of a school system that preached liberal arts in a society that invented the service industry, but could hardly drive a nail or cut a board in a straight line, this crowd, mostly apprenticed tradesmen, seemed a capable group indeed. As one guy said to me, "The Kiwis don't muck around mate, they just get on with it. Tell us to build you a house, we'll build you a house."

The racing, and indeed the living, was hard and good that year. Get togethers were continually being organized by the crews and the camaraderie was strong. We all knew each other and living on board (when boats still had habitable interiors) with everyone in close proximity made for a friendly, 'get to know you' atmosphere that is somehow lacking today with everyone off in hotels. As an added bonus I was on board the 40-foot *Condor*, a Great Lakes boat that won the whole series that year.

After a sobering spring quarter back in Illinois, I managed to land a berth on the 1972 Bermuda Race and Transatlantic from there to Bayona, Spain, on the new 61-foot *Dora IV*. All the big boats were there: *Ondine*, *Kialoa*, *Windward Passage*, *Blackfin*, *Phantom* and others all crewed in large part by the professionals. *Dora* was a Chicago boat owned by a much respected Corinthian by the name of Lynn Williams. Already in his 60's with a distinguished career in law, engineering and later Chicago politics, this long-time yachtsman was planning the offshore passage of his lifetime. The boat was very well built in aluminum by Palmer Johnson Inc. of Sturgeon Bay, Wisconsin and Williams was a stickler for seamanship and preparedness. Some criticized him at the time for the almost eccentric degree to which he carried his lists of tools and spare parts, but he was vindicated as early as the second day out from Newport to Bermuda.

The Bermuda Race is a direct shot, 630 miles, crossing the Gulf Stream on the way. After the first day the fleet was weathering the effects of a severe tropical depression to the south and the going was rough bucking the current. In the rush to prepare this new boat for its first big contest, no one had thought to double-check the cotter pins in the turnbuckles after the last tuning of the mast and rigging. When bashing along under reduced sail, the starboard, leeward turnbuckle on the lower shroud unscrewed itself and fell overboard. Scowling from the hatch, the 'Old Man' simply asked for the spare turnbuckle to be put on and the other ones checked. He was infuriated to learn that it had been left ashore, but his solution was the banding tool.

We all questioned the use of this metal strapping device, the kind you bail up cardboard boxes with for shipping until he proposed the simple solution of passing the metal straps through the eye of the shroud and back through the rail as many times as possible. I will never forget being down on the lee rail with Mike Clancy, usually completely underwater and being washed helplessly about while painstakingly rigging up this clever jury rig. I was seasick at the time but most likely no one noticed as the vomit was washed clear of the deck as fast as it had been deposited there. Without losing any time by favoring the boat (or crew) we made the repair. It permitted us to tack for Bermuda and, in what turned out to be one of the toughest Bermuda Races in its history, we finished 2nd in Class A and 5th overall. Williams might be proud of me if he were alive today; his methods have rubbed off on me. I have the reputation for being ridiculously conservative when it comes to carrying excess weight in spare parts and tools, but also the satisfaction of never having retired from an ocean race for the lack of them.

The Transatlantic to the northwest corner of Spain took the inordinately long passage time of 21 days. Knowing what I know now, I still can't understand why almost the entire fleet sailed right into the middle of the Azores High (the winner took the obvious track up to the north of it). Despite the slow going it was a great first ocean passage for me, out of sight of land for the entire voyage except for a landfall on the volcanic island of Flores in the Azores. With her green and purple hillsides disappearing up into a cloud, the island could have been in the South Pacific, at least for this boy from the Midwest. Among a crew of veterans I was the kid on board. I was already pretty handy around the deck of a boat and what I lacked in experience I made up for in enthusiasm. If someone had to go over the side – I did it. Up to the top of the mast – me again. I dabbled in celestial navigation, learned the constellations and thoroughly enjoyed myself at sea.

That fall quarter in university was an abject failure. I failed most subjects, mainly because of lack of attention and attendance. Wiping that off the record books, I went south again for another SORC on *Dora IV* which had been delivered back from Europe via the Canaries and the Caribbean. That spring it was Jamaica again and than a race to Isla Mujeres in Yucatan.

"How do you get to be a skipper, Clancy?" I asked my mentor of those days. "I don't know, Novak," he said as he took a pull on his Heineken, "You know what they say? Once a mate, always a mate."

I remembered his words while negotiating my first big delivery as skipper; a jury-rigged 40-footer that had been dismasted at the finish of the Mexico Race. I lied to the owner when he asked me if I could use the sextant. The Loran packed in the day after we left for Tampa and soon after the engine quit as well. Narrowly escaping the coast of Cuba in a northerly, we limped our way to the Florida coast and the crew seemed quite impressed with their skipper's dead reckoning abilities not knowing that it was only by the wildest chance that we made landfall anywhere near Tampa Bay.

Every activity, whether profession, sport or hobby seems to go through the evolutionary process of specialization. Just as the Renaissance Man seems to be a scarcity today, so is the ocean sailing yacht that once could sail successfully on all points of the wind and in any waters. Up until the early seventies the ocean racing class had competed in both inshore, day races as well as transoceanic passages, but then the situation changed. A young group of maverick designers with little formal training (and therefore no preconceptions) to realize and prove by experiment that lighter displacement hulls with fin keels would easily knock the socks off the old school, Ron Holland, Doug Peterson, and later German Frers, came to the fore almost overnight with these dinghy-like craft and quickly rendered the older, more conservative designs of the famous Sparkman & Stevens, from 'J-Class' and 12-Meter fame, uncompetitive.

Through new thinking and the use of new technology and materials the new designers could achieve light displacement yachts that were faster on the race course. There were failures; hull skins would delaminate, rudder stocks made from carbon fiber would break and the flimsy rigs more and more frequently would come crashing down. The statistics of the SORC bear this out quite clearly. In 1972 there were 97 entries and only three DNF's (did not finish) in the six race series. In 1978 in an 86 boat fleet, the number of drop outs due mainly to rig and rudder failure was a staggering 24.

Rather than a trend back to integrity, the participants embraced disaster after disaster in the quest for lightness and speed, but at a price. The lighter boats, now suspect in long passages, went offshore less and less. This was in part due to the lack of comfort below decks. In fact, the International Offshore Rule (IOR) has had to legislate through the years against extreme stripping of interiors. It reached a point where racing yachts carried heads which were never used, bunks that were stacked three deep to a side, and were generally fitted out as torture chambers.

Huey Long, the grand old man of ocean passage racing, explained his feelings to me while in Spain in 1983 and summed up the situation in few words. "I still love good seaworthy boats that you can go to sea and feel comfortable with in any kind of a gale. In the old days the rules were not such that you worried about them so far as the rating was concerned. We never had the rules set up so it became much of a factor. But then the thinking about boat building changed, and now we've come up with what? A boat that is a disaster offshore. These new boats are only good for going around the buoys, short races, maybe an overnighter in protected waters, and that's it. And I think it's a damn shame. We don't do ocean races any more; we do Olympic triangles, match racing, trying to do things that belong to other types of boats."

Wiry, tough and known as a 'hard man' in yachts and business, Long was fighting a losing battle. How different the new influx of yacht owners must have seemed: younger, flabbier and with new money and buying their way into a sport he had spent most of his life developing. Certainly this new crowd has never known the ocean and with the newer craft they have little intention of being miserable offshore.

Even others in the old guard had gone the way of light and fast boats on short passages. Jim Kilroy, self-made real estate baron from California had been Long's arch-rival for 20 years with his fleet of *Kialoas*. Technically orientated, he was the first to apply the new, small boat techniques of design and construction to the Maxis. What he fostered was the 80-foot day racer that arguably was unfit to go offshore.

Said the patriarch of ocean racing in 1983, "I've made six Transatlantic, nine Transpacs, three Sydney Hobarts, you name the others. I've done a lot of long distance races, I've done my share. I'd rather now go out and race a hard afternoon or overnighter. I've made and won the long races and would now rather look at a different situation. To look at it another way, the shorter races that Class A is advocating gives you more bang for the buck. And anyway what do you prove on a 600 miler that you don't on a day race? I'll tell you what, you prove that there are more windshifts, more vagaries, your people get tired, etc. Short courses are more competitive and more fun. They involve more yacht handling and sailing skills and I think this direction is a good one for yacht racing."

Consequently, the longer hauls had died out. In that 1972 race from Bermuda to Spain the fleet was over 40 strong. In the race to Cork, Ireland in 1979 there was less than half that number. In that year *Kialoa* and *Ondine* had match raced neck and neck all the way across. *Kialoa* won, and after, both crews agreed that trying to race these big powerful boats like small boats on the open ocean was for the birds. As the Aussie bowman had said to me after the race. "It was a bloody shit-fight mate!"

While this trend was running its course in the States with other international yachting fraternities following suit, the idea of the ocean passage race was gaining new life in Europe, but in a different manner and for different reasons. Europe has always been the center of activity for the experimental and the unorthodox. Witness singlehanding, multihull development, and indeed the Whitbread Race. In America, concepts like the International Ocean Racing rule or the 12-meter rule were developed in its own parameters to a very high degree. In Europe, the tendency was to explore new territories, both theoretical and geographic.

It all came down to the people involved. Certainly France never had a strong yachting tradition in the 'club' atmosphere. Wealthy boat owners were not the ones doing the sailing just for peer gratification. Eric Tabarly, a young, French naval lieutenant, had won the first Observer Single Handed Transatlantic Race in 1964 and had overnight become a legend. He raced for a living and living by sponsorship before the word was ever applied to the sport. It just happened to be the Navy doing the sponsoring and what better public relations for a branch of the armed services? More significantly he was to become the precursor of what is known as the 'French System'. Young people with talent in the sport were shepherded through dinghys, level racing, and on into the glories of long distance and grand prix multi-hull racing, subsidized throughout. Witness recent French success in all facets of yacht racing.

Although English yachting had developed along the same lines as American, a similar movement was also taking place. It was clear to a few individuals that they would never have enough money to own and maintain big yachts and they would have to take a different tack to achieve their goals.

Enter Robin Knox-Johnston and Chay Blyth, household words in Britain for the last twenty years. Blyth with another ex-paratrooper John Ridgway, pulled off the clever stunt of rowing across the Atlantic in a converted lifeboat in 1966. Their instant notoriety must have surprised even themselves, and future projects came one after another.

In 1969 Knox-Johnston, in the wake of that famous Englishman, Sir Francis Chichester, had been the only one to finish an informal, non-stop, singlehanded race around the world. He has never looked back from a career of skippering big, sponsored boats, running long-distance races and training sailors.

The idea of a fully crewed race around the world had been brewing well before the first one was staged in 1973. Two yachting journalists, Guy Pearse and the well-known publisher of *Sea Horse* Magazine, Anthony Churchill, had conceived the race and had worked out the logistics back in 1969. Unable to finance the race themselves, they had to opt out of the organization, leaving the way clear for the Royal Naval Sailing Association to apply its vast resources.

The RNSA is not officially part of the Royal Navy, although it advises the Admiralty on all aspects of sailing, a sport wholly endorsed and encouraged by the RN. Its members number in the thousands worldwide and understandably most are retired servicemen with a wealth of experience not only in sailing, but more importantly in organization and logistics.

Whitbread Breweries agreed to sponsor the event and, in June of 1972, the first Whitbread Round-the-World Race was announced. The course was to be Portsmouth (home of the RNSA) to Cape Town, Cape Town to Sydney, Sydney to Rio and Rio back to Portsmouth. The total distance was roughly 27,000 miles and the committee's logistics set the start date from England on September 8th, 1973.

Sixteen yachts entered that first Race, and fourteen completed all four legs. The big names were there. Chay Blyth entered a 77-footer called *Great Britain II*, built and crewed by members of the paratroop regiment. Tabarly entered *Pen Duick VI*, a French-designed 73-footer especially built for the Race. The Navy entered their Nicholson 55, *Adventure*, while the army entered *British Soldier*, the 59-foot Robert Clark design that Chay Blyth had just used to make his celebrated non-stop singlehanded circumnavigation from east to west only two years before. The first race had a highly international flavor. Poland, Italy, Mexico, Germany and South Africa were represented.

Great Britain II had the fastest combined elapsed time of 144 days 11 hours, but the glory went to Mexico whose *Sayula*, crewed by a cast of international vagabonds, took 152 days 9 hours, but won on handicap by just under two days to her rival, *Adventure*.

That first race had both a colorful and tragic history. Tabarly's mast came down on Leg Three; *Burton Cutter*, another British entry, had to retire from Leg Two with hull damage and several boats had rolled over with dire consequences. The three lives lost from *Great Britain II*, *33 Export* from France and *Tauranga* from Italy served as a reminder once again that the ocean could not be taken for granted.

Butch Dalrymple-Smith, crewman on *Sayula*, wrote wryly about his experience in 'Yachts and Yachting' soon after the finish of what was considered to be, not a race, but the greatest sailing adventure:

Did I enjoy it? No. No, I don't believe anyone actually enjoyed the sailing while it was going on. Like a woman after childbirth who forgets the pain, so we forget the cold and frustration, the perpetual wet and the moments of pure terror of sailing a yacht fast through the Southern Ocean.

It is the pleasant moments that we remember. Ghosting along under the moon with 'Quique' strumming quietly on the guitar; landfall after 40 days at sea; coming off the deck after a hard, frustrating six-hour watch and relaxing in the warm and dry, with Max Bruch's Violin Concerto to soothe the soul and a gin and tonic for the body. The times with the multinational crew laugh-

*ing and joking in an ambiance that can only be found when different people
come together in sharing a deep experience.*

Looking back after 12 years of a multifaceted sailing career, Butch
now remembers what it was like to have done the first of the
Whitbread Races:

"I think the biggest thing was that we were sailing into the
unknown. Although many yachts had sailed through the Southern
Ocean, we were the first racing fleet to sail there fully crewed,
prepared to push the boats through places where traditional stories
tell of giant waves, icebergs and all sorts of unpleasantness.

I remember telling a journalist that we could count the race a
success if all the yachts were accounted for in the end. I thought it
quite likely that a yacht would disappear without trace, as many
other fully crewed sailing ships had done before in that part of the
world. We were of course saddened by the three deaths, but not
altogether surprised. Before the start the biggest talking point had
been the danger, not who would win.

During the race we were more out of touch than nowadays
without the electronic aids to navigation, decent radios and of
course the Argos system. In the event of a problem a man on the
moon could expect help quicker than we could.

We drank a lot. Our average for the entire trip was 6 bottles of
wine every day's sailing, and every day each crewman would have
(at least one) large cocktail as he came off the deck after his 6-hour
day watch. We figured that doing the race was privation enough.
The least we could do was to keep as civilized and as comfortable as
possible. The food was good, much to the surprise of one journalist
who saw 11 jars of caviar still left in the deep freeze at the end of the
first leg. We played up to our image. I don't think it slowed us
down much, and I know it hurt the other crews psychologically,
slopping into their freeze dried curries, knowing *Sayula* would be
having steak again. I should point out that we did take the racing
fairly seriously, once doing 150 sail changes in a 72 hour period.

We were not aware of ours being 'the first' Whitbread Race. It
was conceived as a one-off event, and not until more than half way
round rumors began about a possible sequel. The standard of racing
is much higher now. I guess my best bit of luck was competing in
the first race. It was so much easier to win."

It was the stories from adventures like these that led me to abandon
the American Dream. In the summer of 1976 I delivered a 51-footer
from Bermuda to France, with the vague notion that long-distance
racing was to be my immediate future.

5 · Creating the Monster

"Never before have we had so little time in which to do so much."
Franklin D. Roosevelt

The Colt Cars hull was to be Ron Holland's third Maxi project. His *Kialoa IV* and *Condor* were both tried and tested designs and had had many successes in the Maxi circuit worldwide.

It is a fact that the Whitbread design requirement is very different from the concept which those two represented, being intended more for short course racing.

Through discussions with Rob James about his experience it was agreed that although a Maxi boat was the main requirement, one that was lighter with proportionately more sail area would be more effective, say for example in the light airs of the Doldrums, and also be efficient in light to moderate airs on most points of sail. They felt that a full blown Maxi, like a relatively heavy *Condor* would suffer in what they considered to be the critical stages of the race. Also it was a known fact that the weight and power of the bigger Maxis made them difficult to sail and hard on the crew. The Holland boats were, therefore, very much in the IOR mold, but with minor concessions in tall rigs, a lot of keel area for going up wind, and big propellers and heavy engines.

Of course, we know now that Bruce Farr's philosophy was different, but at the time I easily accepted the Holland view. Ron was one of the top designers, not to mention a personal friend, and of course it was all we had. Besides, I reasoned that Peter Blake, with all the planning time and resources he needed had the same machine in *Lion*, and it was hard to believe that he would be far off the mark.

In the world of custom racing sailboats, shape is one thing, building it is something else. Most modern designers have been guilty of not producing enough proper drawings. In a perfect world the builder constructs the boat to the designer's drawings and specifications which include a lines plan and tables of offsets, a construction plan with detailed areas of importance, rig plan, interior, deck plan, plumbing, wiring, and machinery installation.

The builders should be so lucky. Anybody in the business has

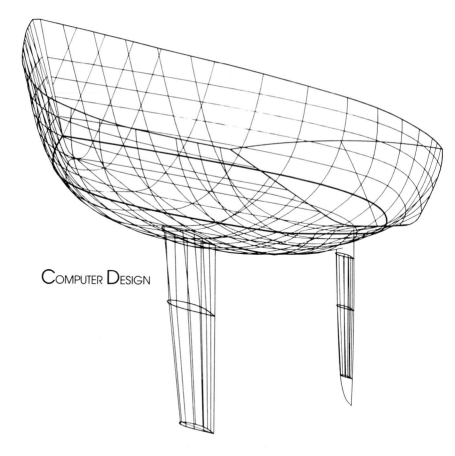

COMPUTER DESIGN

stories to tell. Years ago, building the smaller race boats was largely left up to the builder's discretion. Sometimes he would be given a lines plan and nothing else. Problems would be dealt with as they came up: how to attach the stemhead, the method of rudder installation, and even weight distribution in the structure itself. It was no wonder that few of these boats came out floating on their lines. Items like interior arrangements, plumbing, and wiring? "Do it like you did on the last boat," was a stock directive.

After a time and after numerous failures, when yachts literally fell to pieces, the situation gradually improved. Although the established designers like Ron Holland have weathered this period well and improved their methods, the old system still exists whereby a designer leaves too much up to the builder's abilities. However some long-standing partnerships of designers and builders have produced superb, quality yachts in this way. German Frer's and Ron Holland's marriage with Huisman Shipyard in Holland and Nautor in Finland are probably the best examples.

The *Drum* affair was unfortunate for Ron, and it needs to be said that the project which we inherited had been taken out of his hands

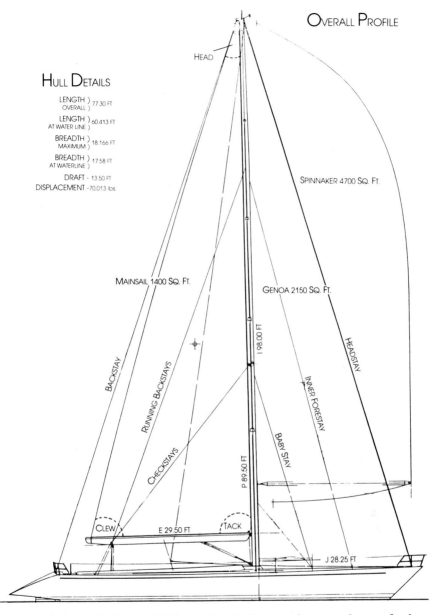

Overall Profile

Hull Details

LENGTH)
OVERALL) 77.30 FT

LENGTH) 60.413 FT
AT WATER LINE)

BREADTH) 18.166 FT
MAXIMUM)

BREADTH) 17.58 FT
AT WATERLINE)

DRAFT - 13.50 FT
DISPLACEMENT - 70.013 lbs

HEAD

SPINNAKER 4700 SQ. FT.

MAINSAIL 1400 SQ. FT.

GENOA 2150 SQ. FT.

BACKSTAY

RUNNING BACKSTAYS

CHECKSTAYS

HEADSTAY

INNER FORESTAY

BABY STAY

I 98.00 FT

P 89.50 FT

CLEW

E 29.50 FT

TACK

J 28.25 FT

after Rob James' death. Without Ron's input, the members of what was then Mitsubishi Maritime would later admit that they didn't have the experience needed in the later stages of the construction.

With Le Bon on the scene and people in charge who he had worked with before, Holland must have been happy once again to be back in control of *Drum's* design program. However the years that had elapsed had taken their toll on what had started as Colt Cars. The hull that was now lying in the shed at Cowes was an inaccurate rendition

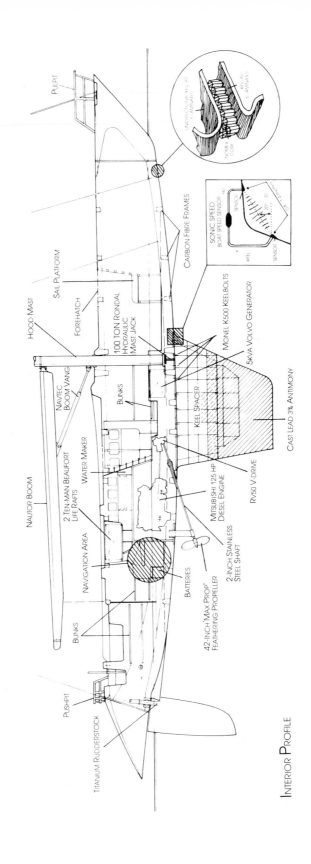

PULPIT

CARBON FIBRE FRAMES

SAIL PLATFORM

HOOD MAST

FOREHATCH

100 TON RONDAL
HYDRAULIC
MAST JACK

NAUTOR BOOM

NAVTEC
BOOM VANG

WATER MAKER

2 TEN-MAN BEAUFORT
LIFE RAFTS

NAVIGATION AREA

BUNKS

BUNKS

KEEL SPACER

MONEL K500 KEEL BOLTS

5KVA VOLVO GENERATOR

CAST LEAD 3% ANTIMONY

RV50 V-DRIVE

MITSUBISHI 125 HP
DIESEL ENGINE

2-INCH STAINLESS
STEEL SHAFT

BATTERIES

42-INCH 'MAX PROP'
FEATHERING PROPELLER

PUSHPIT

TITANIUM RUDDERSTOCK

SONIC SPEED
BOAT SPEED SENSOR

SENSOR

KEEL

INTERIOR PROFILE

of Ron's original lines. While in Plymouth, small modifications were made in the hull, and had had no part in laying out the deck mold or the structural members. The drawings left over from Mitsubishi Maritime were so dog-eared and scribbled on that we realized after one aborted attempt to marry one piece to another that all further constructions would have to be templated off the boat itself. Even the overall length was in question! I saw drawings and correspondence with 76 feet, 78 feet 6 inches and 77 feet. After a quick measurement I can confirm that she is 77 feet 4 inches, stem to stern.

To complicate matters even further the nature of the material we were working in is capricious at the best of times. Unlike a metal boat (aluminium being the classic material for bigger boats) where the construction is by straightforward welding, bonding of plastics, fibers, and resin, known as 'composite', is still more art than science in their use in boat building. Not so in the aircraft industry where the economics of size make the difference. There, the use of Kevlar, carbon fiber, and epoxy resins in a variety of techniques has been made a science. The strength-to-weight ratio of these synthetics has made them a basic material for light airplanes. In the aircraft industry, however, there are rigid controls, inspections and regulations, And, of course, failure has dire consequences. To price a corporate jet built of 'composite' is to experience the price of technology.

Yachts are a different matter. If the carbon fiber rudder stock falls off or the laminate splits and lets the ocean trickle in you simply head back to shore or if you're unlucky, spend a few days in a life raft. Because all racing boats of this pedigree are experimental, it is understood that in the search for the lightest and fastest structure the design will allow, there will be failures.

While the aircraft industry exists in a business environment, yachts, are, after all, a hobby. The game has bred an acceptance of the fact that things do go wrong. Only the forgiving nature of the sea renders these big plastic toys usually harmless. Like a lot of things in this world it takes a death or two to wake people up. In the infamous 1979 Fastnet Race where 15 people lost their lives, for the first time in a long time everyone took a good long look at the designs, the methods of construction and the safety standards. It did a lot of good, but at an extremely high price.

Gary Carlin, one of the leaders in the field in the early 80's described how in *Kialoa IV's* construction, which was the first attempt to build a composite hull of Maxi boat size, the addition of 'exotic material' was almost subjective in nature. In an interview for *Nautical Quarterly* in America he explained how the boat was strengthened and stiffened in certain areas, "You add more Kevlar here, less there. Carbon fiber here and not there. Under the primaries (the winches) there is Kevlar for tension; but it's lousy for compression so you put in glass for com-

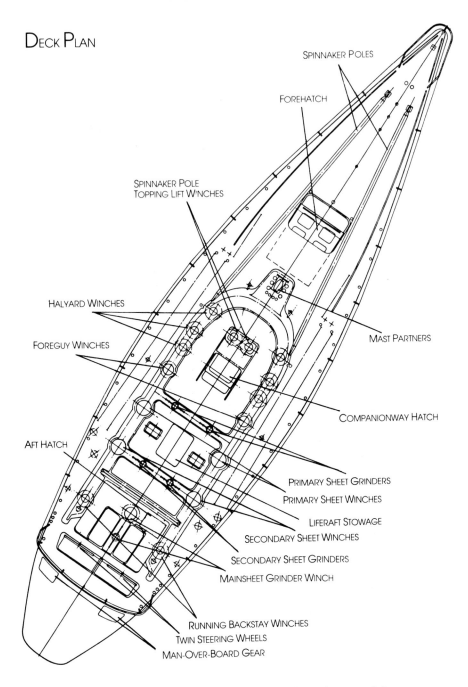

SPINNAKER POLES

FOREHATCH

SPINNAKER POLE
TOPPING LIFT W'NCHES

HALYARD WINCHES

FOREGUY WINCHES

MAST PARTNERS

COMPANIONWAY HATCH

AFT HATCH

PRIMARY SHEET GRINDERS

PRIMARY SHEET WINCHES

LIFERAFT STOWAGE

SECONDARY SHEET WINCHES

SECONDARY SHEET GRINDERS

MAINSHEET GRINDER WINCH

RUNNING BACKSTAY WINCHES

TWIN STEERING WHEELS

MAN-OVER-BOARD GEAR

pression. Stiffness needs some carbon which is also good for compression; but it's lousy for impact. I can't really explain it. You just sort of do it. The laminate on *Kialoa* – that came out of my head. You sit down and work out the logical reason behind the engineering."

That was in 1981. The knowledge and technique of composite con-

Below Deck Plan

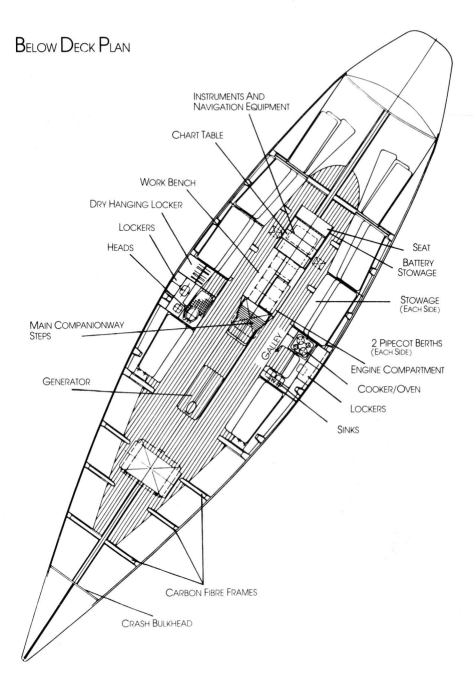

INSTRUMENTS AND
NAVIGATION EQUIPMENT

CHART TABLE

WORK BENCH

DRY HANGING LOCKER

LOCKERS

HEADS

MAIN COMPANIONWAY
STEPS

GENERATOR

SEAT

BATTERY
STOWAGE

STOWAGE
(EACH SIDE)

2 PIPECOT BERTHS
(EACH SIDE)

ENGINE COMPARTMENT

COOKER/OVEN

LOCKERS

SINKS

GALLEY

CARBON FIBRE FRAMES

CRASH BULKHEAD

structions, largely through trial and error, evolved into an accepted building practice in the hands of the right people. The Colt construction, however, once again was pushing the technology (experience might be a better word) of composite to the limit again. Of course, in the original schedule there would have been more than a year of sea-trials before the Whitbread began. We had less than five months to complete the hull, and three months to sail it. We all knew there was a big element of risk involved.

The shed in Cowes, where the composite work was to be completed was, for an American used to the openness of American homes and work environments, comparable to a do-it-yourself work shop in a one-car garage. Fortunately I knew the place well.

With the post war decline of the Royal Navy in Portsmouth and the winding down of shipping out of Southampton, the South Coast of England had been economically depressed after World War II and has only recently come out of it with a revival of light industry. The Isle of Wight, however, has lagged behind. With unemployment regularly 5% above the national average and physically cut off from the mainland by an expensive ferry trip to Southampton, it is no wonder the unknowing think of it as a quaint backwater.

However, possibly for reasons of cheaper real estate and a friendly local atmosphere, Cowes has given birth to not a few of Britain's newest inventions; the hovercraft being the most celebrated – and most noisy. If you have an idea and want to start a small business with a low capital outlay, the Isle of Wight is made for the job.

The Vision Yachts complex is an unimpressive, run-down group of tin sheds on the banks of the Medina River which separates East Cowes from West and is navigable on the tide 4 miles inland to the town of Newport. A chain ferry runs across the mouth of the river and for 10 pence a ride, the five-minute journey is thought to be the most expensive form of public transport on earth – 250% more expensive than a round-the-world cruise on the *QE II* and 350% more expensive than the Concord, mile per mile, so figured one of the Vision staff one day while waiting for a laminate to cure.

When I arrived for the first time, I found that Rob had hired the Mustang Marine shed next door and on the slipway was the hull of our Maxi. Next to it, upside down on the ground, lay the deck. The drafty shed was freezing cold, and the workers were erecting a polyethylene bubble around the boat hung from wire rafters into which hot, dry air would be blown continuously to create the proper environment for the epoxy resins. Minimum temperatures of 35° Celsius (95° Fahrenheit), with as little relative humidity as possible were critical if the materials were to 'cure' properly. The arrangements did not approach aircraft construction standards, but Rob seemed to be confident in what he was doing. I hoped he'd been paying his electricity bill!

Although he was finishing three Admiral's Cup yachts next door, he had shifted workers and hired extras to bring the workforce on the Maxi up to eight and sometimes ten. Ray O'Callaghan, an Irish shipwright, was brought in and agreed to stay with the boat when she went over to Moody's for the fit-out. "Go and have a word with Ray, Skip," said Rob that day. "Tell him how much you appreciate him coming over."

An idealistic boatbuilder from Cork and test pilot from the local brewery, Ray was an extreme example of the frequent fact that if the workers don't like the person they are building the boat for, it just won't get done. Working with materials that can be lethal if inhaled or even touched was a nerve-wracking life. If the workers felt bad vibes they would be likely to walk off the job. They plied their trade with rollers and spatulas like temperamental artists and needed the personal contact that would convince them that they were not just building "Da ting," as Ray said to me over a pint later that day, "But da boot depends on da peeeople involved; it's da peeeople, I tell ya, dat matter." And in a litany I would hear over and over from Ray during pub hours he said to me, "Ya know Skip, most of da people (all the others I suspect) just don't . . . know . . . boots!"

Rick Tomlinson, from the Isle of Man, also had come to work, but he had a motive other than building the boat. Rick had been on the original team of Mitsubishi Maritime in Plymouth and had been conscripted by Jeff Houlgrave as one of *Colt*'s first crew members. When the project collapsed he returned to his self-taught profession of photography, but the desire to do the Whitbread Race lingered, and, in his words, "Photograph it as it has never been photographed before."

A shy, retiring man, he made no bones about his lack of experience on racing boats other than the occasional multihull race or delivery. Few people like to dwell on or even mention disasters they had been involved in, especially when applying for a job. I found out many months later that he had had the misfortune of being at the top of the mast when the trimaran *VSD* had lost her rig in the Bay of Biscay. He just managed to slip out of the boatswain's chair before the mast was pulled underwater. In 1979, he had sailed on a voyage from Norway to the Isle of Man in a replica Viking ship to celebrate the millenium of the Tynwald island government, which was the old center of the Kingdom of the Western Isles. They capsized in a storm off Scotland, but everyone was saved. Had I known he had experienced and weathered these traumas I might have agreed to sign him up sooner than I did, realizing that under that soft-spoken exterior there had to be a strong character. For the time being he was put on hold, a photographer being the least of my priorities.

With the Vision group organized and laminating as fast as Adrian Thompson supplied them with drawings and lay-up schedules, I spent most of my time back in the Hamble with John Irving. The Nautor UK office would be our initial base of operations for ordering the myriad parts and pieces that go into building a big racing yacht. Most of the equipment was custom made, one-off, and had to be negotiated for the best prices, specified to fit our requirement and the deadlines agreed. We spent a lot of time making lists and deriving budgets to be sent to London, sometimes when uncertain, assigning numbers to items from experience as nonchalantly as one would mentally tally up the groceries thrown into the basket at the supermarket, hoping the twenty bucks you have in your pocket will cover it. The only difference being we were working with millions!

Nautor UK is run by the partnership of John Irving and Pat Liley. Overlooking the Port Hamble Marina and the Hamble River beyond, their plush office is a two-room affair with the partners sitting at desks opposite each other. The walls around them display all the Swan half-models and personal memorabilia, some humorously rude, of their involvement in ocean racing for the better part of the last twenty years. Pat had been a boat-bum; then a sailmaker for Bruce Banks. John had done much the same with a short interim in the insurance business. After a few disorderly years on the waterfront he slipped into the Nautor office as Dave Johnson's assistant. When Dave died mysteriously in west Africa during a business trip, John took over.

Most of the figures we could pin down with reasonable accuracy, but some were pure guesswork. "Now what should we say for travelling expenses for the project? £10,000, £15,000?", John would ask me, "Better make it £20,000," could be my reply. "Right, £20,000. What about tools?" "I don't know, £2500?" "No way, better double it." "OK by me." And so on.

Pat, as thick set and burly as John is trim and well manicured, had a sardonic sense of humour. "I suppose," he said on hearing of our food budget, "that includes air dropping the champagne and caviar to the owners during the Southern Ocean legs?"

For all his advice and encouragement it was obvious that Pat had severe doubts about the project. Not only was *Drum* not a Swan, but he knew John's increased involvement in the Maxi meant a greater burden for himself.

While Pat, an active rugby player, is quick off the mark and a man of few words, Irving is garrulous and patient, which may explain his youthful appearance at the age of 46. His favorite hobby, almost an addiction, is talking on the telephone (Pat does a good impression of John taking his first 'fix' of the morning), and for our project it was a blessing.

I used to sit and marvel while John, by pure attrition, ground down suppliers into submissive pulps. Time was of the essence, and lengthy correspondence was of little use other than to place and acknowledge firm orders. He used every trick in the book; "It will be good for your company, good for yachting in Britain, good for Britain! By the way do you have a 14-year-old daughter? Ever hear of the rock group

Duran Duran?" were some of his basic ploys.

One of his best was the fallacy that someone from the Royal Family was likely to patronize the project and possibly christen the boat at the launching. This was not too hard to believe when we first heard about the idea in January by the Whitbread PR people. The Royal Family puts their names to a lot of projects certainly more obscure than ours and it was an established fact that Lady Diana was a big fan of Simon Le Bon. Almost without exception the Brits love their Royals, and if a project received the Royal nod, as it were, the credibility, publicity, and the needed finances from outside sources would be soon to follow.

Shrouded in secrecy, the idea of Royal patronage never went beyond the rumour stage, but it seemed to have the desired effect where needed.

Irving was undaunted, "Did you know that Lady Di is a Duran Duran fan. I can't tell you very much about it, it's a bit hush-hush," mouth cupped over the telephone, Liley staring at Irv over the top of his half rim spectacles, "you know what I mean. All I can say is that the palace is making noises. Now, about those prices you quoted . . ."

By the end of February the priority items had been resolved and if the journalist Tony Fairchild had been upset by an American skipper who scoffed at the idea of a British entry, he would have been horrified by this list: Mast and boom from Nautor in Finland, rudder from the Speedwave Company in West Germany, the engine was a Mitsubishi 125 HP marinized diesel, hydraulics and rigging from Navtec in America, hatches and blocks and other deck gear from Marquip, a Dutch Company.

But the 'empire' was not totally lost; British contributions consisted of the entire winch package from Lewmar, the water maker from Seafresh, rigging from Spencers, electronics from Brookes and Gatehouse, and not least of all, sails, valued at over £150,000, from Hood's loft in Lymington. It would be very difficult (as the America's Cup syndicates have discovered from the 'Deed of Gift' clause requiring the design, the boat and all of its components to be from the country of origin) to build a totally 'British' Maxi, at least one that would be competitive. She would fly a British flag and that's what would be significant.

The keel was certainly British and, as is now well known, had a tragic history. On recommendation from Rob Lipsett we had contacted Adtec Welding Alloys, Ltd. of Plymouth who were originally supposed to do the job for the *Colt* project. Apparently they had been checked out as coded welders and everyone at that time seemed more than satisfied. In fact, as we found out, they still had the plate in stock originally ordered for the job, and it was clear to us that the man in charge knew exactly what was required. It was a simple matter of having Ron Holland's office send them a new set of drawings and they could begin work immediately. This was a logical decision at the time. After all, the other half of the keel, the bottom lead piece, was being cast even farther away, near Falmouth, by Henry Irons. The two pieces would be sent to us separately from these two suppliers and we would fit them together and then to the hull. The results of these decisions would prove to be disastrous.

It was my responsibility to find the crew, and it was a time-consuming task. Although we still had not made our official announcement, the word was out that the project was on, and in no time my house in the Hamble was flooded with mail and phone calls from all points on the globe. Men and women of all descriptions were applying either to Simon or myself. Of course, all the mail directed to Simon was channelled my way, most of which was summarily returned with a formal letter of refusal. Lengthy résumés from bored businessmen (and housewives) extolled a varied career that was as much use on an ocean racing sailboat as a pin-stripe suit and briefcase. "I'm sure I could be an asset to your project," they would plead.

I also received many applications from good sailors. Their resumés were usually lengthy lists of all the ocean races they had done in the last five years or so and reminded me of some of my own I had used in applying for deliveries years before, the kind of resumé that qualified me as a sailing bum and little else.

On this project we needed more than that. We needed the best yachtsmen possible, those who could step on board a big sailboat and slot right into the program. They also had to come armed with the special skills required to maintain the equipment. We would have no time to train them in the rudiments that summer. Of course, they would also have to be easy-going and flexible. I would either have to know them personally or they would have to come recommended by someone I trusted.

My original idea was to have a crew of 14 regulars that would do all of the Race, leaving three slots open for Mike, Paul and Simon who were scheduled only to do two legs each in rotation, making a sailing crew of 17. I already had the nucleous in mind. Dr. Roger Nilsson, Swedish doctor and navigator was my main man. Brian 'Mugsy' Hancock was another prime candidate. Both had been around the world with me on *Alaska Eagle* and Mugsy was with me on the Parmelia Race. These were men I felt very comfortable with after sailing with them for tens of thousands of miles.

When I met Mugsy in 1979 he was 22 years old, fancy free and already an experienced hand with a sewing machine. It took him about five minutes to decide to ship on as sailmaker for the 11,000 miles to West Australia on the Parmelia Race. Years later, and a Whitbread Race already to his credit, enjoying success in America as a salesman and consultant, his life had become more complicated, and he was not so quick to commit.

Said Mugsy's first letter, "I am interested in racing the whole race, but financially under the present compensation situation that won't be possible. I want to do the Whitbread again, because last time was such a fuck-up. This time it will be done properly, and we'll win. But I can't do it at the cost of selling my house so we need to work out a system that I can afford." He followed with four pages of scheming. I reckoned Mugsy was in, hook, line, and sinker.

Roger was in much the same dilemma. Magnus Olsson and Phil Wade were my other two choices for the afterguard. Magnus, 38 years old, had a reputation as one of the best all-rounders in the business, and we had sailed together on a Swedish Admiral's Cup campaign. Phil Wade, a deep-water delivery skipper at home single handing across the Atlantic on a 30-footer or at the helm of the 'J' Boat *Velsheda*, his charge for the last year, was first and foremost a seaman (holding a South African merchant officer's ticket) and at age 40 was fit as a fiddle. Both were interested, but would need time to sort out their personal lives.

For the 'Indians' I had to go for the hard-core boat-bum crowd off the Maxis, guys that could be trusted right away not to cut their hands off tailing a wire sheet nor drop the spinnaker pole on the bowman's head. They had to know how to make and service the running rigging, repair sails, and service the winches and hydraulics without supervision.

As early as January 21st I received a letter from Englishman, Neil Cheston. He had heard about the project early on through the 'old boy network', via Hood Sails at Lymington. At the time he had been working in Italy as project manager, building a 73-foot cruising boat for an Italian owner. He had had a fair amount of racing experience on the American Maxi, *Nirvana*. He said he'd met me before, in Ireland the previous year. "I'm beginning to feel as if I'm wasting my time (on the Italian boat), and I've decided to do the Whitbread if I can, as I've always wanted to. Apart from seven years' racing and delivery experience I have no other skills or degree except that I speak fluent French, Italian, Greek and some Spanish," he said. "I would like to give my boss a month's notice, but if it is only two weeks that's okay." The euphemism of "project manager" for "boat-bum" accepted, he sounded interesting and would be easy to check on. At least he didn't send a typically boring resumé.

UBS Switzerland was our only competitor in Europe. Built in Switzerland the project had made big publicity before the launching when the hull, minus the keel, was flown out of the mountains and down to Nice in a jumbo cargo jet. There she was assembled and rigged and was undergoing sea trials in February. I jumped on a plane to fly down and have a look at their base of operations in Monaco, a likely first venue for their main sponsor, Union Banque de Suisse.

Skipper Pierre Fehlmann also had done the Whitbread twice before. In 77/78 he came fourth in his ketch rigged Swan 65, *Disque d'Or*. In 81/82, with the same sponsor, he built a 58-foot fractionally-rigged Bruce Farr-designed racing machine and came in fourth again. From those experiences, plus his history as a champion dinghy sailor and successful businessman, this third campaign was being advertised as being executed with typical Swiss precision.

The tall, dark, and single-minded Fehlmann did not hesitate when I asked him for a ride on one of their sail testing days. This was more sportsmanlike treatment than I had received four years ago when in New Zealand I asked if I could have a look down below on Peter Blake's *Ceramco*. One of his hunch-back, rugby-playing crew damned nearly pushed me backwards over the lifelines onto the dock. Blake later politely explained that no visitors (least of all competitors) were allowed on board that day.

The Hood Sails team were on board *UBS* when I arrived. Pascal Pellet-Finet was one of Hood Sailmaker's rising stars and we had already discussed his involvement back in London. At the age of 24, he was a veteran of the *France III* 12-Meter campaign and had two years of schooling on *Kialoa IV*, at the time the best institution of higher learning in big-boat ocean racing.

The sail on *UBS* wasn't a great success, or so it appeared. The crew, all young, small-boat sailors from the Swiss lakes, were lost on the big boat and Pierre, with a reputation as a strict disciplinarian, continually vented his displeasure. "*Cette connerie de sac à voile, merde alors! Qu'est-ce que tu fais, toi? Bordel!*" seemed to be his favorite commands.

Sporting the national, the hull was red and white, with pale green decks. It was a beautiful machine, meticulously built. The gear, however, was light and, to my eyes, marginal. They had already ripped the traveller off the deck, and they would have problems with the steering system and other fittings in the months to come.

We returned to the dock early so the crew could get on with their fitting out work. Most of them were in a state of paranoia. The first 'cut' was hanging over their head and would be announced before they left for America next month.

That night most of the crew, with Pascal and the Hood team, went out to the Flash Bar to let off steam.

With the drink talking, a few of Pierre's crew cornered me. They were not happy with his style of leadership and were thinking of baling out. They were interested in signing on with me. I told them to stick it out. I thought to myself at the time, "These guys will never make it around the world like this, even if they do manage to hold the boat together." As events turned out, those dissidents got the 'au

IP NOVAK

MICHAEL BERROW.

NEIL CHESTON

PHIL WADE

SIMON LE BON

revoir' and my supposition, along with a lot of other people's at the time, turned out to be totally wrong. His methods would be vindicated with that old luxury we never had any of, time.

I met Neil Cheston the next day. I was surprised by his sophistication, obviously coming from a British public school education, a thing that is best concealed when you're trying to be a macho sailor. We agreed to remain in touch.

Two weeks later, I was off on another recruiting mission, this time to Florida. All the Maxis were there for the SORC and I could check out their latest equipment as well as see some of the other potential crew members.

I had an arrangement to meet Janne Gustafsson and Micky Olsson in Ft. Lauderdale. Two blond-haired Swedish bombshells who only three years ago had first set foot on a Maxi with the new *Midnight Sun*, they had been on the 'circuit' ever since. I had sailed with them both in Florida and in Norway in 1983, and they had stayed at my house that spring, helping me to replaster a ceiling and fixing the brakes in my clapped-out Volvo in return for rent that the skipper of the boat couldn't afford. We had talked a lot about the Whitbread and I recognized them as good foredeck cannon-fodder. Young, strong and uncomplaining, their only other hobbies besides sailing were fast women. They had no hesitations about the race.

I had never known Bill Biewenga while in Chicago. I first met him in Cape Town in 1981, while he was crewing on *Flyer II*, the eventual winner of that race. For business reasons he had to miss the second two legs, and he was determined to do the whole thing this time. 38 years old, a Vietnam veteran and owner of a concrete pouring business in the western Chicago suburbs who, in his own words, "Had busted ass for 10 years and made some of money," he had had enough of it (money and the concrete business) and was turning his energy towards a career in sailing. Having spent the last four years on Maxis between his business commitments, he also had an interest in doing the single-handed, around-the-world race. He wouldn't be able to join us until after the Fastnet, but I knew he was worth waiting for.

Another steady man was needed. The *Kialoa* crew suggested I talk to 'Filthy,' one of the regulars on board. They said he was a 'good man,' and that's about the best recommendation you can get from those guys. 'Filthy,' is a very common sobriquet around boats. I know of three personally. It either means you have a filthy appearance, you talk filthy, or your name happens to be Phil. 'Filthy' Phil Barrett owned all three. Black, scraggly hair, ring in his ear and one of those perpetual suntans, he always looked as though he had spent the night in the bus station after a bender. His shorts were torn and begreased, and the numerous tatoos on his forearms announced that he was a man of the world.

"I'm from Gosport, mate," he told me, "a Hampshire man, not far from where you're building the boat." He had always wanted to do the race and tried to get on board *Great Britain II* the last time. Attractively rough spoken, he obviously had his heart on it. He was supposed to be an expert in yacht rigging, and his hands looked it. This was no white-collar worker. I left Florida with a good core of men committed and a lot of names pending.

March 20th was the day set aside for the towing of the *Argo* from Cowes back across the Solent to Moody's. Vision had come in one week ahead of schedule. We were off to a good start. The weather was auspicious; one of those blindingly bright clear winter days on the Solent. Simon shipped on board just before departure to complement the boatload of Vision Yacht's staff, reporters, photographers and a multitude of hangers-on. Simon admitted to me he had had a 'hard night' and was obviously still suffering from his chosen poison. He went up to the foredeck and lay down to air out his brain, a pose the Fleet Street hacks loved and made the yachting press wonder.

He later came down below to inspect the interior which was an impressive lattice work of jet-black, carbon-fiber ring frames molded to the yellow field of Kevlar skin. A hollow cavern from stem to stern, in its present state it could easily be described as just plain 'sexy'.

The pugnacious Lipsett, proud of his men's achievements, noticed the rockstar fingering the carbon frames in amazement at the unknown and put what he assumed were Simon's fears to rest by slamming his fist against the side of the boat. As the hull resonated, he bellowed, "Don't worry about her, Simon, she's as tight as a droom!"

"Hey man, wow, 'drum,' yeah I like it, it sounds real strong, let's call her *Drum*," was his response. And after a few weeks *Drum* she became. I didn't think much of it at the time, but it grew on all of us and one of its beauties was that it had nothing to do with the music business at all.

With the project an established reality, the press zoomed in. Big, colored supplement magazines carried the story of Simon's proposed adventure in flowery prose that made the teenagers all agape and the yachting fraternity cringe. British yachting had been on a down-swing for the last decade, and it seemed to some that this was another fiasco in the making. Fraught with internal politicking in their last 12-Meter and Admiral's Cup campaigns, the whole industry was torn between the established amateurs and the lure of a commercial approach like the successful French system. The British yachting world had mixed feelings about what became the *Drum* project.

'Yachts and Yachting' columnist Malcolm McKeag, a sharp-tongued Irishman afloat in a sea of otherwise benign and insipid journalism, had caught the essence of amazement-mixed-with-hope, in the April 5th edition:

MARIO ZIMMERMAN.

BRIAN "MUGSY" HANCOCK

MICKE OLSSON

"FILTHY" PHIL BARRETT.

"Simon Le Bon (can that be his real name?) although admitting to no one publicly that he actually owns the yacht, has bought himself, as his first boat, a 77ft. maxi-rating, round-the-world racer. Well, one has to start somewhere. . . . Simon's first yacht it may be, but his press agent says he's already an experienced yacht race competitor – and indeed he is. He started last year. In Swans. What price your Youth Squad, your Cadet section and your apprenticeship in

Lasers and Enterprises now? It's rather like being able to join the Navy as an Admiral, and more power to Mr. Le Bon's elbow for doing it . . . but behind the posing popstar there is what could turn out to be an enterprise to do our own industry some good: the realities or otherwise of Simon Le Bon's abilities as a sailor laid aside, the yacht herself is real enough and the work going into her . . . Skip Novak, is himself considerably further up the learning curve for this sort of project than any home-grown English yachtsman could possibly be . . . He is in short, a proper, honest-to-goodness professional racing yacht skipper, not one of the self promoting, stunt-men type that this country seems to produce. He sails real yachts in real yacht races with real yacht sailors and when he needs a crew, as he does now, he doesn't rely on out-of-work paratroopers whose first task is to find some crofter's cot in the wilds of the Highlands. He lifts the phone and gets on to other real yacht sailors."

A. H. Moody and Sons' yacht yard and marina is probably the largest such establishment in Britain. At the upper reaches of the Hamble River, a tiny waterway that is already choked on both sides with thousands of craft, the Moody's Marina and boatyard has space for 500 boats in the water and 300 for winter storage. With a complete repair facility and a 40-ton travel-lift able to pull a Maxi boat out at short notice, they have become the center of activity for big sailboats during the summer months.

Hauling the hull out of the water was no strain for the lift. She only weighed 5¼ tons all up, hull and structure, and this pleased Rob and Adrian in coming well inside the target projected weight. They immediately got on the telephone to New Zealand to boast to their ex-partner and now rival Tim Gurr who built *Lion New Zealand* which had been rumoured to have come in heavy.

Moody's, a family concern, has been in the boat business since the turn of the 19th century. Expanding from repair work on commercial fishing vessels, their main activity, in addition to service, was the building of a range of inexpensive fiberglass sailboats. It was in their new, boat-building division that the Maxi would be fitted-out during the following three months.

Graham Moody, marine engineer by trade, was in charge of *Drum*. He already had set out a certain number of man-hours to bring us to completion. This would obviously mean hiring more staff and working double shifts and weekends. The first few days, workmen swarmed inside of the hull and on deck, taking templates for water and fuel tanks and interior bulkheads and fixtures.

Meanwhile, I had moved our base of operations to a hired, mobile office immediately outside the shed. Jacky Dodd-Noble, hired as a secretary, came in with no knowledge of boating, but with many other management skills far beyond the role of a secretary. She quickly grasped the gist of the business. From our headquarters with telex, telephone, and coffee machine, she was soon hammering away at the suppliers in a vernacular that would have made the hardest of the hard-core boaties raise an eyebrow.

Ray and Rick were kept on the Vision pay roll to continue with the composite work, and the more we progressed the more there was. Unlike a metal or wooden boat, a composite construction with a Nomex core means that every single hole drilled to fasten anything requires hours of work of back-gouging and filling with a solid resinous fiber to provide a rigid 'bolting surface.' The major areas, under winches and deck blocks, had been allowed for in the lay-up with solid plywood infills, but what seemed like hundreds of other fittings like thru-hulls, hatches, tracks, and all the equipment not allowed for or even thought of in the original conception required careful work. Ray was already preoccupied with the steering system and aligning the rudder shaft while Rick attended to other tasks.

I decided it was time to give Rick the OK as a bonafide crew member. He worked hard even though he was so allergic to epoxy resins he was covered with sores and welts. If he proved to be ineffective offshore I could fire him later, but I didn't think that was likely; he was a good man all around.

Down in the office, John, Jacky and I had refined the budget and cash-flow estimates. The total came to about £1.7 million. It was a good thing Simon was cutting another album. Mike and Paul were busy negotiating with sponsors, but thus far none were offering the total amount. Mike and Paul didn't seem to worry about it, and we all assumed that we were so deep into it now that nothing could stop us. They had the money, between the three of them personally, to float the project. Work continued in the London offices on the publicity, the graphics, the clothing, and development of the familiar *Drum* logo which went under a few evolutionary modifications under Paul's able direction.

It was a perfect working relationship. We were left to our building and organizing of the race and they were fundraising. Almost weekly I was summoned to London for meetings with Mike and Paul on various aspects of what they were planning while I filled them in on our progress. The more time I spent with them the more I liked their method of operation. From what I had seen of the capricious nature of the rock music business they had payed their dues over the years by hard work and an ability to juggle business, press, and, not least of all, personalities all in the same act.

As managers of Duran Duran their problems were not unlike ours. Multi-million dollar deals and marketing strategy aside, the handling

RICK TOMLINSON

MAGNUS OLSSON.

ROGER NILSSON.

BILL BIEWANGA.

of people was the significant part. I will never forget the first night I met Mike in Paris. After our meeting he was obliged to sit in the hotel bar until five o'clock in the morning patiently listening to one of the band members pouring out his heart about some personal problem.

The brothers complimented themselves beautifully, Paul, at 6' 4" towering over the audience, was the creative one with an incredible ability to put a fantasy into words. Dreaming of novel ways to launch and christen the boat to gain the maximum publicity he almost had me believing that it was possible to drop *Drum* from a military helicopter in the middle of the English Channel closely followed by a nude Grace Jones who would be lowered over the bows to crack the traditional bottle of champagne.

"Gee, that sounds like it could be expensive Paul," was Michael's reply to that idea. Shorter at 5' 11" and of medium build, with his feet firmly on the ground, Michael was the business brains of the partnership and a tempering influence on his brother. It was this combination that steered *Drum* into having what was considered to be the best graphical approach, the best publicity, and the best dressed crew. If all this was not completely how Paul had first envisaged it, at least it was a good compromise.

However I can remember one meeting that did not fill me with confidence. I came up to town to talk to the Berrows about several critical items. Our pre-arranged morning meeting turned out to be 45 minutes in a London Taxi, doing errands before they both flew off to Paris. Every time I tried to get to a point, Paul went off on a tangent, totally preoccupied, for example, with some artwork he had just bought. I was then dumped out somewhere in Kensington as they sped off to Heathrow, vaguely agreeing to my requests. Although I had gotten what I came after, the manner of getting had me worried, reminding me of the Austrian five years ago. Instead of taxi cabs, my meetings with this wealthy industrialist from Vienna usually took place in airports or in transit between European capitals. He had a 76-foot, Frers Maxi boat under construction at Palmer Johnson Inc. of Wisconsin and soon after the hull was finished he decided, seemingly out of the blue, to do the Whitbread Race. Via the shipyard, I was hired to manage the construction and then skipper the boat, which was a sistership of *Flyer II*.

Who was I to question the owner's motives? A rotund little man who happily agreed to all my requests, he did make me wonder from

---

opposite Richard wins the hearts and stomachs of 16 others with a specially prepared dessert on Leg Four (*Photo by Skip Novak*)

overleaf One of the few ways to get off 'the boat' during a month at sea; taken from the boom end while on a fresh reach (*Photo by Skip Novak*)

the beginning. He never visited the yard. In fact, he would never see his boat. Ten months into the construction and a mere six weeks before launching at 'PJ's', his payments stopped. Within a few days he was reported missing along with several million Deutsche Marks. The scandal involved his company, Swiss banks, and the Austrian government. Construction was stopped with thousands of dollars of custom equipment and sails contracted for. It took me six weeks to clear up the mess, a process which included laying off several crew members due to arrive from as far away as Australia. The Austrian eventually was caught by Interpol and thrown in jail. I joined *Alaska Eagle* that same spring. I never thought the Berrows would do a 'runner' on me, but the symptoms had me concerned.

John Irving and I took almost three weeks to discover the problem at Moody's. By then it was apparent that at the current rate of progress we would never finish the boat on time. They did not have the labor they had promised. There was no overtime or double shifting, and company policy required a foreman to be present when any one was on the job, which kept some of the more enthusiastic guys from doing extra time. The British labor environment was a nearly impossible one in which to build a custom boat in a hurry. The elderly foreman couldn't be bothered to put in extra hours. "Some of us want to do longer hours and weekends," a young apprentice carpenter admitted to us, "but we've been told we can't." Apparently the management was unaware of the situation.

An ash-tray-full of cigarette butts later, John Irving had negotiated with the head office that company policy was to be changed. How they sorted it out with their workers committee was their problem. We also had to bring in more people from Vision to work a night shift. Grinding the epoxy resin during the day would prompt the shop steward to pull men out of the shed because they reckoned it was dangerous.

'Plastic Mick' Darby and 'Metal Mick' Corbett to the rescue! Epoxy fumes and dust? These two Isle of Wighters thrived on it! Watching Ray, Ricky, the 'two Micks' and the other 'independents' go to work completely restored my faith in British craftsmen. Their sheer enthusiasm left me in no doubt we would finish on schedule. Without any regard to the time of day, working conditions and impossible timetables they would press on. They paused only to wonder how they were going to deactivate the buzzer that called 'Moody's Men' to their tea breaks.

---

opposite above The damage from Leg One graphically displayed in the Cape Town dockyards for all to see; *below* Filthy stands a half hour watch in the forepeak monitoring the damage after the breakup off Cape Town; the repair held (*Photos by Skip Novak*)

Ron Heazel, the shipwright foreman, got into the act with unflagging energy, and soon this whole change of attitude had started to rub off on the other workers. The young apprentices and the older tradesmen woke up from a long slump caused by building the same Moody's production boats the same way, over and over. With our boat, every day brought a new problem which brought out their real talent. This new sense of pride in the job must have even inspired the management.

On my last trip to Finland to check on the mast (the construction and logistics involved in this 110-foot aluminium tube was a story in itself) I visited Roger in Stockholm. An orthopaedic surgeon by profession, Roger is one of the top yachting navigators in the world. His campaigns have included six SORC's, five Admiral's Cups and four Sardinia Cups. He had navigated *Alaska Eagle* around the world four years before and most recently had crewed for Peter Sundelin in a bid to represent Sweden in Star boats for the last Olympics. They came second in the trials.

Tall and good looking at 37, Roger is single and single-minded about many things, especially women. He is so well known for his philandering I am doing him no disfavor dwelling on a reputation that now preceeds him almost everywhere he goes. "You can trust me, I'm a medical doctor," he will explain as he sallies forth to secure another victim. He is so convincing in his professional attitude that even the mothers of teenagers believe him. His experience as an offshore navigator and the fact that he was a doctor were only two of his several assets. More importantly, I needed someone who was organized, disciplined, and experienced enough to do all the pre-race research on weather, navigation, and tactics, and who could set up our on-board computer system. Roger loves to gather information and file it away. The walls of his Stockholm apartment are lined from floor to ceiling with records of everything he has done and been involved with in his lifetime: School, the navy, yachting, his life is recorded there. Thousands of photographs are arranged in an almost eccentric manner. It is not hard to imagine that he has filed away all his ex-girlfriends and acquaintances under "'W' – women 1977 to 78," and so on.

One gets the impression that Roger is more interested in sailing than in a medical practice that lets him take months and years off for a hobby that has taken him around the world. He pointed out to me then that a friend of his, the doorman at the famous Café Opra in Stockholm, makes more money than he does in medicine. He claimed it would be difficult doing the race financially with a base pay of £120 per month, including lodging and clothing, that our project had to offer. I pointed out the publicity aspect of the project, and we discussed the possibilities of doing a film for Swedish TV. With that and

JANNE GUSTAFSSON.

PATRICK BANFIELD.

PAUL BERROW.

RICHARD FREEMAN.

articles to write for the paper and other yachting journals he thought he could make it. He planned to be in England in May to meet the Berrows and Simon to discuss the filming. He would then give me his decision.

By the middle of May, major items like chainplates, the mast step, the winches and tracks had all been fastened down. Ray had aligned the rudder shaft and was now building the forehatch coaming, his last major job. The two halves of the keel had arrived and were waiting to be bolted on to the hull when she came out of the shed. As the items on the worklist became more minor they also became more numerous and the 'Moody's Men' and our own Vision crowd swarmed over the boat day and night.

Simon arrived for a photographic session and made a big hit signing autographs for all the workers' daughters. During the previous weeks, Duran Duran groupies had been gathering in force, staking out their claim near the building shed, waiting for just such an occasion as this. They were not disappointed. Weird and wonderful people from the music and film business had arrived in town. They made up an entourage of camera men, reporters, film directors and publicity people. The make-up artist suggested she highlight the dark rings under my eyes for my photograph on deck with Simon. Much to my embarrassment Ray and Rick walked into the office as she applied her artwork. Ray was not impressed with this yacht skipper.

While the decks and topsides were being painted the groupies hovered in the doorway waiting for the masking tape to be pulled off so they could collect more 'souvenirs' from *Drum*. In fair weather and foul, mainly foul, they would be there every day. With their punk, pink hairdo's and outlandish apparel they almost became permanent fixtures. "When is Simon coming back down again?" they would ask every morning. "I don't know," I would answer. "But Filthy Phil is arriving tomorrow, you'll love him."

By the end of the month most of the boys were on the job. Trevor Dowe, my mate from a previous summer's Arctic cruise, had joined us and was fitting out our sea freight container with a tool shop and storage. Max Bourgeois and Pascal were working on the sails at Hoods. Janne, in charge of deck gear and Micky, the engineer, were going through their departments and making lists of spares, while Neil and Filthy were making all the running rigging. Phil Wade had arrived after his delivery to Greece and was now in charge of the daily work schedule, taking a lot of load off my shoulders. Things were coming together.

It looked as though the rudder was going to be late, and Ray was beside himself. Every night after work we would retire to our local Pub, 'The Old Ship,' only a two-minute walk from the shed. There, Ray, Rick and the 'Two Micks' had cheap rooms upstairs, but what they saved in room rent they lost every evening in the residents' bar.

Drinking hours in Britain have been unchanged in the ten years I've known 'pub life', and by 1045 the publicans call of "Glasses please!" signals the end for the customers in the passing trade. Most pubs have what is known as 'after hours drinking,' totally illegal, but an accepted practice for regular customers. The Ship, because it has 'rooms' has the right to have a residents' bar. Moreover, for the yachties, the back bar was open slather. We could never figure out how Jim the proprietor managed it, being right on the main road to Southampton. It was always a curious sight to see the parking lot full and people falling out of doors at one o'clock in the morning.

It was here that Ray, with little 'shipwrighting' to do and no rudder every night would drown himself in 'drink,' as the Irish describe it. Jim's back bar was a tiny alcove with stools for only four or five and with the collection of bottles and tap handles for the draft beer aligned like organ pipes it was aptly nicknamed 'Ray's Tabernacle.' He certainly spent enough time there preaching to us about craftsmanship in things that float. After about his eighth or ninth pint of lager, he would close his eyes and begin to sing beautiful Irish ballads that would bring the otherwise unruly crowd to a standstill. Never failing to forget the words half way through he would then fly into a rage, claiming someone had interrupted him and then launch into an inquisition about the whereabouts of 'his' rudder.

Ray was only an extreme example of the way we all felt by that time. After months of 12- to 14-hour days, *Drum* was launched without ceremony on June 18th, only three days behind a schedule that had been made six months before. A few days later, with the mast stepped and the rigging and hardware on board, we motored her down to Port Hamble on the late night high tide.

The crew had worked hard for the last month. When we tied her up downstream, they made a beeline for the crew houses. They would have to be back on board for the first sail by 0800. John Irving, Ray, Rick, the two Micks, and I stayed behind down below and looked around us. We had made it! Pat Liley and his girl friend had arrived with champagne and we proceeded to get completely shitfaced. The unlashed wheel suddenly spun to starboard as the changing tide caught the rudder, just as the sun was coming up. And Ray O'Callaghan, blind drunk with satisfaction, was still trying to remember the words to "On the Banks of Mine Own Lovely Lee."

6 · Tuning Up the Beast

Interviewer: *"Are you pleased with* Drum's *progress?"*
Interviewee: *"I certainly am. I never thought things would go this smoothly."*

July 20th 1985

Most sailboats seem fast when they're new, especially when none other is beside you. *Drum* was no exception to this gratifying illusion as she effortlessly slid through Southampton Water at 10 knots during her first days of sea trials.

Only one week later she entered her first contest. The Round-the-Isle-of-Wight Race is a favorite for South Coast boats. Early in the season it attracts hundreds of entries and fortunately for us there were no other Maxis around. We would be first to finish, barring disaster.

With all three owners on board, my girlfriend De attending to the galley, and a crew of 26, the gun went off at 0730 from the Royal Yacht Squadron at Cowes and we hardened up for the beat out through the Western Solent.

I think it was on the second tack when the wire sheet was cast off the winch that we were all abruptly reminded what it is like to be on the deck of a Maxi in a breeze. Peter Sweeney, a hulk of a man at 6′ 6″, was standing to leeward of the mast and right in the firing line of the clew of the No. 2 Genoa. The weighted stainless steel ring attached to the clew of the sail which in turn is as stiff as hardboard struck him on the head. He was knocked to the deck and his blood ran down the lee scuppers. He was helped below where he promptly passed out, falling on top of De who was trying to attend to him.

I assured Mike, Paul, and Simon that accidents like this didn't happen often despite the nonchalance of the rest of the crew who weren't phased in the slightest. After the thrash out through the Needles Channel we set the 1.5oz. spinnaker decorated with a large eagle, and a blooper to leeward for the run down the backside of the island. It was a beautiful clear day, and we easily ticked along at 13 knots on the surfs in the gentle sea.

There can be up to a half mile of ropes, wires and other pieces of rigging draped across the deck of a Maxi. On a long race you have the time to keep it organized and plan maneuvers accordingly. On short courses, tacks and gybes follow in quick succession and at the best of times we have all experienced some horrendous tangles. With a new crew, and the boat not yet fully rigged, with all the fiddly bits of trip wires, zipper pulls and other gadgetry that, when properly handled, makes the most complicated of acts seem like clockwork, we were, in spite of ourselves doing incredibly well, gybing close inshore, out of the tide.

At the age of 33, already old to be a bowman, Filthy Phil spent most of the run in the boatswains chair bouncing up and down in the rig like a yo-yo. Out to the end of the spinnaker pole, the clew of the spinnaker or up to the masthead, he kept ahead of the endless 'snafus' being created down on deck. By the time we reached Bembridge, at the eastern corner of the island, he was soaked with sweat, bleeding and exhausted. His acrobatics and good humour earned him the respect of the entire crew that day. He was proclaimed the 'Hero of the Day' at dinner and awarded a red and white life ring stolen from the Royal Southern Yacht Club. It became a perpetual trophy for acts of bravery or foolishness.

As expected, we won the race handily on elapsed time, coming only seven minutes short of the record. Although we had proved only that *Drum* had met another critical part of her schedule, the press acknowledged us as a going concern.

I had drafted a strict sailing and work schedule for the summer; a week back at Moody's, finishing the endless list and then it was a sea trial to Ireland for the pilgrimage to Ron Holland's lair in Currabinny, County Cork. After an uneventful passage out to the west coast and around the Skellig Islands that gave us the needed 500-mile qualifying run for the Fastnet Race in August, we motored into Kinsale for the evening. Ron and his office staff went out for a sail the next day down to Crosshaven in Cork Harbor and that evening we had a barbeque at Ron's place.

Holland had come to Ireland from New Zealand in 1973, when a local Cork syndicate gave him his first chance to break into international yachting. There, among the fairy tale world of leprechauns and with the luck of the Irish, he designed the famous one-tonner *Golden Apple* and has never looked back. Strand Farmhouse, where he has lived since shortly after that initial success, overlooks the tidal mud flats of the Owenboy River and across to the village of Crosshaven. The office next door is the old pig stye, now well appointed with drawing offices and climatically controlled computer rooms, and in this rural setting his staff now conjures up some of the most successful and impressive racing and cruising boats on the market today.

It is difficult to leave the hospitality of the Irish, especially with a massive hangover. But the schedule had to be adhered to, and *Drum* departed early the next morning to beat the ebb tide over the sand bar and made her way back to the Hamble with Phil Wade in charge. I flew back to catch up on office work accompanied by a sheepish Micky Olsson who had overslept somewhere on shore.

Once back in the Hamble, I called a crew meeting with the regulars. Subject: publicity. Yachties, especially those used to sailing in the amateur world of Corinthian yachting, have characteristically disdained any form of attention outside their peer group. In a situation now rapidly changing, they would consider media hype and public relations unneeded and embarrassing. This might be a problem, but with the *Drum* project we all would have to deal with it. A few of them were already worried about what Paul was rumoured to have in mind for them.

Only days later, Paul arrived and we had our first fashion shoot, wearing the *Drum* uniform, down at the marina. With a London photographer of doubtful gender prancing around the foredeck in baggy trousers, they all saw the lighter side and cooperated.

And then *Lion* came motoring up the river. Having arrived only days before from their passage from New Zealand, they were justifiably full of themselves, having won the Sydney-to-Hobart Race last winter which saw most of the fleet drop out due to severe weather. Tanned and broad shouldered, they had that smart-ass, wholesome look of an American football team, and as they motored past us to their jetty you could almost hear them snickering at our crew of what a yachtie would describe as a bunch of 'poofdas.' To stir us up they launched into one of their many renditions of an old drill song:

"I don't know what I've been told
Digby's mast is goin to fold
I don't know what I believe
We'll be in on New Year's Eve
Well I don't know about *Cote d'Or*
Cote d'Or never been offshore
Well I don't know about the *Drum*
They're ain't no way they can be number one
Well I don't know about *Atlantic Privateer*
Atlantic Privateer will be near the rear
Well I don't know about *UBS*
There's no way they can be the best.
Well I don't know about the rest
Cause *Lion New Zealand* is the best!"

We waved to them as they went by, shouting good-natured obscenities. Our crew, older, worldly, and mature for their years, knew the real test would come soon enough, out on the race course.

Nevertheless, the arrival of *Lion* and the knowledge that she had sailed over 20,000 miles to get there, was a sobering thought. Metallic grey hull, with an impressive list of sponsors' names neatly laid out below the sheerline, *Lion* was born out of one of the most thorough public relations campaigns ever staged in yachting sponsorship. We would find out later that a conservative construction technique had given her an estimated weight 15 per cent over her designed displacement. However, back then she was truly a tried and tested machine, and, with Blake's experience, she was the odds on favorite.

A week later, *Atlantic Privateer* arrived from South Africa. Hers was a different philosophy in both design and personnel. A big, 80-foot Bruce Farr with a mast-head rig, she was crudely fitted out above and below decks. She had a home-built appearance. Rather than designing an *IOR* type hull, the Farr office was specific in its thinking of the Whitbread requirement with long, lighter hulls; smaller keels and more 'form' stability (the shape of the hull) rather than relying on ballast stability to achieve the desired displacement. Sponsored by Apple Macintosh Computers in South Africa, they too had drawn first blood on the Cape to Uruguay Race in January with an overall elapsed time prize.

Ringleader of what appeared to be an ad hoc South African organization was David Bongers, a frizzy-haired gorilla whose heavy accent left no one in doubt about his origins. A crack helmsman who had lived, on and off, in the UK for years, he had a reputation as a man who didn't take kindly to criticism of apartheid. More than once he and his mates ended the discussion out in the parking lot of some pub, the antagonist exiting with a bloody nose. As far as we were concerned, and we knew a lot of them personally, they were straight-forward guys and had no need to impress anyone. It was not surprising that our crew fell in with theirs and, initially, avoided the *Lion* crew.

While we raced to St. Malo on the Britanny coast, '*AP*', as she came to be known, was hauled out at Moody's for the attachment of a solid lead bulb to the bottom of her keel to increase her stability. *Lion* also was changing her keel to a smaller, lighter one, with a sightly elliptical shape. *UBS Switzerland* had just arrived from Newport after a Maxi Series and another transatlantic shakedown cruise. *Lion's* modification was a success, but the bulb had to come off *Alantic Privateer's* keel the night before the Seahorse Maxi Series. With it, she rated over the maximum allowable of 70 feet under the International Ocean Racing measurement rule.

The first big test of what these boats and crews were made of was a four-race series in and around the Solent. In addition to the four Whitbread Maxis, *Condor* was also taking part as well as *Philips Innovator*, the 65-foot Dutch entry.

Maxi-racing around the buoys is a world apart from the Whitbread style. At least 25 men are needed for the day's outing. Every man has a specific job, including two people below decks who do nothing but pack sails. Tacking and gybing maneuvers are not discussed; they are executed. There is nothing more frustrating, and little more dangerous than trying to race a big boat with an unskilled crew. However, with the right people it can be poetry in motion. To lead the afterguard, we invited Harry Cudmore on board. Reputed to be the best in the business, Harry has an unusual ability for quick thinking and decision making. He is definitely one who is not afraid to stick his neck out in practice as well as opening himself up for ridicule and reprisals later in the game. His belief seemed to be that if you are right 6 out of 10 times you are doing well. It proved to be a good team.

It blew 40 "bags of shit," as they say, for the first race. Upwind with two reefs in the main and a No. 5 jib was exciting, exhausting work. With the tide against us, the fleet made for the mainland shore and short tacked up the mud flats, sometimes touching the bottom as we stood upright in the eye of the wind. *Atlantic Privateer* had got smartly away from us on a tactical move while *Lion* and ourselves battled it out neck and neck. We were certainly just as fast if not faster on the straightaway, and in tacking we were significantly better. *Condor* had pulled in front, half way to the mark off Yarmouth, and *UBS* got herself tangled up in someone's anchor line before the start. There is nothing quite like helming a Maxi in close quarters, especially in a blow. You can hardly see through the flying spray from your own bow, and the closer you come to your competition the faster the adrenalin pumps.

"Starboard!" yells someone through the gale from *Lion's* cockpit. "Hold your course!" we acknowledge with sign language, signalling that the onus is now on us, either to clear him full ahead if we can, reach off behind him, or tack underneath him.

"Standby to ease the main! Cast that leeward runner off! Can we make it? I think we can make it!" I yell to the crew aft with only a gut feeling that we can cross his bow by a few feet. Our bowman, 75 feet away perched in the bow pulpit, waves me on like a railway platform conductor and I decide to go for it. Nobody's second opinion can help me now. With 30 tons of boat a mistake here and you can kill people and destroy one helluva lot of equipment.

As the suits of red foul weather gear come into view on *Lion's* weather rail, her bow slips neatly behind our transom and everyone on board breathes a sigh of relief. "Tacking!" and before the word has been fully articulated our bow swings sharply to windward as the wire genoa sheet is cast off and snarls its way along the deck. Aggressively, the port side genoa tailer gathers handfuls of rope and then wire and as the load comes on he is already being berated by the sharp-tongued

Cudmore for not getting it in fast enough. "Trim on genoa, come on trim on I tell you; you there, what's your name? When I say trim on I mean trim the bloody thing!" No sooner is the clew home, with the four grinders huffing and puffing, than the command comes again. "Tacking, tacking, runner on!"

On one of these maneuvers, the port side runner winch jammed completely. I will never forget how impressed I was, how impressed everyone was when Janne, in charge of deck gear, was on the spot in seconds with his repair kit. He took the winch apart and replaced the broken cog without uttering a word. When Cudmore shouted "Tacking!" the next time, Janne had just dropped the winch drum into place. The tailer wipped the line on and gathered it home. This was professional sailing.

With *Lion* tucked away behind us we made it third to the mark behind *AP* and *Condor*. We all set big spinnakers in marginal conditions, but they soon came down. A sharp gybe at the mark put *Condor* aground on the mud bank with her spinnaker in tatters. We tried to gybe well before the mark so as not to repeat her performance, but the boat broached while the pole was being dipped through, and the spinnaker came down around us like confetti. Rounding in good form with only the mainsail we reset a storm chute soon after and pursued *AP* down the Solent at 16 knots in flat water. We finished a creditable 2nd place and had a great day's racing. Tied up back in the Hamble we politely waved to *Lion*'s crew motoring up to their jetty. They didn't sing us any more songs.

The second day was to be the Round-the-Island Race, exactly the same course we had done on our maiden regatta in June. Our routine in the mornings was to pick up most of the crew at Port Hamble and then another load off Cowes where Harry and others were staying. Maxi boats can draw over 14 feet of water and are unwieldy beasts in shallows and tidal waters. With spring tides the whole week we had to choose our departure times carefully. A controlling mud bar down channel made it impossible to leave the Hamble at low water.

With an early start of 0730 off the Squadron the crew should have been there at 0530 for an 0600 departure. Simon was 15 minutes late, and we cast off without him only to find him waving to us from the fuel jetty downstream. He jumped on board and I put the throttle down and in a cloud of smoke we blasted down the river with a full ebb tide underneath us. The guys had unflaked the mainsail so that they could adjust the battens and be ready to be hoisted at the entrance to the channel. It also partially blocked my vision. Then Paul, standing to one side of me began to tell me the story of the latest film he had seen a few days before in London, and I lost all concentration. I ran her right out of the fairway and onto a mud bank near one of the right-hand markers.

I have never run hard aground offshore in dangerous waters, but I'm famous for pulling this stunt when it least matters in rivers and estuaries. Although the landing was a soft one, this time the consequences were serious. We had an hour to make the start in a series that only had four races. I cringed at the thought of the press getting a hold of this one. I could almost see the water level drop on the piling. In an hour we would be hard over on our beam ends. I mentally kicked myself.

Motoring in reverse turned out to be wasted effort even with the crew out on the boom to heel her over. There was no wind and so no point in hoisting sail and little chance of another boat coming along at this hour.

In what would be a pattern in the year to come, when all looked lost, a saviour had arrived. A well-found motorboat from Poole was off on the ebb for his home port and gladly took our towline in an attempt to warp the bow back into the channel. The skipper driving was good, but the man in the stern dropped the towline as the boat was swept downstream, and anxious moments elapsed before the line was recoiled and cast again. This time it was secured and after maneuvering upstream of the current, the skipper laid into it. Then the rope parted. With the minutes ticking by and the boat starting to list, I decided our only hope was to pull her off by the masthead.

With the towline now made fast to our spinnaker halyard, and the crew still out on the boom, the motorboat pulled us over a good 45 degrees so the rail was submerged and with the engine full ahead she slid off the mudbank and charged into deep water. As she righted, the boom flew across the deck carrying its entire gallery of pigeons. They were launched into the air with howls of laughter. I waved the skipper goodbye. Since he could not have been impressed with our seamanship, I have to thank him for not selling the story to the London tabloids.

After picking up Harry and the others who came to meet us in an inflatable well out in the Solent, we just made the five-minute gun, turned the engine off and took to battle stations. After another temporary halt to clear the prop, we reached up to the fleet in light winds at the Needles, sailed through *Lion*'s lee and went on to finish second again, this time to *UBS*. All in all, an interesting and not bad day's work.

The other races were some of the best maxi racing we had done, short tacking and gybing in and around the Solent in close quarters. Simon was doing fine, trimming the mainsheet with Mugsy, and Mike and Paul were aft on the running backstays. The results were clouded by the fact that with only 7 boats racing there were two classes, one for the sponsored entries and one for the private. We had done well in winning the unsponsored group, but the salient point of the week was that *Atlantic Privateer* was obviously the fastest boat on the race course and well sailed to-boot. Pierre Fehlmann was still an unknown quantity as the entanglement with the buoy and another incident when he ran aground on the Brambles Bank had confused his true potential. Only *Enterprise New Zealand*, overdue from 'Down Under,' and *Cote d'Or*, due to arrive for the Fastnet for her maiden voyage, were unknown adversaries.

The work program leading up to the month of August was no less relentless and we worked seven-day weeks. The only races left were the Channel Race, a Cowes Week course race and then the 630-mile Fastnet. After that we were off to Iceland from Plymouth for a 10-to-12-day sea trial to test gear in the rugged conditions of the North Atlantic. It was vital to put more sea miles under our belt; a few days offshore would be worth a month of Sundays in the Solent. In addition to this, we still had not had the opportunity to calculate fuel, water and propane gas consumption rates; how the living arrangements would work, and of course, the proposed menu of freeze-dried foods. As *Lion* sat sedately at dockside, her crew off touring and propping up local bar stools, our decks were belaboured with tools, people and confusion.

The Channel Race is an overnight, 200-mile triangle starting off Cowes with legs over to the French coast and back. The night before, as a guest of the Royal Southern Yacht Club, Simon pulled a stunt that is not out of the ordinary, but one that the gutter press love, that is if your name happens to be Le Bon. It certainly made his reputation secure and positive with the boys on the other boats.

"LE BON, THE BOAT CLUB AND THE BARMAIDS FROM THE BUGLE" read the headline in the *Daily Mirror* on August 4th. "Duran Duran heart-throb Simon Le Bon rocked the boat when he smuggled two pretty barmaids into his bedroom at an exclusive yacht club. . . . The club (the Royal Southern) has Prince Philip as its Admiral and includes former Prime Minister Edward Heath among its members".

The bemused club secretary was quoted as saying, "He was allowed to stay as a special favor. We do not expect Mr. Le Bon to bring waitresses from the Bugle Pub into the club or take them to his bedroom. This is an esteemed and respected club with a long tradition."

The girl who had blown Simon's cover and sold the story, probably for a fiver, to some sharp talking reporter, sensing her mistake hastened to say, "We did not get up to anything in the room. I was dead worried when he suggested we go to his bedroom, I felt a bit of a tart at first. But I needn't have worried. Simon was wonderful – so polite and charming. He must have known I was not that sort of a girl."

We never did the Channel Race. Shortly after the start in a 40-knot beat, the mast, which we had returned only the day before, was dangerously out of alignment. There was nothing for it but to retire and sort it out. The American Maxi *Nirvana* and *Atlantic Privateer* fought it out side by side across the Channel and back with *Atlantic Privateer* reported to have blown off *Nirvana* on the reach back to the English shore. This was more indication of things to come from the Farr boats.

On the Cowes week day-race, again problems. When I took the engine out of gear to feather the prop, the inertia of the blades had sheared the teeth in the gear and they were, after a quick check through our perspex window in the hull, stuck fully opened. Back to the dock. We let off a few journalists near Cowes and sailed back into the Hamble River. The boat would have to be hauled out immediately.

Just having arrived from France and occupying our space was the new, red hulled, Joubert-Nivel designed *Cote d'Or*. Maneuvering up the Hamble River constrained by your draft and dodging pleasure craft of all descriptions is tricky at the best of times in a Maxi. It was with some satisfaction that we brought her alongside *Cote d'Or* under sail without a hitch. The French hero, Eric Tabarly, a man of few words, and one who is used to the inconvenience of not having auxiliary power, must have been impressed with the coolness of our crew during this episode. A man very rarely given to emotion, I caught a glint of respect in his eye as he simply stared at us, massive arms folded across a massive chest. "Bonjour, Eric!"

"Bonjour, Skip". As in all the eight years we have known each other, so ended our usual conversation.

Our crew obviously was disappointed and I could see doubts on a few faces that afternoon. Neil Cheston wrote in his diary that evening:

We seem to be paying the price for trying to do it all too fast with this boat. During the Maxi series we had a couple of reminders of the lack of a proper shakedown for boat and crew, and now retribution has struck again. The morale on board, which up to now, has been pretty good has taken a bit of a dive, since even to the untutored, Drum *does not really look like a boat ready to race a marathon.*

August 10th was the start of the 630-mile Fastnet Race from Cowes to the south coast of Ireland, around Fastnet Rock and back to the finish in Plymouth. The definitive ocean-racing sprint in an English summer its recent history had included the tragic race of 1979, in which 15 sailors died. We had gathered an interesting crew of sailing personalities to fill out our regular 17-man staff. It would be our first big test offshore against the other Whitbread Maxis.

7 · The Capsize

I cannot imagine any condition which would cause this ship to founder. I cannot conceive of any vital disaster happening to this vessel. Modern ship-building has gone beyond that.

Capt. E. J. Smith
Master of the *Titanic*, 1912

Drum departed for the starting line off Cowes that afternoon of August 10th with a crew of 24 on board. Fresh southwesterlies were proffered for the 180-mile leg down the English Channel to Land's End. As we reached across the Solent from the Hamble river, we tucked in two reefs, nice and tidy, and laid out the No. 4 genoa on deck at the ready. The air temperature was cool and bracing, and we all knew there was a tough night ahead of us.

The Fastnet is always started on an ebb tide and with wind against current, the Channel water was churned up good and proper as *Drum* pounded her way south west with the other Maxis, up in front of the fleet. Early that evening, in the fading light, it was obvious we would not make the 'tide race' at Portland Bill so we and most of the others held offshore to stem the current where it was least for the next 6 hours.

Roger, watching our progress on the radar with *Condor* and *Privateer*, reckoned we needed more sail and with a slight decrease in the wind-speed I called for a change up to the No. 2 headsail. The reefs in the mainsail had been taken out hours before.

It took almost the whole 16 men on deck to control the sails up forward as the seas continually ripped the unruly Kevlar out of their grip, threatening to take it over the side. I, and no doubt others, must have been wondering how in the hell we were going to do these changes with only a watch of 8 on deck in the Whitbread.

With a flashlight I crawled back near the rudder shaft to find the whole quadrant heaving and rolling from side to side. Closer inspection revealed that the top shaft bearing had dropped free from its housing at the deck level, leaving the entire steering system unsupported.

I sadly reported the news to the watch on deck; there was nothing else to do but drop the sails and attempt to relocate the bearing. With the top of the stock supported by a halyard, two men below and two on deck painstakingly 'fished' the bearing back into place using bits of string and needlenose pliers. Time lost; just short of three hours. By 0900, when we were able to make sail, the westerly had so freshened that we could carry only the No. 5 jib and three reefs in the main. In a race of this length we all knew the wind would have to go light and variable if we were to catch up to the leaders. We had no idea just how fortuitous this little interruption would be.

The Cornish coast is notorious for shipwrecks. Steep cliffs and some difficult entrances to harbors, which are few and far between, have been witness to many wrecks in on-shore winds and seas roaring in from the North Atlantic.

The famous Eddystone Rocks were well astern that morning, our next piece of real estate to haul down was the 'Lizard,' a rocky promontory marked by the equally famous lighthouse. Traditionally, transiting the Lizard marked the end of ship passages from foreign ports and an entrance into local waters. For us it meant another tidal gate and with the tide once again against us, we elected to stay close inshore, inside the main flood, and hoped to have it with us by the time we were off the Race.

Beating in the relatively flat water in the sunshine was a relief from the night before. The crew were sunning themselves on the windward deck watching the coast go by. Just after rounding close aboard Dodman Point and entering Falmouth Bay, we overtook the Swedish Admiral's Cupper, *Carat*, a 50-footer who was doing well, far up in the fleet. As we passed them, the blond Swedes waved, especially Magnus Olsson, due to join *Drum* as a watch captain for the Whitbread.

Only about 6 of the crew were in their bunks, hard asleep. The others not on watch were milling around the galley just having finished their round of breakfast, and taking off their foul weather gear. Roger, in a state of exhaustion, not having slept at all since the start, was in his bunk and with bleary eyes and slurred speech rambling on about the tides and courses. I had just poked my head out the aft hatch to suggest to Phil Holland, Ron's brother, to steer her off a little more to achieve our target speed. We would tack back in ten minutes. John Irving had just sat down beside me when we heard the first bang.

"What the fuck . . .?" and then another bang. Thinking the rig must have gone we both rushed forward and the few seconds it took to

---

opposite The steel substructure, an object of much controversy, goes into place only days before the restart (*Photo by Skip Novak*)

overleaf The expression on Magnus's face on Leg Two is what surfing in the Southern Ocean is all about (*Photo by Rick Tomlinson*)

make the companionway ladder was time enough, if not to realize exactly what had happened, then enough to know it was not the rig, but something far more serious as the boat just kept on rolling over, sure and steady.

Phil Wade was shouting to everyone, "Get out, just get out!" And it was literally, every man for himself. My first reaction was that the boat would capsize and sink immediately and there was only one thought on my mind; make that hatch. Trevor, with his pants around his ankles, emerged from the head cubicle and we both floated out at about the time the deck was at 90 degrees.

As the rigging cascaded down on top of me I had a very brief, strangely peaceful feeling of imminent death. Struggling to swim clear while being dragged under by ropes and wires, I managed to reach up for the starboard side gunwhale and grab it with both hands. Like a veritable coffin door, the deck slammed shut as it hit the water and at that time I knew I was safe and that *Drum* was upside down. Then the horror started. I looked around me, Trevor, Phil Wade, "Where are the others?" And all you could hear was shouting from below decks.

Neil Cheston, in a fitful sleep in the port side, middle upper bunk, recalled the scene below:

"I don't think I actually heard the bang. But I remember the boat heeling over and that must have woke me up. My first thought was that we'd been knocked down. Then the bunk started to fold up on top of me, but I still had this feeling that it would come back. It didn't actually occur to me that the keel had fallen off until we continued to roll and about five seconds later I knew we were completely upside down when the bunk fell on top of me. Although my head was clear, I was like in a cocoon, not being able to move anything else. I heard distant voices. Then the water started swirling around the back of my head and with the fact that I was trapped I came to the realization I would drown when this thing filled up. I panicked and was lucky enough to kick myself out through the lacing in the pipe bunk and I can remember pulling a sail bag off of me and all the gear that had been in the rigging locker. I emerged into a twilight world of chaos."

Back outside, more and more heads began popping up around me. Standing on the lifelines like on the footropes of a yard arm, the boat would continually roll dragging us under. I looked up; there was Phil Holland and John Wooderson, hanging on to the propeller and attempting to pass down a safety harness tether to us.

---

opposite Running rigging repairs kept two men busy around the world; here Neil Cheston reworks the end of a Kevlar sheet (*Photo by Skip Novak*)

'Woody,' an afterguardsman of long standing in Britain, is a senior insurance broker for Willis Faber in London. An ex-dinghy champion, he was on deck, in the after cockpit when the roll began. He was clever enough to walk up and over the topsides as she rolled. He would write of his experience:

"Phil Holland on the wheel asked for some more 'grunt' and I went forward to free the leech of the mainsail. As I walked back towards the wheel I heard a horrendous tearing noise and the boat seemed to rise up in the air. At first, I thought we had hit a submerged container, but then the angle of heel became more and more acute until it became obvious that the mast was going to hit the water.

My years of inexpert dinghy sailing instinctively persuaded me to step over the lifelines and stand on the side of the hull. I even suggested that someone free the mainsheet! The mast then began to sink and I realized the boat was going to turn 'turtle' so I walked up the hull and clung on to the propeller shaft. I was immediately worried that the trapped air inside the boat was escaping and the hull would soon sink. We had just passed *Carat* so I stood up to wave in their direction. Their jib soon fluttered down and it was apparent that they had seen us and were motoring full speed in our direction. Phil announced that in his opinion the boat would not sink so I rigged up my life harness tether around the boss of the propeller to enable the rest of the crew in the water to climb onto the upturned hull."

By this time, others, who had swum out through the open companionway hatch, had drifted astern and managed to grapple their way up on to the stern counter getting a purchase on the up-turned rudder blade. Of course, when more people climbed on board back there, the easier it became for the others as their weight depressed the transom, so in effect they were literally washed up like beached porpoises. Little did they know that this stern down trim had almost drowned a man below. Continues Neil:

"In the diffused light coming from the main hatch and a few overhead lights beaming up from the deck-head, the first thing I saw was Terry Gould sitting there. I said to him, "Couldn't you hear me when I called for help?" And then we heard Pascal, his voice muffled, but it was obvious he was yelling his head off. We worked our way back aft to where he was, I think it was the port side upper bunk aft; we were totally disorientated at the time. Micky was already there trying to drag the spare dacron mainsail off of him, but he was completely trapped. With the water inside of the boat all rushing aft from the guys on the transom he was close to drowning then and there. Micky shouted for a knife. I made for the galley and in the mess, quite by chance, found a bread knife. We cut the mainsail bag open and forced the sail off him; he was in pretty bad shape as some battery acid must have splashed all over his face and he certainly came close to swallowing water."

As I grabbed Woody's life harness tether and prepared to climb up I saw 'Chas from Tas' beside me. He politely informed me he couldn't swim. A man I had met in Spain in 1972, he was one of the original boat niggers of yesteryear, he had already collected an incredible portfolio of stories to tell, some of them classics and quite famous, about disasters he'd been involved in and around the world. Although I didn't think of it at the time, I remember he had that unmistakable look about him as he gasped for air, almost a wry smile that said, "I can't believe this is happening. Why me again?"

As I hand-over-handed it up the tether, Phil Wade pulled off my trousers and boots and I made the hull with not a little effort. With three of us aboard we could pull up the others. Phil Wade and I took a head count; 18 on board or in the water. We made contact with the guys below and asked them how many were there. "Five," they kept repeating, and I almost became sick. It was not surprising that someone had been trapped in the rigging or possibly was still tethered to the upturned deck by their life harness.

Neil Cheston recalls:

"We then began to take stock of the situation. There was a lot of smoke from the generator that had been running and continued to do so for at least 10 minutes. Fumes from the battery acid and the smoke made it hard to breathe. Simon was OK and we gathered around the main hatch. Terry took charge, probably out of natural authority, and began talking about finding the diving gear and trying to get at the liferafts. At that time we didn't know if anyone was out there or what. And then all of a sudden we could hear Phil Wade shouting, "How many are you?" "Five," we kept shouting back, and then we found Max stumbling about.

I went off to get some lifejackets up forward and Micky went for the dive gear. At that point we could hear the guys on deck shouting to stay where we were and not try to get out. And then we could hear the chopper."

It must have been only 20 minutes from the capsize to when the rescue helicopter had arrived. Apparently several cliff walkers, one, a retired coastguardsman, had seen us go over and got on straight away to the Culdrose Air Sea Rescue Base, literally just over the cliff tops from where we were. Hovering low, they immediately put a diver down. The rest of us huddled together freezing in the cold wind. Some of the guys who had swum out after the capsize had on nothing more than a tee shirt and shorts. Phil Holland was passing out cigarettes. I looked at the keel plate, still firmly bolted on to the hull and could not believe this was happening. Keels just do not fall off racing boats. We anxiously awaited the diver.

Neil continues:

"The boat had gone down about a foot in that ten to fifteen minute period and the breathing was becoming increasingly difficult. Then, like a man from outer space, this head popped up out of the hatch – the diver. Simon went out first followed by Pascal, Max and Micky. Terry and I came out last together and when we hit the surface I came face to face with the chopper which was incredible close. I turned around and then saw all of these happy faces looking at me and throwing lines down. And from relief I thought to myself, what a huge joke!"

With everyone accounted for – all 24 of us, it had been a minor miracle. I don't think any of us gave a thought to the boat at the time. It was just so good to see everyone alive, nothing else mattered. About that time, *Carat* had overhauled us and was standing by. I can remember Magnus standing on the foredeck up by the mast just staring at us. He wasn't smiling then. He recalls his feelings at the time:

"Someone had shouted down below that *Drum* must have lost her rig because all of a sudden we couldn't see the sails anymore. As we approached the hull from a distance to investigate we called the Race Committee and informed them that we would apply for a time dispensation. Then, we could see that the boat was upside down. Your eyes saw it, but your brain just could not figure out what was going on. It was such an unbelievable sight you had to pinch yourself to see if you were alive. We stood by until the rescue helicopter had ferried the crew off and then continued.

For hours the crew was only talking about that and nothing else. We were sailing very badly for a long time, with the wrong sails, totally preoccupied about what we had just witnessed. It was very much later in the day before I even thought about the fact that I was supposed to join *Drum* for her sea trial to Iceland in a few days and then go on to the Whitbread Race."

When the diver was up on the hull, down came the helicopter's lifting strop. By chance I was sitting right there and, I am embarrassed to remember, the skipper was the first to be winched up. I don't think the diver would have been impressed if I demanded to be the last one off my 'ship,' nor did the thought cross my mind. Within five minutes the first load of six of us were dumped in a cow pasture where a Land Rover was waiting to take us to the little village of Portscatho. Pascal, who, more than any of us, came the closest to losing his life that day, fell to his knees and kissed the ground. I had to agree with him; never had cow dung looked so beautiful!

By the third trip out, a coastguard life boat had made the scene and offered to take more people off. The yachting journalist, Malcolm McKeag, who was on board remembered those last to leave:

"We shared out the oilskins to keep the more lightly clad from shivering to death and were lifted off one by one and then two by two. The lifeboat arrived to help and took off four: two who don't really like flying and two more. "I'm going in the lifeboat," said Woody, "they'll have grog on board, and a helicopter's a dry ship." John Irving was sliding down to the lifeboat's waiting Zodiac before Woody had finished speaking.

Phil Holland and I were the last to leave, save for the Navy diver. What do you say to a man who has just swum six of your friends to safety and who now stands, smiling, waiting to put a noose over your head? 'Thank you very much' seems somehow inadequate. As two of us swung aloft, up, up and away, we glanced back down at our great white whale, the seas washing around her."

Within minutes, those that were rescued by air were whisked off to the Gerrans Bay Hotel, one of those typical Cornish guest houses famous for hospitality and cream teas. Without hesitation they provided the crew with hot baths, an endless tea service, and boiler suits and old clothing, no doubt gleaned from their neighbors' garden sheds. The episode had only lasted about an hour and a half before all 24 men were once again, dry, warm and happy. No one had to remind us that if it wasn't for the three hours lost with the rudder incident that morning we might have been out around Land's End, with no one to see us, no rescue call and the proposition of spending the night in the Bristol Channel with no protection for those on deck and water rising around those below.

Almost as soon as I touched land, the problem of salvage hit me. Terry Gould suggested we get to a phone and call David Carne, local Falmouth businessman and racing yachtsman. By the time we got through and David had organized a boat to go out and attach a line to *Drum*, we were too late. We heard via the grapevine that some enterprising dive boat was already there and had waved our man off.

We couldn't have been more than an hour at the guest house when the reporters arrived, also by helicopter, to reap the rewards of one of the most spectacular accidents in sailing history. Having Simon Le Bon on board was an added bonus. Mike, Paul, Simon and I prepared a statement and were subsequently interviewed out on the front lawn. Hundreds of spectators lined the sidewalks. I had telephoned De just minutes before and she was busy back in the Hamble calling the relatives of every crewmember, before jumping in the car and driving down to meet us. I recalled how, in the Fastnet disaster of 1979, the press made a complete botch-up of the casualty report and I didn't want someone's parents seeing this little adventure for the first time on the six o'clock news. We couldn't be sure what they would say.

Chartering a bus, we were chauffered back to Falmouth, a picturesque, two-hour drive through the heart of Cornwall. With an air of bravado, we all proclaimed that if there was any chance at all we would try to refit the boat and make the start of the Whitbread. It was only six weeks away. The words were not entirely hollow. The fact was that the majority of the capital had been spent and most important of all, reputations were in jeopardy. For people who live and depend on public opinion, Simon's head was now on the chopping block and the Berrow's, and my own, credibility as organizers was now in question. We all knew that if *Drum* was not on the starting line September 29th, the critics would have a field day.

Being celebrities now, the crew billeted in the best place in town that night, the Falmouth Hotel. Built in Victorian times, it is high up on a hill with a sweeping view out to sea. Out on the stately front lawn you could damn near see where *Drum* had foundered. Someone commented that putting us up here, with a view like that, was a sick joke. Water was the last thing we wanted to look at.

The management welcomed us with open arms. Where the *Drum* crew walked, publicity was sure to follow, and they hardly blinked an eye at this motley crew that, in normal times, would probably have been turned back at their tradesman's entrance. We even had our own area in the dining room cordoned off from the public so we could at least have a meal in peace. Leave it to one of the Fleet Street hacks to sneak in and demand an interview.

Michael Berrow, a man far handier at dealing with the press than all of us put together, asserted his authority by grabbing this clown by the arm and ushering him out of the room as one would walk an unruly dog. We settled down to get completely pissed, a process we continued at the hotel bar far into the early hours.

While most of the crew were sleeping it off, De and I came downstairs for breakfast with John Irving who was thumbing through the array of newspapers. "Pop Star Simon in Sea Terror," "Pop Star in Sea Rescue Drama," "Simon Le Bon Yacht Sinks" and "Pop Star is Trapped in Tomb Terror," were some of the front page headlines on

Monday, August 12th. The only one that bothered me was not in the tabloids, but in the quality *Telegraph* where the cameraman who had been in the helicopter is quoted as saying, "All those that the helicopter had lifted off were very cold and obviously very frightened. It seemed to me that not many of them knew very much about the sea." I was right in assuming this would not go down well with the guys, most of whom have spent most of their working lives offshore. As it turned out, this little jibe made them even more determined.

MONDAY AFTERNOON: It was decided that most of the crew would return immediately to the Hamble, not least because of cheaper rent. Only myself, Phil Wade, Terry and Magnus, just up from Plymouth, would stay behind until there was work for them to do. Simon, after a raucous interview in the hotel, had to bail out of a back window into our waiting van to escape the fray. Of course, one enterprising photographer caught him in the act and that made the Tuesday morning papers. John Irving and I, accompanied by the three owners, took a small runabout out to *Drum* to negotiate with the salvor and regain control of the operation. John had spoken with the skipper of the sport diving boat *McAlister* on the radio telephone and the man sounded as though he had had enough.

It only took about a half hour to come to an agreement. I looked around. This stout and seaworthy little craft was tethered to the 'great white whale' by a very short towline. Already, his towing bits back aft had ripped off the bulwarks and had damaged the afterdeck. The mast, now apparently broken, had snagged on a reef that night while he was trying to 'make' against the tide, and it was quite likely the forestay had given way, leaving the rig unsupported. The crew, consisting of a few of his own and four guests who had just returned from holiday diving in the Scilly Isles, were weary from what appeared to be a losing battle. It was clear he was not able to move the boat at will and did not have the proper towing equipment.

It is a point of salvage law that states if one attaches a towline in order to claim salvage, one must be able to have the ability to tow it. For example you can not expect to salvage the *Queen Mary* with a 30-foot motor cruiser. Here was a marginal case. He had attached a line, had moved it (mostly when the tide was in his favor), and indeed had stood by in some nasty weather. We wrote him a letter to guarantee what was a small, but fair sum in the circumstances. The owner-skipper Stuart Farmer, I believe, had the best of intentions and was not greedy. ("Well honey," he would later say over dinner, "I guess we'll now be able to afford that holiday to America we always dreamed about.") He made an offer, and we accepted it without hesitation. The others were winched aboard another Wessex rescue helicopter to fly back to the hotel, a measure not too popular with the taxpayers, or so the press would claim. I stayed on the *McAlister* to await our own tug, which Irving and Mike had arranged to finish the tow into Falmouth. Strong southwesterlies were forecast.

The mast having broken free from the reef, we began to drift back out around Dodman Point and into Mevagissey Bay. We motored against wind and tide all night fearful of parting the towline in the squally weather. Eight hours later, just before dawn, the *Girl Lisa* found us in a rainstorm on radar and took over the tow. It was just in time; we were only about one mile from the beach.

TUESDAY: A miserable day at sea. An old rust-bucket of a beam trawler, the *Girl Lisa* had the equipment to do the job. We began to creep slowly ahead at a half a knot, back in the direction of Falmouth. On board were skipper Steve, a seasick mate, Dougie Rowe the salvage diver, and his assistant.

With the mast and probably broken pieces of rigging dragging along the bottom we had to fight to stay out of shallow water. We grounded and snagged for two hours on a rocky ledge called the 'Field' off Dodman point and had to back track losing three hours in the process. Chugging away yard by yard, sometimes gaining with tide, sometimes just breaking even, we hauled up into the Helford River entrance south of Falmouth and ran the rig aground in 15 meters. It had taken us 32 hours to cover 18 miles.

Dougie Rowe, salvage diver of the old school, is the Falmouth port authority favorite and that is no small accolade when your business is diving in Cornwall. We were informed by the port captain that to enter the harbor with this 'derelict vessel' we would have to insure it for third party liability as such and make every effort to insure it did not become entangled or block the shipping channel into the harbor. Dougie was in charge as he was the man they could trust. He and his mate took only about a half hour to cut the rig loose and drop it on the sandy bottom. We were clear to enter.

WEDNESDAY AFTERNOON: With *Drum* safely tethered to a harbor buoy we retired to plan how to roll the boat over. John Irving had secured the services of the Falmouth Dockyard for any cranage required. Dougie had an elaborate plan to empty the interior and then, by using air bags, right the hull with a small lift.

THURSDAY: A wasted day. After repeated dives it was clear that to untangle the contents of the hull was impossible. The divers recovered a few crew duffel bags and about four sails and miscellaneous gear after half a day's work. Dougie described the problem:

"It's as if someone has put the entire contents of the boat into a giant washing machine. Everything (sails, bedding, ropes) is all twisted and tangled together, snarled and jammed around the interior fixtures. Amongst that, all the floating stuff, floorboards, panelling, is in a thick layer on the surface and you have to force your way through to reach the air bubble in a visibility of about two feet. And on top of that, there's diesel and oil over the lot . . ."

FRIDAY: Clearly more bold steps had to be taken. Dougie was very reluctant to try and roll her over with the contents still on board. I signed a release in his favor taking over the responsibility if my plan damaged the hull or she sank and damaged the rudder. There was little to lose and time was running out. John, Dougie and I met with Dennis Pascoe, the director of the dockyards, and he promised us cranage and labor at 0700 the following morning. Meanwhile, Phil Wade had gone offshore on the *Girl Lisa* to recover the mast which was lifted by air bags. The crew was summoned back from the Hamble for the big day.

SATURDAY: With two slings cradled underneath the hull for safety if she sank when vented, we dove on the hull and attached two more strops from the true starboard gunwhale, down and across the deck and then lashed them on to the port gunwhale. With salvage pumps standing by, the load came on and after a slight pause and a gasp from the spectators as the overload bells on the cranes signalled trouble, she rolled smartly over and her decks washed clear as I jumped aboard. With an audible sigh of relief, the crowd broke into applause. It was over in seconds.

The crew formed a human chain to offload the gear as the salvage pumps quickly lowered the water level inside as if revealing for the first time a long forgotten geological disaster, strata by strata. Sails had been stripped of their bags and some of the spinnakers had wound themselves around the interior in knots that would have impressed Houdini, and had to be cut away. Jars of food, knives, forks, and spoons were stuck in almost inaccessible nooks and crannies in the overhead. Afterguys, sheets and other bits of running rigging were tightly wound around the engine; clothing and personal gear was spread out everywhere. It was obvious that a lot of equipment, most notably sails, had slipped out through the hatches and mast partners and were lost. Although the engine, the genny, and the batteries were still fixed in position and the interior in general not damaged structurally, everything was incredibly abraded.

From the floating pontoon the collection of gear was hoisted aloft on to the main jetty and organized into piles. It's only natural that we would keep a close eye out for our own sea bags. Only Terry Gould, one of the six trapped below had the presence of mind to find his sea bag and rescue his wallet and passport before swimming out. Any time we found something belonging to us a big cheer went out whether it was a rigging knife, a toilet kit or a pair of undershorts. Again, it was already obvious a lot was missing.

Out came a little stuffed animal that one of the carpenter's kids had given us as a going away present. It had been hidden in the chart table and I casually tossed it into the cargo net with the other debris. When Max saw it on the jetty he immediately turned white. "What is that?" he asked De who was sorting that pile out. "It looks like a drowned bunny rabbit," she answered.

"That should never have been on board. Don't let Pascal see it, please." He then went on to explain how the French sailors have an old tradition about rabbits. Apparently in the old days, rabbits had chewed through ropes securing a cargo down below and the ship had lost her stability and had foundered.

SUNDAY EVENING: Steam-cleaned, steadied by five tons of sand bags in the bilge, *Drum* picked up a tow in Falmouth Harbor, bound for the Hamble River. Magnus and Phil Wade shipped on board with sleeping bags, a camping stove and little else. 20 hours later they were berthed at Moody's. The draft in the river had been of no concern!

THE KEEL FAILURE

The Suppositions

The cause of the capsize was reported as *Drum* having hit a rock while beating close inshore in a Force 8. That was the Monday morning story, and it was obviously pure guesswork by the journalists trying to beat their deadline. It wasn't a bad guess seeing that rocks were around and one could easily assume that the only way for a keel to break off was to hit something hard.

Finding the keel would obviously clarify all of this, but as far as we were concerned it was 35 meters down on the bottom to stay, at least in the short term. Positions from the coastguard, the helicopter and our own reckoning had disagreed wildly, making the recovery unlikely.

If you could believe our estimated position and after inspection of the keel plate still attached to the hull, the assumption then turned in favor of a structural failure. The designer and builder of the boat were at once under suspicion by the general public for obvious reasons. The controversy would rage on for months.

The Implications

When even the cloudiest of facts came to light, there was only pity for the crew and the owners. It was acknowledged that we had been victimized by what we had considered to be reliable suppliers. The man that would take the brunt of the accusations was Ron Holland, because quite simply, it was a Ron Holland Maxi. Even as *Drum* still lay upside down he was besieged with inquiries from his previous and future clients about their keel designs.

The Facts

Upon return to Moody's two separate sets of investigations were carried out to determine the cause of the failure. Professor Brian Hockenhull from the School of Industrial Science, Cranfield Institute of Technology, commissioned by the owners; and Messrs. Farrar, Wigley and Claughton from the Wolfson Unit for Marine Technology and Industrial Aerodynamics, Southampton University, acting for Ron Holland Yacht Design.

After a visual inspection of the top plate and the surrounding hull on August 19th and 20th, the top plate was removed and sample sections were divided up by the researchers who retired to their laboratories. Although the two reports vary slightly, they both agree in principle that the cause of the failure was due to poor fabrication technique by the Adtec Welding Alloys Ltd. Importantly for Ron Holland, his design as specified was well within the safety margins for such a structure.

Ron Holland struggled to clear his name and a summary of the report appeared in the October issue of *Yachting World*:

1. The top plate is distorted at the forward and aft ends. This indicates that the weld in these areas was among the last to fail so running aground, either at the time of the accident or at any time before, had no influence on the loss of the keel.
2. Analysis of the welds revealed that some of them were porous and had insufficient penetration. (In one case less than 1mm, in another none at all.)
3. If all the welds had been of full cross sectional area they would have been of adequate design strength, but they were reduced to some 20 per cent of this area.
4. The 'worst case' situation (the boat 90 degrees to the vertical) used in the initial design was reasonable, representing a realistic maximum load possible on the keel.
5. The weld strength figure used in initial calculations was a conservative representation of the welds which would be achieved using normal workshop practice.

The Wolfson Unit was very specific: "It must be said that the general standard of the welding was quite appalling and was not fit for

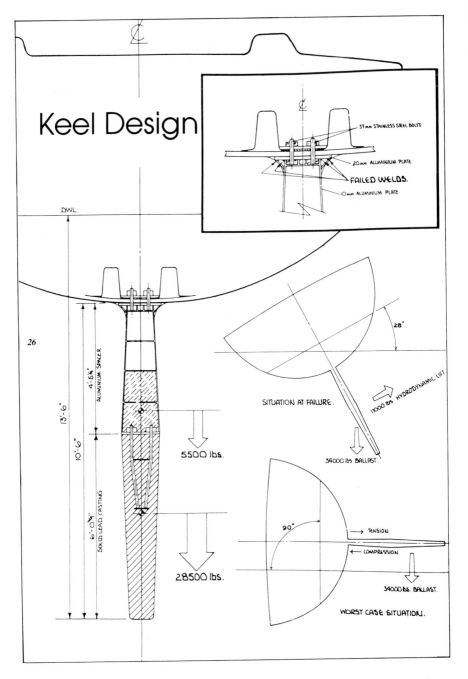

Keel Design

37mm STAINLESS STEEL BOLTS

20mm ALUMINIUM PLATE

FAILED WELDS.

10mm ALUMINIUM PLATE

DWL.

26

13'-6"

4'-6½"

10'-6"

ALUMINIUM SPACER

6'-0¾"

SOLID LEAD CASTING

5500 lbs.

28500 lbs.

SITUATION AT FAILURE.

28°

HYDRODYNAMIC LIFT

1000 lbs

34000 lbs BALLAST.

90°

TENSION

COMPRESSION

34000 lbs BALLAST.

WORST CASE SITUATION.

the purpose of fixing a critical component such as a keel spacer. They had been executed with little care and attention to the requirements of the job at hand. If a simple test sample had been inspected during the fabrication period, it would have been quite obvious that these welds would have failed at an early stage in their life."

Although Ron's drawings had specified that "marine grade alloy" was to be used and that "all welds are to be structural," both reports point out that in the future more information must be supplied to the fabricator in the way of a proper 'weld specification' and that sample weld testing must be done as a matter of course.

The reports go on to say, "It would appear to us that the boat building industry has, in a number of respects, adopted the materials and construction techniques pioneered by the aircraft industry, but without also taking over the documentation, quality control, and inspection procedures used to ensure reliability of the end product. For example, we believe that modern finite-element analysis techniques were used in the design and stressing of the keel in question. These calculations must have involved assumed values for the yield and tensile stresses of both the parent metal and weldments and must therefore be related to the values achieved by specific materials and welding consumables."

The marine industry has been carried along by trial and error. Keels, similar to *Drum's*, have been built for years without problems. There is complacency: you order and pay for a piece of equipment from what you believe and have been told is a reputable company. There is time pressure: mix the two and you have the makings of tragedy.

It can be argued that Ron Holland and indeed ourselves should have exercised more quality control during the keel construction. But if you were to commission a carpenter to build a flight of stairs and the first step you take collapses the first tread, it would be hard to believe the carpenter if he tells you he didn't have enough information to build the stairs strong enough or realize what the stairs were for.

In what should have been a simple case, responsibility still has not been legally determined, one and a half years after the event. Once again, only the lawyers' ship has come in!

For the short term the financial situation was disastrous for the three owners. Just getting out of Falmouth cost the project £30,000. Irving and I reckoned to make the start it would require another £270,000. Most of the sails were lost or damaged beyond repair. All the electronics except some of the Brookes and Gatehouse instruments (guaranteed down to 4 meters) and all of the ship's wiring was a write-off. A new generator, a refit of all the other machinery, strengthening of our spare mast, and, of course a new keel, would stretch the available resources to the absolute limit. And we still had no sponsor, nor was one likely to surface at this stage under these circumstances.

After independent surveyors had declared that what remained of *Drum* was repairable, we were left with only five weeks until the start of Leg One. However, I knew that the real problem was neither time nor money, but morale.

The first ten days were the hardest. We still didn't have the go-ahead from the owners, although we were proceeding at a furious pace. It was hard to persuade the crew and workers to attack the refit with enthusiasm without total commitment by the owners. I realized the gravity of the situation when I was having a chat with Phil Wade.

"I think quite a few of these guys are shaky, Phil. I doubt that Pascal will come back; he admitted to me he still doesn't feel confident and thinks going on the first leg may be a bad decision for the boat as a whole. He needs more time. And I think Trevor is doubtful as well. He says he has to go to Denmark to see his girlfriend to get his head straight. What do you think about the rest of the guys?" I asked him. "Hey," he told me, "I'm pretty shaky myself. I can't see how in the hell we'll do any good in this race if we do make the start. The whole thing looks futile."

I knew that if he went the others would soon follow and I told him so. It was time to put someone on the spot. In the weeks that followed we would lose Pascal, Max and Trevor, and under the circumstances I could hardly blame them. They were, however, all good enough to stay on until the start and help us get ready.

I invited Richard Freeman to join us as the cook, having scrubbed any notion of the crew taking turns with a strictly prepared menu. Because he was English, doubts were expressed about his cooking ability, so he gave us a trial dinner in one of the crew houses one evening. The meal was met with a mixed reception, but with more important things on our mind we were glad to have him.

With still no answer from the Berrows and the crew putting in 12-hour days dismantling and reassembling literally every nut, bolt and ball bearing for inspection and lubrication, another saviour arrived down at Gosport. Weeks overdue, *Enterprise New Zealand* pulled into Camper and Nicholson's Marina in a horrible state. The last of the Farr trio, she had been held up in Florida to repair damages suffered in a grounding off Nicaragua after transiting the Panama Canal. Apparently, skipper Digby Taylor had navigated the 80-foot missile straight into the lagoon of an atoll and spent the night impaled on a coral head. The story goes that he was navigating with a small scale chart that covered the entire Caribbean. The lighthouse he planned to round turned out to be miles inside a barrier reef. They were lucky not to have lost her.

"If some of you guys want to make yourselves feel better, go down to Gosport, take the time off, and see *NZI*," I told our crew. With her mast out, machinery in pieces, everything corroded and inoperable, cracked frames up forward as well, I reckoned she was in worse shape than we were. Certainly her crew were not happy nor confident.

Sometimes it's the little things that give you the incentive. I remember when Paul Berrow's girlfriend, Miranda, called me up for the crew's waist sizes for new uniforms she was ordering, I knew the game was on. Later, with the go-ahead official, we all sprang to life. Magnus was put in charge of the mast and his enthusiasm and 'fresh blood' had helped to carry the day. He recalls those hectic last weeks:

"I think when we finally got the boat out of the water at Moody's and cleaned up, a lot of people started to get some kind of a special feeling for *Drum*. It just had to do the Whitbread. For me, because I was not involved in the accident, it was very easy to approach the job with a clear head. In the beginning I must say I thought it was impossible. But I figured it was only five weeks of effort and it would be very easy for me to work hard for that time and just see what happens. Although a lot of my friends were wondering what I was doing there, I found it a very interesting proposition to get that boat ready on time."

Suddenly everyone seemed to be behind *Drum*. It all came down to pride. The Moody's people pulled out all their stops, forgot about all company policies and put their hearts into it. Foreman Ron Heazel was once again a tower of strength, bombarded from sun up, right through the night with impossible requests to have things made or modified for 14 demanding yachties. Rob Lipsett and Adrian Thompson donned workclothes and tended to some composite jobs free of charge. Irving talked ceaselessly on the telephone and Jacky tried to keep the books straight in a quagmire of deferred payments, unorthodox discount procedures, and just plain promises. If I had been British, I would have been proud to be so during those days.

The Moody's Used Boat Show was run in conjunction with the Southampton Show from September 12th to the 20th and during the last week we were in the yard we became a side-show attraction. Filthy Phil, working in the container on the running rigging had become the groupy's favorite and they would crowd around asking him silly questions as he threw in the splices. 'His' container, fitted with tool bench, lockers, stereo, coffee machine and pin-up calendar was festooned with going-away presents of stuffed animals (no more rabbits!), outsized cards and other paraphernalia.

On the 17th of September *Drum* was relaunched, her rig was in by early afternoon. Ten interviews for radio, television and the papers had me frazzled by the end of the day, and I collapsed in a heap early that evening. By the 19th we were sailing. And by the 21st we had buzzed the Southampton Boat Show under full sail. The loudspeaker had announced that *Drum* was sailing past and the show came to a standstill. Thousands of people cheered us as we rounded up in the river and came back at the dock at 12 knots, the wake submerging the pontoon overloaded with well wishers. We would make it!

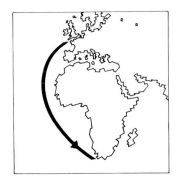

8 · Leg One: As Ready As We Could Be

Roger: *"How are you doing today, Patrick?"*
Patrick: *"How am I doing? Just fine. It's the next 27,000 miles that I'm worried about."*

September 28th, one hour after the start.

A going-away present from the proprietor of the Old Ship Pub had arrived on board. *Quis nos separabit* on the brass plaque when translated from the Latin says, 'Who will separate Us.' Jim, a bronze caster in his spare time when the pub was 'shut,' had supplied hundreds of these to the Pacific and Orient line for their lifeboats. I immediately nailed ours to a prominent bulkhead on *Drum*.

We thanked the Moody's people and our supporters with a party for 500 the afternoon of the 23rd of September and that evening we made our way down the Eastern Solent to Gosport for the race check in.

The other boats were already there. *Atlantic Privateer* had landed a sponsor at the last minute, and a sign painter was applying the ungratifying name and colors of *Portatan Ltd, UK*. Although the reason why a company selling portable tanning equipment would want to sponsor a Whitbread boat is not completely clear, the reason why owner/skipper Peter Kuttel happily changed the former appealing name of his boat certainly was: money.

Enterprise New Zealand also underwent a name change at the 11th hour. The diversified NZI Corporation of New Zealand had offered major sponsorship to Digby Taylor's campaign, that up until now had been relying on small contributions from several companies and in large part from a public funding campaign by selling raffles, paraphernalia etc. Rumoured to be roughly $1 million NZ, the sponsorship was in large part contingent upon the newly christened *NZI Enterprise*'s performance.

---

opposite It takes two people to do anything on a Maxi (*Photo by Skip Novak*)

overleaf Another wet sail change on Leg Three; all available hands are needed to get that headsail on board safely (*Photo by Rick Tomlinson*)

Even the nearly prehistoric *Great Britain II* found essential capital – 12 hours before the start. Under-rigged, antiquated and staffed by a crew of inexperienced charter guests as paying crew in the typical British tradition, this dinosaur was salvaged from the embarrassing position of not being able to start the race for lack of funds by the Norsk Data GB company. What would be clear in the months to come was that the amount must have been a small sum indeed.

Unfortunately, we began the race with no sponsorship other than the benevolence of Simon, Mike and Paul. Their offices were still working on digging up support, but so soon after the capsize this was as unlikely as finding hull insurance.

There were 15 paid up, bona fide entries (see page 143).

On every one of them there was frantic activity; stores to come on board, last minute modifications, radio tests and the installation of the Argos transmitter supervised by the Race Committee. This little dome antenna, mounted on the transom, was a self-contained beacon that would transmit our position to the Argos satellite system (run jointly by the Americans and the French) twice daily to the Race Office which was then relayed to the news media.

Although we appeared to be relatively ready, it was exhausting for all of us trying to pull everything together at the last minute. Replacement sails were arriving one by one right up until the day before the start which meant taking the boat out to check them for fit. Four new crew arrived during the last week and they had to be medically and dentally checked, indoctrinated and issued with the standard kit of foul weather gear, thermal gear, boots, safety equipment and crew uniform. In spite of the best attempts to get them right, the sails, like the clothing, had to be sent back for modifications, and we were getting down to counting not the days, but the available hours left.

We would sail with a crew of 17:

The Regulars

Skip Novak	Skipper	American
Roger Nilsson	Navigator/Doctor	Swedish
Phil Wade	Mate/Watch Captain	S. African
Magnus Olsson	Watch Captain	Swedish
Patrick Banfield	Boatbuilder	British
Phil Barrett	Rigger	British
Hans Bauer	Sailmaker	Swedish

opposite Not only physical, but also mental fitness is required to make repairs 100 feet off the deck while hard running; Janne and Mario struggle to fix the leech cord of the mainsail during Leg Three (*Photo by Skip Novak*)

Bill Biewenga	Deck gear	American
Neil Cheston	Rigger	British
Richard Freeman-Cowen	Cook	British
Janne Gustafsson	Deck gear	Swedish
Micky Olsson	Mechanic	Swedish
Rick Tomlinson	Photographer	British

Extras for Leg One

Espen Aker	Norwegian
Chris Barker	New Zealand
Michael Berrow	British
Lawrie Smith	British

It is hard to imagine a worse place as a venue to stage a big race than Gosport. On the morning of the start thousands of people, milling around the docks in the confined space of Camper and Nicholson's Marina, made it almost impossible for the crews to get down to their boats.

One by one, we pushed and shoved our way through the throng, stopping to sign autographs along the way. We were allowed only one sea bag per man, specially made, that was supposed to contain everything we would need for the next five weeks off shore. It is essential to limit the weight in personal gear as multiplied by seventeen the problem becomes an obvious one. Two books maximum were suggested and five cassette tapes per man. Phil Wade was to check us out before we came aboard that morning. Some toted their bags nonchalantly overhead down the jetty, but when they swung them over the lifelines the strained zippers and bulging biceps attested to the density of the contents; weighing them would have been a better situation.

Around *Drum* was sheer pandemonium. Simon had arrived to see us off. He would only be joining us for the last two legs because of music commitments. Aficionados of rock music, and there were several that morning, would have known that both he and keyboard player Nick Rhodes had splintered off from Duran Duran and were cutting the new Arcadia Album while the other three Durans were in New York assembling the Power Station, their own answer to the substantiated rumours of discontent in their original ranks.

In spite of the little girls making it very difficult, the crew tried to appear calm and collected, casually chatting with friends and relatives.

I was leaning against the mainsail cover when Chris Barker came out of the hatch to tell me he couldn't find any hacksaw handles on board. With half an hour to departure I sent him against the tide of humanity, already dangerously submerging the pontoon, to run over to the hardware store to buy two. Now alert to the problem like a Scoutmaster, I asked Richard in passing if he had remembered to buy

Entry List (8/9/85)

Race No / Yacht	Rating	Rig	Type	Construction	Designer	Skipper	Age	Flag	Approx. Dimensions	Approx. Displace't
Division A										
1 *Drum*	68.9	Masthead	–	Kevlar	Holland	Skip Novak	33	Britain	23.5/19.4/5.64/3.96m 77/63.6/18.5/13ft	30,845Kg 68,000lbs
12 *Atlantic Privateer*	69.4	Masthead	–	Kevlar	Farr	Peter Kuttel	46	USA	24.32/19.25/5.74/3.75m 79.8/63.1/18.8/12.3ft	30,000Kg 66,140lbs
14 *UBS Switzerland*	67.6	Fractional	–	Kevlar	Farr	Pierre Fehlmann	43	Switzerland	24.3/21/5.65/4m 79.7/68.9/18.5/13.1ft	28,000Kg 61,730lbs
18 *NZI Enterprise*	70.0★	Fractional	–	Kevlar	Farr	Digby Taylor	43	New Zealand	24.32/19.25/5.74/3.75m 79.8/63.1/18.8/12.3ft	30,000Kg 66,150lbs
19 *ex-GB II*	67.4	Cutter	–	Foam s/wich	Gurney	Bob Salmon	49	Britain	23.53/20.78/5.63/2.75m 77.1/68.1/18.5/9ft	33,122Kg 73,020lbs
22 *Lion New Zealand*	68.6	Masthead	–	Kevlar	Holland	Peter Blake	36	New Zealand	23.77/21/5.67/3.96m 78/68.9/18.6/13ft	35,000Kg 77,160lbs
27 *Cote d'Or*	68.0★	Masthead	–	Kevlar	Joubert/Nivelt	Eric Tabarly	53	Belgium	25/5.95/4.5m 82/19.51/14.8ft	33,990Kg 74,935lbs
Division C										
4 *Philips Innovator*	52.2	Fractional	–	Aluminium	Vrolijk	Dirk Nauta	40	Netherlands	19.1/15.3/5.25/3.2m 62.7/50.2/17.2/10.5ft	29,065Kg 64,075lbs
9 *Fortuna Lights*	49.5	Masthead	–	GRP	Vislers	Jordl Brufau Toni Gulu	26 23	Spain	18.87/15/3m 61.9/49.2/16.4/9.8ft	18,840Kg 41,535lbs
13 *Fazer Finland*	53.2	Masthead	Swan 651	GRP	Frers	Michael Berner	54	Finland	19.98/16.8/5.3/3.55m 65.5/55.1/17.4/11.6ft	31,000Kg 68,340lbs
20 *L'Esprit d'Equipe*	46.5	Fractional	–	Aluminium	Briand	Lionel Pean	28	France	17.6/14/4.9/2.8m 57.7/45.9/16/9.2ft	16,000Kg 35,275lbs
Division D										
6 *Sas Baia Viking*	42.6	Masthead	–	Steel	Elvstrom & Klerulf	Jesper Norsk	30	Denmark	15.0/12.5/4.4/2.8m 49.2/41/14.4/9.2ft	20,000Kg 44,100lbs
7 *Equity and Law*	44.4	Masthead	Baltic 55	GRP	Peterson	Pleun van der Lugt	33	Netherlands	16.76/14.44/4.92/2.92m 55/47.4/16.1/9.6ft	17,500Kg 38,580lbs
17 *Shadow of Switzerland*	41.3	Masthead	Swan 57	GRP	S&S	Nora & Otto Zehender-Mueller	–	Switzerland	17.5/14.0/4.8/2.8m 57.4/45.9/15.8/9.2ft	21,700Kg 47,840lbs
23 *Rucanor Tristar*	45.5	Fractional	–	Kevlar	Ribadeau Dumas	Gustaaf Versluys	56	Belgium	17.63/14.5/4.9/2.9m 57.8/47.6/16.1/9.5ft	16,500Kg 36,375lbs

★Not confirmed.

matches. (I had already seen the toilet paper come on board.) He had forgotten! Up to the marina shop he went, while I thought to myself, "God, what else has he forgotten?"

By arrangement with the committee we had to leave at a precise time, and that time was now. Simon came out the hatch and when he made the deck I had him plant his lips on a bit of discarded ceiling batten lying in a cardboard box of garbage the last to go ashore. Knowing only too well the circus aspect of the publicity game, the little girls roared with anticipation as I held this quality souvenir aloft.

When I hurled the bit of wood to the crowd the gentle little creatures tore it to splinters while photographers, mature in age, but no less predatory looked on in fits of laughter. With deck speakers blaring the Duran theme song from the Bond movie, *View to a Kill* (parodied by many into *Keel*) sung by Le Bon himself we backed out of the marina and quit the shores of England.

We would only find out much later the drama on other boats. Digby Taylor's generator packed up the morning of the start and he had to decide to sail without the primary system to charge his batteries. Apparently the mate on *Norsk Data* finished attaching the mainsail track to the mast only 30 minutes before they left the dock and *Cote d'Or's* doctor to be, Luc Frejaques, arrived to do the Round-the-World Race only an hour before the start, disappointing the replacement already on board. Luc had been in jail in France for dodging his military service, but in the nick of time managed to convince them he was a bad risk, having drugged himself into a near suicide state only days before.

It was so hazy you could barely see across Portsmouth Harbor. A light southeasterly was forecast, which suited us down to the ground. With only 172 miles clocked up since the refit we were hardly what you would consider to be tried and tested and an easy start would be a bonus.

The entrance to Portsmouth Harbor and the immediate Solent was choked with craft of all descriptions. The Race Committee had arranged for the Royal Navy to patrol the starting area, but it was obvious that they had lost control early on. To make matters worse for us, most of the spectator boats seemed to be following *Drum*.

Hadn't they read the papers? Simon, Paul, John Irving, and the others were on a big power boat somewhere in the vicinity. It was impossible to put sail on until we were in mid Solent where there was breathing room. We managed to leave behind the kayaks, windsurfers and dinghys, but the runabouts and cruisers dogged us without mercy.

Roger popped his head out of the aft hatch to announce a postponement due to the congestion. Seconds later a ferry boat with tourists backed into our port bow, luckily damaging only the paint.

Bill reckoned a postponement was a bad move, "They'll only get drunker," he speculated.

For some unknown reason, the crowd suddenly pulled back and at 1220, September 28th, Naomi James fired the cannon and the Whitbread fleet surged through a corridor of boats, bound for the Needles Channel with light spinnakers. In what was a major coup for *Drum*, we pulled past *UBS* just off Cowes and led the pack out through the Needles, not an insignificant part of the race for a local boat.

The blond-haired and sun-tanned Englishman Patrick Banfield had just joined us days before the start after a three-year flirtation with life in Southern California. He would make his mother very happy when he would later admit to her that on that day, leading the fleet through home waters, he was proud to be British.

The big Bertram with Simon's entourage was the last to leave us off St. Aldhens Head on the Dorset coast. As they were waving us farewell, the old 'Diesel 3/4 oz spinnaker, a remnant from the capsize still smelling of fuel, blew out and fell to the deck in tatters. "Sorry about that, Paul!" I shouted over. I'm afraid it was a grim reminder of what he had to face on shore; a project that in the end would cost the triumvirate over £2 million. The motorboat pulled away and left us to our own devices.

The light easterly was the best condition we could have hoped for. With spinnakers we managed to hold our lead on the Maxi fleet until the Brittany coast was passed at 1500 the next afternoon, *UBS* and *Privateer* were on radar down to leeward, and the others trailed astern in the fog.

Eric Tabarly on *Cote d'Or*, possibly trying to beat the tide, possibly having a last look at La France, decided to cut inside the Ile d'Ouessant off Brest and had to kedge off of a buoy in some little bay when the wind quit. We found out the details later in Cape Town when one of the crew described this lack of judgement as the other Maxis, on the outside, left them quickly behind:

> "The crew, especially the younger guys were in a completely depressed state. While we waited for the tide to change that morning, a little motorboat came alongside with a journalist on board who came to interview Eric and have a cup of coffee; we just couldn't believe it!"

Up until we went on the wind shortly, we had high hopes for *Drum*. The replacement keel, modified to be 3,000 pounds lighter, had 10 per cent less area and with the center of gravity moved slightly aft, certainly wasn't doing us any harm in these conditions. The spare mast, strengthened and modified for the Whitbread requirement was also considerably more stable than the original, and easier to tune. Had the capsize been a blessing in disguise?

By midday on the 29th, the wind had swung through the south putting the fleet hard on the wind. With the change we had lost our lead, but were still right up at the head of the pack. The other Maxis would drift in and out of radar and sometimes visual range, tacking on the windshifts and with the breeze strengthening throughout the day and a major weather system in the offing, we had reached our first big tactical decision. My log on the morning of the 30th:

NZI *below to leeward at about 1.5 miles.* Portatan, *who we thought was* UBS, *is now 4 miles to leeward and slightly ahead. Tricky business coming up with these North Alantic lows that are marching up towards the northeast. A 72-hour prognosis has the Iberian Low developing and lighter winds offshore. That says we should cut close in to Cape Finesterre and get on the inside of the fleet. However, if that condition doesn't materialize, westward is the place to be with more wind and SW'ly shift first.*

Roger and I had spent a lot of time thinking about the Iberian Low. This heat low over Spain will give rise to a strong northerly wind down the Portuguese coast. It was these 'Portuguese Trades,' four years ago, that pushed the Swan 57 *Berge Viking* up in front of the fleet all the way down to the Canaries. We, on *Alaska Eagle*, had stood out to the west, anticipating new westerlies and were stuck in fluky winds for three days.

The morning we left Gosport, Jim Allen, a meteorologist from the Southampton Weather Center, had briefed Roger and me on the current situation and we spent most of the time discussing the Iberian Low. With that firmly planted in our minds, our past experience, and a prognosis to back us up, we decided to go for the coast, as did *NZI* and to some extent *Portatan*. *Lion* and *UBS* stood offshore, with *Cote d'Or* trailing behind to the northwest, still suffering from the Ouessant fiasco.

My log entry for October 1st:

Explorer/sailor Major Tilman would have smiled on us this morning; left-over curry to compliment a meager breakfast of powdered scrambled eggs. The eating seems to be fairly spartan on this voyage compared to the last go-around. Richard seems to be panicking a bit; short rations of powdered egg, milk and who knows what will be next are making the crew somewhat wary of his provisioning. Bilge water sloshing around the galley sole completely threw him last night after the tack. It's all in keeping with my philosophy of one cook, one leg at a time.

We had changed to the No. 3 jib early that morning and it was a bitter taste of things to come for the next 27,000 miles. Not yet routine, the drill, when perfected, went something like this:

It would take at least 6 of us to get the sail out from down below if it wasn't already on the weather rail. In the worst case it might be on the bottom of the pile. No place for a bad back here. As the helmsman was counting his lucky stars the seven others would drag the 30-foot long sausage bag, in this case weighing in at 200 pounds dry, up to the foredeck; the point men, Bill, Janne or Filthy leading the gang with the luff end. It is almost impossible to move anything with three people, let alone by yourself, on a Maxi. Phil Wade, used to driving guys in the gang system, would lead the slaves with a loud "Two. . six! Two. . six!" strategically timed to the roll, pitch and heave of the boat, using, rather than fighting the inertia.

With the new sail on the lee rail and tended by at least two, the others would scuttle back amidships; two to get the halyard forward, one to lead the new sheet, one to lay out the bag for the sail coming down. With a double grooved headstay system, we always did 'double changes' whereby the new one was hoisted either inside or outside the old one and then the old one dropped. What's known as a 'bald-headed change' would flog the Kevlar irreparably in the long term and is also a 'slow change'.

Riding the bow, the 'pointman' feeds the beginning of the lufftape up into the headstay groove and with the halyard tail led aft from its usual winch back to one of the four primary grinders, four men now wail away on the halyard while another tends the wire sheet, soon to be flogging like a bullwhip. It's a long grind up the 105-foot luff and still huffing and puffing, these same four, without a second's respite, run up forward to gather the old sail. With the new sheet trimmed on and the old one eased a bit, the halyard tailing man lets fly the old halyard as fast as the six men up forward can gather it without letting go over the side. One wave catching a yard of fabric at the wrong time and the whole thing, sail, sheets, stanchions and possibly crew can be sucked over the side with alarming rapidity.

They have had sail ties strung across the foredeck before the drop and with the bailed up sail safely under control and the halyard made fast to the pulpit, every one goes forward to drag the old sail aft. Probably the most unpleasant part of the whole exercise, the heap of Kevlar, stiff as cardboard, invariably gets caught on the inner forestay, babystay, and anything else sticking out of the deck. Bill Biewenga, an old man to be forward at 37, but no less aggressive, seemed at times to will the inanimate sail aft foot by foot with a stream of obscenities that only an American can muster, especially one who spent ten years pouring concrete in Chicago. With water still coaming the decks forward the sail is struggled into the bag, and lashed down on the weather rail amidships. With a job well done, we immediately collapse on top, holding it down as if it had a mind of its own. The whole operation can take a half hour in bad weather, and in variable conditions, we may do a change every hour.

Although still weary the crew seemed to be settling down to sea routine. It usually takes about three to five days to acclimatise. The watches and the bunking system below were confused and not a great success in the beginning. In the past we have always worked on the Swedish system, whereby two watches are split evenly, standing alternate six hour tricks in the day and four hours at night. This way, the system is rotational and 'dogs' itself so that in subsequent days a watch stands alternate mornings and afternoons and either two watches or one watch of four at night. Meal times are fixed, at say 0800, 1400 and 2000 and taken at the watch changes.

For many reasons we had decided to try a more complicated system:

A WATCH:	C WATCH
Skip, Janne, Neil, Mike	Lawrie, Roger, Filthy, Patrick
B WATCH:	D WATCH
Magnus, Rick, Hans, Chris	Phil Wade, Micky, Espon, Bill

The theory is that 8 men are on deck at all times. A watch changes with C and B watch with D. Therefore A and B are together and half way through B's full watch, A would go down and C would come up. Half way through C's full watch, B would go down and D would come up, and so on. The big advantage to this system is that every change of watch there are 12 men available on deck and continuity is not lost in replacing one team with another as in a two-watch system. The watch not 'in change' will brief the watch coming up about weather conditions, the set of the sails for the wind conditions and sea state and the rigging of the deck. It also prevents the most common cause of interwatch animosity that goes something like this, more often than not on a dark and miserable night:

On coming watch: "Feels like we need the No. 4, what do you think?"

Off going watch: "Yeah, we thought about that, but the wind has just come up in the last ten minutes. Might be better to wait until this cloud has passed."

And later, down below getting ready to crawl into a dry sleeping bag, we have all felt the guilt rise up inside of us as we hear the new sail being dragged up to the foredeck only minutes later, just as we have, when on deck, cursed those just gone below.

We also tried to pair up like capabilities on opposite watches, i.e. A against C and B against D: Magnus and Phil were opposite watch captains. Roger and I opposite navigators, Filthy and Neil opposite

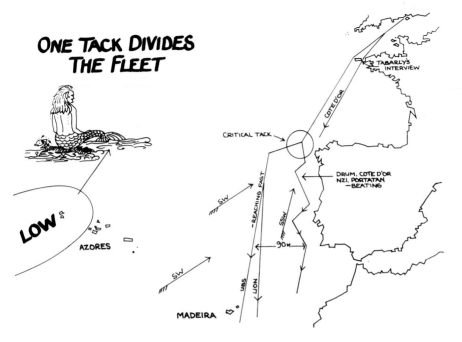

ONE TACK DIVIDES THE FLEET

CRITICAL TACK

COTE D'OR

TABARLY'S INTERVIEW

DRUM, COTE D'OR NZI, PORTATAN —BEATING

—REACHING FAST

SW

SW

SSW

90M

LOW

AZORES

SW

UBS

LION

MADEIRA

riggers, Hans and Espon opposite sailmakers, Filthy and Janne opposite bowman and so on.

Some of the advantages weren't even realized till we were offshore. *Lion*, seemingly overburdened in every department, carried 22 crew compared to our 17 and 16 on the other Maxis. On the Holland boats, which were not that spacious below, I could hardly imagine 10 men trying to get dressed or undressed at one time. In our case it was only four to get dressed, four to hit the coffee flask, four to get out the hatch.

Of course, Richard the cook, did not stand a watch, but was on call to help pack and shift sails below in addition to his normal duties. He also had the pleasure of having to wake up the watches for mealtime and rouse those due to go on deck.

Complicated by having to 'dog' the watch manually, and allowing for time changes, we left the task to Phil Wade to keep the whole thing straight. During the first week's endless debates on the success of the system with speculation about what was happening next kept everyone completely confused. We all accepted Phil's word that the treatment was fair, trusting in his integrity and endless lists and bits of paper.

By the afternoon of October 2nd it was obvious we had blundered badly. The night before a south-southwesterly had headed us slightly on port tack and, playing the 'Portuguese Trade' card, we had a good excuse to flop on to starboard tack and lay into the coast. *Portatan* kept going and just managed to catch the wind line with a southwesterly shift so she could then 'lift up' on starboard and steer south while we were still in the south-southwesterly sailing well east of south. Both *Lion* and *UBS* were way outside, 60 and 120 miles respectively to the southwest and it was quickly apparent they were reaching fast in the new wind. Only *NZI* had been foolish enough to stay in with us and to make matters worse she was showing incredible speed and stability on the wind in the breeze. She was pulling away fast.

Ignoring one of the biggest lows of the season, albeit still in mid-Atlantic, we had gone the wrong way and were left behind, wallowing inshore, looking for a wind that did not exist. Jim Allen, if he was watching the Argos positions, must have thought we were simpletons.

Forgetting the grand scheme of things for the moment, we were reminded of our own vulnerable little world. I recorded it all in my log that day:

Had a real fright this morning. The seizing wire Magnus had used to 'mouse up' the turnbuckles for the diagonal shrouds, aloft had broken (the single strand cheap shit) and all the diagonals had unwound themselves, some as much as an inch on the leeward side. Luckily, Magnus himself spotted the problem from the deck and spent most of the morning aloft putting it right and taking a beating in the boatswains chair.

Espon has come down with stomach flu and Hans now has a back problem, a strained muscle he thinks. In spite of it he struggled successfully to repair a hole in the foot of the medium genoa punched through by the 'babystay' toggle; but he is already showing signs of depression, lying there in his bunk, eyes wide open staring into the recesses of the overhead.

The Argos position reporting system has not been a great success as the committee has restricted its release of positions to the public to 12 hours after the reception – totally useless for tactical purposes and totally English in organization.

Still hugging the Portuguese coast, pushed in by the south-southwesterly, with *UBS* and *Lion* ahead by 120 and 80 miles respectively, it was understandable that the spirits on board were not buoyant. Roger, in an almost annoying manner, mulled over and over about our decision to stay inside. He was convinced that it was clouded thinking because of the stress we were both under during the last week ashore. I must admit to not having given the tactics the slightest thought then.

We carried on and by 2000 that evening, south and clear of Cabo St. Vincente of the southwest tip of Portugal, the wind flicked into the west-southwest, and we careened along on a reach at 10 knots. Things immediately looked a little brighter.

Although I didn't think about it often, the food situation on board was already causing concern. The main problems were that the portions seemed a bit short. We all know we eat far too much on shore, but when you're doing hard work, it is difficult to get used to the idea of leaving the galley still hungry. Actually, I had never felt better and as Neil so aptly put it, "more mentally alert." The ever-articulate Filthy, with his bulging midsection, reckoned it was OK as he pointed out, "Our stomachs are always leading our minds." But Phil Wade, a big man with not an ounce of unneeded ballast at the age of 40, was showing what he said were the first signs of starvation – acute mental alertness. As if to disprove his own theory, he dropped his dinner all over the cabin sole that night and retired to his bunk even hungrier.

Navigating with only a sextant is time-consuming work, at least in good weather, which is the only time it's possible to find out where you are. Eight years ago on *King's Legend* it was all that was allowed. The now familiar Satellite Navigation system was just beginning to appear on pleasure craft. Four years ago, the job became much easier; Sat Nav became a proven entity allowed by the rules. Position fixing was greatly eased and speeded up. On *Alaska Eagle* we had not had to take a single sight, so well did it work.

Now Sat Nav is interphased with the Brookes and Gatehouse compass and boat speed functions; the Brookes and Gatehouse is interphased with the Sharp 5000 performance program; the Sharp 5000 is interphased with the Sailor Single-Side-Band high seas radio for weather facsimile and telex facility. Radar, Ham radio, Decca, VHF, performance readouts littered the boat, above and below deck. It's all one can do to keep up with it; in fact, one can't . . . it requires two.

Since the start, Roger and I had rarely been on deck. We were below, struggling with user-unfriendly manuals, trying to master the advantages of all of this electronic wizardry. Computer equipment that costs £15,000 obligates you to get the most out of it. It needs to be initialized, calibrated, monitored, fed with recording paper and some-times talked to and stroked, to get it all to work at the same time. Then there is the weather-data-gathering side. We had two facsimile machines on board which issued forth a steady stream of information, some useful, like surface analysis and prognosis and other more questionable graphics like the satellite picture over the Canadian arctic and swell condition in the Gulf of Bothnia. Roger worked under the premise that it was better to get it all than to take a chance of missing something, especially in the beginning of the leg. But, he had failed miserably in underestimating the size of garbage can needed under-neath the chart table. And to complicate things further, as it seems to be in everything between the two countries, the French weather maps did not agree with the English.

Possibly we had suffered from a simple case of over-information in the beginning. After all, *UBS* had merely taken what is the average track recommended for any cruising passage to the Canary Islands from the English Channel. By October 4th we were back to basics:

I took a round of star sights last night with Roger's little sextant. Three days ago the Magnavox (Sat Nav) blew up, showing no display. Magnus fooled around with it and could find nothing obviously wrong except a few loose washers which were flying around inside the case. So – back to celestial. I feel more than a bit foolish. Only months before I had written, "In these modern times, electronics are as basic to navigation as pencil and dividers . . ." Now I was left with only one inferior sextant on board; no spare, no plastic job, no nothing.

On the 6th day out the wind had gone aft and light. We were still in good spirits and confident of catching the leaders by the Doldrums. It was a long way to Cape Town.

October 4th 2300
Phil Wade hid one of Richard's freshly baked loaves of bread last night. The bullish cook got up to slice his masterpiece and prepare the rest of the breakfast, only to find an empty baking tin full of crumbs and a buttered knife.
We had to stop the boat and put Micky over the side to remove a meter long plastic fishnet caught on the prop. We thought it was an insignificant bit of string as we were easily reaching out predicted polar speeds. We must in future stop immediately at the slightest sign of fouling – I hope this will not be a problem down south. At the 1200 positions we had gained on Lion, *but had lost ground to* UBS, NZI *and* Portatan.

1100 and 2300 GMT were the agreed times the fleet would communicate with each other on a daily basis. The fleet was split into two groups for purposes of radio scheds; the Maxis and the others. Under the terms of the race instructions, each group had a 'duty yacht,' an assignment that rotated daily. Section 5.5.2 of The Notice of Race reads:

Duty yachts shall carry out the following duties:

(a) Maintain a constant watch on 2182 KHZ using the Watch Alarm.
(b) Listen to the 0900 GMT and 2100 GMT Radio Telephone Traffic List from Portishead Radio and take action to alert any yachts for whom there is traffic.
(c) Control the inter-yacht schedule for her group in conjunction with other duty yachts.
(d) On completion of duty make the report required to Race Headquarters.

The idea was not only to keep the boats in contact for safety, but also to inform the Race Committee of the fleet's progress for publicity reasons. On Legs One and Four, however, it was not mandatory that each boat gives any information to the duty yacht, so quite often when it suited us for tactical reasons, we would listen, but not divulge our position.

Of course, the Argos Satellite System pin-pointed the positions twice daily and if someone didn't report, the others would stand by on the 'traffic list' from Portishead Radio in England to receive the Argos positions where all would be revealed. Withholding your position at the right time without unnecessarily aggravating the others could have tremendous advantages. We would see that some were more adept at this ploy than most.

After every position report was reduced to a common time, either by Argos or the intership schedule, Roger and I would carefully compare the daily runs of each boat and their gain or loss on us with respect to a common 'waypoint' somewhere in the far distance, the present case being near Las Palmas in the Canaries.

To say the least, we all anticipated these reports as one would a death sentence or a reprieve, depending upon the outcome. Roger would carry the log with the results and the weather maps up on deck and then attempt to explain these successes and failures of what could be a mile, sometimes 50 or 70, to our expectant, sometimes elated, sometimes disillusioned crewmembers.

October 5th   position 32° 30′ N 9° 41′ W
0900
30 miles due west of Cape Beddouza, and we can see the red smog layer of the Sahara. Looks like sunrise over Manhattan, but instead of chemicals and poisons its only windblown sand and quite romantic, unlike the New York variety.

Pleasant smells come out of the galley, more fresh bread on the go for lunch with another obscure freeze-dried mess. Most of us have admitted feeling fine, although consuming only half our normal intake. The workload, at the moment is very light and the climate mild. Sleeping bags are being stowed and swapped for sheets. Shorts and shoes are all that are needed for the on-watch now. Pretty soon we will all be complaining about the heat above and below decks (typical of these north/south passages from one extreme to the other). We are the duty yacht today so for us the 'jig' will be up and we will see if this easterly position, that we have held since Finisterre has paid off at all.

Approaching the Canaries in light, following winds was nerve racking. The North-east Trade Winds are established just south of there and we knew that if the leaders were lucky, they would soon be even further ahead. With our lightest spinnaker, the gossamer, wispy bag called the 'floater' (0.5oz per square yard), we would gybe in one direction thinking we had found fresher wind only to have it die off, gybe back and find wind on the other side. Roger was keeping meticulous control of the gybing angles, as it is totally inefficient to sail dead down wind in light air. Instead we had to 'reach up' maybe 40 degrees to either side of the course line as the increased speed when reaching would justify the extra distance sailed. Without any other conclusive information, we tacked down wind forward to a point somewhere in mid-channel between the island of Lanzerote and the Sahara mainland shore.

October 6th 0230
Our latest theory is to sail 'fast' somewhere roughly to the south – a noble conclusion after much deliberation.

Lawrie seems to stay cool during this whole exercise. He admittedly does not have much open ocean experience, but he certainly seems to be versatile. I threatened to blame him for our tactical blunders, as he would be the obvious scapegoat back in England and he took it all as light-hearted amusement as indeed it was intended.

Lawrie Smith had joined our crew only days before the start, a move instigated by Roger, who thought we would definitely need a man of his talents for Leg One. His credits include numerous championships in small boats cluminated by being given the helm of the ill-fated *Victory* 12-Meter campaign of Peter de Savary's.

Almost white blond and well tanned, Lawrie looks more like a 1960's surfing bum from Hawaii than the Englishman he is. A member of a small group of the world's top-level racing sailors, 12-meter skippers and tacticians, Lawrie is one of the new breed who are openly professional. He didn't come cheap. On the other hand, as Roger had correctly pointed out, he was a skilled helmsman capable of long, intense concentration, admittedly unlike most of us. Putting him to the ultimate test, the computer confirmed this; his line on the graph, a function of boatspeed versus wind data, had run the straightest the longest, with Magnus a close second.

Some shipboard observations in my 1400 Log entry:

Magnus came to Roger this afternoon complaining that he, like Phil Wade, was 'hungry all the time.' Roger donated an orange and I a bag of peanuts.

By 0600 this morning we had to gybe back again in a dying breeze, but again it filled and by noon we had 16 knots of true wind speed and were sliding along nicely right on course. Lion and Portatan are committed to the passage between Fuerteventura and Gran Canaria and it is possible that if we are right and they are wrong, we could be in second place tomorrow.

We have been trying to contact Las Palmas radio for local weather, but are told they don't give the weather report on Sundays. Rumour has it Fazer Finland, who has been leading on handicap, will have to stop in Las Palmas for a generator repair as he is having trouble charging his batteries. NZI also has problems with her radio and has been silent the last two days.

Scandinavian sailmakers Hans and Espon have begun to repair the 'Diesel 3/4 oz spinnaker, blown after the start; two able hands indeed. More graffiti is appearing in the head every day and that is always a good barometer of morale.

The 300lb spare mainsail is now back aft again in the fresh running condition, completely blocking the radio set. No doubt this will become the bane of the ship, moving this unwieldly sausage to and fro to adjust our fore-and-aft trim.

Physically, thus far, this is one of the easiest ocean races I've done. Superb crew, no maintenance problems and easy weather conditions. After 1800 miles of sailing we have hardly seen a squall. Although we are racing efficiently, it's more like a delivery.

On the morning of the 7th, just emerging from the achipelago, we raised *Portatan* on the VHF radio at the incredible distance of 70 miles. Various Greeks, Turks, and Arabs were having a go on Channel 16, 'buggering each other's mother', a common pastime for bored operators on ships and very similar to what I've heard in the Red Sea.

We, nor does anyone else, I believe, have the slightest inhibition about listening to other people's conversations on the high seas radio, especially those of our competition. It's a great hobby gaging the skipper's mood and the ambiance on board from the most simple of dialogues.

Skipper Padda Kuttel of *Portatan* wasn't happy to the west that day in light winds. In a long conversation to his wife in Cape Town about the family, business and the Race in general, he sounded like a man who could not believe he wasn't leading the Race; like he had been promised something we all had not been. In a state of depression, and unlike the man known for his limited spending on the boat, he easily succumbed to his wife's request to buy a few thousand Rands worth of furniture for the house; no doubt with more important things on his mind.

By the 1200 'chat show' as it has become called, it seemed that everyone had found the wind and was running free in the Trades: *UBS* was 270 miles ahead, *Lion 93*, *NZI 83* having made a spectacular run through the islands, and *Portatan* only 22, *Cote d'Or* was 85 behind us, the only consolation.

On the morning of October 8th the easy life was over. The wind had filled in at 30 knots true and we began our first taste of hard running. We realized that this was probably the only chance we would have before the Southern Ocean to test the equipment for these conditions. We capitalized on it.

Racing hard downwind requires different thinking and sometimes a completely different way to rig the boat for maneuvers. Rather than attempt dip-pole spinnaker gybes we rigged for a two-pole gybe. It required another topping lift, foreguy, pole guy and in the case of some of our crew, an open mind. Even the big Maxis who day-race would never consider a two-pole gybe because what is gained in safety is lost in time. However, in a 30-knot wind a fast, dip-pole gybe required full crew of 26 on deck. For most of our team, some of the tricks of a double-pole gybe were forgotten or had never been learned. It took an hour to organize the first one.

With the boat becoming slightly unstable with the 'blooper' flying to leeward, we dropped it and the 1.5 oz 'chute' and reset the heavier 2.2 oz, right in the middle of a mackeral fishing fleet just after midnight. Their red-over-white mast lights whizzed by us one by one at an alarming rate as our speedo hit 16 knots, then 17, then with Magnus on the wheel topped 19, as the spectators perched on their pushpits cheered him on.

Racing yachts, by their own exercise can rightly be considered unseamanlike by people who use the ocean for something other than a playground, but what we were doing at close quarters with that fishing fleet was marginal even by our standards. Deep water delivery skipper Phil Wade reckoned they would have been Spanish, South African, Portuguese, the lot; hanging right off the continental shelf.

Owner Mike Berrow was completely stoked by this sort of weather and seemed very pleased to be there. He had turned out to be an exceptional shipmate for an owner; he did the dishes twice the following day! He said he would never go on another rock music tour again, not for any money. Apparently their Duran Duran tour of America and Japan had been very successful, but he reckoned it has taken ten years off his life. Egos and personality problems had been killers but at 33 he didn't look worse for wear and was enjoying himself. He gave no evidence of wanting to use the radio to contact the family and office he had left only nine days before – a common syndrome for the uninitiated.

Only hours before he had told us not to worry about blowing out spinnakers, a fairly regular occurrence I had warned him. As if to test his mettle, the big 2.2 oz *Xargo* 'chute' exploded in full flight that morning. He had no hesitation yelling forward within seconds, "Don't worry about the money!"

During the next two days spinnaker halyards were run external to prevent chafe inside the mast, custom spinnaker pole ends were installed incorporating a 6″ sheave with a housing rotating in a thrust bearing, also to eliminate the chafe on the afterguy. They were the only two of their kind. The two-pole gybe system was, if not yet perfected, improved on and a pragmatic Phil Wade and Patrick, a theoretician of the first order, were experimenting with an automatic 'trip-out' system for taking down spinnakers.

It is easy enough to hoist a spinnaker in any weather; keeping it up there can be tricky; taking it down in a blow, is usually a nightmare. The normal way is to let the pole end down to the foredeck where the afterguy shackle is 'tripped out' and the sheet is winched in, the sail then gathered underneath the main boom. Attempting this in a big sea and marginal steering conditions usually courts disaster because when the spinnaker becomes asymmetric it immediately makes the sail plan, or center of effort, unstable. It will only be a matter of time before the helmsman loses control and broaches into the wind, or worse still gybes her 'all standing.' In an emergency, the afterguy can be let go, thereby creating the same effect as tripping out, but instantaneous. We have all had to do it at one time or another, but to let loose an 11mm coil of wire on a big winch and then dive for cover while it snakes its way around the deck, through blocks, fairleads, and carrying away anything it gets caught on (a stanchion, a winch pedestal, someone's leg?) is a most humbling experience.

The accepted Whitbread tactic is to attach a trip line through the trip mechanism of the shackle, lead it down to the deck and then to a winch. This can then be winched home at a moment's notice (for a sailchange, a squall, someone going overboard), tripping out the spinnaker tack, the sail then gathered in the normal way. Of course someone must go aloft out to the end of the pole to rig it up after the sail is set and also to unrig it when a gybe is in the offing.

Janne, who was proving to be an exceptional bowman, accepted any idea cheerfully. Whether it required him to go out to the end of the pole or up to the masthead; he just got on with it in the finest tradition of uncomplaining Scandinavian seamen from the days of Gustaf Erickson.

Filthy, the other bowman, no less adept and even more fearless, was not so easily convinced we needed all of these gadgets and what seemed like miles of ropes all over the deck. Dumbfounded by every new variation on another new theme, he would often say shaking his head on his way forward. "That's not the way we did it on *Kialoa!*"

My October 8th Log Entry   21° 00′ N 18° 20′ W
2200

A warm and balmy night; T-shirt weather on deck and an impressive array of tropical stars overhead.

It is a comfort to observe how relaxed this crew is in these heavy running conditions after a few days. With an untried boat, caution dictated policy when the wind filled in hard. Now, with confidence that the gear is up to specification and the boat relatively easy to handle, we live at ease with the familiar creeks and groans of the blocks, rigging, and deck coming under load. When we hit our first 15 knot surf the crew hooted and hollered, but now they all stroll about the deck, casually balancing coffee mugs while the helmsman lights a cigarette careening down the face of a wave at 17 plus. It is simply due to a vast depth of experience on board which gives me great confidence. Before the start, Marco, the young sailmaker on Portatan, had admitted to Phil Wade that although they had rough and ready guys willing to push it to the limit, he felt they lacked our depth of knowledge and wisdom. I hope we can justify the compliment in the months to come.

By our noon position on October 9th we had run 301 miles in 24 hours, with the wind slowly on the down swing. *NZI*, duty yacht for the 8th, had not reported for the second time, and we discussed protesting her for the infringement.

We had also heard via race control that *Norsk Data* had pulled into Las Palmas to replace a damaged headstay. They had not been having an easy time of this ocean sailing business with their crew of beginners. Later, Tracy Edwards their young but experienced English cook later explained the difficulties they had faced during the first two weeks:

"It cost each of those crew £8,000 to do the race on the boat. Karl and Chris, the two mates, and the only two who knew what they were doing, were on a different scheme. When I joined the boat, I was told that all the crew had sailing experience, but it wasn't true. Then I discovered we were out of money. I was so busy provisioning and caught up in the whole affair that it wasn't until the morning of the start that I had second thoughts about going.

No one had sailed together before the start. They couldn't even get the sheets and guys rigged for the spinnaker, so Bob (the skipper) decided not to bother with the headsail because it was too complicated to hoist the chute then drop the genoa during pre-start maneuvers. Consequently, at the starting gun we were facing the wrong way and crossed the line 10 minutes late. As I sat back aft on the stern, with my legs dangling over the side, I remember thinking, 'Oh God, I wish I was on one of those other boats!' It took us 38 minutes to do the first tack.

Trying to get the crew to work together as a team was very difficult in the beginning. They were all such individuals, trying to prove what they knew, or trying to hide what they didn't. On other boats, even though people come from different backgrounds, they usually are very clear about the common objective. Our people just didn't have a clue about what was going on. You would tell someone to stand by that winch, and he would go there and say, 'OK what do you want me do with it?'

The moaning started about two days out . . . people complaining about the cold, the damp, about getting wet! They were doing things that were hard to understand, like putting a tea mug on a counter top at 20 degrees of heel and getting upset when it slid off onto their laps, not once but two or three times.

Then we discovered the headstay problem and pulled into the Canaries for 14 hours. Bob had me reprovision and then someone suggested we should stay and have a crew dinner, seeing as they were in Spain. I was so disgusted I packed my bags and was sitting on a bollard on the jetty when Karl found me crying my eyes out. I told him I just couldn't set foot back on board that boat. He took me by the arm and said, 'Yes, you have to, you don't expect me to do it all by myself?'"

On the morning of October 10th we were down to 9 knots. When I woke up after a deep sleep it sounded as though we were in a dead calm. The wind had dropped considerably and with it the noises of wailing winches and terse commands from the deck. The sky was dotted by fluffy cumulus clouds, typical of Trade Wind conditions. The light and variable days of the Doldrums were with us now, and with the pressure of high-speed sailing temporarily off, the minor trials and tribulations of shipboard life reappeared.

It was the first real scorcher. We were 15 degrees from the equator, and the temperature was over 85°F. The watch on deck passed around the bottle of sun tan lotion, the smell giving me a hint of nostalgia for the beach at Ft. Lauderdale on spring break. Almost everyone was at least a little sunburned.

A stomach flu bug is still going around despite the Doctor's efforts. Magnus is the latest victim with a case of the runs, although even this unpleasant condition has not affected his unshakable high spirits. Hans now has problems with his neck, unfit for duty and lapsing deeper into reverie. Roger treats an endless line of people with rashes on asses; Filthy Phil, not surprisingly, is the worst case, and the doctor is prescribing bare ass sailing, plenty of Ultra Violet and frequent bathing.

We had a hot seawater system on board so we could shower in the head in cold weather, but in hot weather a bucket on deck was much more enjoyable. I took my second deck shower in 10 days, far below my average. I was beginning to smell myself. I must admit to a certain little boys' pleasure in quitting the shore and with it the demands of personal hygiene. It is almost ludicrous to shave out here, although most do it. That goes for combing your hair and even looking in the mirror. There's no one to impress. However, after a week of being a slob, a desire for order does creep back into the system, reminding us that we are not in fact animals of the lesser order.

It was cold cereal and fresh bread again for breakfast that morning. Phil Wade, on the dawn watch, had harvested 8 prime flying fish from the lee scuppers and when I awoke at 0700 he was busy frying them up for us, claiming he had to have a greasy food fix; he was having withdrawal symptoms. We were amazed to find that few on board had ever eaten flying fish or wanted to (much to our satisfaction, as there were only 8).

The Doldrums are usually found between 5° and 10° North in October. From the position reports we could see some signs of the leaders slowing down by October 11th. *Portatan* ahead and *Cote d'Or* behind have both favored the inshore gybe while the others are strung out dead ahead. Nearing the bulge of Africa, the temptation is to 'cut the corner' to the east, but it is an axiom that the farther east one crosses the Doldrums the wider they are.

Roger noticed that for the third time the day's Argos positions showed that *NZI*'s was a day older than those of the rest of the fleet. It was a point of fact that Blake as well as Kuttel were also displeased with Digby's failure to comply with the Duty Yacht requirements and now with his suspect Argos we never know where he is. The night before we had heard him claim generator and battery problems and then give a 10-minute interview with Radio New Zealand via Portishead, but for some reason he refused to come on the air with the fleet. It seemed to us that a protest was justified.

We changed mainsails that afternoon. Not only did the Kevlar main need some slides restitched, but I decided that the spare Dacron main would be more forgiving in the slatting conditions of the Doldrums for the next few days. Kevlar suffers from flogging and as surely as it is bad for a sail to flog during reefing in a blow, the same can be said for slatting in no wind. The drill took 24 minutes with 10 men on deck. The drawback is that any Dacron sail on a maxi boat is like a gunny sack at the best of times, and after staring into a perfect shaped main for the last two weeks, some of the crew were grumbling that this one is slow. They had a point, but we had to think about the sail surviving the distance. Chris, a true sea lawyer, pointed out that it was illegal to change sails, but the IOR rule book is vague:

851.2 "Spare Mainsails. These are not permitted to be carried on board with the expectation of improved performance, as for varying weather conditions or points of sailing, but rather a second mainsail can only be carried on board as a bona fide spare for emergency replacement."

If one can change the main if the original one is damaged, the broken slides would be the reason this time. The IOR rule is frequently ambiguous concerning transoceanic races. Changing mains, water makers, and the stowage of sails above and below decks are only some of the examples. In what certainly can be considered a non-development rule in the strict sense of the word, I remembered when the IOR measurer last summer warned us that because our propeller strut was 0.5mm too narrow, we would incur a rating penalty. This was nothing that two heavy coats of anti-foul paint couldn't cure.

My October 12th Log Entry   8° 30' N 20° 15' W
1200

There were minor aggravations like the heat and Roger leaving the top off the 'backwash' jug (aptly named the 'backwash' from the Maxi boat custom of passing a communal drinks container down the weather rail, the last in the line of 25 getting a tantalizing mixture of cookie crumbs, spital, and cigarette smoke with the liquid), and upending it all over the freshly washed cabin sole. They, however, have taken a back seat to the good news on the 'chat show.' Talking in north-south terms, we are 60 miles ahead of Portatan and only 32 miles behind UBS. We ran up on the leaders in a big way, covering 200 miles noon to noon to UBS's 80 and Portatan's 112! East-west which is soon to become significant is a different matter as we are western-most boat. We must, by design, break out of the Doldrums first and then attempt to sail across their bows toward Cape Town on starboard tack before they are released.

I informed Race Control of our intent to protest NZI this morning. Race secretary Brian Evans from the Race Committee said they were well aware of the problem.

With towering cumulo-nimbus clouds on the southern horizon I was certain we would be in the variables by that evening. The crew would need all the moral support they could muster for the next few days.

Hans was still wearing a neck support, but getting better. I suggested to his countrymen Magnus and Roger that he be woken for all of his watches, even if he just sits there in the cockpit and does nothing. Otherwise, he would just lie in his bunk, staring into the overhead for hours on end no doubt thinking, "Why me?"

On a more light-hearted matter, Filthy's pimples on his 'blurter' as he calls it, were getting remarkably better under Roger's disinterested (can you blame him) attention. We had allowed the drying of underwear on a makeshift clothesline from the radar bracket to the antenna pole, and an untidy row of multicolored men's undershorts dangled unaesthetically behind the helmsman, not pleasing photographer Tomlinson who was desperately trying to capture the essence of round-the-world racing.

In the galley liberal helpings of chicken supreme and mash were ladled out that evening, again like always, without ceremony, like in prison or the military. After two weeks at sea, everyone seemed to be reasonably fit with what was considered to be an inadequate diet. Either they had been getting used to the rations or it was just stoic resignation seeing there were still three weeks to go. Even the gannet Wade had not been seen lately foraging around under the lower bunk stores, stealing packs of peanuts and other assorted snacks. Could this have been a revelation for 'western man?'

My October 13th Log Entry   6° 00′ N
0830
Speculation about the Doldrums not being present this year were laid to rest at sunrise. A panorama, in clear unlimited visibility, the kind where the clouds are sharp on the horizon, revealed a sky boasting every imaginable cloud type. Hostile shapes of nimbo-stratus and cumolo-nimbus of immense proportions lower down dominated the wispy cirrus and stratus clouds high overhead; no artist could ever hope to mix or match the blues and grays and while Rick struggled to capture the images in the coming daylight, that would never do justice, the rest of us just sat there in silence and absorbed it the best we could.

NZI must have realized they had pulled a boner, because all of a sudden, they had reported their morning position to Race Control. They also claimed the switch on the Argos has been faulty. This was interesting since the switch was for use only in emergencies for a Mayday call.

That evening we changed back to the Kevlar main after an aborted attempt to save it for use later, after the Doldrums. We had sailed for four days with a slow mainsail and the message to the skipper pinned to the head bulkhead the following morning was plain:

> "We ease the sheet, then trim it on,
> As regular as Quartz
> It matters now how hard we try,
> Cause Dacron sails, eat shorts!"

Still in light weather the next day, we fought through the heat by day and the tangle of rigging and sails on deck by night. Light weather can be frustrating at the best of times, and after a four-hour night watch it may be surprising that with little or no wind it is quite common to do maybe 12 sail changes, and then collapse into one's bunk exhausted.

My October 14th Log Entry   3° 00′ N
PJW, master of the rolls, has solved an annoying problem by hiding most of the plastic glasses and half the cups. The 'dishnigger,' one who does the dishes

on rotation, had to cope with literally every mug and glass after the watch change. Last night the deck was like a mine field of empty cups, the mere sound of them rolling around was enough to drive me right up the rigging. First signs of losing it? Maybe just a pet peeve, similar to the marbles Mr. Roberts had put into the captain's overhead.

One of our two, ten-man Beaufort liferafts has developed a slow leak in its gas cylinder and has inflated the raft enough to blow the lid off the locker – which is how we discovered the problem. Safety officer Wade has it on deck, bleeding it off and restowing what is now but a rubber bag, useless in an emergency.

That evening we had a solid downpour for an hour, and all 17 of us, stark naked, slipped and slid about the deck and rigging, washing our hair, clothes and everything else we could think of. We wallowed in pockets of rainwater in the bight of the main, running off the headsail and in the scuppers. This simple act of child's pleasure lifted everyone's spirits and cooled off brains that had been baking for the last four days.

Science has labeled this area of the world as the Intertropical Convergence Zone. For myself, and I hope for the others who have just frollicked in one of God's biggest and cheapest fresh water showers, it can only be and will always be . . . the Doldrums.

Because of the Coriolis Force, which bends all winds due to the rotation of the earth, the Southeast Trade Wind below the equator changes to a southerly at the equator, then veers west of south until it reaches the convergence well up in the northern hemisphere. This southerly allows a sailing yacht to bear off on starboard tack, initially being able to point the bow just about in the direction of Cape Town. But the further south one goes, the more he will get 'headed off' until, when he is well established in the Southeast Trade below the Equator, he will be steering east. At some point he will have to elect to tack on to port tack and stand down the length of the South Atlantic in hopes of getting around the inside of the big South Atlantic High, the last major obstacle before the finish. That tack is one of the most critical decisions to make on Leg One, possibly on the whole Race.

The option of sailing an extra 1200 miles to go around the western edge of the high, as the old sailing ships did to stay in free winds, had been discarded long ago as a gamble not worth considering with a modern yacht efficient sailing into the wind. The chances of being stuck in the high out to the west were just as great as they were to the east, so there was no point in sailing extra miles.

Surprisingly, the true variables had only lasted 14 hours. By early morning of October 15th, while I was still sleeping, the expected southerly had filled and we bore off on starboard tack with the No. 2

genoa, salt spray once again peppering the foredeck. Cape Town was 3,000 miles away.

Unfortunately, most of the other Maxis had been released across the east-west board at the same time and without anyone getting a major advantage, we all sped off toward the header and the penultimate tack point.

Of course, the intership radio schedule at these times is less than successful, even if you allow yourself to believe some of the positions. Again, NZI had failed to make her Duty Yacht report on the 15th, and I assumed they were still playing the generator card. No surprise then, when the Argos report, now working, had them in first place on direct mileage to Cape Town.

On the morning of the 17th, as Phil Wade pulled in his fishing line, after the 20 minutes per day he was allowed, Roger and I were listening to the radio and by chance tuned in to Peter Blake talking to his wife in New Zealand and caught the words, "And yes, we are two degrees south of the Equator."

We made contact with the Race Control via Portishead and confirmed the 0300 Argos report as both NZI and Lion being well south already on port tack. Against Roger's judgement and indecision, I called for the tack at 1015, reckoning that we couldn't let them get away. As we were in the middle of the fleet, it would have been risky to go all the way over to the east side of the course; by the time we would get to Portatan's line of travel, (they succeeded in slipping through the worst part of the Doldrums unscathed) we could have been 200 miles on their stern.

Roger had been very disappointed with this tactic and he wrote in his log that afternoon:

Skip made a strange decision today to tack south, without even consulting me. I feel completely out of it and run over. We had always decided together to go to the east. Now the whole situation is very tense and I feel disappointed. I get the impression he was not happy with our tactics further up the course and he wants to take all the responsibility. Already the crew notice the confrontation.

The decision I had made seemed logical to me, and I recorded the reasons at 1100, just after the tack:

Alarm in the nav area has run rampant when we calculated the day's runs in this steady weather – the Maxi fleet is reporting the same wind speed. Speculation and fear that the boat is slow has fueled ideas of going east, 'to do something different', but as I reckon, accepting the fact that the Farr boats seem to be 2 to 3 tenths of a knot faster on the wind, we are talking about 50 miles in 10 days of fetching – not the end of the world, and certainly

retrievable in the variable conditions near Cape Town. But to be 200 to
300 miles behind because of taking a 'flyer' would be a disaster for the race
as a whole.

Roger had told me Janne has body lice. He predicts it will be hard to
avoid infecting the whole crew. Other than that piece of unwelcome
news, life had been going on as normal, the cook cheerily going about
his business, mildly bitching about how starboard tack is the pits
because bilge water regularly sloshed about his shoes. On port tack,
his bulk supported by the safety webbing, he was all smiles.

At 1320 GMT, October 17th in 8° 50' of West Longitude and 0°
Latitude, King Neptune and his 2 pirates 'came over the bow' to give
us safe passage across the 'Line'. Even considering he had never done
any open ocean sailing or cruising, I will never forget the look of
complete puzzlement on Lawrie Smith's face.

Struggling to keep his identity unknown and his beard of red yarn
from blowing away, King Neptune summoned the skipper to 'bring
forth all the scumbags who have not been this way before.' They
were: Patrick, Lawrie, Mike, Janne, Micky, Magnus, Richard and
Rick. Hard on the wind with the No. 2 jib and with the lee scuppers
awash, the unfortunate bastards were lined up naked on the mid deck,
given libation, then made to haul the heavy Kevlar No. 3 down
below, around the mast and then back on deck a few times to test their
physical capabilities. The rest of us, who had been through this
before, berated them without mercy.

They were then each accused of being out there for ulterior motives
(financial gain, peer group gratification, criminal records) and had to
prove their sincerity. Mike Berrow was told a Live Aid Concert in the
middle of the Atlantic wouldn't work, "Cause there ain't no power
out here! Douche 'em!"

For every unacceptable answer, the two pirates would 'douche 'em'
with a disgusting mixture of bilge water, baby powder, soy sauce and
engine oil.

Their last task was to untangle balled up light spinnaker sheets to
test their seamanship, again suffering heaps of abuse from the rest of
us. Bottles of champagne were cracked, Neptune took a long pull and
they were given permission to cross into the Southern Hemisphere,
that is after they cleaned up the mess. Up ahead a black cloud and
possible squall were threatening.

We were now faced with the prospect of a twelve- to fourteen-day
beat and it was clear we all had apprehensions about it. We were
right; as soon as the wind filled and we had a press of sail, the leeward
main shrouds went incredibly slack. The 100-foot mast was the big
fear and during that first day on the wind we fiddled with the tuning
in an effort to stabilize it. Less bend and more runner tension helped a

bit and Magnus took up one and a half turns on the mainspan shrouds during the next few tacks.

Imagine a weather leg of 2500 miles! The weather mark was Cape Town, 2500 miles away. We can 'see' our competition through the Argos and the inter-yacht position reporting. The wind heads and then lifts; we tack on the shifts. Do we sail hard on the wind or with slightly cracked sheets, anticipating a wind shift that is probable far further down the course?

The weather facsimile station in Pretoria was coming in loud and clear with pictures of the South Atlantic High squeezed right up against the South African coast, well east of its normal position in the middle of the ocean. If it stayed there, *Lion* and *NZI*, far to the west, could possibly get around its western edge on a reach. On the other hand, if it moved off, they would get stuck in the center.

We tacked back to starboard for 70 miles that night and crossed *UBS* only 30 miles behind. Obviously she too was short tacking on the shifts. *Cote d'Or* and *Portatan* have held starboard, making only 20 degrees off the course line while the two Kiwis have held a bad port tack, but making southing.

We heard Blake on *Lion* talking to Peter Montgomery at Radio New Zealand, full of confidence that he was doing the right thing. With his extreme westerly berth after the Doldrums he had to convince his supporters that it was good tactics, not simply the result of splitting with the competition and banking on chance. He reported that all was well on board (was it ever not so?); his gorillas just had a good breakfast, slight problem with the water maker, but glad to have a sturdy boat in the pounding conditions. He surmised he was in the lead, but he had spoken too soon. The 1100 schedule revealed that *Portatan* was 115 miles closer to Cape Town.

In the previous two Whitbread Races and the Parmelia Race, the port tack 'header' only lasted a day or so after the Equator and a steady lift soon justified the initial unfavored board. This time it was different. It did not lift us, and instead headed to the extent that several times we had to tack back on to starboard, a most disconcerting proposition, while Blake and *NZI*, on a better slant a few hundred miles further south, just kept on going.

Lawrie Smith, tactician first and foremost, and Roger and I debated endlessly about how to play this situation. Lawrie favored a straight game of small boat tactics, always tacking on the slightest shifts. For 36 hours, we steered very close to the wind in an effort to make what is called the best Velocity Made Good, or VMG in the direction of the true wind. A debatable tactic in the open ocean with long legs, it had not only served to put us further behind, but for some unrelated reasons caused intense and unfavorable speculation by the crew about our abilities.

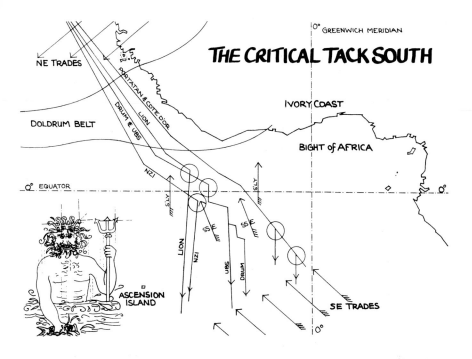

THE CRITICAL TACK SOUTH

Neil spoke for most of them as he wrote that day:

We've crossed the Equator in reasonable shape — fourth or fifth place depending on how you judge the distance to Cape Town. If I've understood the situation correctly, we are now faced with a tactical conundrum, whose outcome will more or less decide the first leg. We need to make southing, but the favored tack is the one going east. We've already got all the easting we need so it looks like the 'bad' tack must be favored. That seems simple enough, but the management group is unable to agree. It's quite obvious that we are tacking too often, apparently with no clear plan. Each tack involves the bloody headache of shifting a dozen or more wet sails up to the weather side. The popular feeling is that we should hold on for a day or two, and see if we get lifted.

October 19th   5°43′S 7°38′W
0930 Log Entry
Although the gear is holding up just fine, wear and tear is beginning to show up in the personnel, most likely born out of complacency during the last three weeks of easy going. Short tacking in the shifts has been a subject of much controversy, not for any valid tactical ideas, but simply work related. Each tack involves shifting all the sails below (over half a ton) to the new weather side and rousing the sleeping off-watch to move to the weather bunks. We shifted four times on my off-watch. It has to be done, and I am losing patience

with a few of the guys who are not playing the game aggressively. Granted it is rugged going, but we certainly have not experienced any hardships yet.

At 1800 we made our last tack to port, deciding that we will stand south in any event. Lawrie, trained from years of sailing on level racing boats, instinctively wakes up as the boat comes level and rolls out of his bunk to change sides without being asked, trailing his sleeping bag behind him like a six year old with his security blanket.

Jimmy Buffet tunes wail away up forward, serenading Richard while he peels tonight's quota of fresh onions. The BBC World Service squawks from the SSB radio back aft of the nav table where we sit and discuss tactics, our shaky dead-reckoned positions and the strange weather situation to the south in the high. Another sunset behind total overcast descends on Drum as cabin lights below brighten up the dismal scene of piled up sails, running rigging, and listless bodies, apparently organized in some logical fashion. Reminds me of the Southern Ocean days, except everyone is wandering around in shorts and deeply suntanned. Hans, in his upper bunk, scribbles furiously in his logbook in the fading light. His face is twisted by thought and his clothing, loosely hung rags on a gaunt frame reminds me of a starving Bohemian author, Paris, circa 1920s.

We were caught in an empty area between good winds to the west and to the east, and it cost us a loss of 60 miles with most of the fleet. The wind had headed us for most of the evening hours giving us no bias on either tack, then quit completely for one hour before filling in firmly favoring the port board, at last. *Lion* and *NZI* looked very strong to the southwest with the high still persisting in the eastern part of the ocean. I was not pleased with myself. That day, I wrote:

Morale on board is very low and from my standpoint it is now very hard to push the crew when those of us back aft are making such monumental fuck-ups. All that screwing around short-tacking as if we were trying to beat to the Nab Tower from Bembridge has been a complete waste of time. I kick myself for not trusting my own judgement of the obvious. I just hope we can get out of this mess without embarrassing ourselves, which is a possibility. It only takes one more stroke of bad luck or stupidity. I feel I have let myself down, failing completely in making a success of this leg – something I am supposed to know well.

We were well on the way 24 hours later; no more tacking for a while, making well east of south. Again, like the days before, thick stratus clouds covered the sky from sun up to sundown making celestial observations impossible. The Sonic Speed, working on the Doppler principle between two sensors in the hull and keel, had also packed up temporarily and our back-up impeller logs we knew were underreading by 8 to 12 per cent. Frankly, this didn't matter so much for position fixing because we were in the middle of the ocean, but a loss of accuracy aggravated the problem of comparing our position to the fleet, which was a practical and a morale problem of great significance.

My theory was that because the high was so far east, we were experiencing continental air that had picked up a lot of moisture as it moved out across the ocean. Consequently it had become unstable and had condensed to form the massive sausage-shaped stratus cloud lying directly over and in front of us.

I was afraid that if the high was a closed cell to the west, *Lion*, already 200 miles further south, had left us for dead. They reported eased sheets that evening, but, wonderfully, we had gained about 30 miles on them and were steering a closer tack towards Cape Town, still biting up into the wind. Phil Wade wasn't worried, saying that this nebulous high must stretch right across to South America and that they would all get caught at some stage. He and I put a 'fiver' on it.

In the variable wind the crew spent a frustrating night constantly changing the sail trim as the wind went up and down from 5 to 15 knots true. They did a good job. Micky was awarded a 'Dunce Cap' by Filthy the next day for spending a solid 3 hours tending the 'down fucker' on the clew of the genoa, a menial task if there ever was one.

I spent 6 hours at the SSB radio on the morning of the 22nd. Communications are almost a full-time job for a skipper these days. Weather reports, Argos positions, Duty Yacht functions, calling the office, radio, newspaper and TV interviews, and the intership schedule can easily take up most of the day. Roger and I usually split these duties.

Still, I was fortunate in not having the responsibilities of Peter Blake. In what is without doubt one of the best orchestrated publicity campaigns in yachting, we heard Peter talking to New Zealand via Cape Town, and his shore contact gave him a list of 12 numbers to call. Chris Barker reckoned it had to do with a certain subscription that for $1000 Kiwi dollars, the 'bloke' 'down under' would get a half model of *Lion*, other assorted paraphernalia and a personalized telephone call from the skipper in mid ocean.

The life of a skipper: Yesterday we had heard Blake again, this time to his wife Pippa who ran through a few minor details about how the crew had burned a lot of holes in the carpet in one of the crew houses in the Hamble. "I guess we'll have to buy a new one; bring the details to Cape Town." She went on to say that they had also run up a big telephone bill there during the last day ashore. A deep sigh, "Bring the details to Cape Town."

The 'Chat Show' had some bad news that day. Word was passed

that the 55-footer *Equity and Law* was on her way to Monrovia in
Liberia with a broken spreader fitting. One of the smallest boats in the
fleet she was also one of the best prepared. She would fix the fitting
and eventually arrive in Cape Town, but she was effectively out of the
running for the entire race. Ex-Nato fighter pilot in the Dutch
airforce, skipper Pleun van der Lugt would later describe what it was
like:

> "Up until that happened the crew was supermotivated and we were
> confident that we had more than a fighting chance to fullfill our
> ambition to win our class and to be in the top 5 on corrected time.
> The dream was shattered when that spreader fitting broke without
> warning. We were lucky not to lose the whole rig.
>
> Our feelings are hard to describe. We just could not accept that
> this could happen to us. At the time we were too busy to be
> emotional about it, but during the next five days needed for the
> repair in Monrovia and to get back on the course the demotivation
> bug started chewing on us with some success.
>
> During training we had carefully worked ourselves up to a
> mental framework of quiet confidence that fitted our ambition. On
> a race like this where the crews get just enough money to stay alive,
> you feed on motivation to achieve your goal, your dream, your hot
> air balloon. Take away that hot air balloon and you have a huge
> problem. It took the rest of the trip to Cape Town to recover from
> it. My peptalk to the guys was, "What happened to us was terrible,
> but to give up now is even worse." Looking back on it now, the
> conclusion is that good organization doesn't necessarily exclude you
> from disaster."

At 1245, October 22nd, we made a fortuitous landfall on the lonely
island outpost of St. Helena. Phil and I couldn't believe Roger's sun-
line and DR from the last Argos position in that he reckoned we were
seeing the island at 50 miles out. Phil put another 'fiver' on it (his
standard wager for everything, significant or not, was a fiver) and
Roger got very annoyed that we didn't believe him. Coming onto
radar range 36 miles out ended the discussion and luckily we were
both wrong, in almost equal doses. I would have said 20 at 36, Roger
still insisting 50.

Rising out of the mid-Atlantic ridge, this volcanic plateau occupies
only 47 square miles in an otherwise vast, lonely expanse of the South
Atlantic. Discovered by the Portuguese in 1502, but not claimed, it
was then occupied and occasionally fought for by the Dutch and the
English until the East India Company and later the British Crown
established themselves as a permanent colonial government. For no
other reason, St. Helena, population 5,000 (1975 census) and little

known to the outside world, is familiar only to students of French history. It was there, in 1815, that Napolean was exiled, to spend his last six years in benign tranquility.

Of course, Phil had been there many times, along with, it seemed, every other island and rock sticking out of the Atlantic from a career in the delivery business. Directly on the Trade Wind passage from South Africa to Europe or North America, he explained that they were supplied only by ship, once every six weeks. It had no airport, which was important because, as anyone who has travelled by boat in the last twenty years will tell you, once a place gets an airport, the romance is finished.

Phil described it as one of the most interesting places he had visited. As the lump of rock slipped by some 10 miles off our port beam, he spun yarns to the less worldly youngsters of the old antique cars still in use, the inbreeding, the local hootch, and the sex-starved females of all shapes and colors.

St. Helena Radio came up loud and clear on the VHF and then later on 2 Megs and we made a flurry of calls, as I recorded in my log, to London, Paris, New York and Auckland, kind of like those joke business cards.

Mike spoke to brother Paul in London for 40 minutes about record albums, concert tours, and rock videos. He briefly mentioned our bad tactics, but hastened to add "The boat is OK."

Although everyone on board had been in good spirits lately, Mike was a bit depressed, obviously disappointed with our progress; maybe expecting too much too fast. Part of the problem was his view that yachting was totally disorganized, with too much left to chance. Our inconsistent tactics and what must have seemed the whimsical way Roger and I went about making decisions could only have reinforced his view. The fact is that the ocean and its weather are so variable by nature that hard and fast tactics are all but impossible and any skipper with experience will agree that the majority of us follow general guidelines, but that much is finally resolved by circumstance and gut feelings.

Mike is handling the situation superbly, but he is no doubt getting tired, as we all are, of hearing on the Argos report that we are 6th out of 6 Maxis – and, no doubt, so is Paul back home.

Wade won the 'fiver.' On the 23rd, it was clear that *Lion* was slowing up first and would not be able to reach around the outside of the high. The Maxis were only 90 miles apart on a distance calculated to Cape Town and from the last weather map from Pretoria it looked as though everyone would be on the wind with no escape. The Argos positions that night had us 5th after a long spell at the bottom of the ladder, however close the rungs might have been spaced. Later that evening we started to run out of wind as we pushed against the northern edge of the high.

My 2200 Log Entry

Another epidemic of what appears to be food poisoning is running rampant through Drum, *Mike, Neil, Magnus and Micky have all succumbed, with Micky spending 36 hours in his bunk. Richard wears a sheepish grin every time somebody mentions food poisoning and we reckon it could have been the red kidney beans in the freeze dried chili two days ago, if not a dirty galley and/or head. The Doctor continually lectures the guys on personal hygiene, but I'm afraid it's all in vain, not because they are unhygienic, but because I don't think it's the problem at all.*

We ran the main engine for 12 hours to burn off unneeded fuel. Of course we could have broken the rules and pumped it overboard. Or even, like Digby Taylor, not even departed with the required amount. Burning it off, like dumping our water by 'showering' and not just dumping it straight overboard only complies with the rule and not with 'the spirit' thereof. Because long ocean races have been neglected, you could say, almost ignored by the rules committees, a lot of what is reasonable for shorter races is simply not complied with in round-about ways. The rules state quite clearly that water cannot be used as ballast, and yet everyone on the Whitbread carries a watermaker, a device that allows you to create and discharge ballast at will. There is nothing in the rules that says watermakers are illegal or even an acknowledgement that they exist.

The Whitbread rules require every yacht to embark with at least 12 imperial gallons of water (in any form) per man per leg. Few carry that much for long. I know of several skippers who have dumped the lot right after the starting gun, relying on the watermaker, a full spares list for same, and maybe a Doldrums shower to survive.

At that stage of the leg we were down to 1 liter per man per day (inclusive of cooking water for freeze-dried food) and planned to cut it down even more, relying on the watermaker to supplement our intake over and above this survival level. I reckoned 1500 miles was not too far to suffer a little in the event the thing packed up.

On October 24th we ran only 134 miles noon to noon, our slowest of the leg thus far. For the 27th time the sun was setting on *Drum*. The watch lined the leeward rail, each man with his own thoughts, as the

---

opposite A view from the end of the spinnaker pole, rigged specifically for enthusiastic cameramen (*Photo by Skip Novak*)

overleaf Simon and Magnus crack a bottle of champagne with an obscured but recognizable Cape Horn in the background (*Photo by Skip Novak*)

light No. 1 genoa lazily slatted in the non-descript ocean swell. Phil Wade tried to inspire the guys with things to come in Cape Town, but was immediately mocked by Micky: "Imagine a white sandy beach, steaks on the grill ('freeze dried chili,' says Micky), a bottle of wine ('bottle of backwash and a dirty cup') and a beautiful woman ('a spotty bum and a soggy *Playboy!*')"

The trend was for *Portatan* and *Cote d'Or* to the east to make good while *Lion* and *NZI* to the west were dying a death. The fact that we gained 35 and 38 miles respectively on those two boats was not enough to appease the crew; the fact that we let *UBS* take a short hitch to starboard and thereby gain 15 miles, was discussed so endlessly that I noted it in my log *as a pain in the ass.*

Of course, disdain for the afterguard's tactics has always been a comfort for the forward hands and they happily while away the hours on the weather rail justifying their theories of the obvious solution a day later. I had hoped for their sake we would pull this off and place well.

With the wind increasing I could remember myself becoming more and more nervous. Frequently Rick and I would bump heads in the dark of the forepeak while furtively listening for odd noises and shoving our fingers in between the mast step and the carbon beams in a not-too-scientific analysis of monitoring what the designer and builders had assured me was an 'acceptable amount of movement' in the area. Rick had been in on the construction from the beginning and seemed to be worried, but then again he always looks worried. I though to myself, "Does he know something I don't?"

The step area had worried not a few of us last summer. We had made the usual measurements of loading the back stay and checking the deflection in the hull. The fore and aft plane was incredibly stiff as we noticed little movement with backstay tension on or off. Athwartships was, however, suspect. We were pumping up our hydraulic jack underneath the step to over 50 tons pressure to achieve the proper tension in the shrouds. We could measure 10mm of deflection when we released the pressure which had become a point of great speculation.

Ron's office, Adrian, and Rob all had thought it was not out of the ordinary, and they suggested I contact Ray Butler at Scicom if I was still worried. He had done the original computer model of the structure and should know what was acceptable.

"What do you mean you have a jack with 50 tons of pressure under the mast – nobody told me about that!" was his first reaction to the

---

opposite   This custom made spinnaker pole end was the only one of its kind in the fleet and must have saved us countless hours repairing chafed spinnaker afterguys; notice the 'trip line' running through the guy shackle (*Photo by Skip Novak*) problem. I couldn't quite understand his alarm as the ultimate loading on the rig could have been achieved without a jack, just by tuning the lee shrouds in a fresh breeze, the jacking device only a convenience.

I tried to explain how the mast partners were connected to the step with four tierods . . . and in mid sentence he asked me what mast partners were. I soon realized he had not a clue what a sailboat was about in what struck me as a prime example of theory with no practical input. I politely cut off the conversation, even more confused. Back then it was too late to do anything about it anyway.

I was right about Rick's concern; he wrote in his diary that evening:

I checked the structure again this evening. I prefer to do it in the dark so people can't see me. Maybe I'm just paranoid; I know a few of the guys think I am prowling around the bilges with a torch when I should be sleeping. The mast step is still moving and that worries me. It can't be right.

With a worsening hernia condition, diagnosed just before I left England, I was not in a good mood then, not being physically able to do my share of the work. Most skippers do very little on the deck, but I chose to stand a watch and pull my weight (hell, I thought before the start, I'm only 33) and this deficiency bothered me.

Running a Maxi boat and trying to win a popularity contest are not in the least compatible at the best of times, and in those days I must admit to being a complete dictator. But as the Arab proverb has it, "The camel driver has his thoughts, the camel he has his." I was not, however, completely insensitive to the crew's situation, as I recorded on the night of the 25th:

28 days out. Food getting very monotonous and in short supply. But that's the idea, arrive with sweet fuck-all and the crew chomping on the bit for a steak, a piss-up and pussy.

Conditions are once again squalid now that we are back hard on the wind. Not having a salon table is still a good idea, but I can see it in their faces that they are tired of living in a shit heap, taking dinner on their laps. The guys aren't exactly fastidiously tidy either and the last straw was finding an olive pit, no doubt casually spat out on the head counter top and then forgotten. Even these annoyances don't bother me much. Only the results matter: boatspeed and crew performance. All else stands insignificantly in the background and I couldn't give a damn if the dinner is good or bad or if the head got a good cleaning today. Keeping the pressure on in the good and the bad times is vital to the results.

With the wind on the increase the 6 Maxis and their crews hammered hard into it with determination and singular minds. Three days later we were devastated.

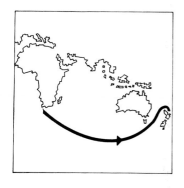

9 · Leg Two: And Now For the Southern Ocean

The mutual conquest of difficulties is the cement of friendship, as it is the only lasting cement of matrimony. We had plenty of difficulties; we sometimes failed, we sometimes won; we always faced them – we had to.

Apsley Cherry-Garrard
'The Worst Journey in the World'

The four weeks we spent in Cape Town was the most difficult period we had to face while on *Drum*. Still only a quarter of the way around the world, the multitude of problems both past and present already had taken their toll. The discovery of new cracks in the keel spacer was almost too much.

"How can that happen? I have never been on a boat that has had so many problems. I just don't know who to believe. One thing's for sure, I have lost all faith in this boat," explained Magnus at another crew meeting and I though for a moment, "Well that's it, the beginning of the exodus."

Hans had turned in his resignation only days before, the only one thus far of the regulars, and he sat in the corner staring into the blank wall opposite as I tried to explain things the way I saw them and that this little hiccup was no more than that. I could only offer the facts:

1. The keel as designed was correct as scrutinized by two independent research institutions. (I felt a bit of a fool using anybody's advice as an argument, even theirs.)
2. *Lion*'s keel spacer, built by the same company, was actually inferior to ours since ours was slot welded, rather than butt welded to the top plate (not bad reasoning).
3. The logical conclusion was that the cracks in our spacer were caused by a lack of stiffness in the hull under the mast step (what else could it be?).
4. When a spacer like ours had been attached to a rigid hull, as in the case of *Lion*, there were no problems. (This is what we were trying to achieve.)

Patrick, a practical engineer and sometime naval architect, lent needed support when he said exactly what I was trying to say but, not being an engineer type, had no right to, when he said, "You have to look at it as an objective problem that is easily solved." Capturing the essence of the feeling, he would write:

The problem is that most of the guys just don't understand anything about yacht engineering and quite a few are still unconvinced. To me, the whole bilge repair has been way over-engineered without any thought to weight or performance (or aesthetics for that matter). I can't blame Skip since I suspect his judgement was dictated by the thought that he might not have a crew for the second leg! I'm not at all impressed with Butch though. His whole approach has been to basically cover his (and Ron's) ass. He hasn't shown any real interest in helping us win this race. Adrian and Rob seem a good deal more switched on, but Skip seems convinced that Adrian is glossing over the issue, saying there's nothing wrong with the hull (his bit), the problem being entirely with Ron's engineering of the keel; but I take Skip's point that he may be less than totally objective. It's hard to figure out who was responsible for what – there's a lot of mud-slinging going on right now.

Expecting the worst, they filed out one by one, each with his own thoughts on the immediate future. It was a tribute to the team spirit that we all held together. Another successful meeting was adjourned.

With only two weeks to the start of Leg Two there was still a mountain of work to be completed. The bow repair and the internal steelwork were just scraping by on schedule. A day lost there would have meant dire consequences.

Phil Holland had arrived two days later, shouldering a 5-foot bar of Monel K 500 for the new keel bolts. Of course, with the keel spacer needing another 20mm top plate sistered to the cracked one, the existing bolts were not long enough. Unobtainable in South Africa, we had found the piece Phil brought with him in England. It was barely long enough to cut and turn 14 bolts.

Phil had just posted a letter to New Zealand. "I've got some good news and some bad news, Mama; the good news is that I'm coming home; the bad news is that I'm coming home on *Drum*." It was obvious from the beginning that this new victim, for want of a better word, was nervous about his prospects. In the parking lot of the machine shop he carelessly let the 2-inch bar of Monel drop on his instep. While he jumped up and down muttering kiwi oaths, speculating it was broken, I shook my cane at him (still recovering from my operation) and told him flat out, "You're not getting out of this that easy, Phil!" We were a most unlikely pair of ocean racers.

Meanwhile, other, minor dramas occurred almost daily. Looking back on them they have their humor, but at the time, well . . .

Then there was Patrick's preoccupation with improving the

steering system. He was convinced he could improve the gear box with very little effort. A machine shop made the gears interchangable and attempted to eliminate the annoying backlash in the system. When they reassembled the steering gear, only a few days before the start, it seized up and wouldn't turn at all. Patrick worked all night to get it right, and I had to ask him not to make any more experiments before New Zealand. "Don't ya know," said his old mate Filthy. "He's famous for doing that type of thing."

Just as we had our hands full, so did the other boats, as well as the Race Committee. *Cote d'Or* was now bolting on her new keel, willing to accept a 96-hour time penalty on the overall results for doing so. It is not allowed to change your rating during the race, but Tabarly reckoned the boat was dangerously bow-down to continue as they were. They agreed to be penalized and hoped instead to win a leg or two. Tabarly himself was back in France, leaving the running of the project to his sailing master, the Belgian Luc Heyman.

The protest we had lodged against *NZI* was thrown out on a technicality. Trying to explain himself during the inquest, it seemed to me that Digby dug his own grave. He had broken the rules by not reporting. By his own admission, he had started the race with a faulty main generator (illegal under the Notice of Race); departed with insufficient extra fuel for his back-up generator, hence his lack of radio communication (illegal under the Notice of Race). Nevertheless, he had frequently contacted Radio New Zealand and his sponsors, claiming that this was more important than fullfilling his obligation to the rules, having missed 3 out of 5 turns as the Duty Yacht.

We only found out in the meeting, that Digby, as verified by the Committee, had requested and had been given unauthorized dispensation early in the leg by some fool on the Race Committee for his lack of reporting. The Committee had undermined itself by its own error. We on *Drum* were made to look foolish, and the protest as lodged was thrown out.

Rear Admiral Williams then appealed the decision to the International Yacht Racing Union in London, but after lengthy correspondence, involving high court lawyers, the appeal was refused. How misguided was the original Protest Committee and how easy it would have been to find him guilty in the first place, holding the rules to the letter, and award him with a token penalty. They had set a dangerous precedent.

And on the Cape Town favorite, *Portatan*, there was controversy in the air. David Bongers was dismissed from the crew; fired say the boys, by Skipper Kuttel as he held him personally responsible for the dismasting. Dr. Julian Fuller, veteran of the winning *Flyer II* campaign four years ago had kept a good diary of his thoughts during the disaster on *Portatan*:

October 28th
Tempers are getting short now as everyone has had enough of this bashing to last a lifetime. We continue to hold our lead of 64 miles on UBS and over 100 on the other boats.

October 29th
Ludde and I sit on the weather rail and discuss this heavy sailing. I think we are both in agreement that it's too much. Certainly on FLYER Connie would never allow this type of pounding. Trouble is we sailed like this in the Fastnet and survived. Therefore everyone says that we can do it again. I have my doubts.

October 30th
It is whispered that Padda eventually has told David to stop breaking the boat and to slow down. The pounding is now unbearable and down below I am hitting the deckhead above my bunk on each wave as we crash down 10 feet.

Go on watch at 0200 and at 0445, with Arthur at the helm, and myself, Greg, Paul, Ralph, Ian and Dave sitting miserably to weather, we fell off another wave. Crack!! With an almost unbelievable surrealistic ease, I watch in horror, astonishment and almost déjà-vu as the mast suddenly topples straight down to leeward into the sea.

After thay had jettisoned the rig and cleaned up the mess, he wrote:

Several of the crew, myself included, are ready to throw in the towel now, and there are not many aboard with the resolve to try and sail to Cape Town. I mean how can we? 230 miles to windward in 30 to 40 knots. And so a decision to temporarily abandon the race is taken and few could admit afterwards that we could have heaved to and waited for the wind to drop.

Several of us feel we were pushing the boat much too hard for those conditions. But if we want to win we have to push hard. The problem is knowing when to stop. Ultimately David is sailing master and therefore responsible. Padda and Ludde argued with him a few hours before that fateful moment and I think he should have realised that we had a 100-mile lead with 230 to go and were in a virtually unassailable position.

The crew had mixed feelings about his dismissal as one of them told me later, "Everyone blames David for the rig, but when we were doing so well last summer winning all the races, no one gave him the credit. I think he got the short end of the stick."

So it was announced that Kim 'Shag' Morton, an Aussie veteran would take over in David's place. Another old-hand delivery skipper well known just about everywhere, 'Shag' was one of the popular favorites during the race. At 40, with perrennial sun glasses perched on the top of his head, and an open fronted lumberjack shirt worn in any weather, he exuded an air of boisterous confidence. A lot of people thought he looked like he had 'been there' from the beginning.

But there is always someone more venerable around the corner: "Shag, oh yeah, I took him on his first delivery from SA to the Seychelles about 13 years ago and taught him how to sail," the boyish Phil Wade explained in the bar that day.

The season of Cape Town 'soaps' culminated when *Norsk Data* had lost their cook, Tracy, not to *Portatan*, but to *Atlantic Privateer*. Yes, the name was changed back to the original when the sun tan company reneged on the sponsorship deal. Rumour had it that it was all about apartheid.

With only ten days before the start disaster struck *Drum* yet again, but we had no idea it would be for the last time. We had been working late preparing to bolt on the keel. The new keel bolts were in place and the canoe body of *Drum*, all 78 feet of her, was suspended above the keel by two mobile cranes slung fore and aft. We had just made a successful dry fit and were getting ready to apply a thick layer of epoxy mill fiber onto the top of the keel to 'mold' in a perfect bolting surface. The plan was to lower the hull onto the epoxy, spin the keel bolts medium tight and leave the thing to set until the following morning. With a releasing agent on the hull, we could then lift her off for the last time to apply a sealant in the joint, before bolting the keel home.

It was then that the aft sling, the one we had used before, the one *Cote d'Or* had used earlier in the day, suddenly parted with an agonizing rip. *Drum* settled back on to her keel, crushing a sound, 12-by-12 inch wooden bilge block under the foot of the keel and settled by the stern, but not before folding the bottom third of her rudder (Patrick had just finished repairing it after it had blown off the horses) like a piece of tin foil. It was hard to hold back the tears.

We jumped on board and, with the deck 25 degrees to the horizontal, rigged up a wire strop to our backstay chainplates and within minutes she was safely at rest and level once again. Luckily only the alloy extension of the titanium rudder shaft was bent and not the exotic shaft itself; it still swivelled freely in its bearings. The hull appeared to be OK, so there was nothing for it but to finish the job we had started, a routine we were all used to. We dropped the rudder out at about midnight and hid it under a tarpaulin anticipating the press who would welcome another free meal on *Drum*. We all went home with an air of resignation, a few philosophical, most heart broken.

Late for the dinner party De had put together for our friends from Cape Town, I arrived at the apartment door begreased from head to foot. Surely they had all gone home by now, I thought, but I opened the door to find them all still there – the last thing I wanted to face. While Phil Holland entertained them, De ushered me into the bath-room where she cleaned me up and fed me in the bath. Emotionally shattered, I had to take to the bottle in order to face the guests.

We literally threw the boat together during those last few days. It blew 60 knots again the weekend before the start which didn't brighten our prospects of going offshore for a test.

On Thanksgiving Thursday, we didn't get the repaired rudder in until 2200, which made me late for another dinner engagement. Fortunately our Thanksgiving dinner was at a Greek joint De and Alice had found. To blow off steam the crew broke every plate in the place. Friday the boat went in and the mast was stepped. The start was on Wednesday.

It wasn't until the Monday that the wind had allowed us to leave the dock. It was a sad joke that there was no wind and I had to motor in reverse to get the spinnakers to fill. Some wise guy suggested we all come back into the dock wearing our lifejackets. As a practical joke it wasn't bad, but under the circumstances one that could go badly against us later if the slightest thing went wrong. So it was with 10 miles of sea trial we would begin Leg Two, notoriously the roughest leg of the race. Roger recorded his thoughts:

I will never forget the morning of the start and my thoughts of one of the most emotional departures I can remember. I saw quite a few of the people we had gotten to know, both male and female openly crying their eyes out when we left the dock, as though they would never see us again. I thought to myself when I saw Hans standing there, "Maybe he is the only one who has done the right thing." I certainly didn't feel very confident at all.

My mind was occupied by worry about what we might have forgotten. I had repeatedly urged the guys to have everything in their departments checked and rechecked and on board for keeps.

We were scheduled to leave the dock in ten minutes: "Are you in a good mood?" asked Phil Wade.

"Not bad, how about yourself?"

"Micky forgot to fill the water tanks."

After an embarrassing 30-minute delay we were the last to leave the jetty at 0930 as if we were unsure of the way.

The Southern Ocean begins upon leaving the shelter of Table Bay and ends 7000 miles away at the North Cape of New Zealand. The starting gun went off on time, and we left the small fleet of spectator craft astern. Once again we led the fleet down the coast in the midday sunshine. *UBS* eventually overhauled us in a tacking duel and by nightfall the fleet had split inshore and offshore, the Farr boats again running in front.

There had been some crew changes. Mario Zimmerman, French sailor and veteran of the *Charles Heidsieck's* Whitbread Race of four years before, flew down to take over sail repair from Hans. Mugsy, his brother 'Topher,' J.J. Provoyeur (local boatbuilder who had fixed our bow), and Phil Holland filled out the list of 17 regulars. The watches were:

A	B	C	D
Phil Wade	Skip	Magnus	Phil Holland
Micky	Janne	Topher	Roger
Mugsy	J.J.	Rick	Patrick
Bill	Neil	Mario	Filthy

It was a beautiful first day. The Cape of Good Hope, on our port bow, was our last sight of land. The sharp contours of the South African coast faded away in the distance and we were left that afternoon with a sunny sky, gentle ocean swells and the reassuring company of the other boats close aboard. But as darkness came on, the wind freshened. The boat was now under load. She heeled to 25 degrees and dipped her rail in the water for the first time, I could not help wondering to myself, "Will this thing be alright?"

We were all physically and emotionally exhausted and as I sat below having a cup of coffee, my eyes opening and closing intermittently, I looked up at the overhead to the giant size 'best wishes' card we had received from Clair and Tracy, two of our loyal *Drum* groupies from the days at Moody's. "You'll make it this time!" they had assured us with hearts and kisses. We almost hadn't on the first leg, and now here we went again. As the pounding increased we all listened for any strange noises. So far, the repairs were holding.

By December 6th we were surfing hard at 40° South. After a few good off-watches, we felt a lot better, and everyone seemed in good spirits. Down below was better organized than it had been on the last leg. There was better stowage for mugs, tapes, tools and for Richard's food bags aft. So as to concentrate the weight further aft down below, no one slept up forward. Richard had a permanent bunk aft where he kept his sealed plastic garbage bags, each with a day's menu for 17. This method soon proved itself appropriate, garbage being the operative word.

I will never forget when on *King's Legend* in 1977, the first front filled in with a vengeance at about this same place. Until then we had had no idea what the Southern Ocean was about. With the 1.5 oz chute and 2.2 oz blooper we all looked at the black cloud astern and agreed with an air of bravado, "Let's ride this one out, boys!"

Four hours later, humbled and sheepish, we were still cleaning up the mess after the inevitable broach/gybe that pinned us on our side for what seemed like forever. The score for our boldness: blown chute, blown blooper, broken spinnaker pole, topping lift, foreguy, and afterguy as well as a few holes in the mainsail. We had lost about

25 miles. Years later, the Kiwi cook we had conscripted out of the bar at the Royal Cape Yacht Club admitted to me that this first experience of yacht racing had convinced him he was done for, at the complete mercy of a bunch of lunatics.

It was hard for these experiences not to have an affect. I was determined to be ultra conservative in sail handling from then on. I had no immediate worries because within a few hours the wind was again forward of the beam, a relatively safe point of sail.

Lion was still in sight, broad on the starboard bow and it was obvious we were catching her in the heavy reach. Her crew reefed in and out in an effort to stay ahead of us, but it was no use. In the late afternoon orange light of a Southern Ocean sunset, we got within 10 boat lengths of her. Almost in hailing distance, we could easily read her sail numbers and the spray and spume glistening on the bright red foul weather gear of her crew lining the weather rail made for a most impressive sight. Before dark they bore off a bit and let us through.

Our plan was to try and stick with her for as long as possible, as difficult as this was now proving to be without slowing down, not only to pace ourselves, but also for reasons of security, not a bad idea and seemingly very popular with the crew.

Twenty-four hours later, with *Lion* still on our radar but safely buried 7 miles behind us and *Cote d'Or* well to the north and struggling, the wind suddenly quit and we painfully slatted our way to the southeast at 1 to 2 knots. Worse still, we then had to watch as *Lion* slowly regained the lost ground, ghosting with her Windseeker staysail, an almost see-through ultra light headsail. Our Windseeker was unfortunately in the container along with a lot of other sail we left behind in an effort to lighten the boat to offset the extra weight of the repair. We were all tired and preoccupied, when Mugsy held his meeting to decide which sails to leave behind, for the next two legs. They were the Windseeker, the Light No. 1 Genoa, the Diesel 3/4, the .05 oz, spinnaker staysail and spare, old No. 3. Our inventory included:

Kevlar main	storm trysail
Dacron main	genoa staysail
Kevlar Medium No. 1	No. 2 jib top Dacron
Kevlar No. 2	3/4 oz spinnaker
Kevlar No. 3	1.5 oz spinnaker
Kevlar No. 4	2.2 oz Flanker
Dacron No. 5	2.2 oz full size spinnaker
storm jib	storm chute

For the second leg we added:	3.0 oz spinnaker (new)
another 1.5 oz spinnaker	'Chicken Chute' (new)
another 2.2 oz spinnaker (new)	2.2 oz blooper

Not having the Windseeker (it was in the container on its way to Uruguay) was more of a psychological problem than anything else, and the miles lost were not too significant. The extra spinnakers pile aft when the wind was 'in', made for difficult living conditions – which was especially aggravating sitting there in a calm.

A few, very few of us even took a swim at 41° South. 16°C (61°F) was not too bad as we were still in the warm Agulhas Current that sweeps out from the Mozambique Channel and rounds the Cape to fight the colder waters of the Southern Ocean Drift. I dove, ever so briefly, to inspect the keel joint and recorded what I had found in my log:

All is well below, except for a distinct crack around the leading edge of the keel again; not so alarming as what the Fleet Street papers had described as the ½" one when we hauled in Cape Town, but there again, none-the-less. The top flange plate on the keel spacer has left an impression of its outline in the fairing compound, like a reminder that once again, the mast step is trying to push its way through the keelson. I assume it is only cosmetic; it must be, as there is no sign of movement in the bilge. Nevertheless, I didn't tell anyone what I had found.

In the Southern Ocean, under a high pressure sky, I remember thinking that it was a perfect day, if one was cruising and could relax. The water was clear and as deep blue as any I've seen in the tropics. Sooty Albatross, White Chinned Petrels, a few Arctic Terns and the occasional grandaddy of them all, the Great Wandering Albatross, boasting a wing span of 4 meters, were all gliding with some difficulty around the boat in wide circles. In a dead calm, they too, like us, can go nowhere, and are forced to land on the surface of the water. Like our towering sails, their wings are too heavy to support themselves without some breeze to supply the necessary lift for gliding. For hours on end they would watch us while we watched them.

After the blow, the calm. After the calm, another blow. The whole fleet went on a tight reach briefly on December 8th. It was not much fun with the No. 4 and three reefs in the main, the water temperature now dropping rapidly and big waves regularly combed the beams.

Just after a sail change, Magnus fell backwards and just caught himself on the leeward lifelines. This minor incident almost went by unnoticed. With the weather sheet not yet attached to the No. 4, it could have been serious if he'd gone overboard. I constantly preached preparedness and safety. I found that lecturing came easily because I was in charge and had the ultimate responsibility. It was clear that the crew were getting fed up as I constantly pointed out the obvious, but in these matters I am thick-skinned to criticism, like the cook seemed to be about his stock-in-trade. We lost a few miles to the boats to the south. *Privateer* was making big gains, with *NZI* not far away. As fast as the NNE'ly had moved in from this weak low to the north, the quicker it moved off and I awoke at 0500 the next morning to absolute chaos on the level deck.

After an icy rain squall, the wind had flicked around from ahead to a dead run in 15 minutes. It was Phil Holland's watch, and apparently they had postponed setting up the spinnaker gear and weren't ready when it became apparent that a change was needed. Mugsy was adamant that they should set the 2.2 oz spinnaker immediately, but the tangle of ropes and wires and the general confusion made it an impossible proposition.

Mugsy was not happy the way things had gone that day and described things as he saw them in his diary:

Within seconds the rain had stopped and a warmer wind started blowing. I knew immediately we were at the front and needed to run spinnaker gear as a chute set was imminent. Had my second row of the trip with Phil Holland, when I called for some reefs to be shaken and the gear run and a quick set to the 2.2 oz. Phil disagreed saying it wasn't prudent to push the boat and that it was too soon to be contemplating a chute. It took three hours to eventually get the boat going, not until after Skip appeared on deck and kicked some ass. Who knows how much we lost by Phil's and Phil Wade's hesitation for that matter. I do resent having Phil Holland above me on the crew, not that I dislike him; quite the contrary. I respect his sailing ability – he is good, but he is not familiar with this type of ocean.

We passed close to Prince Edward Island at dawn on the 10th, while *Lion* chose the channel separating Prince Edward from Marion Island. A South African weather station in this remote and vulnerable piece of real estate at 46° South takes the full brunt of all that the Southern Ocean's Roaring Forties have to offer. If the albatross, who nest on this dubious bit of shelter could talk, they would tell you so.

The first cold night was, as J.J. said "Fucking cold!" with the water temperature down to 6°C as we closed in fast with the Antarctic Convergence. Around 50° South, there lies a distinct boundary layer of very cold water to the south verging on the extreme limits of the polar pack, and to the north, just cold water, the difference in survival times insignificant for anyone who happened to fall overboard.

As the boat careened along at 10 knots with the rail underwater I noticed myself becoming even more cautious than usual. I even began to distrust the 'pee' strap, a makeshift chest harness hanging from the backstay which allowed us to relieve ourselves without hanging on. Instead, we just let it flow freely into the bottom of the cockpit. Since it was continually awash, it was as good as any modern flush toilet. Phil Wade reckoned getting at all the zippers was the chief problem; he counted four, all formidable barriers when your hands are cold and you're in a hurry.

Again we experienced another lull in the wind as high pressure to the north and weak fronts tickled the fleet. A 3/4 oz spinnaker in the Southern Ocean? Unthinkable, I would have said, and did say to the crew during Leg One when we talked about what Leg Two would bring. After a week out it had been nothing like my forecasts, and now they jokingly disbelieve whatever I say about weather. Filthy reckons the Southern Ocean is such a "piece of piss," that he is going to "invite his Gran along on the next race."

I had no doubt that we would see some heavy downwind running, but the prediction that we would run hard for weeks on end already had failed to materialize. This unexpected weather system that seemed now so dominant might be explained by the fact that we started this leg one month later than we had four years before, and the South Indian Ocean High is further south than it was then. On *King's Legend* we sailed down to 56° South, ran hard for 30 days and spent 10 days in iceberg country – a grand adventure. On *Alaska Eagle* it had been less exciting, with more variable winds, but still it had been off the wind in the main.

Many of our crew had no desire to push the boat far south to look for better winds and risk tangling with icebergs. I can appreciate the reasoning but it makes little difference safety wise whether you sail at 48 or 52 degrees in ultimately getting to shore if you have problems. There was still the race to think of and I felt then I had to take almost a radical approach to balance the mood – a totally opposite situation with respect to my attitudes about sailhandling and safety on board.

Richard had a bad go in the galley on one of those first blustery days. He served out a disgusting mess of leftover lunch, described by someone as 'rice topped with baby's shit,' and passed it off as a bolognese applied over undercooked spaghetti. One by one, dissatisfied customers ushered out the hatch to deposit the contents of their bowl overboard, some alarmingly full. While waiting on deck to go off watch and sample his fare, I was amused by the first unhappy patron, curious about the second and third and downright worried when a few late arrivals appeared. It wasn't inedible, certainly not to a truly hungry man, but I immediately saw their point.

It was revealed that only two breakfast menus existed, cold muesli and hot porridge. Roger ordered the cook to change from muesli to porridge the next morning because by now it was bracing on deck. Richard's response was to test us with hot muesli. It reminded us of the fruity taste of the previous day's lunch. Again, his customers were not impressed.

Once again, I saved my piece of fresh bread for lunch instead of breakfast, taking great pleasure in wrapping it in a bit of paper and

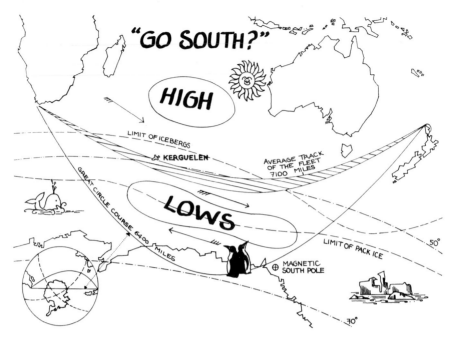

"GO SOUTH?"

HIGH

LIMIT OF ICEBERGS

KERGUELEN

AVERAGE TRACK OF THE FLEET 7100 MILES

GREAT CIRCLE COURSE 6400 MILES

LOWS

LIMIT OF PACK ICE

50°

MAGNETIC SOUTH POLE

30°

hiding it in the chart table.

Anybody who has been there before will tell you that there is only one important tactic in the Southern Ocean: don't get stuck having to go to windward. Weather systems in the famous Roaring Forties travel from west to east totally unimpeded right around the world. An endless cycle of travelling low pressure cells; really a circumpolar trough, lies around 50° to 60° South on average, and herein is the navigational problem.

The distance from South Africa to New Zealand as the crow flies is roughly 6400 miles. Passing a string around the school room globe from those two points, it becomes obvious that the track is impossible in anything other than an airplane as this 'Great Circle' course passes over the Antarctic continent itself bottoming out below 70° of South Latitude. Not only would the polar pack ice quickly foil any attempt at even approximating the Great Circle course, but also south of 55° headwinds become likely, which are the established easterlies on the south side of the trough. The tactician's problem is to weigh the extra miles sailed for the security of staying in fast running conditions by remaining north. The Race Committee had selected a handicap distance of 7101 miles as being a logical average track that most people would follow. Any doubters attempting to disprove the theory that in this case the fastest way to get between two points is *not* to follow a straight line, would have, even if they had been successful, found it damned unpleasant.

In the 1977 Whitbread, John Ridgway, skipper of *Debenhams*, illustrated this with great success in his attempts to sail the furthest south; he made it down to 59°, but was stopped by the pack ice and had to steer northwest for 24 hours (back in the direction of Cape Town) to get out of brash ice. Hardly a justifiable situation when racing, but as Ridgway, an adventurer first and a yacht racer a distant second, said of the experience in his book *Round the World with Ridgway*, "All the worry of building the boat and entering the race was worth it for this single twenty-four hours of indelible memory. I turned in at five in the morning, a tired but truly delighted man. My feet were completely numb."

Even in small doses, the temptation to cut the corner to save 150, 100 or even 50 miles, can have disastrous consequences. On *Alaska Eagle* in 1981 we only reached 53° South, but that one degree turned out to be too much that year. The boats just to the north had strong following winds while we languished under a trough for 36 hours. The distance lost between surfing or poking along at 5 knots is easily and painfully calculated.

This year, the dangers seemed to be coming from the north. The semi-permanent high in the South Indian Ocean was ridging down to 50°, and light winds were right across our path for the first two weeks. Two lows had already moved through but without a strong westerly flow established further south, they had meandered north, butted up against the western edge of the high and then slowly slipped southeast around the bottom. Hence we had light headwinds this time. The 'surfing' corridor was narrow indeed and hard to find.

It was strange then that on the 12th of December, with the Maxis still hard on the wind, pinned on to port tack making south, still under the influence of that second low, *Cote d'Or* suddenly appeared to be on starboard making northeast having left the Crozet Islands well to starboard. "What did that old fox, Tabarly, have up his sleeve this time?" I asked myself. Little did we know of the problems on board. A week later we found out over the radio, although we didn't learn the details until we arrived in Auckland.

At 2230, December 11th, on board *Cote d'Or*, François Carpente had gone forward to investigate a terrible noise. Tabarly was woken to inspect two broken ribs in the forepeak. Disgusted with another structural failure, he decided at once to steer northeast, laying a course for Tasmania. It was only the beginning of a string of problems. With broken frames, and soon after, more delamination in the bilges, they were unable to go to weather; but they still pressed her hard in running conditions with the spinnaker. The day after they clocked up a 320-mile noon-to-noon run (the rest of us very puzzled by her track), the mast head spinnaker cranes collapsed; no more spinnakers. That was on the 16th. On the 19th the steering quadrant started to crack, but they continued to limp along, jury rigging that as well. We considered ourselves fortunate; we were still in one piece and very much in the race.

Approaching 50° South the water temperature was down to 2.3°C (36°F) and the air frosty at 8°C (46°F). I don't think Filthy's Granny would have been very happy. Getting dressed to go on watch became a major project. There was the basic clothing: thermals, polar suits, socks and bootliners; hats, gloves and finally heavy foul weather gear, with possibly a dinghy dry suit over the top. Then there was the hardware; safety harness, rigging knife, strobe lights, mini flares and flashlight making pockets bulge and rendering quick movements on deck cumbersome.

In what is almost an ironical situation, the weight of this rig, ballasted by heavy, leather-lined sea boots, would surely send you right to the bottom if you did go over the side, not a bad fate I suppose, given the water temperature (life expectancy in that water would have been no more than a few minutes). On the other hand, if you go on deck with empty pockets after a while, it's as if the weightlessness makes you feel helplessly naked.

Gloves, hats and balaclavas of every description adorned us all. Gloves, as always, seemed to be a real problem when handling wet sails and rigging, and the merits of each type of glove were discussed endlessly. Neil and Bill have trendy, brightly colored climbing mitts. Wet suit gloves are popular while most of the stuff you can buy in a chandlery we found utterly useless. My solution is having many pairs of light wool gloves (they only last about 5 or 6 days) worn under rubber over-mits. Roger had passed out some black, gauntlet type rubber gloves, something that looked suitable for a veterinary proctologist, if there is such a speciality. But the variety of gloves was a blessing; nothing could be worse than 17 pairs of matching gloves, hats and socks and the ensuing arguments over who owned the dry ones.

In what I can only describe as very rugged sailing we all had our difficult times. Neil recorded one:

What the hell am I doing here? Shaken out of a fitful sleep to go on watch, my eyes dried out in their sockets from the prickly air of the diesel heater. My socks and gloves so carefully placed on the heating duct three hours ago have fallen into the bilge and are still cold and wet. Struggling to my feet I reach for my boots, just as the boat hits an apartment block, and my head cracks against the clothes peg. I hear the watch on deck laughing at the hilarity of it all and curse them roundly. Almost weeping with frustration I fight off sleep and wonder why I can't move my arms until Janne tells me my harness is on back to front. Sort that out and bless them, the on-watch has remembered to fill the coffee flask. Grab my mug, light a cigarette in the hatchway and out into the pitch black of the Southern Ocean. Crawling along the mid-deck to take my place on the weather rail a wave comes over and does the 'double fill', out goes the cigarette and 'splush' goes the coffee, all over the deck. Who says this isn't a good time?

The low was finally on the march across our bows, but not before giving us one last blast on the morning of the 12th. I was feeling the strain myself:

Lost my cool with the crew today. Have been 'asking' them to run the third reef line through the sail for over an hour, while guys were down below making cups of coffee, taking shits and other less critical maneuvers. We were starting to pound and it was time to take sail off. With the boat obviously burdened, they just sat there.

The shift went through earlier that same morning and on starboard tack the wind gradually freed into a beam reach. Although the pounding had stopped with the new seaway smoothing out, it was bad enough. A wave carried away the spray dodger for the main hatch at noon and now, with the dodger down below being repaired, there was a continuous cascade of water coming through the coamings flooding Richard's galley which still was turning out substandard food.

Phil Holland also lost his bet with the *Lion* crew. The 'bow foil' he had rudimentarily made out of aluminium and fastened to the bow in Cape Town to keep the seas off the foredeck while surfing, disintegrated that afternoon. Half of it sheared off with a headsea and while Wade and Phil tried to hacksaw through the bolts to jettison what was left, another greeny buried them waist deep in water. When they surfaced the job had been done for them.

L'esprit d'Equip sighted the fleet's first iceberg that same day at 49° South, 41°30′ East; they reckoned it to be 300 meters long. We posted an iceberg watch on the weather deck for the first time that night and since there was a bit of a moon I reassured the guys we would be able to see the big ones. "What about the little ones?" they asked. "Don't hit any," was all I could say.

Friday the 13th passed uneventfully – almost. While *NZI* blew a chute, a pole and tore a reef in the main, almost our only damage was a broken thermos flask. The wind had flicked into the SW and with some apprehension knowing the day, we carefully set the undersized Flanker; it opening with a distinct lack of report. Immediately after we tried the big 2.2 oz chute, but 30 minutes later the halyard parted sending the sail luckily clear to leeward where we anxiously gathered it aboard. The full size 3.0 oz was tried next and it stayed up there, it's sheer weight barely defying gravity.

In anticipation of another low now brewing off South Africa and already on the march, we gybed to port late that afternoon at 51° South. We didn't want to be on the wrong side of this one. It was a great pleasure to be off the wind for a while. Once again, with the boat upright, the decks relatively dry, hot showers being taken and clothes and bedding aired, we felt less sorry for ourselves.

Surfing hard, at 15–22 knots, closing up under Kerguelen Island in the middle of the South Indian Ocean was an exhilirating sail. It was a Southern Ocean that I remembered well. On deck, dangers were all around; an overloaded afterguy ("Don't stand near it!"), same for the Kevlar sheet; the helmsman steering a bit too shy and ready to roll out ("Call him down!"), guys up on the foredeck swept aft to the mast ("Glad to see they're clipped on."), and worrying about the halyard ("Better put two on.").

Down below that feeling is lost as soon as you slide down the hatch. Now, lying in your bunk it's fear and loathing. I slept below the afterguy block when on port tack and as the deck strained and crackled I had this vision of a whole piece of it being torn away and the next wave quietly lifting me up and out through the lifelines.

Mugsy slept opposite me under the Kevlar sheet, where the winch howls continually as they trim and ease to keep the marginal spinnaker under control. We both lay there experiencing the weightlessness, the shuddering, and dreading the violent crash, instinctively hanging on, pinned to the overhead and very helpless. If we're lucky, they avoid the broach, the boat instead charges down the wave at 25 knots, the boys on deck yelling their heads off; if you didn't know better you'd think it was screams of terror in some tragic disaster.

J.J. had become a bit of a worry after only two weeks out. He wonders what we are out here for. He told me that he thought this was not a happy crew, "I don't hear a lot of laughter here," said he. Although I didn't agree, I saw his point. I assumed J.J. had known what open ocean racing was all about, but he did not seem comfortable. Judging this experience from his 'Cape Town-to-Uruguay' set of values (his only yardstick); tropical sunsets, cocktails on deck, no worries; this Whitbread must seem like a nightmare. Still, he must have known what he was getting into.

He got all bent out of shape when I yelled at him to ease the sheet the day before. I thought it was a fair way to go about things seeing the bow was about 4 feet underwater. "That's what crew are here for, to be yelled at!" was my emotional response as if to say, what the hell do you think you are doing out here? He wasn't pleased nor was I with myself.

Possibly a quick sight of land would cheer us both up. Late afternoon of the 15th we were reefed down to the sail numbers only 30 miles off Iles Kerguelen. Although that surely was land on our port beam, it wasn't a cure for homesickness. Mount Grand Ross's 7000-

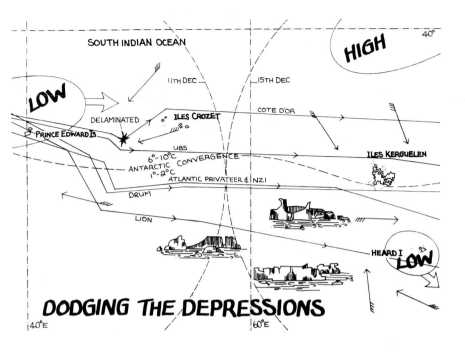

SOUTH INDIAN OCEAN

HIGH 40°

11TH DEC 15TH DEC

LOW

DELAMINATED ILES CROZET COTE D'OR

PRINCE EDWARD IS

UBS ILES KERGUELEN

6°-10°C
ANTARCTIC CONVERGENCE
1°-2°C

ATLANTIC PRIVATEER & NZI

DRUM

LION

HEARD I LOW

DODGING THE DEPRESSIONS

40°E 60°E

foot summit was obscured in the blow and we just caught a glimpse of the lower ice slopes and some rocky crags. Discovered by the French in 1772 and soon after visited by Cook on his 'third' voyage of discovery, this archipelago, claiming 300 islands in a rough circle 60 miles in diameter, remains under French sovereignty. They maintain a weather station in one of the fiords on the eastern flank.

The Antarctic Pilot Book describes the place in few words; "The interior has been but little visited due to the rugged and boggy nature of the ground, the severity of the climate, the absence of trees and wood, and the want of supplies. All necessaries have to be carried by exploring parties."

Within 30 minutes of the landfall, another squall swept through forcing us to change down to the No. 5 jib. The main already had four reefs in. It was blowing a solid 50. Then suddenly the island was gone. There was a miserable night ahead of us.

We were determined to be on the right side of the approaching low and so Roger and I decided to hold about 10 degrees higher than the course until the low was due south of us. *UBS* would be safe passing north of the island. *AP* and *NZI* were a touch south of our position while *Lion* was down at 53°30′ South. We were hoping for the low to put *Lion* on the wind temporarily and push her back even farther behind than the 80-mile lead we already had. With the other two it would be marginal.

Headsail reaching with the wind forward of the beam was some of the most unpleasant sailing conditions we would face. I recorded my thoughts that evening:

Fully pressed at 60° apparent wind angle. It is almost as bad below as it is on deck. Dodger again carried away. Condensation is getting to be nasty, sleeping bags damp, foul weather gear needed in the main saloon as it's like a tropical rainforest, without the heat. Bilgewater is a constant problem and we have to pump every hour to keep up with it, seems to be coming in from everywhere. Although it's no joy ride, I can hardly imagine what it's like on NZI; no bunkmodules, no floorboards, no heater, just one big drafty cavern.

Suddenly, to our horror, given the time and place, we heard a deep clanging sound coming from the bilges. Rick and I started to investigate, he with 'keel' written all over his face. What a pleasure it was to find only one of the small stainless steel water tanks, then empty, floating around in the bilge water, having broken free from its mountings. Like Richard's 'Edible Boat,' a parody of the galley now appearing in written form in the head (spaghetti-type seizing wire, crispy Nomex honeycomb biscuits), we easily repaired and secured it using bits of wood from the overhead framing, ready at hand, having only to reach up and rip off a piece through the voids in the overhead, not yet replaced from the break-up off Cape Town on Leg One.

On the 16th we got one of the first weather fax maps from Canberra in Australia and the news was not good. Roger recorded it and his feelings about the tactical situation in his log that day:

Well, the weather map indicates that the low has gone as far south as 53°, very close to our longitude. We obviously should have reached off for more speed, as did NZI and AP, UBS was pretty scared off the low having held north and I was sure Lion would get stuck, but they all escaped. I feel very tired after these last few stressful days worrying about that low and I am now a little disappointed when I realize we have committed our first tactical error of the leg. I try hard to keep my spirits up as we are still only half way. I wonder how NZI and AP knew to bear off south?

Roger and I seemed to be working a lot better together this leg. We had decided to take no big risks, stay on a conservative track and make small gains with sharp tactics. It was proving to be successful, despite our boatspeed problem. But Roger was showing the strain from all his heavy thinking. He began to claim that no one was listening to him again. They say he is fatigued and needs more sleep, his symptoms being ceaseless talking and repeating himself over and over. At least he was preoccupied with the race, unlike some of the guys who, instead of paying attention, would sit in the cockpit while on watch and ramble on about anything that came to mind. I was accustomed to

Roger's peculiarities and knew that his saving grace was an unshakable interest in the job at hand. I was less pleased with his critics.

My 1430 Log Entry December 16th
The first really tough day down South for the boys this morning, which is as much as to say things did not go well at all.

Probably from a reaction to the losses we made by holding too far north for too long, the 0300 to 0700 watch this morning shook three reefs and hoisted the flanker, only to have the halyard break one hour later. No second halyard was rigged.

Again I came on deck to absolute chaos. The storm chute was just going up, and I was shocked to find the spinnaker net was not rigged. This little device had saved us hours already by preventing a spinnaker from becoming tangled around the headstay. Made from Dacron webbing and hoisted up the luff groove like a sail, it had been ultimately successful, but like someone who is loathe to try the vaccine if he has never experienced the disease, some thought it only a nuisance. Rather than let them find out through example, I made the medicine mandatory.

Not only that, I found the mainsail had a big gash in it below the first reef where the spinnaker sheet had chafed through it. The watch in charge had not noticed it. It seems once again, Mugsy had forced the set, and the two watch captains, Phil Wade and Phil Holland didn't have the deck ready in time. With only one halyard attached, the storm chute came thundering down only 30 minutes later. J.J. almost went overboard while gathering the sale and badly cut his hand. Roger laid in five stitches and he retired to his bunk with a condom over the affected appendage.

I had to admit to being not completely happy with the watch captains at that time.

It's as if they are almost afraid to tell people what to do when decisions have to be made. On the first leg in the straightforward conditions it was nothing more than an annoyance, but now when things really matter this inability to get on with it means blown sails and possibly worse. I know full well I will never be a popular figure like Magnus, but I never was, never claim to be. For me, Magnus, and Phil to a lesser extent, are far too polite for the job. I'm not sure what it is; afraid of responsibility, of making a mistake, of being too hard with their friends? We've discussed it several times and I keep saying that in the eyes of everyone their ability is beyond question, all you have to say is "Do it" and they'll do it.

This problem had been bothering me a lot. Our original concept had always been for the two main watch captains to run the deck completely, leaving Roger and myself to attend to the weather, the radio and the navigation. Every time there is a flak it seems I had to go out and clear it up. I have no problem ordering people about and never have. There are times when 'please' and 'what do you think guys?' are about as helpful as an umbrella on the foredeck in a blow.

Roger is aware of the problem but not really in a position to do anything about it. He keeps complaining that Magnus is spending too much time doing menial tasks like packing spinnakers, fixing things, and grinding when he should be steering more and just taking a back seat and watching the big picture. Of course, he is more than right. One thing I have learned on a project as big as this, as soon as you put your head down to a task, catastrophe is waiting behind you.

For all of his attributes; crack helmsman, sail trimmer, electronics wizard and the best all round athlete I know, Magnus is happier as a team player; a doer, not a delegater. Phil Wade suffers a little from the same but they are not men to turn their backs on any kind of work. I suppose this trait was better than its opposite, but it was almost ironical that I had to be more autocratic than I liked to be. It didn't help me in the popularity polls, either. In any case, imperfect as it was, it worked, and from what I have heard about the other boats we were damn lucky we were who we were. Personally, I've never sailed with a more able, compatible and pleasant bunch of individuals.

Phil Holland and Roger had a go at each other about the same problem. Roger reckons Phil, for all his experience, is too complacent and does not think ahead enough during the major shifts. Phil reckons we are short on guys, citing the *Lion* example of 22. All the more reason to be ready, says Roger.

Roger thought Mugsy would have been a better decision-maker as a watch captain because his thinking was clearer and he wasn't afraid to put his judgement on the line (the bad decision to not take the Windseeker had been a good example), but although I agreed, he still was possibly a bit too wild for this boat and prone to carelessness. As Phil Holland rightly says, "We definitely have to make it this time."

Although satisfied that we had done the right thing in the circumstances by holding high, we had in fact lost a lot of ground to *AP* and *NZI* who had steered lower and faster gambling that the low would pass well south. Another low was on the weather maps, brewing a storm to the west and with it, another chance for us to catch the leaders and widen the gap with those behind.

It was a battle to keep up at the best of times, as it was for everyone. All the boats had gear failures, made wrong tactical decisions now and then and sailed with varying degrees of efficiency. It was, however, plain as day, that the Farr boats were noticeably faster in reaching and heavy running conditions. For example, when straightlining against *NZI*, close together and in the same winds, they had run 333, 313, and

330 miles on consecutive days. We had to struggle to make 300. Even *AP* had trouble keeping up with *NZI* at that time and we can only presume it was a matter of control, their fractional rig being easier to handle than *AP's* masthead configuration in big seas.

Phil Holland had been taking a fair share of abuse and fending off snide remarks lately about how slow this boat was. After initial attempts to blame our tactics and praise the high caliber of the crew on *NZI*, he finally admitted that the Farr boats indeed were fast, certainly Blake and his Holland-designed *Lion* were no help to him in his reasoning then 80 miles behind on what was definitely a flyer. He had reported icing in the rigging and a lot of snow at 55° south. He even admitted being "too far south" on the radio that day. If he had a fast boat it is clear he wouldn't have been down there then.

Had a good day's work in the Southern Ocean today. Janne re-ran a new spinnaker halyard. Magnus inspected the rig (found a bolt missing in the headboard car). Mario and Mugsy sewed up the gash in the mainsail in situ, balancing precariously on the boom. The cabin sole was cleaned, the bilges inspected, and a general drying out which gives us a good break to face the next weather system on the way.

In addition to gaining 20 to 40 miles on all the boats, the 19th was a special day – Filthy's birthday. He got a hand-drawn birthday card, a custom-made 'young rigger's' smock with all the tools, a cake and a bottle of whiskey with a custom label: 'Old Nigger Riggers', 'A Most Carelessly Blended Scotch Whiskey from the Southern Ocean.' There were so many of us taking photographs of him that this man, usually so full of repartee, was totally speechless and wore an amazed smile. His old friend, Patrick, described him well when he wrote:

We had a great party for Phil's birthday. He is an extraordinary chap though he can be the most anti and negative person you'd ever want to meet – particularly towards those who don't conform to his own code of behaviour. Yet, when he's cheerful I've never met a more popular guy, and everyone – myself included – wants to be his friend. Even though I've known him as long as anyone on the boat he's still a source of endless frustration to me.

Again on the 21st the wind blew northerly and in another heavy reach it was miserable on deck. We hadn't seen the sun for days, but the Sat Nav just kept ticking off our position.

My 1845 Log Entry: position 53°30' South 113°40' East.
By 1900 the light is fading fast, what there was of it. A fogged, heavily condensed port light and aft hatch, cold to the touch, makes a cozy atmosphere below. I'm not ashamed to say that I enjoyed spending most of the afternoon

on my watch doing navigation, radio links, and the chat show.

On his off watch, Mugsy, cramped up in his upper bunk, was thinking of home when he wrote in his diary:

Only four days till Christmas and another one at sea. Last year it was on Fazer Finland with Skip, on our way to Santo Domingo. It's such a pity because I really enjoy Christmas at home; shop windows nicely decorated, hot cider and cookies to munch on while browsing the gift stores. Snow flurries and icy winds; all bundled up, nose running and turning pink with the cold. Then home to long evenings in front of the fire and then Christmas day-out to the Cape (Cod) to Erin's parents for dinner. I wonder if they think I only visit them to eat . . . Well this year, only the snow flurries. It's not very Christmasy aboard Drum with 16 other dirty, smelly guys packed into 78 feet of plastic! My choice to be here.

As miserable as it was, with the wind again forward of the beam, I could not help but see the humour in a typical slice of life at sea below decks.

It's breakfast time, 0630 at 53° South:
Four men struggle to get dressed for the upcoming six-hour watch. Heeled over 25 degrees and with the dodger gone again water pours through the hatch like a waterfall. "Where's the hell's my other seaboot?" Neil asks at large. Wade is struggling to take a leak in the head and the steam rises up and out of the head module as Richard announces that breakfast will be late as no one filled the day watertank up last night. Micky and Bill slide down below to gain a little warmth – they'd been freezing their asses off on the dawn watch and are dripping wet. Richard shakes Patrick up for the third time, a heavy sleeper with a miserable disposition in the morning, he finally sits up in his bunk staring ahead struggling to keep his bloodshot eyes open, scowling all around him. "I can't find my bloody seaboot" Neil reminds us, but no one is listening. Like a mountain climber losing a mitten and then realizing he doesn't have a spare, he begins to panic until Filthy announces he's got another pair with a hole in one.
Bodies swing wildly to and fro to the rhythm of the roll and heave of the boat, the old hands like Wade moving effortlessly around while the less experienced crash into the bulkheads and each other. A hiss hiss sound is reassuring as Richard pops the lid off the pressure cooker and a vapor cloud issues forth from his grease pit; breakfast is ready.
Rick grabs ahold of an enginebox fiddle and the whole thing comes away in his hand; another casualty in what was once the interior joinery. The hatch slides open and along with the cold draft of air, a wave pours down below on Filthy forcing down his porridge, but he doesn't even flinch as he is already in his dry-suit. He shakes his head of black, scraggly hair and wipes his mouth on

his sleeve and chucks the bowl in the slops bucket, the bowl making it, the spoon landing somewhere in the pile of wet sail bags. He looks as though he walked out of the pages of Conrad.

The bilge water sloshes to and fro announcing that once again it is time to pump for those below, and Magnus announces from the hatch that it is blowing even harder and, for those due to come on deck, it is time to change sail.

Not everyone saw humour in this as Pat wrote in his diary that same day:

We've just had a couple of the most miserable sailing days of my life. Fetching with 3 reefs and the storm jib at 53° South is not my idea of fun. I think one of the problems is that everyone is getting really tired; it's cold; and the food is just disgusting. Richard's cooking this leg has been dreadful. Half the guys are living on coffee and Mars Bars (of which we seem to have thousands), not exactly the recipe for sustained energy and good health – no wonder everyone's a bit down. Phil Holland's earlier enthusiasm seems to have waned, not surprising since he's hardly eaten for three weeks and is definitely looking a bit on the gaunt side. My shoulders and arms ache like hell and my enthusiasm for steering is evaporating rapidly.

It was Christmas Eve. For the occasion the wind had backed into the northwest and lightened to 20 knots. J.J. had just resurfaced after a record-breaking three days below with some virus, and we were sitting in the cockpit. His spirits were up, we having reconciled our differences over the definition of a 'good time'.

We were chatting away, staring to leeward when the rogue wave hit us. Without sound or warning, an old beam sea had rolled up and over the entire deck and as the boat pitched on to her starboard beam ends we were both washed down to the leeward rail completely at the mercy of the wall of water. J.J. fetched up on the binnacle and split open his forehead, while I caught myself on the mainsheet grinder pedestal before ending up a lifeless form in the bottom of the cockpit with the wind knocked clean out of me. As the cockpit, full to the deck with ice-cold water emptied slowly down the scuppers, like a tide in time lapse, I remembered clearly having a vision of peace and solitude as I was swept away, if only for an instant. With my eyes open, blue all around in total immersion, something told me just go with the flow, as trying to hang on against an irresistible force probably would have resulted in worse injury. Phil Wade had also almost gone over the side while hanging on to the backstay. None of us were clipped on.

Pale as a ghost (they said) I was poured down the hatch and rested below, the pain of cracked ribs to get worse before it got better. J.J. earned another 5 stitches and as the Doctor, in his underwear, casually picked his nose while he deftly laid in the stitches our amateur photographers popped their flash units happily. Roger, a born showman, was amused; J.J., the victim, was not and I could but hardly help in sympathizing with his sometimes negative opinion of us.

On Christmas Day, 1985, we were in the heart of the Southern Ocean. The longest day of the year in the Southern Hemisphere gave us only four hours of real darkness at 50° South; with very few clear nights there was not much chance to see the Aurorae Australis, which was a pity. The compass variation was up to 50° and hard under the bight of Australia, it would be the closest we would get to the South Magnetic Pole, normally an area of difficult steering due to the vertical 'dip' in the earth's magnetic field, causing a sluggish compass card. For those of us who actually enjoyed being there in all that misery, it was a 'Boy's Own' adventure.

Richard's gallant attempt at a Christmas cake in the rough going turned out to be a sad story, except for one member of our crew. Even though our microwave, mainly used as a convective oven, is mounted on a pivot, the violent conditions made the cake set with a strong bias to starboard and the bottom had burned and stuck to the pan. Then, when he tried to cut it, the cake fell to pieces. Finally, it fell off the counter top and landed on Bill. Happily he picked up and ate the crumbs. The crew was less enthusiastic about licking the frosting off his trousers than they were at grappling for the crumbs, needless to say. Again, cameras came out.

Roger spent an exhausting day at the radio attempting to put through link calls to parents and girlfriends for the crew. Sitting there in the swivel chair for hours on end is incredibly tiring as you struggle to hear garbled replies, wait for hours listening to other conversations and just when your turn comes up, the reception on that frequency goes bad and you have to start all over again on another; more often than not you have to try to raise another station. Roger described a touching conversation Magnus had with his elderly parents in Stockholm. He promised them he would spend some time at home that coming summer to help paint their old wooden house. For a man who had spent the last seven seasons skiing in Aspen and the rest of the year sailing all over the world, the Whitbread Race was already having the affect it does on almost all of us. It makes us want to settle down one day.

The crew awoke on Christmas morning to red stockings, not neatly hung by the chimney but tossed into their bunks. Hot brandy and spice were ladled out on deck that afternoon and Santa finally appeared. His Scandinavian accent told us how far he had come to see us. Patrick and Filthy, wearing Musto boot gasket seals over their heads and dressed like Santa's helpers grilled us before they would hand out our presents. If not to test our intelligence, the questions were certainly designed to embarrass us. Phil Holland: "What 2 out of 3 drugs are common: morphine, cocaine and amphetamine?" Rick: "The clitoris is found where with respect to the female vagina?" His answer, "bottom right hand corner", had the crew in fits of laughter. Mario: "What is special about Beaujolais Nouveau." For this Frenchman who does not like bread or cheese, and has Zimmerman for a last name, it was not surprising to find that he didn't realize that the grapes are not crushed.

Boxing Day did not go as well. The wind was aft and had again strengthened. Phil Wade, in a good move, changed early to the storm chute at 30 knots of true wind. All went well until just after dawn. I was below and had just pumped the forward bilge when *Drum* started to become unstable. I started aft for the hatch but by the time I got there it was too late. Neil, who was on the helm, described the chain of events:

I came on watch at 0500 and it was obvious we were on the edge of control. The seas hadn't had time in the new wind to build up from astern, and without the help of following waves, Drum was laboring along like a sick cow, but at a steady 15 knots. I took over the wheel, not yet fully attuned to the conditions, and realized immediately that disaster was imminent. Mugsy was riding shotgun on the other wheel and on some of the puffs we were both struggling to hold on to her. After about 15 minutes with the crew looking nervously over their shoulders at me, a stronger blast hit us and we spun right into a flying gybe. Everything seemed to happen at once; the main boom came flying across and hit the runner, the spinnaker pole dug into the water and we were lying over on our side. I let go of the spinning wheel and looked helplessly about me at the carnage I had created. No question about it, I was scared shitless, convinced I had sunk the boat and everyone with her. Water was dangerously close to the open hatch, and I imagined clearly what was going on down below.

I remember looking at Mugsy, almost directly above me at the other wheel. "Now I've done it!" He said, "Don't worry, she'll come up," and at that moment the spinnaker blew out and Drum struggled to her feet.

As I gathered my wits and gybed the boat back on course, the off watch came up, white-faced and bewildered, to survey the mess of tangled sheets and shredded sails draped across the deck. Patrick appeared at the wheel with a huge grin on his face and told me I looked as though I'd seen a ghost. I remember thinking he didn't look too relaxed himself. There was no point in dwelling on what had gone wrong, so we got down to setting the reacher on the pole and set off again. Despite the gleeful leg-pulling and the guys making Chinese faces at me (what we had executed is called a 'Chinese' gybe) during the next few days, I knew it could have happened to anyone. Skip stood up for me by giving our whole watch a bollicking for not changing to the Chicken Chute or the reacher sooner.

We roared off at top speed averaging 14.8 knots for 4 hours that day – a pace that would give us a 353-mile day, although it would be nearly impossible to keep up the pace, given the handling difficulties. Sporting an enormous grin even enormous by his standards, Magnus hit 25.46 on the speedo that afternoon, the fastest yet recorded although we were certain that our top speeds while surfing were far above those recorded by the Brookes and Gatehouse speedometer which had a long time delay in processing.

Mario and Mugsy reported that the storm chute would take 36 hours to repair. Mario reckoned some of the cross cut panels were missing and this coupled with the fact that it had been blown and repaired several times arguably made the job fruitless.

To add to the list of mishaps, Patrick was down below with his knee in a cast from an acrobatic trick gone wrong. I was beginning to understand Blake's theory that we should assume, with 22 crew members, a casualty rate of 25%. Patrick recalls what had happened:

After arguing with Mugsy that the blooper would be faster (I reckoned it wouldn't) in the end I capitulated and offered to go out to the end of the boom to reeve a sheet, I was standing in the fold of the main (we had one reef in) and as Drum *surfed off a wave at about 20 knots she heeled slightly dipping the boom in the water. Since I was standing facing outboard my left leg which was below the bottom of the boom took a 90 degree turn at the knee which neither it nor I appreciated.*

Roger, after an extremely painful examination, thought it was strained, but later admitted that the ligaments might be torn. With the crew looking on like vultures he put my leg in a cast. Less painful, now that it is immobilized I can only steer and trim (no bad thing!)

Roger's medical kit was getting a good hammering on Leg Two. His list of ailments included:
tonsilitis
finger infection requiring draining
5 stitches to cut in hand
virus infection in four cases
wax in ears
infection of the penis
herpes infection
5 stitches to cut in forehead
torn ligaments in knee requiring a cast
cracked ribs
2 cases of sea sickness
finger infection followed by an allergic reaction to anti-biotics
several cases of 'spotty bums'
reports of fatigue

Although these were all minor ailments, it is alarming to think of what can happen on a big sailboat on a long voyage. Boasting the most comprehensive medical kit in the fleet, weighing 70 kilos in 5 waterproof black, plastic boxes, Roger was prepared for the worst.

At 45° South, we were now south of Tasmania, with 1200 miles to go to the North Cape of New Zealand. The wind was moderating, and so were the temperatures of both sea and air. *Lion* was a good 190 miles behind; they had shot their bolt by holding to the southern course. On the other hand *AP* and *NZI* were neck and neck, 160 miles ahead. They would match-race all the way to the finish. *UBS* was only 60 miles ahead, but with high pressure in the Tasman Sea it was likely that the whole fleet would 'concertina' together as the front runners slowed up first.

Up went the 1.5 oz spinnaker for the first time in a long time. As the sail filled and the sock came fluttering down, so did Neil's missing sea boot, having been packed with the sail. Landing in the water with a splash not three feet from the side of the boat the crew rolled about the deck in hysterics, while Neil retired below, apparently not seeing the humour in it all.

I talked to Peter Montgomery from Radio New Zealand on December 30th, which was a morale booster. He was extremely positive, saying that the people of New Zealand think we are doing great to have gotten the boat back together and to be doing so well.

What a difference the New Zealanders' way of doing things was to that of the British. We did several radio interviews with UK commentators during the following few days. They were all depressing. Hugh Marriott, Whitbread's PR man talking from the Boat Show in London could only muster inane questions like, "How's the weather out there?" and "Have you had any mishaps?" The interviewer from BBC's Radio Four was completely uninformed asking me only, "Is Simon on board?" "Oh, I see, is Leg Three, then, the one where you go around Cape Horn?" And this, coming from a country that is sponsoring the race and has always boasted of being the foremost seafaring nation! By contrast, the sailing population in New Zealand was going wild, following the battle for first place between *AP* and *NZI*. They had been in sight of each other, on and off, for a week. Dr. Julian Fuller on *AP* made these observations in his log during that last week:

December 27th
Suddenly at suppertime Paul spots a boat on our starboard beam on the distant horizon! It is soon apparent she has a blue spinnaker and is thus obviously NZI! Pandemonium aboard as we realize we have caught the Kiwis at last after 5,000 miles of sailing.

December 29th

During the afternoon Henry goes aloft and spots our foe again on the horizon just forward of the beam! Much to our disgust, positions at 1100 and 2300 show that yet again NZI is slowly pulling ahead. We really thought we were faster in light conditions, but not so.

December 30th

In the late afternoon Arthur goes aloft and yet again spots NZI as a speck on the horizon. Absolutely becalmed that night. Fighting for every mile. 100 position shows NZI 22 miles ahead, but by 2300 it was back to only 10.

December 31st

We are only 280 miles from Cape Reinga. But what a blow at breakfast as we are now knocked 35 degrees off course and feel that NZI have it all in the bag, assuming she is now 7 miles dead ahead.

Then the call goes up, "There she is!" And there on the starboard beam is a sail coming over the horizon towards us. What incredible luck as we realize she will pass 1 to 2 miles astern of us!

January 1st

Isn't it amazing how New Year's Eve can come and go without really being noticed. We missed a whale by 5 meters again today. Wish the radar was working so we could accurately compare our progress hour by hour.

January 2nd

Arrive off Reinga at 0300 about 5 miles ahead of NZI. In the light headwinds, we watch to our horror as they whittle that lead down to 60 meters at the point! It will be a reach and then a run down the back side of the North Island. At first light two planes and two helicopters buzz us as a few large motor yachts roar out to witness this incredible piece of match racing.

The wind nears the critical wind angle and up goes our chute first, lasting only minutes before blowing out. We hoist the 'all purpose' 1.5 oz. Minutes late NZI also blow theirs, and are very quick with a replacement.

There is so little in it now, and the good news for us is that it will be a square run down into Hauriki Gulf and the finish. NZI being fractionally rigged finds she must reach out more to sea to keep up boatspeed.

What an armada of ships and planes, as folks have dropped everything to come out and witness this battle royal between two Maxis, offering us a liberal supply of beer. Only later we learn that it is reported that spirits on AP are high with lots of smiles while on NZI it is all seriousness as Digby realizes his 'first into Auckland' is hanging in the balance.

The 'Hen and Chickens Islands' are the next mark, and to our joy, NZI, who have gone far out to sea to the east, have gybed back and fallen in two miles astern of us! As the light begins to fade, our lead is looking good and all hands are still on deck, manning all possible positions for quick sail changes and gybing. Eventually we are able to set a course for the finish line. We cross first at about 0100 local time doing about 12 knots with the spinnaker up missing the pier full of spectators by 50 yards. What a feeling of relief and utter collapse! And then out of the misty gloom, 800 yards behind, NZI steams over the line only 7 and a half minutes after us!

That was the big story of Leg Two. I couldn't help but be jealous of those two crews. In 1978, *King's Legend* and *Flyer* had finished only an hour apart, and we could see the Dutchman behind us in the light winds as we struggled over the line. However, we on *Drum* couldn't complain; our perseverance was beginning to pay dividends.

In our hallowed hall of grafitti, someone scribbled the passage, "All Ye Sinners Come Forth, So We Came Fourth." And so we did, which was a respectable finish being only 10 hours behind the two leaders. *UBS* did an outstanding job of catching up and finishing only two hours behind them, thus retaining overall first place by a wide margin.

Lion had also closed up to within five hours of our finishing time, finishing a disappointing fifth place – more disappointing as the New Zealand publicity game swung into high gear. An astute player, Blake was already making the most of the whale they had hit, which rendered their rudder almost useless two days before their finish. Indeed, they had gybed and broached their way down the New Zealand coast and blew out every spinnaker they had.

For *Drum*, we did what we set out to do: make it in one piece. Pleased with ourselves and with the thousands of people who came out to greet us on a rainy, miserable afternoon, we all felt great. For the first time in six months, we looked forward to some real holiday time. It was sorely needed. For me it was the first in a year. I could truly relax.

10 · Half Way But Whole Hearted

Ma roto hoki kia ora ka pa te korero.
If the inner man is refreshed, the conversation will be agreeable.

Maori Proverb

We looked forward to a full six weeks ashore in New Zealand. What a pleasure it was to make out a worklist of nothing other than the normal servicing of the mast, the equipment, and sails. Chris Barker was contracted to be in charge of the cosmetic work, including repainting the deck and the interior, hiding the battle scars of the less pleasant times *Drum* had faced.

There's an old saying that suggests that if you really want to get away from the sea and settle down, put an oar over your shoulder, walk inland and when the first person asks you what you're carrying, then you know you've arrived. Although not taking it to that extreme, suffice to say that few of the crew were seen around the boat for their two-day leave after we got in. They preferred sleep, heavy drinking, chasing women and dining ashore.

In fact, the whole fleet except *Cote d'Or* would arrive with surprisingly little damage, and, in New Zealand where there were some of the best and most enthusiastic marine tradesmen anywhere, and six weeks in hand, there was nothing much we all couldn't accomplish. While the dockside pundits inspected the damage to the Belgian monster, the real attention was on Digby's success and *Lion's* failure.

---

opposite Needlecraft on the high seas: *above* Almost washed overboard with a freak wave, J.J. got off lucky with only stitches to the forehead during the middle of Leg Two; *below* In a sailoft the size of a well appointed broom closet, the temperamental but persistent Mario Zimmerman struggles with an equally temperamental sewing machine while repairing the storm chute on Leg Three; man beat the machine that day (*Photos by Skip Novak*)

overleaf Roger drives while Chuck rides 'shotgun'; Mugsy and Micky grinding, chatting to Filthy while cameraman John Toon waits for interesting material during a beautiful day's sail on Leg Two (*Photo Skip Novak*)

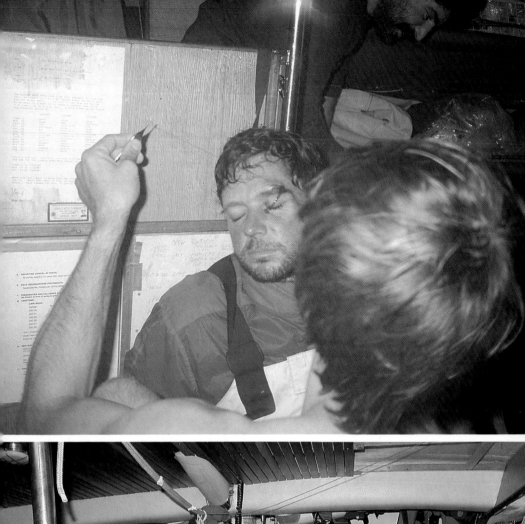
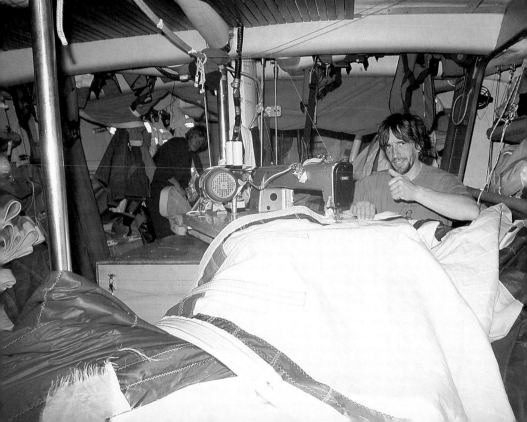

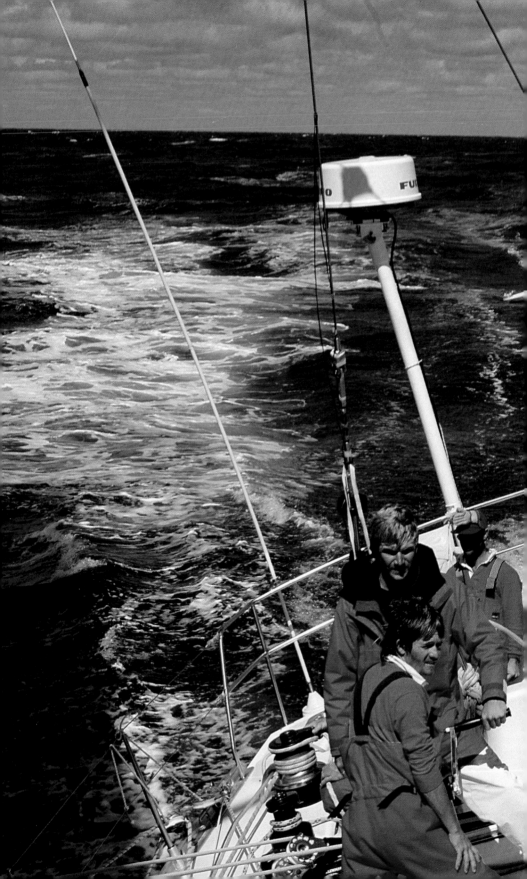

Hitting the whale off the North Island was possibly Blake's saving grace in an otherwise uninspired passage. The day after she arrived, *Lion* was hauled out at McMullen and Wing boatyard for all to see the damage the whale had done to her rudder. The two Kevlar skins had indeed been stripped away and not much was left of the foam filler of the blade. Grant Dalton, watch captain on board, explained the collision and his near death as a result.

"It was about quarter to ten at night when we hit the whale. We first hit him with our bow, then again with the keel as he slid aft while the boatspeed fell from 11 to 6 knots just like that. We checked everything below, there was no problem so we carried on. It wasn't until the next morning that the boat began to wander on a reach and we then suspected that something must be wrong with the rudder. We put a man over the side and sure enough, the bottom 4 feet was gone, and the Kevlar skins were delaminated from the rest of the blade. As we continued we could see that every now and then more would break away, so we took off the head doors, sewed them into a sail bag and with *Lion* dead in the water, attempted to sink this 'sleeve' over the stern with the anchor chain and slide it up and over the damaged blade, as it was obvious at that rate we would soon be left with only the alloy frame and shaft. The idea didn't work because it was impossible to maneuver it in position, so we decided just to 'go for it' and hope for the best. Going to windward around the North Cape it was OK as we could balance it out with the sail plan, but on the reach and run down the coast the problems started.

On one spinnaker peel, the boat wiped right out. With both kites still up we decided to let the second halyard run as well as all the sheets and guys and jettison the sail (our support boat was standing by to pick it up) and just start over. I went forward to cast it off, but instead of the halyard tail falling in the water after it went flying out the masthead, it instead fell straight onto the deck right on top of me. The spinnaker was now well astern in the water like a big trawl net, and as the boat took off the halyard wrapped around my waist and started to pull me aft along the deck at 10 knots. I smashed straight into the steering wheel, bending it into a pretzel and just as I was about to be literally sliced in half, spread eagled straddling the backstay, my body went horizontal and the loop of line ripped off me, destroying my foul weather gear and tearing off both my docksiders. It was close to being a very nasty accident."

The Maxis had all arrived within a day and a half of each other, as

---

opposite Janne sips a bit of warmth as Mugsy drives on (*Photo by Skip Novak*) usual getting most of the publicity. More than two days later, *Philips Innovator* made the finish and helped by light winds for the next 24 hours, her arch rival for the handicap prize, *L'esprit d'Equipe* drifted down the coast, not only losing her one-day advantage from Leg One, but incurring a net loss of 12 hours for the two legs combined. It is a tribute to the New Zealand people that they fully understand the handicap system and their interest in yachting rivals or possibly surpasses their interest in rugby, football or cricket. They not only turned out in thousands to welcome those two handicap leaders, but also as a matter of courtesy, did the same for tiny *Baia Viking*, the last boat in, almost 10 days later.

An overhead view of the east coast of the North Island and especially the Hauriki Gulf outside Auckland makes it obvious why it is a sailor's paradise. While the west coast is rugged, wind- and wave-swept with little natural shelter, the Auckland side is deeply embayed, has little swell and most importantly a rural atmosphere. By European standards, it is an area unaffected by over-development, pollution, or congestion. Most of the offshore islands, carpeted in lush, green sub-tropical vegetation, are protected, but accessible, so that within a half day, the Auckland businessman can be surrounded by a panorama equal to anything in the South Pacific. It is hardly surprising that most of the population is waterborn at one time or another, and it is a fact that New Zealand has more pleasure craft per capita than anywhere else in the world.

Princess Wharf in downtown Auckland, normally used for cruise ships, was Race venue. The yachts were tied up on one side of the 1000 foot pier, moored to floating pontoons which rose and fell with the tide. The Race Office was conveniently located on the second deck of the wharf warehouse, directly overhead of the Whitbread Cafe, a bar-cum-restaurant provided with a temporary license in order to dispense liberal quantities of what the folks Down Under call the 'amber fluid' of life.

More a large town than a big city, Auckland boasts 1 million residents in a vast sprawl. Anyone had free access to the jetty, and not a day went by when the area was not teeming with spectators. Of course, *Drum* was once again a center of attraction with a special following of teenage girls. Daily, we would have to run the gauntlet of questions about Simon and when he was due to arrive. "Soon," we would say. Almost as a concession, they would ask *us* for our autographs. As we looked at the girls one day with their pink, punk hair-dos all spiky, and some of them with their mothers in tow, Bill made the observation that it would have been far more interesting sailing for Julio Iglesias than Simon Le Bon.

After 10 days in port, the action at the jetty was quiet. Most of the other boats had pulled their rigs for the compulsory inspection and were hauled out in and around Auckland for refits. We, instead, repainted the decks in the water and generally spruced the boat up for the filming of our TV commercial for Sasson clothes, that most important financial committment that had been on our minds since the end of Leg One. One January 14th we slipped the lines and made sail north for the Bay of Islands with a volunteer, skeleton crew.

I had suggested everyone take a good, two-week holiday while in New Zealand, preferably away from the boat. Magnus was already off to Sydney to sail 6-Meters with Pelle Peterson and most of the guys with girl friends had declined the 8 day junket to do the film, which was not surprising since they had just sailed 7,000 miles. It was no problem conscripting others; one look at the quality of the New Zealand models involved and the boat was full.

Australian director and rock video pioneer, Russel Mulcahy, had assembled a mixed production company of people from the UK and New Zealand. The plan was to use the boat as a prop, with a commercial featuring Le Bon and the models wearing the summer and winter collections of Sasson casual clothing. The Bay of Islands with their hilly, green islets and superb sandy beaches was the perfect backdrop for Russel's entourage. Ace camera man and veteran of our Fastnet capsize, New Zealander John Toon would do the filming. He had been originally scheduled to do the third leg with us around the Horn, but he was still searching his soul about that proposition, and this was a perfect way to get him back into the swing of things.

Simon had arrived up the coast by seaplane to join us, a bit flabby and pale as a ghost from a heavy recording session in Europe. Most of us who knew him from last summer were confident that he would be OK when it came to the crunch, but for someone who wasn't familiar with our celebrity he didn't exude much confidence upon appearance as Patrick (who had joined the boat at the end of the summer) observed in the hotel that evening, "I don't think he's got the slightest idea of what he's letting himself in for." This was a view widely held by the press and therefore most of the public.

In a hectic schedule, he had also managed to find time to marry his new girl friend, Jasmin, a beautiful anglicized Persian girl and already a top fashion model. The rumour had it that she was pregnant. If so, he would have a lot on his mind during the next two months.

On the first day, while Simon relaxed at the hotel breaking himself in to the brutal summer sun, I, and the film crew, went out in a motorboat to recconoiter the islands, sound the channels, and plan a schedule of stunts and sequences for the next four days.

The first day went like clockwork, the only problem being trying to evade crowds of curious spectators and keep them out of the line of the cameras. An old climbing friend from the South Island, Bill Rainey, spent the whole day in our Zodiac, fending off inquiries and making polite gesticulations to beer swilling 'diggers,' Le Bon aficionados, and the casual public. We were now used to this type of thing because for a variety of reasons where *Drum* went, people were sure to follow and we made it a point of always being on our best behaviour. A local and a lawyer by trade, Bill was the best qualified to politely tell people from what seemed all walks of life, to 'get lost'.

Simon spent most of the day in a harness standing on the third spreaders, about 75 feet off the deck, while Toon, hanging out of a helicopter buzzed him from every angle conceivable. Meanwhile, we would sail the boat over and over through an especially narrow channel (with about 2 feet of water under the keel) at nine knots flying our special Sasson Spinnaker.

Chopper pilot, Alan Grant, was the real star of the show. We marvelled at the free-form way he flew his machine, sometime coming alarmingly close to the rigging. He seemed to find it impossible to fly anywhere in a straight line, but we realized he was no fool – just another flamboyant Kiwi bush pilot, weaned on rough terrain, open country, and few restrictions. It was a pleasure to watch him.

Ten hours later, tired, burned out, but happy with our first performance we motored back towards our anchorage in front of the Waitangi Hotel. Roger decided to try a different channel than the one I had used without him on board the day before. At six knots, we ran gently aground on the mud flats in the last light before dusk. The tide was still rising, the boys were having a good time with the models, and there was plenty of beer on board, so it was not a serious proposition having to wait an hour to float off and try again. Simon and Paul were still on board and for the first time, we all were enjoying the boat with light hearts. We didn't have a care in the world – until the ferry boat came. Down to the gunwhales with tourists, you could almost hear their sighs of satisfaction when they realized who we were and how lucky they had been to have caught this ferry and not the earlier one. Giving his customers real value for their money, the boat captain decided to park his vehicle directly in front of our bow and didn't budge when I politely asked him to move off.

We had the entire cast, crew, models and producers out on the end of the boom to heel her over. We launched off of the bank with the engine in full ahead. Not realizing what was going on, the ferry held her ground. To avoid impaling our boom in the ferry's afterdeck, thereby ending the commercial then and there as well as probably injuring innocent bystanders, I had to veer sharply to starboard and once again ran back up on the mud bank. I then told the captain what he could do with his ferry boat, in a language a Kiwi understands perfectly well. He left us to our own devices and in 20 minutes we had *Drum* back in her anchorage and were headed for shore in the dinghy.

By dinner time that evening we had all forgotten the grounding. But we had forgotten who we were, and had to pay for it the next morning. At 0600 sharp, I got a telephone call from the *Auckland Star*. The caller asked me if I could corroborate the story that we had grounded and damaged the boat yet again, and what about the rumor that Le Bon was injured. I tried to convince them it "was really nothing," but, half asleep, I probably sounded like the proverbial drunken captain sleeping off the hangover after the disaster.

Late for breakfast, I had the pleasure of then reading all about it in the *New Zealand Herald*, front page, in a story just about eclipsing the one about the ticker tape parade the crews of the other boats had got down Queen's Street that same day. Of course, someone had reported not only how foolish we had been to run aground, but also how 'ungrateful' we had been to refuse an offer of assistance from the ferry. This didn't seem to worry Paul or Simon in the slightest; they had experienced much worse in the music world.

The remainder of the commercial went well. While we sailed *Drum* in and around the islands, Simon was made to ride bicycles and cars on water, tow the boat with a bow line (while walking on water) and generally fool around with the models who were always visible somewhere in the background.

We had only one incident that gave me a real fright. John Toon and Russel wanted to film Janne, who was a 1980's version of Sterling Hayden, while he was 'halyard flying in the boatswain's chair'. The plan was for Janne, suspended from the top of the mast by the spinnaker halyard, to pull himself out of the water and soar over the dinghy with the camera. Instead, they almost ran over him with the 25 HP outboard. When his sun-bleached, blond head appeared from under the boat and he gave the 'thumbs up' sign, I was relieved to know that if he did make Hollywood some day, he wouldn't have to make his 'B' movies with a wooden leg.

Times have changed in the sailing world. Ten years ago I never would have imagined that I would see a group of hardened, macho, boatbums prancing around the deck, coiling lines and grinding winches to the canned Sasson music while wearing scimpy designer 'T' shirts; but they all seemed happy as could be. After a job well done, sunburned, well fed and relaxed we headed back down to Auckland. Patrick wrote his friend back home about that enjoyable week:

The last four days have been just great, it's the first time we've had the boat to ourselves purely for fun. Naturally we all spent the first couple of days letching over the six or so models who are here for the commercial. They've turned out to be good company and lots of fun and after we realized (to our chagrin) that they weren't going to fall into bed with us, we've got along together famously. Needless to say Janne had different ideas and has been putting the bite on one of the more attractive of them who I'm maliciously happy to see has (so far!) resisted his Scandinavian charm.

Roger, too, is like a kid in a candy store while we've been here. Most of the time he's serious to the point of boredom but with women around he turns into an oversexed schoolboy. It's almost embarrassing to see him fawning all over them – or would be if he didn't enjoy the success he does – I can't see what women see in him. It is, however, great to see everyone get along so well – especially after the amount of time we've all spent in each other's company over the last few months.

We had a big welcoming committee upon arrival, but once again they were disappointed. Simon had returned to Auckland by air and had gone to Sydney for a few days. The work schedule began in earnest and that next day we pulled the mast out by mobile crane and jibbed it up onto the roof of the Princess Wharf warehouse where an impromptu mast repair facility had been organized. Magnus and Neil would again strip every fitting from the rig for inspection and look for signs of fatigue.

In a shore facility that left little to be desired, one level down from the masts was the sail repair loft. There Mugsy and Mario, having staked their claim to floor space by marking its boundaries with duct tape, and with our Pfaff sewing machine in a proper stand and their repair kit neatly laid out, began to survey and service our sail inventory. Outside on the first floor terrace, Filthy set up his rigging shop, consisting of an old wooden wire spool for a seat, a few hand tools, and like the Old Salt he already looked at 33, he dispensed a wealth of stories, jokes and advice for the kids and for anybody else who was interested. With his ability to talk easily to anyone, Filthy soon had an enormous following.

Nursing an outrageous sunburn and his usual good natured, but boisterous notoriety, Simon dutifully showed up at the boat for work as we were in preparation to haul out at McMullen and Wings. As Simon was trying to 'get in shape' and toughen himself up, the young girls loyally stood guard on the jetty, and I couldn't help speculate that possibly their female emotions were being stirred not by the rockstar, but by the deeply tanned, hardbodied crew working below. This theory was strengthened when after a time, the girls would not ask the usual everyday, but instead, "Have you see Janne or Neil today?" Or "Do you know when Micky is coming back?"

I will never forget the day when we had pulled out the mast and we had to motor back down to our berth at the other end of the jetty. Filthy suggested I invite about 20 girls, who had watched our every move, on board for the ride, a distance of about 100 yards.

I no sooner than gave the nod, than they were jumping down onto the deck like lemmings over a cliff. Worse still, word got around down the jetty and with already 60 girls on board I could hear screams coming from around the corner. Just as I shouted to "cast off quick!" another group came thundering down the dock like a herd of buffalo. Remembering we had no liability insurance for this type of thing I started to panic and as we eased ourself off the wall the stragglers were still falling over and across the lifelines and impaling themselves on stanchions and winch pedestals. We must have had a 100 girls on board. We gave them a proper, 20 minute ride around the harbor and as an added attraction we let them off on board *NZI*, not pleasing her crew who were servicing the winches. The girls thanked us, proclaiming we had made their summer holiday. Unfortunately, the ones who didn't make the boat showed no restraints in their displeasure in such a way that made the hardest of our hard core cringe a bit. What a feeling of power to make people laugh or cry with such little effort.

With Phil Wade and Roger in charge of the work schedule, De and I flew down to the South Island to visit friends and were soon joined by Filthy, and two crew from *Cote d'Or*. The four of us had planned to spend a week in a high mountain hut and from there climb Mt. Aspiring, one of New Zealand's classic alpine peaks.

Although Filthy had never climbed before, he was extremely competent with his hands and in his ability to handle ropes properly. We had little difficulty in making the top after being weathered off twice. The four of us scarcely discussed sailing all that week, and I can think of no better way to clear your mind of the sea than to go into the high mountains. A few of the crew, especially Roger, had questioned the wisdom of taking this risk and when Filthy arrived back in Auckland with a cast on his left leg they quickly claimed foresight. As it happened, he had not fallen on the climb, but was knocked over by Alain of *Cote d'Or* who slipped during the long walk out of the valley. Fortunately, Filthy's problem was only torn ligaments, and in no time he was fit again.

A lot had been accomplished while we were in the mountains, and the boat was already back in the water. Patrick had completely redesigned the rudder, incorporating more balance and also had rebuilt the entire blade, it having been repaired so many times before that it was suspect. He also completely eliminated the gears in the steering boxes making it a simple, direct, sprocket to chain system.

The story goes that they were backing out of the travel lift slip after launching with Roger at the wheel. As the tide nipped the stern he turned the wheel to port, but the stern went instead to starboard. "Turn the wheel the other way, fer Christ's sake!" said the naval architect to the poor doctor. "I am turning it the right way!" he said.

By eliminating the gears, the direction of travel of the steering cables was in effect reversed, a gross oversight by our engineer and the cause of much embarrassment for him amidst fits of laughter and ridicule from the others. To make it work properly, that is, to make it 'as easy as steering a car,' he had to completely dismantle and realign the brackets. Assisted by Micky and accompanied by much cursing and bruised fingers, they managed to get it back together for the one-day Maxi Series in Auckland Harbor scheduled for February 6th. Largely instigated by Paul Berrow and Pierre Fehlmann, the Maxi skippers and their sponsors had organized the event purely as an exhibition for the New Zealand public. Two short, in-harbour courses were scheduled and the promoter, Andy Hayden, a former New Zealand All Black rugby star, had arranged live coverage. His estimate was that 100,000 people would be watching.

In what is a difficult thing to conceive, promote and pull off at the best of times anywhere else, in less than two weeks the game was on, with Hayden not only having landed the event sponsor, the Town and Country Inns (a chain of hotel/restaurants) for $50,000 NZ, but also had secured several sponsors for the boats for a set price of $20,000 NZ to cover our costs, insurance, and a kitty to be divided up equally at the finish. For the day we happily became *Drake's Drum*, Drake's, being the New Zealand branch of an international personnel employment agency.

With a day-race crew of 26 and an afterguard including the Managing Director of Drake's as well as the Mayor of Auckland, Dame Cath Tizard, I discreetly reminded the crew to take it easy with the language. The Drake's house flag was flying from the backstay, the Drake weather cloths were tied to the lifelines and the crew donned their bright green Drake T-shirts for the day, while I thought to myself, "Hell this is an easy way to make $20,000."

Just before we left the dock to do battle, the Managing Director pulled me to one side and humbly asked me if his two teenage daughters could come along, promising they would stay below out of the way. "They're big Duran Duran fans," said the father. Understanding what makes a sponsor tick only too well, I invited them aboard, making their dream come true, and I'm sure removing any doubt the Managing Director might have had that his money was well spent that day.

The first race was sailed in squally conditions which was a shame, if not for the thousands of spectators on the water, than for those watching from land farther away. The start was chaotic and the first leg up to the Harbor Bridge was a confused mess of spectator craft of all descriptions.

Our crew was obviously a bit tense with our guests on board. Cath Tizard, a good-looking, gray-haired lady old enough to be Filthy's granny, must have sensed this and understanding men, particularly sailors, shouted forward, "What the hell's he doing? Tell that bastard to get his boat out of the way!" This had the desired effect; the guys immediately relaxed and acted like themselves.

In company with boatloads of cheerleaders à la American Football, we came second behind the then infallible *UBS*. *Lion* was miles behind, but worse than that, *NZI* had run aground after the first mark and then succeeded in running down an anchored trimaran injuring a nine-year-old boy who had to be taken to the hospital. With a gaping hole in his starboard side from the collision Digby retired for the rest of the day. The second race was called off when the wind dropped and we retired to Princess Wharf and on to the evening's festivities. It was a great day for us, but not for the two local boats.

Kiwi pride was divided along interesting lines between *Lion* and rival *NZI*. While Peter Blake's *Lion* campaign was backed by Auckland 'city money', Digby's was more of rural origin, the funding originally coming from a syndicate of farmers down island. Blake had been organized early, the boat was professionally built and conservative by design and construction. They toured New Zealand in grand style for many months prior to their departure, acting and looking confident and invincible.

Although impressive, *Lion* was the antithesis of *NZI* which in a lot of ways appealed more to what New Zealanders are all about. Digby Taylor had done the race four years ago with his home-built *Outward Bound*, a Laurie Davidson 58-footer, and had great success for a first time effort finishing 5th on handicap and winning the 'small boat' division.

With limited backing initially, he tried to build the Maxi along the same lines, using his own ingenuity, volunteer labor and, for most of the time, his own two hands. A laminator by trade, Digby was the archetypal Kiwi craftsman; he knew how to do most things himself, and if he didn't he figured it out along the way. This grass roots approach appealed to many people and Digby found backers who believed in his methods.

The project had not gone completely according to plan, however, even in the early stages. The boat was, if I may use the description, 'agricultural' in appearance, and their homespun philosophy left them usually late for deadlines and often in chaos. After the first leg, Blake's superior organizational skills carried the day, while Digby's mast nearly came down but then Digby's stellar performance on the second leg not only saved *NZI* from the critics, but also cast a dark shadow on *Lion*.

Some difficult questions were asked of the 'establishment.' For example, how could *NZI* be so much faster than *Lion*? What was Blake thinking of, with this design and with what was then considered an overbuilt construction, especially after his earlier success with

Ceramco, the Bruce Farr 67-footer of four years ago? The story has it that Blake had gone back to Farr for a Maxi design, but wanted an exclusivity clause in the contract, stating that Farr would not design any other Whitbread Maxis.

Farr agreed, providing *Lion* paid the design fee in triplicate. He already had three other tentative orders from Whitbread customers and after all, Kiwi pride or not, he was in business. Blake and Co. declined a Farr boat altogether opting for fellow countryman Ron Holland, their theory being that they wanted an advantage in design first and foremost and not just a pace horse.

As an underdog, Digby would have been hard to criticize in any case, but Blake, as favorite, had not come through. The people in the know and there were many, as well as the public (ask any cab driver), who knew enough, were putting tremendous pressure on his *Lion* camp. At this half-way point, although *Lion* was only 26 minutes behind, it seemed clear that, if *NZI* could hold together, it would be no contest – and no mercy for the Auckland 'city slickers.'

All this could not have come at a better time for *NZI* or at a worse time for *Lion*. Both syndicates were stretching their resources; Digby's by normal practice and *Lion*'s because of the rudder and spinnaker disasters coming up to the finish. Blake claimed he blew $30,000 *NZ* in sails – and with a $500,000 overdraft still outstanding.

NZI religiously went sailing most afternoons, taking the general public for a few dollars each, lending an appealing air of poverty to their efforts, while Digby and his syndicate negotiated for the real money behind closed doors. Given the facts of boatspeed, their tenacity, their public appeal and the results as evidence they had a strong bargaining chip. Blake stuck to his theories of the 'bomb proof' approach (he could now do little else) hoping publicly for as much bad weather as the Southern Ocean had to offer. Nobody realized just how soon his methods would be vindicated.

At the other end of the publicity spectrum, *Norsk Data GB* was again looking for new crew. Some had left on schedule while others had opted out with a gutful of being wet, cold and in a muddle for the privilege of an £8,000 investment, a tidy sum by anyone's standards and one that some journalist pointed out was more expensive than an around-the-world-cruise on the *QE II*. Skipper Bob Salmon was not to be deterred, however, and went public in his 'conscription' campaign offering berths on a 'first come, first serve' basis for the voyage around Cape Horn.

Malcolm McKeag, writing in 'Yachts and Yachting' recounted an incident in Auckland that, even if is not completely true, revealed Bob's unabashed methods:

'A hopeful recruit arrived on the boat one afternoon: 'Have you got $6,000?' asked Bob.

'Yes'

'Welcome aboard.'"

"Later," writes McKeag, "the lad turned up with his seabag in one hand, the $6,000 in the other. Bob shook his hand, extracted the money, showed him where to stow his gear and turned to his wife Beryl, 'Here you are, darling, take this and pay so and so will you?'"

It must be one of the few (if not the only) anomalies in colonial communities that the aboriginal population has not only survived and become a cultural centerpiece, but also held in great respect. So it is with the Maoris of New Zealand. For a variety of reasons the Maori Wars in the 1800s didn't have the completely disastrous effect on the natives as did comparable conflicts in Australia, America, and everywhere else for that matter. Although the Waitanga 'Treaty' of 1840 was far from the end of the conflict, it was the official inception of the territory of New Zealand into colonial status and an official acknowledgement from the Crown of certain Maori rights including the ownership of land. Of course, then as now, that treaty was resented by many Maori chiefs as unfair, but what was left was enough for them to rebuild their culture itself into what we know today. In a mixed population of 3 million people, the Maoris (also now largely of mixed descent) account for over 300,000, and most of those identify with their ancestors rather than with what they call the 'pakeha', white visitors.

It was a great privilege and an honor when the Oreiki Maori, the local chapter in Auckland, invited the crew of *Drum* to a welcoming ceremony – five weeks after our arrival. Their 'Marae,' or assembly place, the highest ground in Auckland, overlooked the entire gulf. The Maoris are of Polynesian origin. Legend has it that they arrived by canoe in antiquity. Their spiritual beliefs are based on natural phenomenon and their Gods of all living things are remembered through elaborate carvings and totems adorning the Marae.

We were told that we were being honored with a 'Three Challenge' welcome, which apparently is only reserved for, as they explained it, "people as high up as the Queen of England." The Maoris, like everyone else are smart enough to be moving with the times; Simon Le Bon, a rockstar, had been elevated almost to royalty that day.

We made every effort to make sure Simon, our spiritual leader, was there on time, but of course, in rock music protocal, he was so late to the extent that the show had to go on before he did. So it came to be that this humble yacht skipper from the suburbs of Chicago had to confront a fully dressed Maori warrior (with the sun in my eyes) at the entrance to the Marae.

The drill was that each time this warrior of severe aspect offered a branch by placing it in front of me, I was to pick it up and advance on him. All the while he would yell and spit at me testing my nerve with a wooden sword with which he damn near took my nose off (an easy target reckoned Patrick). He must have enjoyed himself coming as close as he dared and I can hardly imagine him taking the chance with Le Bon, let alone the Queen, as the press was of course, standing by in the wings. I made it with flying colors, but I had no idea that the big test was still due to come and would cause us great embarrassment.

We were summarily seated and entertained with a Maori 'haka' or tribal dance, the men, women, and children enjoying it all as much as we were. Someone once said that there is no worse museum in the world than the human one, and I normally loathe native people being put on exhibition, but this was quite different. We were on Auckland's highest ground, looking out to a blue sea, green islands and pure air. The confident smiles, the music, and the speech by the old man who spoke no English had the effect of leaving us in no doubt of whose country we were in, and that we were welcome.

I was invited to make a speech on our behalf which in those circumstances was easy for me. The speech I was prepared for, but not for the tradition that requires a song from the group after the leader has said his piece. How sad it is that most of us had no ability in this simple form of impromptu expression.

After a painfully embarrassed silence, Chuck Gates grabbed one of the Maori guitars and deftly led us in 'Blowin in the Wind,' which we barely struggled through. Having joined the boat only three days before, the crew was suspicious of him, as was natural with any unknown entity, especially one who is the skipper's 'friend' and who had admitted to them he hadn't been ocean racing for over six years.

My oldest friend from Chicago, and one of the most talented natural sailors I know, Gates soon enough proved his ability on the race course, but this simple demonstration at just the right time had not only earned him the immediate respect of the others, but saved our face with our Maori hosts. Simon eventually arrived, thereby fullfilling the obligation of signing hundreds of autographs for the kids. So ended a successful and interesting day.

The time to depart had come all too soon. At least this time we were supremely well rested and truly ready for the second half of our odyssey. While the crew put the last minute touches to the boat, I came home depressed, something quite minor having gone wrong.

Instead of sympathy, De gave me a good dressing down that evening when she told me, "Listen you, what do you have to complain about? You're a Maxi skipper in the Whitbread, making TV commercials, flying around in helicopters, just did a Maxi series in front of hundreds of thousands of people, wined and dined by the city of Auckland, welcomed by the Maoris and took a holiday and climbed a bloomin' mountain! – what more do you want out of life?" She was, of course, only too right.

11 · Leg Three: Leave Cape Horn to Port

You gone too far this time
But I'm dancing on the valentine
I tell you somebody's fooling around
With my chances on the dangerline
I'll cross that bridge when I find it
Another day to make my stand
High time is no time for deciding
If I should find a helping hand

Simon Le Bon 'The Reflex'

February 14th was billed to be the biggest spectator sporting event in the history of the southern hemisphere. 25 aircraft and 22 helicopters were licensed to fly that day (twice the number assigned to the seventh race of the America's Cup in 1983) with journalists and camera men bringing the start live to all New Zealand. In addition, 200,000 were expected to be there in person, in boats and on shore.

It is difficult to say goodbye to New Zealand, even after a six-week stopover. Furthermore, tackling the rigors of the Southern Ocean did not make this the best of times. Bob and his wife Anne, owners of the Westhaven Motel where we were billeted, had sent us off with a champagne breakfast that morning. I had no appetite, however, and can remember an uneasy feeling of foreboding. Perhaps it was purely reluctance to leave what had been exceptionally good times on shore. For a traveller who loves the place, but has had to endure three English winters, it is ironic that the British had sent convicts and undesirables to colonize this paradise. It was clear to me who has now had the last laugh.

There was little to think about that last morning other than to get down to the boat on time. Our spare parts and unneeded sails had all been neatly boxed up the day before and were in the customs shed, ready to be shipped back to England by sea freight. A few smaller boxes with other spares were in a different pile waiting to be air freighted to Uruguay and to this we added all our shore bags and personal gear, now bursting with mementos we had collected along the way. Our sea-freight-container cum workshop had gone direct from South Africa to Uruguay.

Rick arrived with double his allowance in gear bags, and he explained that half were Micky's. Sharing a room with three others he was the only one to sleep there that night and while Richard and Mario eventually surfaced to collect their things at the 11th hour, Micky had not made the last car load. I was not particularly worried about this or anything else for that matter as we pushed and shoved our way through the crowd choking the seawall.

On board, the mood was different. All those weeks of undivided attention from our fans and supporters suddenly became too much, and I was anxious to got away from it all. I had refused to sign any more autographs and even the little girls on the jetty noticed it when they shouted "Smile!"

"Becoming a pain in the ass," said Filthy, expressing in his own way my exact sentiments. And even Simon, on board at the appointed time, could manage only half-hearted waves and forced smiles. This was no ordinary gig he was about to perform, and I'm sure it wasn't the fans he had his mind on at that moment. I could sympathize with him.

The Oreiki Maori had come down in full dress to give us a Maori farewell. They did their best to dance and sing to us while balancing on a barge rolling and heaving from the wakes of what appeared to be thousands of spectator craft. With only ten minutes until departure time, I did a head count. With 18 on board we were one short. It was Micky. The guys said something about a new girl friend, and I started to have a sick feeling. His on-time record was not impressive and I was quickly reminded about how he had missed the boat in Ireland and how he had forgotten to fill the water tanks in Cape Town.

However, he turned up with the girl in tow soon after. There were tears running down her face when he jumped down the ladder, and I noticed that he looked better than the others who had been on the drink until the early hours. We cast off and made our way to the starting line.

A light northeasterly blowing down the gulf would give us a short reach and then a beat out through the islands. The gun was scheduled to go off (fired by the Prime Minister David Lange no less) at 1100 and we had no problem maneuvering among the spectator craft. A few of us carried walky-talky radios linked in to Peter Montgomery, and we gave interviews both during and after the start live on TV and radio which was an incredibly well organized and clever way of making a sailboat race interesting for the public, an activity described by many as one compared to watching grass grow.

Anything that could float was out in the harbor, but most of us had few problems. Not so for Digby Taylor. He complained to the Race

Committee that the spectator boats were constantly getting in his way. His lack of rapport with his own countrymen was picked up by a journalist who later wrote:

> "The ever-whining Digby Taylor, skipper of *NZI Enterprise* complained about the behaviour of a few spectator craft, but then Digby complains about nearly everything. More than anyone else he has appealed for and is relying upon other people's money to enable him to do this race, and he can hardly complain when other people want to come along and watch him spend it. Compared to the shambles laid on by English yachtsmen in The Solent at the race start itself, Auckland's sailors were as well drilled as a Fleet review."

As he did in 1981 with *Ceramco*, Blake and *Lion* won the start to leeward. Briefly we were second, but the bigger *Cote d'Or* soon passed both ourselves and *Lion*. *Cote d'Or* was first to the turning buoy and had no trouble maintaining her lead on the beat for the rest of the day.

It was a sunny, warm, southern hemisphere afternoon and by 1500 we were well through the archipelago and only our personal support craft stood by us. There is an old tradition among sailors and their girlfriends, and so it was that all the women lined up on the side of the cruiser and when Filthy shouted "Come on girls, show us your tits!" they dutifully bared their chests to a big cheer as the coxswain peeled off to starboard and headed for home. Once again we were left only with memories and our own company. Cape Horn lay 4,000 miles away and we all knew there would be some heavy going on the way.

Tacking on the shifts all day in the medium air was pleasant work, but what was surprising was that although *Cote d'Or* and *UBS* had established a small lead, we were holding *AP* with no problem. Upon closer inspection we discovered that they were flying an old Dacron Medium No. 1 genoa while we had a new Kevlar jib. As expected, when the wind did freshen she began to roll through us.

Red Mercury Island was our last turning mark and from there we sagged off on a beam reach out into the Bay of Plenty and the endless Pacific Ocean beyond. A large anticyclone was established to the east, very similar to the situation in the Second Leg and in the steady reach the standings had taken on an all too familiar pattern by the next evening; the two leaders had done what's known as 'horizon job' on us, while *NZI* was also ahead, but her stern light was still in sight. Once again, both *Lion* and *Drum* brought up the rear of the Maxi fleet, almost as if we were designed to do so.

It was ironical after our protest with *NZI* on Leg One that only 10 hours after the start our battery charger packed up. We normally ran our Volvo 5 KVA generator several hours every day to boost our service batteries. We still would have been able to run the watermaker, the electric kettle and the microwave, but we would have to run the main engine to charge the batteries through the 125 amp alternator. Of course, the big engine gulped 12 liters of diesel per hour in comparison to the 2 used by the downed generator. Fuel consumption would require austerity measures. First on the list would be the charging of the batteries for the camera and video equipment.

On his own initiative, Roger had been compiling a video record of our trials and tribulations, and the results were so good that he had landed a contract with Swedish television. He lost no time in organizing a spare charger to be flown out to the Chatham Islands which we were due to pass that evening. It would be our last piece of real estate until the Horn.

The rules state that you can put in anywhere for repairs without penalty, but the proposal of an airdrop would incur a time penalty equal to the estimated time it would take to get into port. This same request had already been denied *NZI* on Leg One from the Canaries.

Roger was adamant that we must pick up the spare somehow, penalty or not. We would probably lose upwards of three hours in doing so, and I knew this would not wear well with the crew, nor with myself for that matter. I could already see the scenario of missing a place in Uruguay by one hour because we were penalized four. On the other hand, there also was John Toon to consider. He was on board, shooting 16mm movie film for the revived *Drum* movie to be produced by Mike and Paul. He had to have the charger for his battery packs and ancillary equipment.

I was about to resign myself to the decision knowing that it would be unpopular, when I discovered that the tenacious Magnus Olsson, who had been tinkering with the charger for the last 6 hours, had jury-rigged it so it was putting out 40 amps, or half power. With un-flagging enthusiasm and almost treating this electrical problem as a mental exercise, he was delighted with his success, and we all were delighted with him. The movie makers decided to risk it, and we cancelled the attempt to pick up the spare.

I was feeling relaxed, almost redundant in a way, as we were reaching along in benign conditions. Patrick had taken over my role of B watch captain. My plan was to spend less time on deck and paying more attention to tactics.

The watches were allocated as follows:

A	B	C	D
Magnus	Patrick	PJW	Mugsy
Paul	Skip	Micky	Roger
Rick	Mario	Bill	Chuck
Neil	Simon	Filthy	Mike
Janne			

Richard, cooking; JohnToon, camera

At 1930 local time we crossed the 180th meridian and earned another February 16th and another Sunday. But unlike Sunday at home with a long sleep-in and a big pancake breakfast, it was just like any other day: up at 0630 for the bowl of muesli and on deck by 0700. At least the weather was beautiful.

On my last two trips through these same waters, it had not been so easy. On *King's Legend* there had been controversy about date-lines, time changes, and the effect they had on celestial navigation. It was New Year's Eve, to boot.

"Shit, we're more than half way around the world," I can remember Mike Clancy declaring, "we've crossed the Equator with no party and in miserable weather, no celebration at the Tropics or the Greenwich Meridian and I'll be damned if I'll let this opportunity slip by." At the time, everyone thought it a great idea.

To make things even more interesting, by now it was blowing 45 knots from the southeast – dead against us. Nevertheless, the atmosphere below decks rivaled any at dockside as we charged along under a storm jib, with four reefs in the main, in a dangerous situation and treating it all in a manner I could hardly see myself encouraging now.

I will never forget the feeling coming back on deck, high as a kite, to stand my four-hour watch from 0200 to 0600 (2 of the others never made it, having passed out below). I sat there in the cockpit, listening to the storm as the Southern Ocean seas combed the entire deck, and checked my lifeharness clip every two minutes. All one can say about foolhardy experiences one was lucky enough to have lived through is that they were fun at the time.

On *Alaska Eagle*, it had been much the same; the International Dateline and New Years' Eve on a double bill, but then we had been downwind. On some boats New Year's celebrations were delayed until the wind abated. This time on *Drum* I can hardly remember the dateline being acknowledged at all, the complimentary case of 12 oz bottles of Long John Whiskey from the Race sponsor lying untouched in the bilge.

The North East corner of the Chatham Islands was 20 miles off the starboard beam in the early evening of the third night out. 1300 miles off New Zealand's South Island, the few permanent residents raise sheep by the thousands and provided a port facility for the offshore fishing fleet from the mainland. John Toon had been there, and he said there was little else.

Only 25 miles long, the island was dead on our track. It split the fleet early, precipitating a tactical pattern that would be adhered to throughout the leg; *UBS, Cote d'Or* and *NZI* were up the middle with us trailing, while *Lion* was already 60 miles to the northeast of us skirting the edge of the high. *AP* had different ideas and soon was 60 miles southwest of us, obviously going for the option that favored the shorter southerly track. This was attempted by *Lion* on the second leg with disastrous results. On the other hand, they might get a good jump on the fleet at the beginning by finding better winds farther from the high that was already tickling *Lion*.

We had cleared the corner of the island with the spinnaker set, but just. During the approach I had the unpleasant task of asking Paul to relinquish the wheel in this critical stage. Roger had got me up, all in a state, fearing that if we didn't keep the best helmsman on we would not clear the foul ground off the headland. I was not happy having to do the dirty work; it was the watch captain's responsibility to administer the helming. In an afterguard/owner's meeting in Auckland, we had all agreed that the best helmsman should steer whenever possible and certainly we should take no risks with beginners (i.e. the owners and a few others) in marginal conditions.

I came on deck to find Magnus sitting to weather, looking apprehensive, but unable to do anything about it. It was not surprising that half the time we were either close to broaching with the spinnaker pressed to the breaking point or were steering too low, too conservatively. The sad part of it was, that Magnus, with his courteous, jovial manner, would have done a better job of relieving Paul than I did. It is no easy task and certainly thankless, telling anyone to stand down because he is steering poorly, especially if he is the owner wanting pleasure for his massive investment. However, there would be many other times ahead where he would get his fill.

Watch Captain Phil Wade was having his own problems. I heard the first harsh words spoken on board when he asked Filthy to man the grinders. He was told to 'fuck-off' and then got slapped in the chest, almost like a hesitant love pat, really. Apparently Filthy had remembered the chain of command as well as the size of Phil Wade. "All I told him to do was go to the winch and he turned around and hit me!" explained Phil seeing the humour in it all. For some reason Filthy had been in a foul mood from the start, leaving himself wide open to be parodied in the head. The list eventually would read:

Filthy is on the 'rag' because:
1. He has a spotty bum?
2. He hates foreigners
3. He is a foreigner!
4. Got no pussy in New Zealand
5. He's a frustrated mountaineer
6. Mario cut up his light spin sheet for a leech cord
7. Somebody used the changing sheet for a 'down-fucker'
   ad infinitum

These minor altercations were to be expected. We knew each other too well for disagreements to be taken to heart. For better or for worse we were stuck with each other for the duration. Neil would write in his diary during the third leg:

Not so long ago, I remember, we were falling over each other in our enthusiasm to make our mark. During last summer in England, many of us, despite lengthy experience in ocean racing, were aware of the fact that this was something slightly different. If we were to spend the next year in close quarters with these people, many of whom were complete strangers, then we wanted to establish the ground rules early. All too aware of Skip's right to get rid of anyone at a moment's notice we determined to shine. Those dismissed were reminded to return their foul weather gear, and Skip's warning to us at an early stage not to write our names in the newly issued clothing became a standing joke among us lads. However, after 12,000 miles of racing together, we hold no more surprises for each other, and a more relaxed atmosphere prevails. Observations from Skip which six months ago evoked open-mouthed admiration are now greeted with the far more natural howls of derision. He's stuck with us now and our names are boldly printed on every item. As for the others, we are lucky enough to have a very friendly atmosphere on board, and have so far avoided serious argument. There is plenty of healthy piss-taking, and any of us attempting to put on airs is rapidly deflated. It's all rather like being at boarding school, or on National Service; not exactly a big happy family, but certainly relaxed and enjoyable company.

It was good news indeed, that Richard had weathered what was a difficult period for him as well as for his clientele. His new-found popularity in the galley had been the outcome of a long, uphill battle from his culinary nadir on Leg Two. I recorded first impressions of the new Alliance Freeze-Dried menu from New Zealand that night in my log, making the point however good it was, it was freeze dried, none-the-less:

We had a tasty, completely freeze-dried meal tonight, the Fish Supreme swimming in liberal quantities of potato mash sprinkled with peas and corn; an homogenous mixture that would have done credit to the best of old people's homes where eating usually requires no chewing and a fast, clear passage through furred up plumbing.

To say Richard had been given more than an ultimatum in Auckland was putting it mildly. The crew did not hesitate to berate him in public and expose his shortcomings to Mike, Simon, and in particular to Paul, a self-proclaimed gastronome. Paul made it his personal crusade to oversee the provisioning as he had no intention of 'roughing it.' We could easily have replaced Richard, but though there was much talk of giving him the 'bullet,' I decided that we should keep him for the simple reason that, although what he had served had been absolute rubbish, he at least shovelled it out on time without fail, even under some pretty appalling conditions. In addition to this he was good on deck and strong as an ox. Most importantly, he weathered the most abusive treatment with an air of resignation, getting along with everyone far better than could be expected.

The 'day bags' of food, each in their own sealed garbage bags, weighed about 14 kilos (30lb). The vacuum-packed meats were stowed in the bilge to keep them cool, while the fresh vegetables, fruits and eggs were stowed in wire bins aft where they would be dry, safe from bruising, and have plenty of circulation. In the southern legs spoilage was virtually nill.

We were a testament to the notion that one can survive without refrigeration. Dr. Johnson once said, "Conveniences are never missed where they were never enjoyed." Admittedly, for most of us it was difficult to adjust to not having cool drinks in the tropics. However, this was a minor matter since most of the race was sailed in cool parts of the world. Actually, there is very little indeed that needs refrigeration and the saving in weight of the machinery and the peace of mind of not having to repair it when it inevitably goes wrong far outweigh cool drinks – at least to my way of thinking.

This business of weight-saving is certainly first and foremost on everyone's mind in a yacht race. Our main difficulty on *Drum*, however, was due to the fact that our designed displacement was about 12,000 pounds more than the Farr boats. This we could do nothing about. Assuming water and fuel are kept to acceptable minimums and the sails, rigging and tool inventories are adequate, the quantity versus the quality of the food always remains as the great topic of discussion. Although a few hundred pounds seems insignificant, it is 'extra' none-the-less.

NZI seemed to carry the weight problem to extremes claiming a total food supply of 350 kilos for 16 people per leg. Although we had three more mouths to feed, *NZI* was carrying only half of our estimate for Leg Three. Part of this was also due to having modified our original spartan theories (abandoned would be a better word). Assuming we could find good quality freeze-dried food I had been in favor of a completely freeze-dried menu plus dried rice, pastas, and potato flakes, supplemented only by fresh onions and garlic.

We all know that food is a great morale booster when sailing over distance. On cruising passages when, for long stretches of time, there is little else to do or think about, the subject of food is a dominant one, and I take pleasure in spending time in the galley conjuring up meals to test on my victims. Racing is different, however, if you assume we have our thoughts rivetted on the race and boat performance first and

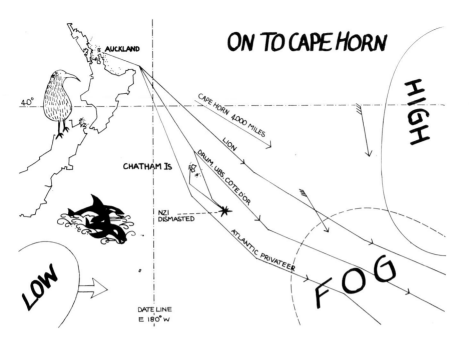

AUCKLAND

40°

CAPE HORN 4000 MILES

LION

DRUM UBS COTE D'OR

CHATHAM IS

NZI DISMASTED

ATLANTIC PRIVATEER

HIGH

FOG

LOW

DATE LINE
E 180° W

on our stomachs second. Possibly I am more suited and used to limited privation for long periods quite content to shove down whatever was going (and complimenting the cook as a habit without thinking about it) and immediately focusing my thoughts back to the race. Of course, if you are winning the race it is incredible how minor even significant irritations become in the grand scheme of things and I admit I was not, at times sensitive to the fact that for most of the first half of the race since we were not doing well, better food would have improved the crew's spirits. For these reasons the galley had to improve to avoid a mass rebellion.

Paul was completely justified in saying that a few tins of this and few tins of that would make not the slightest difference, and in this he had the majority of the crew's whole-hearted support. But when the dam is breached, the flood will follow, and we left Auckland with about 15 per cent more weight in food per man than we had carried out of Cape Town. It was equivalent to carrying an extra crewman (we already had 19) and all his gear.

For example, I completely lost out on the issue of carrying fresh eggs. With 19 in crew and assuming it takes three eggs per man to make enough scrambled eggs, it would require 57 eggs for a breakfast! Egg powder, which we had used before, seemed to make far better sense as I could hardly imagine the cook willing to fry 19 pairs of eggs individually, even in good conditions, or so I had thought. On the morning of February 18th we had a most inspiring breakfast, and I recorded the events in my log:

This morning Richard cooked a fried egg breakfast with bacon and two loaves of fresh bread — the answer to almost everyone's complaint. When Paul surfaced, a little queezy, complaining about the spicy sausages of yesterday, he asked Richard, would you believe it? for scrambled eggs! The cook was taken completely aback, having just busted his balls for two hours frying up individual slices of bacon and eggs in a galley heeled over 25 degrees and this guy comes along and wants scrambled! After the ensuing fray where the cook gave in, I came below to hit the head, thoughts of clever grafitti running through my mind, when I found Richard, alone in the galley, just shaking his head. We looked at one another and broke out laughing.

Little did we know that while the great egg controversy was raging, *NZI* was cleaning up after a disaster and heading back in the other direction. In the early hours she had been reaching along quite happily when the mast buckled and then broke in two places. They would ascertain later that what was an old fashioned rigging terminal, swaged on to the rod of the jumper stay, had simply pulled out and with that *NZI* was, as 'Drumspeak' had it, 'Reg Bistry' (cockney slang for history). By the time we had received the news on the mid-day 'chat show,' the disheartened crew had secured the pieces to the deck and were already under jury rig and motor, bound back up to the Chathams.

Of course, this was a shock to us, but I remember my immediate fascination of what it must have been like on *Lion*. It was no secret to anyone that there was no love lost between Digby and Peter, both poles apart in their methods and attitudes. Unfairly or not, I imagined a perverse scenario on *Lion* when they got the news; yelling and cheering, party hats, fog horns blaring and general celebration, with Blake sitting there in the center of it all in silence, like a guru, with an 'I told them so' look on his face.

It turned out that I wasn't far from the mark. One of the more senior members of the *Lion* crew told me later that the behaviour of the younger guys was, in his word, 'disgusting.'

"We know how you feel," said Peter to Digby over the SSB, referring to the *Ceramco* debacle in 1981, "My commiserations. Enjoy the Chathams. *Lion* clear."

It is hard not to derive some pleasure from competitors' failures. I think that during Leg One all the crews would have been truly sorry if *AP* had not continued after her dismasting. She was good competition and good company. But as time wears on and the war wounds accumulate, one finds oneself less benevolent. We had had our share of problems, and now for us, *NZI*'s dismasting meant a safe third place, that is, if we could hold together for the rest of the race.

A Whitbread axiom holds that most of the race is won or lost through organization before the start. It was common knowledge that

NZI was not as well managed and had not had the luxury of long sea trials like *UBS* or *Lion*. After the race, Bruce Farr compared his three designs and described his early misgivings about *NZI* in *Seahorse Magazine*:

> "With *NZI Enterprise* our concern stemmed from the fact that we were never involved in much of the engineering of the boat or its construction so we really didn't know what they had.
>
> There were some aspects of the rig which looked pretty agricultural. That doesn't necessarily mean they were bad, but there were a lot of unusual ways of doing things and there were different systems for attaching things, such as shroud anchorages.
>
> Some of these were simple systems and maybe were good systems. But we couldn't help wondering whether the engineering had been done properly and everything had been thought through. As it turned out, I guess you have to say that maybe they were not."

We all knew that, despite *NZI*'s short-lived effort to fly in a new mast section and repair the rig in the Chathams, we had seen the last of her. Rumour had it that most of the crew had walked off the job, having not the slightest interest in re-erecting what had fallen down twice.

On that same day we also tuned in and spoke to James Hatfield on board *British Heart*, a 25-foot cruiser, at 37°14′ South, 178°55′ West. He was sailing singlehanded around the world to raise money for a heart fund. The skipper, an ex-heart patient himself, had stopped in the Bay of Islands when *Drum* was there and had met several of our crew. We agreed to monitor his progress for the British press. After Roger bored him into a state of depression in 15 minutes, Simon got on the radio and cheered him up.

I can remember this encounter also put me briefly in a state of depression while I thought to myself, "What the hell am I doing out here on these big yachts, and what good am I doing for anybody else except myself?" I recalled reading years ago when a journalist asked a skipper about how he felt being part of the American Admiral's Cup Team. His sobering reply will always stick in my mind as an accurate opinion we sometimes have of our little world on racing boats; "Nice thing to do. I'm happy about it . . . If you discover a cure for cancer you should be impressed with yourself . . . But winning sailboat races? I don't think so. Nice thing to do though." For reasons other than sailing alone in a small boat, I had hoped Hatfield would somehow make it. (He didn't; he capsized near Cape Horn but, luckily, was rescued.)

We crossed south of the 50th parallel on the 19th. Throughout the next 48 hours conditions were so steady as to be almost boring. We changed from the Kevlar to the Dacron mainsail, anticipating some heavy running soon, but after the swap, which took 35 minutes because we had to dismantle the reefing line blocks sewn to the leech of the sail, we hoisted the Dacron only to find out that the leech cord repair Mugsy had done in Auckland was completely bogus. Patrick took one pull on the block and tackle that controls the leech cord wire and the whole thing gave way. He nearly almost fell backwards over the lifelines. Water temperature 7°C (45°F)!

Mugsy went aloft at first light and came down proclaiming the whole thing a mess. The pressed sleeves on the wire were the wrong size, which left us no choice but to change back to the Kevlar and repair the Dacron. With great effort and considerable cursing we struggled the new main out the hatch once again. Time: 23 minutes, hoist to hoist.

Our sailmakers were having a tough time of it on this leg, even though the going was easy. Mario had spent 10 hours fixing and retiming our sewing machine the day before the mainsail episode. Mugsy and Mario are the two smallest people on board and it is only with great effort that they can manipulate and repair these huge, unwieldly pieces of material. To understand what it is like to repair, for example, a blown spinnaker at sea, think of approximately 4700 sq ft of sail, of a complicated panel design, ripped to shreds and immersed in seawater. Next, imagine that sodden, tangled mass in a space the size of a small bathroom with a hair dryer, a pair of scissors, and a sewing machine. Finally, imagine trying to put it back together.

UBS was only 20 miles ahead and we were on line with everyone else after 5 days out. In these moderate conditions, the boat seemed to be performing well and hanging in there. The crew were far more alert, our tactics were sound, and the improved rudder was a big help. I had just hoped we would not have trouble with broken steering cables. I had not known then that Patrick recorded the same thoughts in his log on the 21st:

It seems the steering is a definite improvement; the boat feels more responsive and easier to 'get in the groove.' I was feeling quite smug about all of this until I discovered today that one of the cables had worn completely through due to the chafe because of the appalling 'jury rig' I did in Auckland when I had to realign the whole system. One set of cables gone in one week. Yikes! At this rate we'll run out of spare cables before Punta del Este, which is a bit of a worry. So far I'm keeping quiet about this.

After one week out we had hardly seen more than 20 knots of wind and we were already closing in on 56 degrees South. Visibility was bad as the warm northerly still blowing into the high in front of us condensed to form fog and sea smoke. We had crossed the Antarctic Convergence again and the water temperature plummeted to 2.5°C (36.5°F). With the decks dry and little undue pressure there was little to complain about and we were doing as well as we could hope in the light winds. This was a perfect way for Paul and Simon to get into the swing of things. They seemed to be enjoying it all. Mugsy recorded his impressions of them during these first days:

Paul, Mike and Simon are fitting in extremely well thus far, Mike especially. He's a bit of a mentor to the other two, having done the first leg, and it's great to hear him giving them advice. Both he and Paul have crossed oceans before, but this is Simon's first time at sea for any length of time.

He was on TV AM from England yesterday; his interview with footage of the start in Auckland. He's a bit of a clown and definitely a showman when he gets on the air. He's a very normal guy most of the time, but give him a mike and an audience and his whole personality changes. I must confess I don't know his music at all, but I listened to the 'Arcadia' tape and I really like it. It seems strange to have him on board knowing his status as a rockstar. Still he fits in just great and is doing a good job on deck. He was just behind me on the foredeck last night pulling down the headsail and working like a slave. I think he'll work out just fine.

We were only just beginning to realize the value of John Toon. With three owners on board, all in business and one wtih a pregnant wife, not to mention the normal duties, the radio seemed to be tuned up 24 hours a day. Roger and I had made it clear we could not spend much of our time involved in making telephone calls. As they had to spend their 'on watch' time on deck, it was left up to the unfortunate Toon to spend hours at the radio trying to make link calls on their behalf via Wellington Radio and then later Portishead. It was fortunate for them that the weather was so dull and benign as to make filming uninteresting and unfortunate for John that he was so good at the radio.

After spending hours down below monitoring different channels and waiting for your turn to come up, it is difficult not to acquire what may be described as a 'soap opera' mentality. I admit to a certain perverse pleasure in listening in to personal conversations on the high seas, and can't help being fascinated by some of the tragedies that merchant seaman go through in talking to their wives who are somewhere up in the North of England on a cold winter's day. In the worst case, and not uncommon, the wife has run off with the best friend from back home, but more typically what is usually a one-sided dissertation revolves around the smashed up car, the sick children, the leaky roof and the salary payments not coming in on time. While the woman rambles on with abandon, the seaman, only too aware that people are listening, will usually just sigh or mutter "Uh-huh."

The end is always the same. "Do you love me?" "Uh huh." "Are you sure you love me?" "Uh huh."

This light entertainment is not confined to the British stage as I was humorously reminded when Toon called me to the radio to listen to some of my own countrymen; in this case a 'Good Ole Boy' on an oil rig somewhere in the Pacific, broad of Southern accent and sporting an amusing limited vocabulary:

The wife: "Did you send last month's check?"
The man: "Roger."
The wife: "I've just picked out the new furniture. I hope you'll like it."
The man: "That's a roger on that."
The wife: "Will you be home for Easter?"
The man: "Negative"
The wife: "You know, I just can't go on like this with you away all the time."
The man: "That's a roger."
The wife: "Do you love me?"
The man: "Rrrroger!"

Richard got a 'thumbs down' from Paul for the corned beef hash on the 22nd. Something to do with adding too much water and no garlic. The chili passed the test the next day however, which kept them both happy for the next 24 hours.

With a freshening breeze we changed from the 1.5 oz spinnaker to the 2.2 oz that afternoon, right in the middle of rolling out the pastry. It is an established tradition that I bake one apple pie during the race.

Mugsy, a veteran of three out of my four Southern Ocean excursions, made the observation that the first pie on *Independent Endeavour* in the Parmelia Race warranted a few flash pictures, while the one on *Alaska Eagle* was filmed by 8mm motion picture. As I carefully maneuvered the masterpiece from the oven this time, it was obvious multi-media had arrived in the Southern Ocean as the press core assailed me with flash, studio lights, video and 16mm documentary film camera. Possibly they already knew this sequence was not to be repeated.

John Toon shoved the microphone in my face and asked me where I learned my baking skills. "After the experience on *Alaska Eagle*," I told him, "I retired to my girl friend's parents' place and learned how to bake bread as therapy for acute anxiety and depression."

Levelling off around the 55th parallel, well on our way to the Horn now 2500 miles away, a few incidents occurred that quickly changed the complacent mood on board. *AP* was the first to report 'ice' on the

22nd only 40 miles to the south of us. Thoughts about not going any further south to avoid the danger were soon rendered futile when the next day *Lion* reported a large berg about the same distance to the north. *Philips* and *Norsk Data* reported visual sightings astern. We were left in no doubt that we were right in there with them. Although the wind had freshened from astern and we were running hard, its direction was still well north of west bringing a relatively warm wind over the colder sea. The resulting fog and mist had lowered the visibility to less than half a mile most of the time.

It was interesting observing how the crew handled this news. Most of the guys owned up to a limited enthusiasm at the prospect of seeing ice, while Chuck and a few others were absolutely delighted. "I came on this leg for three reasons," he loudly announced, as usual bubbling over with anticipation, "to round Cape Horn, to do some heavy duty surfing, and to see icebergs. God damn-it, I didn't come all the way from Chicago to be disappointed, ya hooo!"

Careening along at 11 to 18 knots into the milky mist, the air was so thick and the atmosphere non-descript so as to become an homogenous soup, not unlike diving in mid ocean. At times the sky overhead would clear and with dusk approaching the light filtering through the sea smoke cast curious colors on our deck, sails and faces. It took little imagination to understand that a few people on board were becoming increasingly apprehensive about this 'magical mystery tour'.

Paul must have asked me five times about growlers and bergy bits, the former being chunks of ice breaking the surface, the latter can be described as having the aspect of a modest size house. The big bergs I was not worried about because even if we couldn't see them, we would certainly pick them up on radar. In clear visibility I have seen them glow in the dark, irrespective of cloud cover or moon, and there had always been plenty of time to alter course. The small chunks were a worry. They could not be pick up by radar, and on a dark night a growler resembled a breaking wave and might easily be recognized only after it is too late.

"Surely the growlers will bounce off if we hit them," Paul said. It was half statement, half question. "No," I said "They would most likely hole the bows and we would sink in a matter of minutes." That night, with an iceberg watch at the shrouds, we saw nothing, but three came up on radar, the closest 2 miles to starboard.

The 23rd was a spectacular day's sail. Hard pressed with the big 2.2 oz up, on the edge of control, we took the opportunity to change back to the Dacron mainsail. It was not an easy task running dead down wind. We stabilized the boat with two poles on the spinnaker and installed our best driver, Magnus, on the helm. Then the wind swung into the southwest and strengthened, and for a time we had to hoist the jib top and staysail to make course. On the reach, water once again (it had seemed ages ago) flooded the decks and misery re-entered our lives. My log describes the situation below:

As had been usual, water is literally cascading down the companionway hatch once again, Rick's repair in Auckland proving totally ineffectual. Paul, wearing his 'owner's hat' was outraged by this situation threatening to seek reimbursement from Huisman's who made the hatch and/or Moody's who had originally installed it. I could imagine their polite smiles upon hearing this news, much the same stoic smiles the crew are now wearing as they merrily go about their business as usual, like tourists enjoying a bit of annoying spray at Iguaso Falls.

With the water temperature at 2°C (35.6°F) and the night time air temperature at 3° to 4°, out came the 'survival suits.' Made by Helly Hansen of Norway, these one-piece jump suits were developed for the oil rig industry in the North Sea. Through his contacts in Scandinavia, Roger had offered the crew a chance to buy these on an individual basis for an extremely low price. They answered the need for a dry, warm outfit, unlike our foul weather gear but, not he assured me, because of the possibility of foundering on the second leg. Roger seldom wore his on Leg Two because the soles of the boots were too slippery. While in Auckland, however, they were replaced with effective yachting soles.

Since the suits were not normal crew issue, most of the guys couldn't afford them. Although I had bought one, I foresaw the problem they would cause and left mine in its plastic bag to be used only in an emergency, for anyone, at least that's what I promised myself. Neil captured the mood when nasty weather filled in:

The comforting familiarity of our little world has suddenly been shattered, and things will never be the same again. After weeks of coming on deck half-awake and being able to recognize each other under layers of clothing by the attitude of the head or a particular way of slouching, we are confronted with aliens in our midst. Not for them the standard uniform of Red Mustos and blue boots; they are decked out in the very latest in survival wear for environmental extremes. There has always been a kind of solace in knowing that the other guy's collar leaks too, or his boots don't dry, but now, thanks to the invasion, envy has raised its ugly head, and once again we must consider ourselves 'haves' or 'have nots.' Who are the lucky recipients of these perks? Why, the owners of course, and Roger. They have donned their one-piece rubber outfits, incorporating boots and hood, seeing themselves as guinea pigs for future yachtsmen.

Most of the fleet was now sailing due east, spread out along the latitude of Cape Horn. At 55° South, a degree of longitude equals only 34 miles and keeping pace with the time zones was a constant problem of juggling the watch system. A standard time zone is 15 degrees of longitude (24 hours × 15 degrees = 360° at any latitude) therefore, travelling at our average speed of over 250 miles per day, required a change about every two days. For practical purposes we changed two zones every four days.

The local ship's time had been adjusted two days before to GMT – 9, so dawn broke at about 0300 the morning of the 25th. A deep low was passing well to the south of us, and the night before the wind had strengthened with the first significant barometer drop since the start. The seas had built slowly and steadily, and we had had no problem carrying the big 2.2 oz spinnaker in 30 knots of true wind in superb surfing conditions. By first light, however, we were beginning to be unstable, and despite Patrick's opinion that we were not pushing hard enough, I ordered the change to the 90% Flanker.

'Bang!' went the trip shackle on the tack of the sail and one watch gathered the sail to the deck while the other watch rerigged for the narrower, flatter and more manageable Flanker. After a quick check of halyard, guy, and sheet chafe, the new sail was reset on the same gear. Within 10 minutes from 'hoist to hoist' we were drawing hard and once again on our way, barreling along at 20 knots plus on the surfs.

It was a cold morning, the air temperature was at about 3°C (37.4°F) and I remember our watch was glad to get below looking forward to some decent sleep, secure in the knowledge that the right sail was up for the conditions. We were down below for no more than 10 minutes, shedding our foul weathergear in the forepeak and sipping mugs of coffee when *Drum* again became unstable and rolled violently to weather indicating the helmsman was steering too low. He made one recovery, but the die was cast, and as he rolled out for the second time we knew it was curtains. As we grappled to hang on to what ever was handy, while cursing him roundly, we waited for the inevitable crash, but instead *Drum* came quietly to rest on her side, pinned down by the spinnaker gently licking the surface of the water.

For the second time we had gybed her 'Chinese' or 'all standing.' As I made my way aft, Neil had a look on his face that was a combination of fear and one that seemed to say, "Thank God I'm not the only one who has pulled this stunt!"

Pinned over more than 50° it was as much a shambles below as it was on deck. Groggy heads popped out from behind the curtains in the bunk modules, scowling and swearing, only to be peppered by paperback books, cassette tapes, and other carelessly stowed items. Simon had been on the high-seas radio talking to the office and was upended in his chair. He calmly told the secretary in London, "Seems we have a bit of a problem on deck, have to go now." Given the

Englishman's habit of understatement I could only imagine what she must have been thinking.

Struggling out the after hatch and cowering in the bottom of the cockpit, I found Filthy waist deep in water to leeward. He was trying to winch in the trip line while most of the others were fumbling around with the two preventers and trying to get the main boom across. The immediate danger was that if the preventer that held the boom aback suddenly broke it would sweep the deck, well below head height.

The spinnaker was still full and drawing, holding us securely on our side. The sheet and lazy-guy winches were three feet under water and inaccessible. The cleated lazy-guy was taking the sheet load, and the trip line had jammed with the pole-end submerged. In an act of courage Mario went forward and cast off the halyard. In a shower of sparks the wire raced around the winch drum and the tail shot out like cannon fire through the blocks and *Drum* slowly struggled to her feet. With some difficulty the main boom was eased in amidships, but not before a fouled piece of rigging collapsed three lifeline stanchions with the greatest of ease.

With the spinnaker safely fluttering above the surface of the water and no major damage done, I had a feeling that we had got out of this too easily. No sooner had the thought left my mind than the oversize parachute lifted clear of the water as the boat got underway and promptly blew into the after rigging taking out the weatherfax antenna, bending the Sat-Nav antenna and ripping off the after deck floodlight, before tearing itself to pieces on the backstays and again going overboard.

By this time all hands had come on deck and it took all eighteen of us to manhandle the sail up and over the lifelines, heaving and pulling in rhythm, foot-by-foot, sometimes inch-by-inch. A broken spinnaker pole topping lift, a chafed guy and sheet, and one half of the double-grooved headstay foil smashed and useless completed the damage list. The worst was to come.

The deck was a shambles of wires, ropes and hardware in incredible tangles, so the on-watch hoisted the forestaysail that is always hanked on for safety in case we had to go to weather in an emergency, and now served us as rough and ready sail area until the decks were cleared. Instinctively I went below and had a peek through our viewing tube directly above the propeller. My worst fears were justified when I spied what I presumed to be the bright yellow, spinnaker turtle streaming happily from the now fully opened two-bladed feathering propeller. A check at the viewing tube for the rudder aft confirmed that it was the twenty-foot-long spinnaker bag. Not taken below after the last set nor tied down, it had obviously washed off the deck during the gybe.

Things like weed, fish nets, and bits of line caught in the propeller are a constant problem on a racing boat. We knew from experience that if the blades were misaligned and open, the speed loss could easily be in excess of a knot. For this reason I did not hesitate to call on Micky, our diver, to suit up and prepare the mini-dive bottle we carried for just such an unfortunate occasion.

I fully realized what I was asking him to do. The water temperature was just above freezing point, but the biggest danger was the condition of the sea. We were in a full-blown gale in the Southern Ocean. Like one of Conrad's ever-smiling Scandinavians, Micky agreed without discussion. The crew on deck lowered the mainsail and the forestaysail to take the forward way off the boat. Richard was below, firing up the kettle and kicking on the hot water heater for Micky's return. We tethered him to the boat from his Lirakis life harness to a block on the rail amidships and then to a winch. Bill handed him a knife he had just sharpened. When he stepped over the lifelines I was confident we had done what was necessary.

Micky had been a Swedish Navy diver. Perhaps now he regretted the stories he had told us about diving in the Baltic in midwinter. As he jumped overboard, Bill and Rick paid out his line, and he disappeared below the violently rolling hull. He would later recollect what happened:

"As soon as I found out there was something caught in the prop, I immediately knew it would be me going overboard. I was secretly hoping that Skip would not come up and ask me! I knew it was a dangerous thing to do, that it was going to be cold and pretty tough in the sea, but I just got on with it and suited up, not really thinking too much about it.

It wasn't until I went over the side that I realized just how rough it was; you kind of needed four hands down there to hang on and work. I almost got everything untangled and then either the line that was attached to me or the bag came right across my face and ripped off the mask and the mouthpiece, and I figured, that was no big deal, I'll just go up, sort myself out and then go down again. Just then the boat moved violently to one side and I must have had too much slack in the safety line and found myself up on the wrong side. It was then I thought, now I'm in 'deep shit' here, as I was up underneath the transom, getting the hell knocked out of me. Before anybody realized where I was, I had a very hopeless feeling for a while that I was 'history' until the guys realized where I was and gave me slack. Then for a moment things didn't seem so bad, away from the transom. But still I was getting dragged down by the pull of the line and was taking in what seemed like liters of water. I had strange feelings because every time I had a chance to look up I saw everyone standing there trying to do something and I remember getting very pissed off with John Toon filming me almost drowning. It was silly, because he couldn't help me anyway, but it was not a good feeling watching this guy recording what could have been my death."

The mistake we had made was placing his 'lead block' on the rail too far aft and also paying out too much slack that allowed him to be shunted to the other side.

I was the first to hear Micky shouting above the wind and the waves, and as I looked aft I could see him taking a terrible battering under the stern counter as the transom rose and fell 3 feet. Calling for Bill to give him 10 feet of slack, he then trailed aft and I saw he had no mask or mouth piece, and although he was away from the immediate danger, he must have had several mouthfuls of water and was obviously fading fast.

It was clear that he could not come back the way he had gone over the side. As Roger fumbled with the heaving line I called to Mike to pass me the tail of the mainsheet and began to coil it, ready to throw. With hardly room to swing I made a terrible effort on the first toss and the line blew away to leeward. I coiled it again, an agonizingly slow process while I watched him struggling for breath.

Micky wrote, "I even considered at one point to cut my tether, the obvious solution to the problem of constantly getting dragged under, but somehow in those situations you still think clearly, and I knew that if I did that it would be the end of me. When you guys finally got the line to me, I could barely hang on, so I wrapped the line around my arms as many times as I could and at that point I knew I would make it."

I can't remember, I think it was on the third or fourth toss that he caught the line and with one big heave and a lucky wave, we landed him up on the transom like a big black fish. Phil and Bill jumped on to the transom tethered by their harnesses and grabbed him, passing what was now an inert body up to eager hands.

Richard stripped him, and, with dry clothes he put him in the drying locker and shut the door. He was OK, but no one had to remind any of us that we had come close to losing a man. If he for any reason had become completely separated from the boat we would

---

opposite above   Hard running on Leg Three and a couple of tons of water adding to the burden; good for photographs, bad for boatspeed; *below*   up and away, out to the clew of the genoa to attach a new sheet (*Photos by Skip Novak*)

overleaf   Becalmed in the Doldrums on Leg Four, Paul Berrow waits his turn for the bucket, the only form of relief from the equatorial sun (*Photo by Skip Novak*)

have lost him. We had no sails up, and the propeller was fouled.

Fortunately his effort was not in vain. He told us he had managed to unwrap most of the spinnaker sock before he lost control. Never a man at a loss for a solution, Phil Wade lowered our 35-pound Fisherman anchor over the side and grappled up the end of the bag. Leading it to one of the winches they crossed their fingers and spun the handle. Miraculously it came free. Through the viewing port, I could see that the prop was clear and the blades feathered, particularly fortunate as Roger suggested I go overboard and try where Micky had left off!

We put up the storm chute and went roaring off toward the Horn, still a thousand miles away. Like most of us, Patrick was sobered by the experience. He recorded it in his diary that afternoon:

It's an awful feeling to see someone in trouble like that and not be able to help them. It serves to underline how difficult it is to pick someone up out of the sea and how quickly one becomes debilitated from the cold. I suspect we've been a bit cavalier in our attitude to personal safety.

Roger had calculated that the spinnaker bag affair had lost us 16 miles. For the next three days all the Maxis ran before this strong westerly and conversation during the 'chat show' was undramatic.

"How's the wind blowing over there?" Fehlmann might ask Kuttel.
"Oh, probably much the same as you."
"All well on board?"
"Yes, all's well here."

It wasn't until we hit Punta del Este that the stories of the others came out in barroom chat.

Lion: Suffering from the control problems, like our own, they were pushing hard when the shackle on the spinnaker halyard opened and the 2.2 oz went under the bow. They recovered it quickly, but it was in pieces. On the next set, they put on two halyards which was fine, but when they tried to drop that sail, the sheet shackle on the take down opened accidentally on a jammer handle and the sail blew over the side attached by nothing but the halyard. The sail was flying like a flag from the masthead.

Lion's mast-man, Ed Danby, was sent aloft with a retrieving line. The idea was to trip the halyard shackles. As he explained, "You know what it's like in a panic especially in the middle of the night, you whip your harness on and off you go." By the time he got to the first

---

opposite A thoughtful Simon le Bon (*Photo by Rick Tomlinson*)

spreaders he felt the harness, improperly fastened, slip out through his legs and he instinctively grabbed hold of the shroud and landed on the first spreader, unattached to anything. Shaken, he slid down the rigging to the deck.

Watch-captain Grant Dalton was next in line and he succeeded in tripping out the shackles and the sail was recovered, but not before he got the ride of his life. "You can imagine being up at the top of the mast in a 40 knots true, pitch black and no one can hear you on deck. As they were lowering me down, while I was right in the middle of 'no man's land' between the spreaders and nothing to hang on to, they broached the damn thing. With the mainsail flogging to buggery and the rigging shaking the life out of me, I thought then and there the whole thing was going to fall over the side, with me in it."

Immediately after that they reset the storm chute, but with the halyards attached by screw-in 'D' shackles. Neglecting to realize they had no swivel in the system, the halyard twisted, chafed and parted and that sail come tumbling down again. It was some time before they could rig another halyard and fly a spinnaker. Blake reckoned that the whole episode cost them 30 miles.

Cote d'Or: I was surprised to learn they carried as many as 15 spinnakers on board for the middle two Southern Ocean legs, but it turned out that they needed them. In those same three days they blew one of their 2.2 oz sails and the 95% Flanker in a broach. Then they lost the 80% storm chute with all its running gear, halyards, sheets, and guys when Tabarly gave the 'thumbs down' sign to the young cowboys who couldn't get the flogging mess under control.

Recovering a spinnaker in heavy weather is a dangerous job. Everyone has to pull together at the right time and more importantly it is up to the helmsman to keep the sail in the lee of the mainsail during the take-down. Sailing Master Luc Heyman of *Côte d'Or* described a typical incident that has at one time or another happened to all of us.

"I was pulling in and gathering the sail from well up on the weather deck and must have had my feet on a part of the cloth because all of a sudden I was picked up and was flying in mid-air over the leeward lifelines as the whole sail went overboard. Our doctor, Luc Frejaques, caught me just in time and pulled me to safety. When the spinnaker wants to get away like that you can be 8 men, 10 or 12; it doesn't matter, you just can't hold it."

Atlantic Privateer: The boys on *Privateer* were telling about one major incident on Leg Three, nor did they need to tell more. Broaching violently just after a spinnaker set, the headsail was still on the foredeck being gathered and they lost the whole lot over the side, while the foredeck crew, waist deep in water, were struggling to save themselves.

In a situation reminiscent of our own, they discovered they had a 150 foot 20mm rope genoa sheet trailing from the propeller, but at 60 degrees south in severe cold and rough seas they decided not to put a man over to clear it until the conditions changed. They suffered with this streaming warp for three days. Then they risked it.

UBS: Either the Swiss were telling no stories or they had none to tell. In what was like a broken record they simply proclaimed they had no serious problems, and looking at their days' runs during that period, we had every reason to believe them. On the 26th of February they reported a 355-mile day, from position report to position report, and a staggering 370 miles in a 24-hour period. They claimed they could carry spinnakers easily in 40 knots of true wind, in control, with the spinnaker sheet cleated.

Conceptually, *UBS* was a breakthrough Whitbread design. Compared to our own best day's run of 315 miles in that same period, which was similar to *Lion's* and below *Cote d'Or's* 340 miles' day, *UBS* was a runaway. It was fortunate for us that we did not have hard running conditions throughout the leg. A handicap of say 25 to 35 miles a day in rough conditions would have been a staggering deficit after 4 weeks.

Breakages, close calls, and small disasters are part and parcel of ocean racing, and the events of the previous week had all been taken in stride by our crew. Paul, however, was beginning to have doubts. He had the impression that we were the only boat with problems, which is an easy assumption when things go wrong. Neil, Magnus and myself had on several occasions tried to convince him that trouble is quite normal when you are pushing a boat to its limit for protracted periods.

At other times, I readily sympathized with him. The next day, when we hoisted the storm chute its center blew out as soon as it made full hoist, and we were left with nothing but the two tapes and the remnants dangling over the bow. We couldn't really complain about this sail. It had seen service in the *Xargo* inventory and then a hard life on *Drum*, already having undergone three major repairs at sea.

It's funny, how one derives a great pleasure from throwing things overboard, even more so when what went overboard represented a substantial saving in weight and created space below. This, of course, was not true of disposable underwear or socks or well worn magazines with the pages stuck together by the damp, but it certainly applied to the Storm Chute. The Emperors, Simon, Mike and Paul, had given the 'thumbs down' sign to racing sail worth $9,000, which had been reduced to a pile of useless rags. Senators Zimmerman, Hancock and Novak had given their speeches condemning it as irreparable, and no one came to its defence. After cutting off the head and clew reinforcement patches, we chucked it over the side with much celebration and waved it goodbye. Mario presented Simon with the head patch with the inscription that ready simply, "Good luck Simon Le Bon from Mario."

Needless to say, the sailmakers had enough on their plate keeping us in sails. Watch after watch Mugsy and Mario would take turns hemming the edges of the Flanker, piercing this jig-saw puzzle back together and then running the seams through the machine. Not as patient as Mugsy, a continuous stream of obscenities issued from Mario as needles broke and the machine jammed. "Quel bordel! Putain, putain! Cette connerie de machine de merde!" He vowed he would never ship on board as a sailmaker again. After a 30-hour marathon, however, the Flanker was ready to go up.

There is always a tense moment upon rehoisting a repaired spinnaker. Shape is not usually the problem, but only a small hole or a seam left open can, within seconds, reopen the whole sail. The Flanker flew successfully, but the two small holes where Mugsy had put on sticky-back tape but had not sewn it down did not please Mario. His displeasure was intensified because it was his watch, and the sail once again was coming below, and he had to finish the job. This was not their last difference of opinion.

A change of weather brought moderating winds and a shift back into the northwest. We decided not to give any more southing away as we were already one degree (60 miles) below the latitude of Cape Horn and more importantly, *Lion*, our arch rival was still north of us, representing a danger if the wind went into the north giving them a broader and thereby faster reach toward the Horn.

We were still surfing up to 20 knots on the afternoon of the 26th, but the pressure was off and we contemplated dropping the 2.2 oz and holding up a few degrees with the Jib Top. The horizon was hazy but the sun came out overhead as Richard emerged from the companion-way hatch carrying afternoon tea in the pressure cooker – a practical tea pot for the afternoon ration. This was a British boat and we carried out the tea ritual in all but the most severe weather and that day, Bill hàd no problem ladling out the tea into mugs to be passed around.

I was sitting aft, muttering something to Patrick who was driving, when all of a sudden the stern rose up about 45 degrees, and as his eyes popped out of their sockets, I instinctively dove for the bottom of the cockpit and wrapped myself around the mainsheet winch pedestal. He later described what happened in his log:

Skip looked up and barely had time to say "Holy shit!" as we got picked up by and surfed down the steepest wave I've ever seen. We must have hit 30 knots down the face of the wave since the spinnaker was hard aback on the rig and the wind was just a steady 25 knots true. At the bottom of the trough, the boat buried herself past the main hatch and if it hadn't been for Mario jumping across the cockpit and grabbing the other wheel we would have broached since I just about lost it. I was convinced we were about to pitchpole and from the expression on Skip's face I'm sure he thought so to.

Once again a freak wave had hit us when we least expected it and again, few people were clipped on. The afternoon tea session was a wash out. It was almost a relief when the wind swung right into the north and we went off on a relatively safe reach. The message in the head was clear: a gybed boat on her side with a VOID stamp over the top and the words; "Fuck this shit, guys, Let's go home!"

No sooner had we sheeted in the main than the leech started to flutter like a machine gun. Attempts to draw in the cord failed, and Mario went aloft to have a look. His news was not good. The wind strengthened later, and Mugsy's watch was putting in the fourth reef. The boat was fully pressed again with very little sail up. Apparently he was forward up by the mast shouting orders above the wind for the reefing maneuver. He described what happened next:

Everyone's nerves were a bit shot from the last week of shitty weather, however the only one to crack was Mario. We were throwing in the fourth reef and out of the blue (and from behind) the 'fucking Frog' attacked me and knocked me down. I still don't know why he did it and neither does he.

The next morning, with the wind heading even further, we decided to fix the leech cord. Reluctantly we dropped the mainsail to the deck. It was obvious that it was only a matter of time before the sail would open up and then we would have a real problem on our hands. Mario took charge of this miserable job – miserable because it was wet, cold and bouncy, and five in the morning. Mugsy, still smarting from the reefing incident wrote:

I was off watch for only two hours, only to be woken by Skip who wanted our watch to help fix the mainsail. Why in the hell he wanted to fix the thing at that hour and not at a watch change I'll never know. I will say something – there were four very upset people on deck in the freezing rain fixing the damn thing. We had to thread a spare radio antenna through bit by bit opening up the leech every 10 feet, to run a new cord and the operation was directed by none other than that obnoxious, shouting Frenchman whose mood had still not improved. It was all I could do not hitting the bastard, my head still hurting from when I banged it when he knocked me down.

Our last weather map indicated a ridge of high pressure over the Horn so a port tack reach all the way was likely. It wasn't pleasant sailing but it was fast. The survival suits were again in vogue. Roger, smoking casually under the dodger with his suit around his waist, had it completely filled by another rogue wave coming over the beam. He retired below, while the witnesses, who had no survival suits, to what they described as this 'poetic justice' were beside themselves with laughter. Neil wrote down his thoughts on this popular topic:

Our covetousness has taken the form of ridicule – indeed they do look pretty silly with their cone-shaped headpieces and agricultural trousers, but our derision rings hollow when we ask, "Are they better off than the rest of us?" Little things like this serve as a reminder to us all that no matter how far from civilisation you go, human nature is still slave to the same old weaknesses. Anyway, I'm pleased to report that the suits don't work! I distinctly saw Roger shivering with cold during last night's watch.

There was another incident which caused much laughter. Mario, of all people, opened the aft hatch just as a wave broke over the cockpit completely flooding the aft cabin and the Frenchman. Toon was cursing because he didn't get it on film and was planning a retake with a bucket.

I looked at our bearded cameraman lying in his bunk, living and working out of his sleeping bag, surrounded by all his gear and possessions, a nostalgic reminder of pleasant days I had spent storm bound in mountain huts in New Zealand. This observation precipitated the revelation that we had both spent extended periods in Pioneer Hut in Mt. Cook country years before.

John confessed to me that he was worried about the documentary film. Because his budget had been started and then stopped each time *Drum* looked to be in an impossible situation, there was little continuity in the earlier stages. He was on board only for Leg Three and was supposed to get all the necessary sailing footage out of it – no easy task.

One of his biggest problems was setting up his 16mm camera and sound recorder in time to catch events as they happened on deck. Roger, on the other hand, was having more success with his video camera, which could be grabbed and handed on deck and be operational within seconds. Simon, the ostensible star of this film to be, also was not cooperating. He shied away from the camera and John took it personally.

He did make the point that the rest of the crew were superbly cooperative about what can be a difficult job in filming people working, when at times it is expected you should be helping out. He enjoyed telling us the story when on *Lion* in the Sydney–Hobart Race, he was shooting an eating sequence at the salon table and one of the obnoxious Kiwis purposely threw-up his mouth full of food all over the table.

The weather situation was not helping John either. The prospect of light weather at the Horn, little surfing, and the fact that, up to then we had not seen (or would see) any icebergs except on radar didn't make his job easier.

March 2nd broke on the upward sloping curve of what was a continuous sine wave of morale on board. The slamming had stopped and the hard times of a few days ago were forgotten. Once again the decks were dry. Pancakes were scheduled for breakfast, the water-maker was humming away as usual at that early hour, and Russian music from Radio Moscow was loudly telling the off-watch that it was time to get up. Life was pretty damn good.

We had made big gains on all the other boats in the last 24 hours, apparently being pushed along by a private wind. *AP* was still reporting a northeast down at 60° South and Padda sounded panicky for the first time, realizing that in his bid to sail the shortest distance, he might end up due south of the Horn, dead to leeward of it, while the rest of us fetched or reached in. Neither Roger nor I could understand *AP*'s strategy. They seemed to us to have violated a basic rule: don't take risks by going off to one side or another of the course when you are out ahead and you know you have a fast boat.

Lion had also lost a whopping 37 miles. They held the extreme northerly berth finding generally lighter winds close to the high. This was a complete reversal of Blake's tactics on the second leg. Both times, his extremes were costly.

For the last week with the die cast, we had been confident of beating both *AP* and *Lion* into Punta, but then, for the first time, our 200-mile lead took on a new and important meaning. Assuming we could hold this lead to the finish, and then, with a little luck, pull off something similar again on the last leg, it was possible that we could beat them and come in 2nd in the Whitbread. As much as this is dangerous thinking with so long to go and the knowledge that anything at all could still happen to us, Roger and I still could not help but run through the calculations and give the results to the rest of the crew.

Good idea or not, the news injected new life into the ship as did a sunny sky. The deck work and the cleaning up of the mess below was attacked with new enthusiasm.

It was my day to be the 'Nigger of the Day', which meant I had to sweep the cabin sole, tidy up the eating area, clean the head, and organize the forepeak and tool locker. Our sewing-machine box top, cum eating dispensary was, inevitably by its location, a catch-all of accumulated gloves, rigging knives, hats, candy wrappers and neck towels. What I thought to be a disgusting set of black underwear was lying in the corner of the table. They would be thrown directly overboard, my reasoning being that no one would admit to ownership. It is accepted practice on racing yachts that what is not stowed or immediately claimed is thrown away, especially if found by the skipper; and in this case especially if the skipper finds dirty underwear in the eating area.

While I was in the head sloshing it out, Simon surfaced to come on watch and asked no one in particular, "Anybody seen my black balaclava? It was on the table." Sheepishly I had to admit my mistake. Luckily for both of us, he found it impaled on a stanchion on the lee side!

Our first sign of human life since leaving New Zealand, showed on the horizon one night when we were still 350 miles from Cape Horn. It was an unidentified ship, and it altered course to follow in our wake for three hours. I assumed it to be a naval ship from either Chile or Argentina, adversaries in this most inhospitable forum.

The prolonged dispute between Chile and Argentina is partly the result of the complicated geography of the southern tip of South America. Tierra del Fuego, which is, further north, a clear-cut natural border between Argentina and Chile, is lost in a maze of islands, channels and scattered alpine peaks. Years ago this was of little concern, but when oil was discovered in and around the Cape Horn area, these bits of real estate became serious business. Both countries patrol the area with well-manned and well-armed naval vessels, each making sure that the other is keeping to his side of the fence and not establishing either a miltary presence or a settlement in the uninhabited territories.

I dreamed up various horror scenarios based on the Argentine unhappiness over what had happened in the Falklands. We were, after all, a British ship.

I imagined the ship was Argentine and I knew from talking to Naval personnel in Argentina four years ago that duty in Tierra del Fuego was considered similar to a prison sentence of sorts. I saw a drunken Argentine sea captain, possibly who had made some incredible blunder in the Falklands War and now bitter and exiled, was spending his last years of duty benignly monitoring the Chileans while tending the bottle.

The ship on the horizon finally calls us on the radio; we identify ourselves as British. He sends the helmsman and the look-out off the bridge for a cup of coffee ("Muchas gracias, Capitan!"), then promptly runs us down and under in a savage vendetta for La Malvinas!

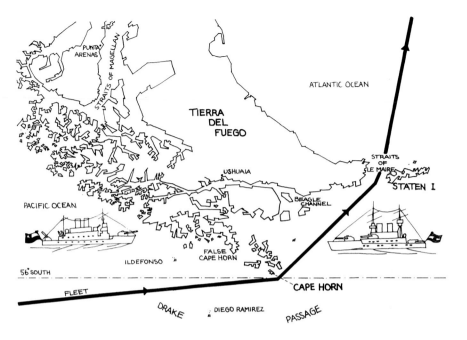

As he didn't respond to our initial calls in three languages I decided not to identify ourselves as British if he did come up (and tried to remember who sold arms to the Argies) and also managed to raise *Fazer* to inform her of the situation. However, by first light, he had disappeared, whoever he was.

March 3rd dawned as gray and foggy as had so many days before. Chuck asked me what we would do if we had to navigate with a sextant down here. It seemed weeks since we had last seen the sun or a horizon clear enough for celestial observations.

Eight years before, on *King's Legend* we had, in fact, been in a similar situation: nine days since the last fix and roaring in on Cape Horn, without a clear idea of where we were. I remember the mood on board was quite different – anxiety, anticipation and constantly questioning our own judgement. Looking at the Cape Horn chart, the same one that now is proudly displayed at home, didn't exactly serve to give us confidence either; Falso Cabo de Hornos, Isla Deceit, Arrecife Peligroso and Isla Hope were testaments to those ships that had gone wrong before us and the fact was acknowledged that in the methods and equipment of navigating *King's Legend* in 1978, we really had no advantage (at least at our disposal) to those unfortunate forebears.

"Cape Horn is still in the same place, I'm happy to report," announced Pierre Fehlmann from *UBS* on the evening chat show. He was 127 miles ahead of us, and 65 miles ahead of *Cote d'Or*. On a straight line distance. *AP* had fallen back dramatically and was now two miles behind us! However, the wind had shifted to the East (a condition the Pilot Book says never occurs), giving him a starboard tack fetch and saving him the embarrassment of beating up from his southerly option gone wrong. Neither had *Lion's* northerly option been worth the effort; he was 237 miles behind us!

With Sat Nav pin-pointing our position and our competition chatting away on their radios, I could not help but feel superior and privileged to have done this race eight years before on *King's Legend* under more dramatic circumstances. On my wall is the chart which carries the fortuitous sun line I had shot back then, confirming that our dead reckoned position, had, in fact, been about 40 miles off. 24 hours later, among the rocks and islands of the Horn area, this could have had disastrous consequences. Also we were certain then that we were completely alone out there. Three weeks before in a broach, a toilet bowl full of water had emptied itself into the SSB radio, rendering the transmitter useless. No one knew where we were, or if we were still afloat. In those days, nobody seemed to mind much. Today, that situation would call for front page headlines.

I have to agree with Hilaire Belloc, who once said, "When the unknown becomes known, it loses that mysterious power of attraction that the unknown always possesses." So it was on *King's Legend* that we had rounded Cape Horn, 5 miles off in the dead of night, never setting eyes on it. It was blowing 45 knots from the west.

Well before sunrise the next day, we had seen a white light that seemed to be following us and it had grown progressively brighter. To our mixed surprise, dismay, but ultimate delight, we identified her as the French 58-footer, *33 Export*, her yellow hull surfing up to us. She also had set a poled out headsail. In what must be some of the most spectacular surfing conditions I have ever experienced, she drew even with us by 1100 and we sparred with her on the waves only a boat length apart. We toasted the crazy Frenchmen then threw the beer cans at them, but they won the contest easily by having a female member of their crew appear on deck bare chested. However, after some marvellous pictures were taken, we hoisted our 'Chicken Chute' spinnaker and, on the very edge of disaster, pulled away out in front and put them back where they had come from.

There was no doubt that those experiences of uncertainty, foreboding, the ultimate relief of having found the way, as well as those last few moments of recklessness which seemed to say, "Up yours!" to the Southern Ocean were difficult acts to follow. Times had changed.

"When do you reckon we will see land?" Mike asked on the morning of the 4th.

"Should be in about a half hour," was Roger's confident reply.

"Be sure to wake us up when the Horn is in view," they had said before they went off watch to sleep as comfortably as babies. Yes, times had certainly changed.

Nevertheless, just after dawn, a dark red stripe of light broke above the eastern horizon and as it brightened to a brilliant orange and then a deep yellow, we could see the silhouette of Diego Ramirez, 25 miles off our starboard bow, an island outpost, alone in the fury of the Drake Passage. The Horn was still 60 miles away to the northeast, but this was as impressive a landfall as one could hope for. Rick had been instructed by our pressman in London to take fewer sunsets and more people. He only had to turn around to do both. The trouble was that we were *all* festooned with camera gear.

Twenty-three miles away, a dark grey headland rose above the horizon. It was topped with the brilliant white snow-capped mountains of the Cordillera Darwin far beyond in the hinterland of the 'Land of Fire'. The wind had been weak and variable all that morning and with a moderate northerly slowly filling, we changed to the jib top and staysail for what was to be an easy reach up to and past what is recognized the world over as the milestone in an ocean sailor's career. In what is more typical of this area than the light weather we were experiencing were the fast-moving clouds, and the mist that had moved in. Within minutes visibility was so reduced that this mighty headland became nothing more than a low dark, nondescript rocky shore, the breaking waves the only indication that we were only a mile away. Of course, the radar confirmed this when we made the transit at 1045 local time.

Belloc might have been pleased at this turn of events, but the photographers (and there were many) were not. The photographs that were produced, blurred and underexposed, were about as insignificant as the attempts to capture the memory on film. So, with much of its mystery still intact, Cape Horn faded into the mist just after lunch. If those on board wished to have a clearer view of this celebrated venerated piece of rock, they now had a damn good reason (those who had never been would later say 'excuse') to return.

Champagne corks were popped and we toasted ourselves, *Drum*, and the sea for good measure, and also for good measure drank our fill. For light entertainment, a 50-foot whale surfaced close aboard to show us the way, and, when we passed within 50 yards of an outcropping called the 'Bocas,' what we had thought were rock 'gendarmes' sticking up at odd angles turned out to be sea lions who delightfully perched and dove into the sea from their rocky ledges. Seabirds were everywhere. I had the pleasure of identifying a pure white snow petrel, a rare sighting this far north. They are one of the few species that actually breed on the Antarctic continent.

From the Horn, it was a 60-mile leg up to the Straits of Le Maire that separate Staten Island from the mainland shore. Once the corner is turned there usually is a sense of relief; the greatest test is over. The Southern Ocean, with its vast, empty stretches, high winds and great seas, has been left behind for the familiar waters of the Atlantic. This was certainly true for us; we had had our hairy moments. However, as the wind went ahead and freshened, with a heavy-weather sail change imminent, some of the joy of entering the Atlantic was lost. We were familiar with what the Atlantic could offer. It was a dead beat through the Straits and beyond. The good news was that *Cote d'Or* and *AP* were only just over the horizon ahead; the bad news was that *Lion*, although still over 200 miles behind was still running free and would recoup some lost ground.

On the evening radio sched the American 65-foot singlehander *American Promise* came up on the 8 megahertz Channel having rounded the Horn only three days before. Ted Hood had designed and built Skipper Dodge Morgan's yacht in a fashion that would have made Bernard Motissier chuckle and Vito Dumas turn over in his grave.

I had seen this boat the year before in Marblehead, and Mugsy had helped Morgan fit her out and conduct her sea trials. She was a new, totally different approach to singlehanding. Formerly, the emphasis had been on simplicity and self reliance. *American Promise* was packed full of diesel fuel to power an impressive array of hydraulics and electronics that steered, navigated, and worked the halyards and sheets. What was even more surprising was that it all seemed to be working, and he was on his way back up to Bermuda on a record-breaking voyage.

I thought at the time, "Poor guy, all he wants to do is to tell us about his boat and the records (some very obscure, others never heard of) and all we want is the wind conditions from him." Pierre, in what was his stock question that we had heard over and over had asked him. "And which kind of wind do you have?"

Obviously not understanding Pierre's accent, Morgan would reply with something totally unrelated that had an amusing effect like, "O yeah, it took me 31 days from the longitude of Hobart to the Horn; 2 days faster than . . ."

The following 24 hours were immensely frustrating as we not only had to go hard on the wind, but were later becalmed in the Straits with *AP* only 7 miles ahead. They, like us, were stemming a foul tide. As soon as we emerged into the Atlantic, a new wind filled in, again from the northerly quadrant. A big high was out to the east of the Falklands and we found ourselves with the prospect of a long beat on a favored port tack, with the Falkland Islands dead ahead. We had about a thousand miles to go to Punta del Este, Uruguay.

The wind had slowly freshened throughout March 6th. By the time

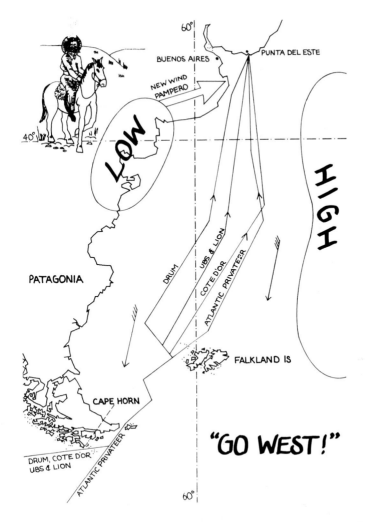

we were off the northwest corner of West Falkland we were down to the No. 5 Jib and three reefs. Patrick made some caustic remark that we "were blowing the race, by slowing up and not pushing the boat hard enough." Pat had pulled this behaviour before, claiming we often were too conservative with the choice of sail. Flying off waves at 10 knots (reminiscent of Leg One) and burying the boat up to her stanchion tops was not my idea of racing the boat right. I was pleased to have Pat standing by the next morning when Padda Kuttel on *AP* came on the radio and reported much the same conditions and exactly the same sail combination. Pat had earlier assured me, his 'mates' on *AP* would be 'going for it.' Possibly they also had learned their lesson on Leg One.

Eight years ago, in those conditions on other boats, we would certainly just have buttoned her down, hung on and, indeed, 'gone for it!' But with these machines, built ever closer to marginal strength, our thinking must now be dictated by paranoia as much as anything.

Roger woke me up an hour before my watch change the next morning. A rapid wind shift had come through, swinging from dead ahead to well aft, and on deck, confusion reigned supreme. I decided not to interfere and let them get on with what was a difficult task of setting a spinnaker while still punching through an enormous headsea.

While I was getting dressed some time later, I could hear Neil and Paul in the cockpit chatting away about pushing the boat in heavy weather as well as an important discussion on the merits of several spaghetti dishes Paul wanted to try on Leg Four. Talking to the helmsman had always been my pet peeve (Magnus was probably the only one on board good enough to carry on a discussion and still steer his best).

I would frequently remind people of this; no doubt I sounded like a broken record at times. This time I assumed when I came on deck that the spinnaker was up and everything was squared away so that I gave Neil nothing more than a humorous reprimand about talking while steering. Instead, when I came out of the hatch and looked forward, I saw that there was no jockey pole on the afterguy, the pole was too far forward, the outboard pole end 4 feet too high and flagging all over the place, and the deck was a complete mess. And these guys were talking about pasta! I blew my stack, and Neil walked off the wheel in a huff. He wrote of the situation and of his feelings that morning:

I'm the first to admit that part of the enjoyment of this race lies in the camaraderie and banter that prevail among the lads, and we've had some good old laughs perched up there on the weather rail. "Do you remember the night when . . . ?" is usually enough to distract us from the business of trimming properly. Still, a far greater degree of concentration is required from the man on the wheel, and the rule about talking to him is very clear. My own performance in this has often been a bit short of the mark and Skip has on several occasions told me to shut up. Fair enough, but nothing rankles so much as a reproach of the innocent.

Most of us are very careful nowadays to stay clear of the helmsman if we want to have a conversation. Paul, however, is the exception, and he will happily strike up a chat with the driver, usually reminiscing about the chef's speciality at his favorite restaurant in Paris. As much as I tried to ignore him this morning I was caught red-handed by Skip. "You're way off course, stop talking about food for Christ's sake and steer the boat!" It was useless trying to explain myself and I thought his reaction was a bit unfair.

Ten seconds after I took the wheel, the temporary strop that held the topping lift block aloft (the fitting was damaged in the gybe) broke and the pole, weighing a good 140 pounds, came crashing to the deck and missed Janne's and Magnus's heads by inches.

I felt frustrated at what most considered little things gone wrong but which, in reality, could undermine the entire effort by a breakdown or serious injury. Although I knew that this was the best and the most enjoyable crew I had ever sailed with, or was likely to, I recorded my thoughts on this subject of management that afternoon:

This lack of self discipline seems to be a continuous problem on board. Of course, my sometimes heavyhanded way of reminding people about this surely does not help the situation and I know my methods only too well. I believe this is a great dilemma when your crew are your friends first, the way I like to go sailing, but when it comes time to remind someone of what is essentially a behavioural problem they will naturally take offence. As Phil Wade says, "It's hard to run a bunch of boat bums who are set in their ways."

We all know Pierre Fehlmann on UBS *and Rietschoten on* Flyer *(both far senior to their crews) ran their organizations like military commanders, and their crews were young and inexperienced enough to be completely subservient. You only have to look at the results to understand that their system surely works well, with the obvious drawback of imposition.*

I still feel that my way is better; finding a crew that is self-motivated enough to get the job done.

We had made a big tactical decision back by the Falklands when we tacked on to starboard and went 60 miles to the northwest, while the others ahead kept on the favored port tack and weathered through the edge of the Falkland archipelago. We found out later that *AP* actually risked running through an uncharted channel in order to stay on the slightly favored port tack; a situation that prompted one of the crew to wear his life jacket.

Roger and I both agreed to gamble on the prospect of a new wind coming from the west eventually, which was not unlikely as we were still in a westerly flow coming off Patagonia. We had little to lose with the three leaders as the finish was only three to four days away and we knew we could not beat them by sailing in the same weather they had. *Lion*, although having caught up to only 90 miles behind was safely out of it, at least for that leg.

On the night of the 7th, we talked to several trawlers and fishing boats with their lamps lit up to attract squid to the surface. They were lined up along the continental shelf of Argentina, just outside the legal limit of 200 miles offshore. Strung out in a dead straight line to the north, they looked like a line of street lights along a misty highway. What we thought were a few dozen turned out to be several hundred. We also spoke to a Yorkshireman on board a Japanese trawler leased to the Brits, who was fishing inside the Falklands exclusion zone, in order, as he said it, "To fly the flag down here."

It was only little over four years before that the Falkland Island War had broken out, only weeks after we had left the Argentine resort town of Mar del Plata on *Alaska Eagle*. I still remember how friendly the Argentine Naval commanders, no doubt 'cognoscente,' were to the Whitbread Race Committee during a party on board HMS *Endurance*. All of them were ex-Royal Navy. I only found out much later that Patrick had lost a brother in the Falklands. He wrote in his diary around that time:

Well it looks like we might even get a result this leg. All the other boats have hung out to the east. Skip and Roger are convinced the wind will fill in from the west and, from the weather maps I've seen, it looks that way. Skip asked for a weather report from an Argentine radio station for the Falkland area and he was reminded they were the Malvinas, much to Filthy and Neil's disgust – and mine for that matter.

For the next two days the wind was flicking around from the north and variable in strength. We played the shifts, but still hoped a miracle would happen. In any case, morale was high as we neared land. Dolphins were often close under our bow and at night their phosphorescent wakes, like the trails of shooting stars, would keep us spellbound. Waves of moths and other insects invaded our little world, and we even had a bat hanging from the second spreaders at dawn on the morning of the 11th.

Head grafitti was in full swing and again I was the subject of criticism: An unmistakable likeness of my nose and moustache bore a caption, "OK guys, come on, we're ocean racing!" It was later overdrawn to resemble a part of the female anatomy, and then graciously changed again with the heading: "An artist's impression of the resort town of Punta del Este, a c--- of a place!"

Dr. Nilsson was like an army surgeon lecturing a group of young recruits before their first shore leave in a foreign country. AIDS was beginning to be a big topic of conversation, and he even had an opinion about that when he romantically told them, "If you use a condom and try not to kiss the girl, you should be safe."

He also wanted to inject the crew with gamogloblyn for hepatitus. Phil Wade, an old South American hand, said he would take his chances, while a few were convinced enough to have the shots. I politely refused, remembering what had happened when he jabbed me four years ago on board *Alaska Eagle*.

We were hard on the wind coming into Mar del Plata, and I volunteered for the shot in order to get the ball rolling. It was hot and sweaty in the head and as Roger fumbled with the cotton swab after the jab, I became nauseous. The next thing I knew I was looking up into about five faces who were asking me if I was OK. Flat on my back in the main salon, it was some time before I came to and realized where I was and who they were. I can remember my acute embarrassment, with my shorts pulled down around my ankles, as if I had done something very naughty and got caught. Roger looked down at me and seconds after I declared myself 'OK', he simply asked them in his familiar drone without any emotion and completely convinced of his methods, "Who's next?" There were few takers.

With less than a day to go and the Maxis jockeying for position just outside the Plata Estuary, a weak Pampero, but still a strong southwesterly had filled in at 0500 that same morning. A small low had developed just to the southwest of our position, and we had no doubt that we had gotten this wind first.

The midday 'chat show' had confirmed what for us was one of the high points of the race: *AP* was 9 miles behind, *Cote d'Or* 12, and *Lion* back to 160 miles, having been becalmed all night. *UBS* was also in light weather, but only 20 miles from the finish and sure to beat us.

At 1300 we could see *AP* and *Cote d'Or* from our masthead, they with the wind, now catching us fast. "What about bloody *Drum*?" asked Thierry Rannou, the journalist on the big Belgian boat. "They're 53 miles out," said Padda on *AP*. "Then we are foocked!" said the surprised Frog, "But we will all have a good drink in the Yacht Club tonight!"

Three hours later the buildings of Punta del Este, disappointingly similar to the skyline of Miami beach, appeared above the horizon. We were ecstatic.

Three miles out a typical South American Naval vessel, belching black smoke and rolling violently, came alongside with the press to lead us in through the channel. The big 2.2 oz spinnaker was up with the *Drum* logo, and with a proud Simon Le Bon on the wheel, we drove her across the finish line and right into the tiny yacht basin with full sail at 10 knots (the only boat to attempt this stunt). Simultaneously all the halyards were let fly, the sails fell to the deck (and in to the water), and *Drum* glided to a halt in front of thousands of cheering spectators.

The sun was setting and it would be dark before *AP* and *Cote d'Or* finished. We hadn't won the leg, but for us a second place was a triumph for our combined efforts. And there was more: *Lion* would finish almost 24 hours later, and we knew that the last leg represented the big challenge – an assault on second place for the entire race. The troubles of months past waned and faded for all of us on *Drum*.

12 · Leg Four: Onwards and Ever Northwards

I want to wish you guys the best of luck; but no more than 18 hours of it.

Peter Blake

The reasons why the South American port of call has changed three times in the history of four Whitbread Races are both unfortunate and interesting. Rio de Janeiro has always been the classic port-of-call for sailing ships plying the length of the Atlantic; it was logical that the first Whitbread fleet in 1973 should stop there.

Hot, noisy and cosmopolitan, Rio was in the height of Carnival when we arrived on *King's Legend* during the 1978 race. We had blown the leg tactically, and, although still solidly in second place overall, we were almost 60 hours behind the race leader, *Flyer*, with not much hope of getting it back. To make the situation worse, *Flyer* and her crew were fat and happy, while we were in desperate financial trouble. Despite our problems, we settled into Rio as best we could, determined to enjoy ourselves with a vengeance, which in Rio is not very difficult.

Unfortunately, our host, the Rio Yacht Club, was less than enthusiastic about a bunch of dishevelled yachtsmen smelling of poverty, who by their very presence appeared to despoil what was not really a yacht club at all, but rather the most elite and snobbish social organization in all of South America.

Most sailors I know and associate with are some of the poorest people in the western world, but they have not the slightest hesitation when it comes to socializing with people nominally far above their station. The club's first mistake was in barring us from the inside bar and restaurant, allocating us the patio bar and grill, which actually was a far more pleasant place. But, as any student of human nature will agree, deny a man something he has not the slightest interest in, and he will quickly become an enthusiast. This and other minor incidents, going strongly against the grain of most of us, caused an immediate resentment that precipitated what was a near riot.

Anybody who has been involved with or has followed the Whitbread, knows the story about the night of the poolside prizegiving only days before our departure. Some say it was the samba music, others the half-naked dancers or a combination of both that made the crowd go crazy. They harmlessly threw each other in the pool along with the lawn furniture and anything else that wasn't bolted down, in a simple act of letting off a little steam. Again, the Rio Club blundered badly by calling in the yacht club guards who started waving their truncheons at us. They were summarily thrown into the pool as well. Then, going a step further, the management called in the guardia militia who lobbed tear gas canisters into the arena. As *King's Legend* crew member, Greg Tuxworth, described the fray, "Being children of the sixties in America, and fairly drunk we weren't particularly afraid of tear gas – so we chucked them back." It was clear to everyone that the Whitbread would never be invited back, nor would we want to be. So much for Brazil.

In 1981/82 the Whitbread was welcomed with open arms into Mar del Plata on the Atlantic coast of Argentina. Not only did this move avoid the calms outside of Rio, but in facilities and efficiency, Argentina is much more European than is Brazil. The Club del Mar also opened all its doors to all of us. Our problem was that five weeks in a place that offered very little other than high-rise apartment blocks and beach cabanas for bourgeois vacationers from Buenos Aires was boring at best, and worse than that when compared to the city of Rio. All things considered, had it not been for the Falklands War, we would have no doubt gone back there again. So much for Argentina.

Like a social worker looking for a home for unwanted refugees, Race Chairman Williams had to look elsewhere for the 1985/86 Race and he had run out of countries on that coast, except for Uruguay. With no facilities in the capital Montevideo the choice of Punta del Este was obvious. It is well down the coast at the mouth of the Plata Estuary, had berthing facilities for yachts, and a resort atmosphere for the crews.

Punta del Este is actually a spit of land formed by Atlantic breakers and forms a natural shelter from the east. Although the name, "East Point", is not inspiring, this former fishing village, now the premier South American resort, certainly is.

On a continent where economic instability and political capriciousness is a way of life, Uruguay, pastoral and lacking a sound industrial base, has somehow remained a pillar of a wealthy South American society, so secure that Argentinians are the largest investors in this Uruguayan resort. Apparently wealthy Argentinians have more faith in Uruguay's politics than in their own.

At first glance, Punta, with its high-rise condominium blocks, restaurants and shops, looks like it could be almost anywhere in the Spanish-speaking world. A foray into the hinterland of this little peninsula reveals what Punta is really all about. Estates that appear to be 'second homes' of the grandest proportions, surrounded by immaculately maintained lawns, number in the thousands. These 'residencias' are evidence for the theory that any South American with anything to hide has probably hid at least a part of it in Punta del Este.

This conclusion, whether fact or fancy, is reinforced when you venture no more than 10 miles out of town and travel into the real Uruguay. Although the nation's population of 4 million is one of the best educated in South America and has the highest literacy rate, once out of Montevideo, life on the rolling, rich, grassy plains of the Pampas can best be described as feudal. Absentee landlords are common for the land-holdings from where beef and wool are exported all over the world. The farm managers and gauchos work the land almost exclusively on horseback. Motorized transport, where it exists at all, is one of the most impressive collection of vintage cars in the world. The fact is that they are not considered vintage at all. Only a half-hour drive out of Punta, it is not uncommon to see a farmer and his family arriving in a village to stock up at the general store riding a dusty Model-A Ford, complete with crankstart and wooden spoked wheels.

It was hard to imagine that some of these proud *campesinos* would have been pleased to know part of their tax money had been spent on such an elaborate jetty and harbor facility in Punta del Este just for pleasure craft. Possibly the government realized this when they installed their Navy as the port authority and ostensible political breakwater there and in all other ports in Uruguay.

With the Whitbread fleet safely tied bow-to on the concrete seawall and open to the public, everything seemed reasonably relaxed until the jack-booted Prefecteur came down to assess us a 6,000 Peso penalty for not flying the Uruguayan courteousy flag the first day. Not intending to pay this fee, we implored Admiral Williams to intercede on our behalf, so as not to start off on a bad foot. There were no problems after this was made clear.

Mugsy, John Toon and Chuck had departed as planned a few days after we arrived and Bill also flew back to the States temporarily to keep abreast of his commitment to work on the BOC Single-Handed Round-the-World Race as a shore manager for the American Warren Luhrs. Mike, Paul and Simon also left for a few weeks to attend to their businesses in Europe. They were to re-join us five days before the start.

For the rest of us there was little to do on board, until we pulled out the partners, the wooden wedges that support the mast at deck level. We had not planned to pull the mast for inspection, because it meant a trip to Montevideo with the boat and a lot of inconvenience. To our dismay, the mast was clearly bent, with a large dimple on the port side and we postulated this must have happened when the boat Chinese gybed; or possibly when we went off the wind in the headsea after the hard beat up past the Falklands. Magnus and I agreed that in order to be completely safe, the mast would have to come out and be sleeved externally with another aluminium section where it passed through the deck. One phone call to Hood Yacht System in America was all it took to order the sleeve and get the plan into motion. We knew it was just the beginning.

Already the problem of transhipment into Uruguay was looming as a major difficulty for boats wanting to bring in spare parts and equipment. Hood Sailmakers had found this out, but very late, as their representatives were still awaiting their sewing machines so they could set up their service loft, and no other facilities for repairing sails were available.

Admiral Williams, completely aware of a problem that could brew up into an ugly situation cajoled the local race officials to somehow organize a system that would by-pass all the red tape. "Come on fellows," I heard him say more than once in his good-natured fashion. "These yachtsmen won't stand for this sort of rubbish!"

It is a Latin custom to appoint a long list of honorary officials for a sporting event; in this case, they seemed to outnumber the participants. The names on the souvenir brochure was eventually put to the real test by Pascal Pellet-Finet representing Hoods and assisted by 'Lobo,' an Argentinian who crewed on *Flyer II* in 1982. Using a local telephone system that was as antiquated as the horse is as a mode of transport, they started at the bottom of the list and gradually worked upwards in a well-known system that says, "I'm sorry, I cannot help you. You will have to talk to my superior." They finally hit pay dirt with a one Cr. Don Enrique Iglesias, Minister of the Exterior, only one down the ladder from the Presidente de la Republica himself, who was the 'Honorary' Race Chairman. Their persistance was rewarded with the delivery of the sewing machines. A basement garage car park was turned into a sail loft. They were soon open for business.

Most of the crews had little to do on board the boats except the usual refit schedules. Accordingly, daily life slipped quickly into the South American standard of dinner after 10 o'clock, off to a night club, in bed no earlier than 4 or 5 and up at the crack of noon.

The Uruguayans were indeed friendly. The bulk of the vacationers had left before we arrived, making accommodations available. However, there was enough 'talent' still around to satisfy the likes of the *Drum* crew. Micky in his usual sincere nature was rewarded with one lovely companion for the month, while his mate Janne, more flippant, played the open field with less satisfying results. He reminded me of some politicians I've met – the kind who seem interested in a conversation, but quite ruthless about breaking it off when they see someone more useful.

Roger also was starting to suffer from a lack of credibility with women in his effort to corner the market of models and other ornamental beach beauties. "Please, come with me, I would like you to meet Simon Le Bon. It will be good for your career," we would hear him say in what had become his usual routine. His methods of rushing around with his boxes of recording and video equipment, documenting and recording everything became a well-known source of amusement.

A former Miss Uruguay Roger had met at a beach party one day turned to Neil after the Doctor's monologue and asked him in Spanish, "I can't understand a thing he is saying; what does he want?" Never a man to let an opportunity like this slip by, the articulate Cheston replied at once. Grabbing her by the arm, he said, "He says he wants to borrow a few thousands pesos for lunch!"

Few of our crew did any traveling in Uruguay, but De and I, with a couple from *AP* spent four days on an estancia up country. It was a thoroughly enjoyable experience. Horsemanship is a way of life on the Pampas, and we rode whenever we could, both there and back in Punta. A few of the other yachties climbed on board the spirited horses at the local country club only to be quickly thrown off or rubbed against poles and fences. Bruised and bloodied they were easily identified as 'Gringos' by the bow-legged walk and the raw skin and bandages on legs and forearms.

Most of the crews had spent their reserve cash in either South Africa or New Zealand, and so it was much appreciated when the Cantegrill Country Club in Punta had given the fleet free use of their facilities.

The club was used by everyone and there was no trouble. Mario and Magnus played golf, Magnus played tennis, Richard used the pool, De and I went riding. Neil, Patrick, Janne, Filthy, and Micky haunted the bar.

As projects go, we were certainly not impoverished on *Drum*, but Mike, Paul and Simon had made it clear before they left that it was unlikely there would be enough cash to commission the construction of a new Kevlar mainsail or a new No. 4 Jib. Although we would need all the help we could get to beat *Lion* for second place, none of us pressed this point of new sails. These three men had done enough financially to get us this far, and I was deeply sorry that they had not, in the end, gotten any sponsorship. With a need to recoup eighteen hours on one leg, it was clear that strategy and tactics would be more important than a new sail or two.

Drastic cutbacks in support and austerity measures are typical of the last port-of-call. By then, most of the yachts are out of the running. *Lion*, under serious threat from *Drum*, lost no time in ordering a new mainsail. *L'Esprit d'Equipe* and *Philips*, seemed unlimited in ordering new sails and equipment; only five hours separated the two from an overall victory, the French having the advantage.

When *Drum's* crew complained that we were running low on money, I told them how we had had to sell old sails, blocks, and ropes from *King's Legend* in Rio to keep us in food money. The Brazilian yachtsmen, suffering from a 300% import duty for yachting equipment and other luxuries at the time, would buy anything. I remember the day Hans, who was the mate on board, brought a father and son below to sell them his wristwatch and camera gear. Bartering like Arabs, Hans sold his old foul weather gear, the ones with the ass ripped out, to a man who seemed only too pleased to acquire them.

With a week to the restart, *Drum* was safely back in Punta del Este after the mast repair at the Naval Dockyard in Montevideo. I called our last crew meeting in the hotel foyer to double check the worklists, discuss the watch systems, and most important of all, to dwell on the topic of saving weight. Leaving the spare mainsail behind was a point of division with the crew, but I vetoed the move on the basis that the little advantage we could gain would be insignificant with the loss if we were caught without one. However, we managed to pare down weight in all of departments, including food.

In closing I made the point that to start this leg with a clear head and the body free from poisons would have benefit. I would have no mercy on anyone dogging it during first few days while recovering from an extended hangover. No sooner had I finished this little speech, than Micky, as if on cue to demonstrate my point, went pale, broke out in a cold sweat in the back of the room and then ran out to throw up. Janne explained he had just gotten in (it was 0930) from a 'hard night out.'

The day of the start, April 9th, came soon enough for us, but possibly not soon enough for some. Three of the crew of *AP* had just been released from a few days in the town jail, having fallen out with the proprietor of the Puerto Banus Bar, the crew's favorite watering hole. I think the Race Committee and the local officials, both visibly agitated, were delighted that we were finally getting underway again.

Less delighted were several new girlfriends. They were there on the dock that morning, in tears, now living on promises. As the world knows sailors' romances are as ephemeral as a squall in the Doldrums. I thought it a bit of honest cruelty when a girl asked one of our crew members, "When will I see you again?" "Never!" came the terse reply. He must have realized that the life he had left behind in Europe was still waiting for him, his tour of duty in Uruguay soon to be over.

For the last time, Filthy turned up the stereo, threw the deck speakers out of the hatch and a "View to a Kill" left no one in doubt what we were about to try to do. We slipped the lines by hand signals, made our way to the starting area, and with few spectator boats on hand, the gun went off on time at 1200. Instead of heading out to open sea, our course took us up-estuary for a few miles to round a buoy near the beach. These little detours have become a common practice in long offshore races, the purpose being to give the spectators on shore a last look at the ocean greyhounds before they charged out of sight. It was no surprise to see the beach just as deserted as the day before.

The fresh northeaster blowing down the coast put us dead on the wind. It was a beautiful sailing day; cobalt blue sky over the Pampas; endless, dark orange beaches stretching up to the Brazilian border glowing redder and redder as the day wore on. As we short tackled in-shore, just short of the breakers, the spray and spume cast a misty veil over it all.

Only forty miles down the coast, with dusk coming on fast, we tacked offshore at Cabo Santa Maria, a move recommended by local sailors who had sailed on numerous Buenos Aires to Rio Races. The accepted practice was to tack out into the Atlantic, even if unfavored, for at least 100 miles to gain an offing for a long starboard tack up towards the bight of Brazil. The temptation to 'cut the corner' and go direct for Cabo Frio, the southeast corner of Brazil, is usually rewarded with light winds and calms up under Rio. By midnight, most of the Maxis were on port tack, heading east.

Unlike the starts of the other three legs which were fairly easy going, this was a bash to windward in fresh conditions. It seems my advice at the last crew meeting had not been taken seriously. Patrick recorded how he felt the next morning in his diary:

Well our four-week stay in Punta has come to an end and it's just as well. The start was great – or rather would have been if I'd been feeling a bit sharper. For the first day, everyone looked like I felt, which was a small comfort. I wonder what it is about boat bums that we feel obliged to abuse ourselves when we're not sailing? I certainly don't feel in any sort of shape to do a long off-shore race and it is just as well the human body has (hopefully) rapid powers of recovery.

Even Magnus admitted it is grim to go back offshore after a month on land. And Mario on the wheel for the first time that day had said he has "Perdu l'habitude" for steering, so different from his perfected golf swing. Patrick later continued on a different subject:

We've really made a big effort to save some weight on the boat. I can't believe how much less gear we're carrying on this leg compared to the first two. Even Roger, who has carried more gear than anyone else and jealously defended his right to do so has agreed to leave a pile behind, though, I might add, only after considerable pressure from the rest of us. We'll look pretty stupid if we need any of the medical gear he's planning on leaving behind – a fact that he'll be sure to remind us of.

Like everything else, we had wittled the numbers on board back down to 17 for this last leg. Our only new entry was a young New Zealander called Sean 'Kiwi' Connolly. He had done the third leg on *AP* as an extra for the Southern Ocean and came highly recommended. The watch system was:

A	B	C	D
PJW	Skip	Magnus	Patrick
Simon	Janne	Paul	Roger
'Kiwi'	Neil	Rick	Mike
Micky	Mario	Bill	Filthy

Richard cooking

All of us had faith in our watermaker, enough to gamble on a very short reserve supply, far smaller than we had ever done before. We decided to carry no more than 1 liter of water per man per day in the tanks and make water daily to supplement the normal requirement which included reconstituting the freeze-dried food. Many of the other boats had carried hardly any water at all, dumping the official requirement soon after the start. This cut-back for us then, was in no way extraordinary and seemed like a good idea – until the machine packed up after the third day out.

While Magnus and Micky were pulling it to pieces, Phil Wade calculated that we could consume no more than a half a cup of liquid three times a day, the remainder of the total of 550 liters being dished out to the cook on a daily basis. This ration was based on the assumption that we would get no rain water in the Doldrums. It would not necessarily be a test of survival, but certainly one of character to cope. In hope of rain, Mike began to wash out our only long plastic hose (last used for diesel) and Mario made plans to sew a funnel in the foot of the mainsail.

A variable southwesterly shift and light winds made the repair on the watermaker a lot easier than it might have been. *UBS* was the only Maxi to jump ahead, then already 30 miles in front of the rest of us. It was decided, because of the water crisis to have Richard divide up the box of oranges into 17 piles, each to be coveted, eaten and bartered with as one chose.

All that day and most of the evening the two indefatigable Swedes, assisted by the amateur electrician Wade, had, after a 12-hour marathon, repaired the burned out winding of the electric motor that drives the watermaker. They did it by removing one of the four windings and soldering the connection to the other three with a cigarette lighter! With our fingers crossed (and our throats still dry) we fired it up and dumped in a few hundred liters. The drought was at least temporarily over.

The next day Blake on *Lion* reported another collision with a whale (no damage) and the wind swung slowly and steadily through the east as the fleet dowsed the spinnakers and went with big headsails to windward in a pleasant beat. "Is the weather always like this?" asked Paul as he sunned himself up on the weather rail, enjoying himself immensely. "Hell no!" I entered in my log only 6 hours later, on the morning of the 13th. We had just changed to the No. 3 Jib and it took all 12 of us on the watch change to do it. *Drum* already was pounding hard and burying her bow. The wind had settled in from the northeast at 30 knots apparent and would last for the next 4 days, slowly lifting us up to course to our way point on port tack. Roger had set our way point at roughly 250 miles east of Cabo Frio, Brazil. And so began the pitched battle with our arch-rival *Lion*.

There never had been much difference in speed between *Lion* and ourselves, but in straight-line conditions we had been certain we had a slight edge. Now, with her new Kevlar mainsail, however, the reverse seemed to be true. She was not losing ground and seemed to have the ability to point a degree or two higher when she wanted. We kept a constant visual bearing on her over the compass and checked her distance off with the radar. There was no need to motivate any of our crew to sail with determination. With only a few miles separating us, every good sail change cost us some part of a mile, a bad one much more – until they had to change, when we would get it back.

Thirteen oranges per man were divided out that afternoon and this simple case of strict allocation in the wake of the watermaker scare had produced some strange behaviour. Some scuttled through the gangways, oranges in hand, to be hidden in their lockers or crew bags. Others had left them in the airing bin cleverly labelled with magic marker, almost an open invitation to get ripped off, if there had been a thief among us. Neil refused to lower himself to such child's play and instead wrapped each individually in tissue paper, his theory being that this would keep them fresher, and it was assumed, provide a handy identifier, just in case.

The morning of the 14th *Lion* had sailed successfully up and over our bow during the night and was only 1.6 miles away. I had the unpleasant skipper's duty of having to take Filthy off the wheel after he lost 14 degrees of bearing on her. He sulked for most of the next few days and would not talk to me for weeks.

The water temperature was up to 28°C (82.4°F) as we bucked the counterclockwise circulation of the South Equatorial Current. Sleeping below was becoming difficult in the heat of the upper bunks, so bodies passed out where they fell in the sail bags lower down. Rick and I had an unspoken war in our bunk module throughout the leg, where he in the lower bunk would direct the fan on himself. In the middle of his off-watch, I would come below, get into my upper bunk and direct the fan on myself, but when I woke up in a sweat later on, the fan was invariably aimed down at him again. My theory was that hot air rises and I needed it more than he did. I'm sure he had a theory of his own.

"We want pancakes, we want pancakes!" the on watch chanted. Richard refused and stoically 'prepared,' as he called it, the cornflakes. With the tank water now the same temperature as the sea water, the milk for the cereal was less than appetizing. Phil Wade bet me an orange that Richard didn't know the recipe for pancakes. It turned out that I gave the cook more credit than he deserved. The pancakes we'd had on Leg Three had been made by instant mix. Neil called his bluff and offered to make them, and soon after the truth was revealed.

The next day, stronger winds forced a change to the No. 4 Jib as *Lion* had done only an hour before. The radar indicated they had dropped .4 of a mile to only .9 of a mile ahead in the predawn darkness. We followed suit, but a blunder up on the foredeck cost us a .8 of a mile, putting us 1.7 miles behind. By first light in a dramatic canvas of whipped water and wind-driven spray, the Kiwis went a step further and changed to what must have been a No. 5. It became clear that they were underpowered. They started to slip down to leeward. Phil and I thought for a moment that it looked like the top of their mast was bent, but it must have been an optical illusion; nothing so fortuitous as that was reported on the chat show later that day.

There they were again at daybreak on the 16th. The night before they had again hardened up across our bow and were ensconced on our port beam, 1.5 miles to weather. A low pressure cell just south of Rio had been funnelling this uncharacteristic northerly down on top of us, but Roger still reckoned that in another day we should be seeing more typical Southeast Tradewinds, filling in from the east.

Instead, after 32 hours with the No. 4, the wind flicked into the west giving us a reach and we hastily set the No. 3 and shook the reefs in sync with the Kiwis. At the chat show, Blake was right in saying that it had been great sailing like this in tandem, which it had, but "Damn it!" I thought, "All we want to do is to get away from you!"

Simon confessed he had had a great day in spite of the heavy going. Unburdened by foul weather gear, most sail changes were done in the raw in these latitudes, with bathing *au natural* on the foredeck, if you can hang on. He spent about a half hour underwater up there, streaming from the inner forestay by his finger tips, with green seas continually burying the front half of the boat. Everything seemed fine; *Lion* still there, watermaker still working, my supply of oranges in good shape . . .

Then we heard the BBC World Service news report about the American bombing of Libya. We were two days late in hearing the news, having been too busy fending off the New Zealanders to have heard about what seemed to us to be an impending World War III. I was immediately reminded of Neville Shute's *On the Beach*. What would we do in our unique circumstances if worse came to worse?

That night a rain squall moved in and we fumbled with the spinnaker gear after so many days hard on the wind. After the second 30-knot blow the visibility cleared. *Lion* was still in sight, but on the starboard gybe going east. That was the last we saw of them until the finish.

Two days later we found ourselves not only hard up against *UBS* and *AP*, having run up to them, but 25 miles ahead of *Lion* and *Cote d'Or* who had lost out on her easterly gamble.

Later that afternoon Neil and I, feeling chuffed with ourselves like everyone else on board, discussed how the *Lion* crew must be carrying a huge inferiority complex load. We suggested that they considered *Drum* an enigma. Neil pointed out that we had beat them fair and square on the last two legs. It was also a fact that we soundly romped them at the intercrew sports contest that they had organized and trained for, and to which our crew turned up horribly hung over. When it came to women they were completely dumbfounded about *Drum's* luck. Neil reckoned the crowning blow came when they challenged *Drum* to an impromptu paper airplane flying contest from the verandas in our high-rise in Punta. After they had little luck, their creations nosediving immediately to the lawn below, Richard calmly

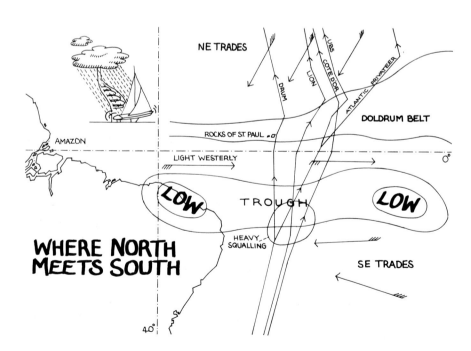

stepped out on his balcony with a piece of work that flew all the way to the Yacht Club car park, some two blocks away.

Our small, 25-mile lead was a good start in achieving what we had set out to do, but there were 5000 miles still to go. The least bit of complacency would let our guard down; the most minor of incidents reminds us of how vulnerable we still were. A simple dip pole gybe that went wrong because of lack of planning nearly did it. 'Kiwi' was left with no one to help him back aft on the new afterguy trim and when the guy didn't come on fast enough, the sheet bolted and with the spinnaker pole unsupported it careened onto the foredeck, narrowly missing Filthy. A direct hit and we would have been bound for Salvador.

Pierre Fehlmann on *UBS* was up to familiar tricks again. He reported his position 25 miles to the east of where he actually was while in visual contact with *AP*! Roger pointed this discrepancy out to Pierre who made some ridiculous excuses for an intelligent man. Kuttel, on *AP*, admitted later that he was so disgusted with this they paid no attention to what Pierre said after that.

Working Portishead Radio on the 19th we overheard another one of those classic conversations that is worth repeating:

The wife: "I know I wasn't supposed to, but I spent £300 on driving lessons."
The husband: "Oh?"
The wife: "I failed the test, don't yer know."
The man: "Don't worry."
The wife: "We've got no more money."
The husband: "Don't worry."
The wife: "But how will I feed little Johnny?" (Johnny is heard sobbing in the background.)
The husband: "Don't worry."
The wife: "You won't be home for two more months, what will we live on, it's getting desperate!" (Johnny is kicked a little harder and wails even louder.)

As heard, the situation appeared to be serious, but the husband did not promise more funds. Possibly he had heard this many times before. They ended with the usual "I love yous" four times over, and even the radio officer signed off offering his condolences to both parties, obviously entertained by this impressive bit of theatrics.

What were or might have been the Southeast Tradewinds did not last even 24 hours. At 8° South we sailed out of the Tradewind sky into heavy squalling conditions changing in one watch from the Flanker to the Medium Genoa, then back to the Flanker, No. 2 Jib Top, one reef, back to Flanker, back again to No. 2 Jib Top and finally to the Flanker. For the next 24 hours it rained solidly with very little wind. Wearing only shorts and a nylon track-suit top and bottom with seaboots full to the brim, I felt like I was back in the warm wet womb.

Still south of the Equator, there was speculation on board that we were in the Doldrums, but this was really impossible. Instead, we had sailed through a trough of low pressure that extended across the track of the fleet and we soon broke free into stable conditions and reached up to the way point line in a light westerly. The Doldrums were still to come.

The next day, on the verge of crossing into the northern hemisphere, the talk above and below decks turned to what we call 'Life after Whitbread.' Phil Wade, the hardest of the hard core, planned to embark on a Hinckley–41 only two weeks after the finish for a delivery to Maine from the Med, and then on to the Alaskan salmon fisheries. Magnus' preoccupation was a short ski holiday in France and then back into his normal mainstream of racing in anything going, the world over. Roger is unenthusiastically contemplating his job back in his Stockholm clinic, while the younger hands like Janne, Pat, Neil, and Micky are undecided, talking about the Bermuda Race on *Nirvana* and Sardinia Cup later in the summer. Mario talks little about future sailing projects and a lot about golf. Richard is back down to New Zealand to marry the girl he had met there. Rick has his sights set on a career in photography, something he had set out to do via this project – no more epoxy, no more sail changes. Filthy was in a real state. 33 years old, getting to that age when going back on board *Kialoa* as one of six deckhands gets to be a decidedly unattractive prospect. A deep thinker under a hard exterior, he knows only too well that this is only playtime. He was seriously talking about buying a house in Gosport for an investment and home base, probably the best move he could ever make. Bill had a full year outlined managing the BOC Race entry *Thursday's Child* and would be off as soon as we hit the dock. Paul and Mike had the straightforward task of getting down to business to help pay for the past year. Simon had to face picking up the threads of his music career. Some said it had faltered badly because of this project.

I had much to contemplate and a lot to do: *Drum's* last refit and finding another skipper were my first tasks. I had this book to write. Also, after the Uruguayan experience, I was tentatively planning to ride across South America on horseback during the following winter. Wade, also impatient to take a break from sailing and thinking about Alaska, gave me some advice on the South American trip. "Don't think about it too much or it will never happen. Make it as unplanned as possible. Just go there and buy a horse." Phil and I think along the same lines about a lot of things regarding travelling, places to see and how to see them.

Talk on the off-watches centered around the ideal cruising boat; cheap to build, made of steel for durability and equipped with a lifting keel and retractable rudder for expedition purposes. It would be about 50 feet overall, big enough for 6 people maximum and freezer capacity for a ton of fish that Phil would catch and resell later as he went. Patrick, sleeping back aft and party to these fantasies began to doodle in a notepad, sketching the profile and interior. So began the drawings that later would evolve into a dream come true. Phil and I and Chuck Gates (although he didn't know it then) would soon break two of the cardinal rules of professional boathands: never own your own boat, and never enter into partnerships.

We crossed the Equator at 2030 local time on April 22nd at 29°41′ of West Longitude. *UBS* had disappeared in a squall the day before, in sight of both ourselves and *AP*, and when she surfaced on the radio she was 60 miles to the north-northeast, having sailed in a private wind. The rest of us struggled across the equator in weak and variable conditions.

It was another big day in the logbooks. Mario was unfortunate to be on the wheel when a small waterspout caught us unawares and spun the boat around three times with the genoa aback. Every time we tried to bear off and sail away from it, the sail would back again and it would draw us into the center. Of course, all of us offered none-too-polite suggestions ("Fer Christ's sake head up!" and "No, no, head down you bloody fool!") that he didn't take too kindly. Finally dropping the genoa and doing nothing, we let this little 'maelstrom' wander off on its own accord.

It was hairy to be in a 78-foot sailboat totally out of control, however briefly, and I could imagine how elaborately this story will grow in future tellings: "We thought we were done for, as the boat spun round and round ever faster. Just as we were about to be lifted off into the ether (or down into the vortex) I released the sheet and we broke free from the whirlpool, by then of immense proportions . . . etc."

That evening we ghosted past the Rocks of Sao Paul e Sao Pedro, which are nothing more than mere outcroppings in the middle of the Atlantic. As expected, Wade 'had been there,' and he told an interesting story of how he had no sooner than dropped his anchor on a ledge to go diving, than hundreds of ocean sharks swam right up the chain and surrounded the boat. Patrick and Neil took great pleasure in givig anyone a hard time and they immediately discounted his tale as another 'fish story.' They pointed out that the voyage was coming to a close and he had not caught anything.

Earlier that day they accused him of cornering the orange market, then in short supply. Apparently, so they claim, he was planning to bring out a few bogus rotten ones causing a run on eating or a cheap sell out. His supply intact, consider the profits to be made. He demurely denied these accusations claiming simply, "I've made out well on oranges."

Phil was vindicated that same night when Mario pulled in a 12-pound Yellow Fin Tuna on Phil's line. Six hours later, this great catch was re-enacted for Roger who had just woken up. They tied a line to the dead tuna and lowered it over the side. "Shit, pull him in!" "I can't hold him!" "Get the boathook, quick!" we all shouted from the deck as the Doctor-cum-camera-man bloodied himself getting out of the hatch, video in hand. Of course the tuna was stiff as a board with a pronounced curve to starboard and tied to the line by his tail, but with this event safely recorded for Swedish Television, we though it a bit unfair if we didn't admit the whole thing was a hoax – some four hours later. Phil did a masterful job of filleting and did the cooking, with Richard barred from this most important of tasks.

Due to torpor from the heat, the Equator celebration took place two days late and was a non-event in comparison to the one on the first leg. Filthy, still depressed, refused to be Neptune so Mike filled in and did a good job castigating Simon, Paul, and Kiwi. The results of the last 48 hours didn't add to the lack of ambiance. *UBS* was gone, over 160 miles to the north, firmly in the Northeast Trades and we had lost big to all the others by staying west when they kept going well east of north. Our plan had been to get north as quickly as possible, but this had temporarily backfired by putting us into the light and variable. *AP* was heading straight over to the bulge of Africa, no doubt attempting to repeat an inside berth as they had successfully done in the South Atlantic on Leg One.

By the next 'chat show', however, everything had once again changed. The boats to the east had been becalmed in a hiccup in the Doldrums and we to the west had regained all that we had lost and more. By the time the Trades had filled in for all of us we were again 35 miles ahead of *Lion*, 55 ahead of *Cote d'Or* and 10 ahead of *AP*. The next tactical problem, and our last chance to outwit *Lion* was the Azores High, almost 2000 miles away.

Two days later, beating to weather in steady Trades, the North Star surfaced 17 degrees above the horizon and north circumpolar constellations that we hadn't seen for seven months announced our arrival in familiar waters.

Mario and Richard had a minor skirmish in the galley as we fought to windward on the 27th. It had something to do with the Frog wasting a whole bottle of dish soap when it drained out in the sink. Mario went for him with fists flying, but the bullish cook immediately put him in a headlock and threatened him with a severe beating. By the time I heard the racket and ran forward, it was over and the

Frenchman sulked off to his bunk. Nobody thought much about this other than inquiring if Mario had eaten his pancake for breakfast or if it was still available. The Englishman wiped the sweat off his brow and puffed and sighed much the same way his two pressure cookers let off excess steam.

The rest of the crew were content to sit up on the sails on the weather rail in the bright sunshine chatting away about the future. I sarcastically suggested to Phil Wade that he should consider taking a managerial job (he had once had such a position in a shipping company in Cape Town) somewhere, possibly a boatyard, and stop wasting his days in the middle of the ocean. "Hell no!" he answered in all seriousness, "What more could you ask for: just had a belly full of flying fish, sunny day, no worries . . ." He had a point, and I recorded similar sentiments in my log that day:

Last week I had finished reading Lee Ioccoca's autobiography and I found it hard to believe this mundane, uninspiring piece of reading had been a bestseller. It's success was no doubt due to celebrity value, but also was a sign of changing times. I could hardly imagine it as popular in the 60s and although I readily admit to needing more than 'a belly full of flying fish' to satisfy my lifestyle, I can hardly see the value of preaching his kind of ambition. It certainly was world's apart from the weather rail I was sitting on this afternoon, and I wouldn't have traded my wet ass and sun tan for anything.

About the same time I was contemplating life's strange way I was also reading Hemmingway's *Across the River and into the Trees*, a depressing, but beautiful little story about an old dying American Army Colonel who falls in love with a teenage Italian Countess. Reading this was poignant after a slight flirtation with a 'Uruguayan Princess' and it made me so sad I almost didn't finish it. I also recorded my thoughts about this in my log:

The good thing is that I am not dying, and if the Colonel's comment to the Countess about 'mediocre writers living forever' is true, I have a bright future ahead of me indeed.

We were fast approaching 30°N on the 29th of April. I can well remember how all the recent victories and failures, like gaining 60 miles in 24 hours on *AP* which was battling through the Cape Verde Islands; like the fact that *UBS* was then a staggering 250 miles ahead of us; and all those little annoyances and pleasures, like catching Patrick asleep on watch that day as well as finding Rick asleep under a pile of sails when we thought he had fallen overboard unnoticed in a photographic stunt hours before. How all of this seemed so minor and petty when we heard on the BBC World Service that a radio active dust cloud had settled over Scandinavia and was spreading over northern Europe. Chernobyl had exploded.

Assuming the effects were much worse than the media – especially Russia's – was allowing, I was a bit concerned about venturing further up into the northern hemisphere, realizing how much the southern one had going for it. But like Neville Shute's submariner who deserted his ship off the coast of a devastated California, the boys on *Drum* were ready to go home, regardless of the dangers. I pointed out optimistically to the crew that we could be telling our grandchildren about this one day. "Yes," said Neil, "If our grandchildren have ears."

The Azores High had been moving around a lot during the last week. Then it finally became stationary just south of the Azores. *UBS* looked to be committed to passing the high to the east, on the wind, while we to the west hoped to get around its backside and pick up the westerlies first.

We were in a good position to do so on May 2nd when we entered the southwest corner of the high and a good degree north of *Lion* and almost two degrees north of *Cote d'Or*. On a straightline course to the finish up the English Channel we were only 25 and 15 miles ahead respectively, but for them to cut the corner meant sailing through the center of the high. All our weather fax maps from Bracknell and Northwood in the UK and Paris had the high well established and ridging to the east towards Europe. We had been maintaining a solid 2nd place, but if we broke free early, as planned, we even had a chance of being first home.

Twenty-four hours later, it was obvious this was not to be. *UBS* shot ahead in a completely different weather system. Early that morning as we ghosted along in a general northerly direction at 4 knots, the tension onboard was thick as fog. Roger leaned toward bearing off to the east and steering the course, while Phil thought we should play out the northerly card and look for the new wind first. It was a difficult decision; Roger made a lot of tactical sense by simple calculation combined with endless study of the weather maps. On the other hand. Phil seemed to be predicting the trends with uncanny accuracy, using only observation, an art developed during a lifetime of offshore voyaging.

Paul and Mike were concerned about getting stuck in the high, and in the end we came to a compromise. In this wind that was verging on non-existent, we decided to steer in a general northerly direction. Roger and I went forward to have a private chat. Under extreme pressure the last two days, he chain-smoked while we discussed the situation in muffled voices:

Skip: "How do you think the crew are holding up?"
Roger: "Some better than others."

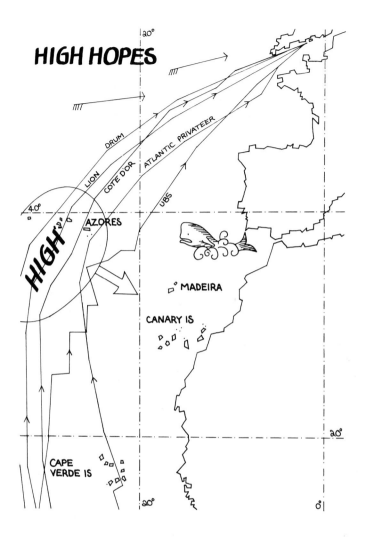

HIGH HOPES

Skip: "Did you explain the situation?"
Roger: "I did."
Skip: "That's good."
Roger: "Some say we took a gamble to the west and that is that."
Skip: "That's a healthy attitude."
Roger: "Others say nothing."
Skip: "Those are the ones to watch out for, they could turn on us at the drop of a hat and become raving lunatics!"

The morning of the 4th a line of stratus cloud approached from the northwest and by late afternoon, sure enough, the wind had filled southwesterly at 15 knots and with the 1.5 oz spinnaker set we bore off on to a course passing through the Azores. With fingers crossed we expected big gains on the others during the next 12-hour period as there was no doubt we were the first to be on the right side of the weather shift.

Morale on board soared to an all-time high. The 18 hours we then needed was by no means out of the question and we raced the boat with a new vengeance. Richard had taken our last 4 days of food and divided them up into 8, just in case, and back aft the radio cooked away to England, announcing our hopes and expectations to family, friends, and the press.

With a new ocean swell starting to roll in from the northwest, the weather maps 24 hours later showed us the painful news that the high had moved right off to the southeast, no doubt releasing not only *Lion* and *Cote d'Or*, but *AP* as well. The gains we had made were substantial, but clearly not enough.

There were still 1400 miles to go to the finish, as Mario pointed out to us that afternoon. "You never know what can happen in the Whitbread," declared the veteran. Four years ago, it was at this very spot that they lay becalmed for two days while *Flyer II* finished in Portsmouth, having come from nearly four days behind to win the

Whitbread Round-the-World Race 1985–1986
Results to Date – 21st May 1986

		LEG ONE				LEG TWO			
				Place	H/C			Place	H/C
Race No.	Yacht Name	Elapsed Time	Corrected Time	In Div	Place O/A	Elapsed Time	Corrected Time	In Div	Place O/A
DIVISION A		DHMS	DHMS			DHMS	DHMS		
1	*Drum#*	36.16.44.23	36.13.44.48	5	11	29.13.31.04	29.10.02.59	4	9
12	*Portatan/Atlantic Privateer*	Retired	Retired	–	–	29.03.04.36	28.22.44.02	1	4
14	*UBS Switzerland*	34.01.39.20	33.23.05.31	1	4	29.04.59.22	29.02.23.34	3	6
18	*NZI Enterprise*	35.09.06.42	35.09.06.42	4	8	29.03.11.56	29.03.11.56	2	7
19	*Norsk Data GB*	39.15.09.53	39.02.31.20	6	12	36.00.02.49	35.11.14.26	7	14
22	*Lion New Zealand★*	34.17.46.47	34.11.45.25	2	6	29.18.58.12	29.12.52.08	5	10
27	*Cote d'Or★★*	34.23.28.26	34.14.49.27	3	7	30.20.07.06	30.18.23.25	6	11
DIVISION C									
4	*Philips Innovator*	36.12.28.11	32.18.38.09	2	2	31.12.57.26	27.17.57.26	1	1
9	*Fortuna Lights*	38.18.46.48	34.08.09.55	4	5	35.12.04.53	31.00.04.59	4	12
13	*Fazer Finland*	36.10.33.09	32.23.15.55	3	3	32.17.45.45	29.05.23.40	3	8
20	*L'esprit d'Equipe*	37.13.41.25	32.07.07.47	1	1	34.01.59.01	28.17.46.50	2	2
DIVISION D									
6	*Sas Baia Viking*	51.18.15.56	44.22.06.47	4	14	44.17.37.48	37.19.20.48	4	15
7	*Equity and Law*	47.18.23.05	41.20.13.22	3	13	34.18.29.03	28.18.28.36	1	3
17	*Shadow of Switzerland*	43.06.12.40	36.09.16.08	1	9	41.13.35.24	34.14.30.25	3	13
23	*Rucanor Tristar†*	42.01.40.04	36.12.49.49	2	10	34.14.23.10	28.23.49.28	2	5

\#   *Drum* sailed Leg 1 on rating of 69.3ft and Legs 2 and 3 on a rating of 69.2ft.

★   *Lion New Zealand* received a time penalty of 25 mins 17 secs on her Leg 2 elapsed time. This has been incorporated.

★★ *Cote d'Or* received an 11 mins 24 secs allowance on her Leg 3 elapsed (this has been incorporated) time and has received a time penalty of 97 hours 56 mins 38 secs (which has been incorporated in the total combined elapsed time at the end of the 4th Leg).

†   *Rucanor TriStar* received a 30 min allowance on her Leg 1 elapsed time. (This has been incorporated.)

   UBS Switzerland has beaten *Flyer's* record by 2 days 16 hours 2 mins 32 secs.

race on handicap from *Charles Heidsieck*. It was such a foregone conclusion that *Heidsieck* had it 'in the bag' that the sponsor had already ordered that the T-shirts and posters be printed in anticipation of their victorious arrival. Mario enjoyed telling us how they sat there, helpless while skipper Alain Gabbay had a nervous breakdown and threw all the winch handles overboard (Mario managed to hide one under his jacket), ripped the weather fax machine off the bulkhead and threw that over the side, and physically destroyed the steering wheel in a fit of rage. He then went forward, put his head in his hands, and sat there in silence.

Just north of the Azores, Paul had no sooner commented on the lack of sea-life this leg, than a 40-foot sperm whale jumped clear of the water right in front of the boat. Ten minutes later we sailed right through the middle of a school of basking sharks, harmless filter feeders, but the one we hit back aft was enough to give Wade a fright as he was relieving himself over the side. For the next 48 hours dolphins escorted us on and off for much of the way back home into the Western Approaches.

LEG THREE				LEG FOUR				LEGS ONE TWO THREE AND FOUR COMBINED			
Elapsed Time	Corrected Time	Place H/C In Div	Place O/A	Elapsed Time	Corrected Time	Place H/C In Div	Place O/A	Elapsed Time	Corrected Time	Place H/C In Div	Place O/A
DHMS	DHMS			DHMS	DHMS			DHMS	DHMS		
24.23.30.35	24.20.27.17	2	8	31.13.08.29	31.10.04.25	3	9	122.18.54.31	122.06.19.29	3	8
25.00.50.25	24.21.00.54	3	9	32.01.55.49	31.22.05.21	5	12	n/a	n/a	n/a	n/a
24.14.11.20	24.11.54.06	1	7	29.17.41.40	29.15.23.52	1	4	117.14.31.42	117.04.47.03	1	4
	RETIRED FROM LEG AND THE RACE			–	–	–	–			
27.15.45.41	27.04.28.50	6	14	34.18.17.13	34.06.57.34	6	13	138.01.15.36	136.01.12.10	5	12
25.22.53.59	25.17.31.32	5	11	31.18.53.00	31.13.29.13	4	10	122.06.31.58	121.07.38.18	2	7
25.01.09.11	24.23.37.51	4	10	31.09.46.12	31.08.14.29	2	7	126.08.27.33	125.19.01.50	4	10
26.09.19.51	23.01.10.20	2	4	32.16.15.12	29.07.45.42	2	2	127.03.00.40	112.21.31.37	2	2
28.05.18.15	24.06.10.21	4	6	35.09.13.00	31.09.41.22	4	8	137.21.22.56	120.19.06.37	4	6
26.12.15.43	23.09.56.43	3	5	32.12.50.24	29.10.12.52	3	3	128.05.25.01	115.00.49.10	3	3
27.00.50.39	22.07.54.53	1	1	33.07.44.14	28.14.20.19	1	1	132.00.15.19	111.23.09.49	1	1
32.14.10.39	26.11.42.17	4	13	41.16.49.06	35.13.44.13	4	14	170.18.53.29	144.18.54.05	4	13
28.00.33.50	22.17.42.47	1	2	35.05.41.40	29.22.18.59	2	6	145.19.07.38	123.06.43.44	2	9
31.21.08.43	25.17.58.04	3	12	37.21.58.03	31.18.10.42	3	11	154.14.54.50	128.11.55.19	3	11
27.21.05.10	22.22.33.21	2	3	34.21.17.57	29.22.16.34	1	5	139.10.26.21	118.09.29.12	1	5

As each day came to a close during the next five, it was more and more clear we would not beat *Lion* in the overall results, especially in this steady weather. They wavered between 70 and 20 miles behind us and, by the time *Cote d'Or* passed us on a heavy run up under Land's End, the game was all but finished.

We would finish third on the last leg and third on elapsed time for the Whitbread Race in 1985/86. On corrected time, *Lion* had beaten us fair and square for second place. I would have traded almost anything to have won, to have exchanged places with *UBS* when she crossed the finish line victorious, breaking *Flyer II's* record by 2 days, 16 hours to make it around the world in 117 days, 14 hours of sea time.

Would I have traded anything to have exchanged places with *Lion* for second place? I don't think so. Not having won I could hardly imagine trading all of those ups and downs, those crazy moments of apprehension in failure, and those joys of limited success in fighting on, for the privilege of saying we 'got second' and little else. Results are one thing, value of memories is something else, and it would be hard to beat ours.

Paul and Mike Berrow, who spent a fortune just to take part in this race, would later simply say, "It's changed us. From out of the depths and drudgery of business life we are totally refreshed with a new outlook to the future. It will give us a lifetime of happy memories."

Simon Le Bon would tell the interviewer at the press conference, "For me, I now have a yardstick to measure myself against, something that I never had before." For the man who, of all of us, had risked the most, he said little more; nor did he have to.

And for the rest of the crew? Heaving, pulling, and stumbling their way down the deck with the same determination they had eight months ago; the look on their faces during that last sail change on the last watch of the last day tells the story of what it takes to go the distance in this Round-the-World Race: determination, knowing that the reward would be no more than self-satisfaction.

The few platitudes *Drum's* crew offered to those there to greet them would fall far short of the way they really felt. But how do you explain to someone who has never been, just what it's like to have raced around the globe and only an hour ago had been roaring up the English Channel, homeward bound on the heels of a spring gale?

Drum finished the Whitbread Round-the-World Race at dawn on May 11th, 1986.

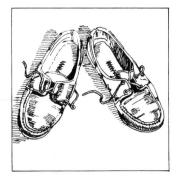

Epilogue

Haven't we, together and upon the immortal sea, wrung out a meaning from our sinful lives? Good-bye, brothers! You were a good crowd. As good a crowd as ever fisted with wild cries the beating canvass of a heavy foresail; or tossing aloft, invisible in the night, gave back yell for yell to a westerly gale.

Joseph Conrad

One year has elapsed since we finished an ocean voyage that had changed most of us in some way or another. For some it was easy to pick up the thread of life they had left behind, others went through difficult periods of assimilation before striking out for new horizons. We would, I believe, agree that all our horizons had been broadened by living and working together through some very difficult times, which made the lighthearted moments that much more enjoyable.

Magnus Olsson for the first time in seven years has not returned to the ski slopes of Aspen. He painted his parents' house in Stockholm last summer, worked as an adviser for the Italian America's Cup Syndicate in Perth in September and then spent the winter building a 50-footer for the Swedish Admiral's Cup Team.

Phil Wade spent his summer fishing for salmon out of Alaska to help pay for his share in the steel cruising boat, now under construction in Southampton. He and Magnus delivered a 61 footer from Finland to the Canary Islands in October and is currently with the same boat in the Caribbean, impatiently awaiting the next fishing season up north.

Roger Nilsson has written a book about *Drum* in Sweden and is now trying to raise money to fund a Swedish entry for the next Round-the-World Race. He has temporarily given up his orthopaedic practice in Stockholm.

Bill Biewenga has followed the fortunes of Warren Luhr's *Thursday's Child* on the BOC Singlehanded Round-the-World Race, managing the support operation at each stop-over. He plans to stay in professional racing.

Patrick Banfield tried out for the British 12 Meter campaign as a genoa trimmer. His chances of making the team did not look good after he fell overboard the first day out, and instead landed a job as a shore manager. After returning to Britain to finish the design details on our steel cruising boat, now christened *Pelagic*, he is hoping to become involved in another Whitbread project.

Rick Tomlinson has successfully landed on his feet as a marine photographer having covered the Sardinia Cup, the Maxi Series in Newport, the St. Tropez Maxi Series and various Swan World Championships. He is now employed full time by Nautor's advertising agency.

Brian 'Mugsy' Hancock returned to Marblehead after the third leg, got married and then sold his house at great profit. He is now investing in real estate in Rhode Island and talks about the next Whitbread Race.

Janne Gustafsson spent the last six months working in a 'salad bar' in Stockholm. After flying down to Sydney before Christmas to race on *Atlantic Privateer* in the Hobart Race he joined the Swedish 50-footer, *Carat*, in Florida for the SORC. A definite candidate for 1989.

Micky Olsson went to work on *Carat* where she was built in France, sailed her in the Sardinia Cup and stayed on board for the SORC.

Neil Cheston co-authored a book with Simon about *Drum* that was sold in England in the fall of 1986. After several Nautor deliveries around Europe he took the skipper's job on the American cruising Maxi, *Nirvana*, joining her in the Galapagos.

Mike and Paul Berrow are still in the music publishing business, but they no longer manage Duran Duran's affairs. Paul married his girlfriend Miranda in July of 1986 and they had their first child last spring. The brothers are beginning to contemplate other sailing projects.

Richard Freeman left for New Zealand soon after the finish. He lasted two weeks with his fiancée and was summarily dismissed as the story goes. He spent the later part of the summer sailing in Hawaii and on the west coast of America and has not been heard of since.

Mario Zimmerman took up his golf clubs immediately upon hitting France and after nine months training is now semi-professional. No immediate plans to go sailing anywhere.

Simon Le Bon and Duran are back in the mainstream of the rock music scene after a difficult period of reconciliation. He and his wife Jasmin spent six weeks cruising in the Caribbean aboard *Drum* last winter and then went on a world concert tour.

Phil 'Filthy' Barrett never bought his house in Gosport. Instead he took over as skipper of *Drum* after the finish and has become a living folk hero 'Down Island.' One year later he was still on board.

Drum competed in the Round Ireland Race in June, 1986, the St. Tropez Maxi Series in September of that same year and has sailed Transatlantic to the Caribbean this past fall. Back in the Mediterranean she was still up for sale as of last summer.